FALLEN FOURTH DOWN

TIJAN

TABLE OF CONTENTS

DEDICATION

This is dedicated to all the Fallen Crest fans! You guys are amazing! You love Sam, Mason, and Logan as much as I do and sometimes, I think you love them more than me.

CHAPTER ONE

SAMANTHA

Logan loves me.

Tate's words had been haunting me for three months. They could destroy everything. I already lost one family; I didn't want to lose another. It would fuck everything up if my soul mate's brother loved me. I thought about those words even now, sitting in bed as Mason slept next to me. As I watched him sleep, tears threatened to spill.

The fear, terror, paralyzing horror—you name it, I felt it— surged up in me again. Mason was leaving for college today. This was the day that would start my most challenging year ever.

Mason had become my rock, my soul, my way of living. Some say that I depended on him too much, but I didn't give a damn. He and his brother, Logan, protected me when everyone had abandoned me. If Logan did love me, everything would be destroyed. The family unit we had would be gone. Jealousy and mistrust would take its place. I couldn't shake the fear that Mason would follow through on a threat he said a year ago: No girl would come between him and his brother.

Well. Hello. Here I am.

He opened his eyes, and it was like he'd been awake the whole time. His green eyes looked right into me, like he always did, immediately alert and focused, and he reached over. Trailing a hand up my arm, he tugged the blanket down, then curved his hand around my waist. He pulled me down, and asked, "What's wrong?"

He positioned me so I was laying on top of him, and I just savored being with him. Mason Kade was beautiful to look at and even more beautiful to touch. He was all muscle, so solid and powerful, all right beneath me. He was over six feet tall. Sculpted broad shoulders. His back was contoured, and his muscles tapered down to a trim waist, making him look like a perfect specimen. With black hair cut in a crew cut, chiseled cheekbones, a strong jaw, and a perpetual smirk that tugged at the corner of his mouth, he could've been a model. He wasn't. Instead, he was the future star wide receiver for Cain University's football team.

He'd been a god in Fallen Crest. He and Logan both were. I'd endured hell over the last year just because I was his girlfriend, but he was going to a Division One school. That meant his games would be televised nationally. ESPN coverage. Future NFL talks.

"Hey," he murmured, his nose nuzzling my neck. His arms tightened their hold on me, pulling me tighter on top of him. "Talk to me."

"You're leaving. Enough said right there."

"Sam."

I shook my head. We'd been inseparable over the summer. I wasn't sure if it was on either side, or more from me. I should tell him my fear, what Tate said to me, but I couldn't. Couples are supposed to tell each other the bad stuff, even if it might hurt. I knew Mason would want me to tell him, but my vocal cords shut down. I couldn't say a word.

I wanted it to go away. Logan didn't actually love me. It was all a lie or a horrible joke.

"Hey," he murmured again, catching my chin and turning me so I was looking right into his gaze. "Tell me what's going on? I know something's up. You've been off all summer, running more than usual." He paused. "What is it?"

Tell him. Just tell him, let the chips fall how they're supposed to. Then his voice came back in my head, *"I'm not going to let anyone get in between my brother and me."*

I couldn't say anything. I was a coward.

"Sam?" He cupped the side of my face, and his thumb brushed a tear aside. "Everything will be fine. We're going to talk every night. Eleven at night, every night. It's set in stone for me, no matter what. And you're in a good place. David was a fuck up before, but he's coming around. He's trying to be a good father to you, and you have Malinda; she's awesome. Analise is still in that treatment center. My dad said she's going to be there for a long time. Logan's across the road. There's no Kate. No one will mess with you this year, and if they do, just tell Logan. He'll deal with them. You and I are good. There's nothing to worry about. I love you." He sat up. As he did, he held me in the air, holding me in place, and he rested against the headboard. I was placed back down, straddling him. Feeling the strength of his muscles underneath me, a rush of adrenalin went through me.

My hand fell to his waist, lingered there, and he trembled under my touch. That was me. That power over him, was all me.

He was mine. So many wanted him, but he was all mine. I let that filter in. That gave me reassurance. That made me feel like I was on top of the world, having him love me so much. When I thought about that and felt Mason's love, Tate's words were shoved to the back of my mind.

What she said didn't matter. It couldn't.

"Assholes, get up!" Logan's voice came from the hallway, and he pounded a fist on Mason's door. "He's not just yours today, Sam. You have to share. He's my brother, and he's leaving me too." He pounded again on the door. "This is your thirty minute notice. You have a half hour to do your deed, ride him hard, and then get dressed. I want my time with him."

Mason's chest moved as a laugh came from him. His hands went to my legs, and he pressed them down, moving me so I was grinding on him, and he said back, "You want to ride me?"

There was a brief pause before Logan's response. "Only if Sam isn't getting the job done. I'll pull on my brother shorts and make you feel all girly and pleasured."

I rolled my eyes.

Mason called back, "Go suit up."

Logan groaned, and his voice muffled through the door. "How did this conversation take this turn? This is very weird."

I shook my head and yelled back, "They always do with you. You're the common denominator."

Logan laughed. "Denominator. Don't you mean dominator? Come to think of it, take your time. Where's Kris? I feel like finding my own dominator. I like being submissive. It makes me feel special and precious all at the same time." As he kept talking, his voice faded when he walked down the hallway. Then he called back, from further down, "Be done in two hours, Sam! I call dibs with my brother after that."

Mason chuckled, and the sound of it acted like a caress, rushing through me and making my insides curl. He cupped the back of my head, anchoring me as he looked into my eyes again. "Everything will be fine. I promise."

I wanted to believe him. "I know." But I didn't. I should tell him, but I couldn't. Not yet. It would come out, though, and that was the day my world would be threatened. I closed my eyes again and let my head fall forward so it was resting softly against his. Moving to kiss me gently, he whispered, "I love you, Samantha."

"I love you, Mason." I would relish this moment with him, go with him to help him move into his room, and I'd come back to start my senior year. It'd be me and Logan in Fallen Crest.

I'd have to figure everything out later, one day at a time. With that final decision made, I moved to meet his lips with mine and applied pressure. He groaned, meeting my command for more, and it wasn't long before he slid into me. As he did, I held onto him. I didn't want to let him go.

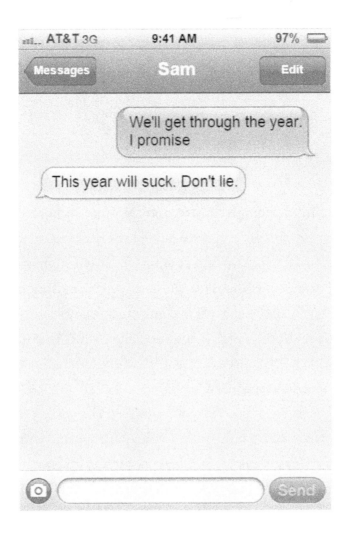

CHAPTER TWO

Three weeks later

It'd been almost a month since we took Mason to school. He had to go early for football, and since being back, I'd been on an emotional lockdown. I worked at Manny's. I went running, and I avoided Logan, but earlier today he cornered me at work to make sure I was going to his party. I had gone to a few over the summer, but when I said, 'a few' I really meant a few. I think there'd been three that I'd been coerced into attending and two of those were before Mason left for college.

Heather had promised to come later, but she needed to run to Channing's for a little bit. Lovely. Without Mason and with Logan lip-locked to his girlfriend, I flashed back to the first month of my junior year. Alone. A little hesitant. The need to run was climbing high inside me. As I crossed the street, I watched as a car stopped and a bunch of people hurried out of it, running towards Logan's house. I had to laugh at the irony. It was Becky, the one person who had been my friend the beginning of junior year. The laugh stopped abruptly as I recognized the rest of the car's occupants.

It was the Elite. When the hell had Becky started hanging out with them?

They were at the front door now, and I paused behind them, stepping onto the curb outside Logan's house. For now, they were clueless of my presence. Becky glanced back and froze. Her eyes got big, and her mouth fell open slightly.

She looked different. She had lost weight. Her frizzy red hair was now a dark auburn and sleek. Her face had been clear of make-up when we were friends, but I saw a tiny bit there now. It suited her. Her eyes were more captivating. Her lips looked cute and adorable. The rest of her matched that description. Adorable. She was almost petite now. She wore a short skirt with ruffles on the bottom. A black camisole was peeking out from underneath her jean jacket. I couldn't remember what kind of shoes she had worn before, but it hadn't been the glitzy sandals she had on now. They were pretty and pink.

"Your friend's undergone a makeover," Cass said from behind me. She had stopped beside me, playing with the car keys in her hand.

I groaned inwardly right away. Another lovely change. I glanced over and saw the smug hostility in her gaze. She flicked her blonde hair back and gave me a cocky smirk. She added, "Hurts, doesn't it. To know that your friend—sorry—someone who used to be your friend is now in the enemy's camp."

"That's what we are? Enemies?"

"We're not friends. Since I'm dating Mark, and you got me banned from my own boyfriend's house, I wouldn't say we're acquaintances."

Becky's eyes remained wide as she watched us. Fear darkened them.

Cass waved her hand and plastered a fake smile on her face. "Things are fine, Becks. Go in. We're cool."

I rolled my eyes. We were not cool.

When the door shut and it was just the two of us, Cass started forward. She turned around and sauntered backwards, as if mocking me. I glared right back at her and followed, pushing her to go faster and faster. Cass didn't seem to mind. The other side of her mouth lifted up, and her cocky smirk transformed into a smug, triumphant smile. As we drew closer to the door, she taunted, "I took your friend, Strattan. I wonder what else I can take from you?"

"You're this pissed because Malinda banned you from the house? What did you expect? She's Mark's mom, and she's going to marry my dad. You threw wine on me one night. You've known Malinda most your life. Did you really think she wouldn't react to that?" I shook my head. "You're stupid. I'm going to be her stepdaughter. She's going to take my side."

"Yeah, well," her eyes narrowed, "we'll see. Since most of the old crew graduated, I'm the leader now. It's me, Amelia, Adam, and Mark. We had a spot open and Adam vouched for Becky. I figured, what the hell? Anything to piss you off, especially after that night."

"Newsflash, bitch. Becky and I haven't been friends for a while." I stepped closer, purposely invading her space. This wasn't a Tommy Princess. I wasn't worried a knife would be drawn by this one. No, Cass was Fallen Crest Academy through and through. She thought she was more than she was, and I had already taken them on—and won—once. I smirked at her. Mason was gone. Things with Logan were uncomfortable, so that meant I had a whole host of bad shit rolling around inside me. She thought she could target me? Oh no. I had found the perfect target. As my smirk grew, hers faded. I leaned in closer. She was now pressed against the door, all that bravado gone. I asked, "You want to take me on? Do it. I'm going to enjoy this because, honey, I need a distraction from the real turmoil going on in my life."

She swallowed.

I tilted my head to the side, scanning every inch of her to make her even more uncomfortable. "I should thank you for volunteering. After taking on the Tommy Princesses from FCP, you're going to be a treat. For real."

She froze, and I rolled my eyes. I shoved her away from the door and headed inside. That game could start later on. It was my senior year. Even if Mason was gone, I should enjoy some of it. I headed for the kitchen. Maybe it was time I tried drinking. Everyone else seemed to enjoy it.

"Hey, Sam." A guy passed me, but I didn't recognize him. As I drew closer to the kitchen, more and more people said their hellos. The hostility wasn't there from the girls, and the guys weren't tense around me anymore.

"It's because of us."

I drew back as Natalie, one of the remaining two Tommy Princesses at FCP, stood beside me. She was leaning against a counter with a beer in her hand and a scowl on her face. Her black hair was tucked behind her ears, and her eyes were heavily made up with mascara. With a black corset top, her breasts almost popping out, and tight jeans that were ripped near the crotch area, she looked scary.

"What do you mean?" I asked.

She gestured around the house. "It's because of us. We're not in force anymore. Kate and Parker graduated. It's just me and Jaz. You and the Kades took care of our threat so the girls are going to be nice to your face, since you're still close to Logan Kade, but don't be fooled. The guys will all wonder who's going to bang you now that Mason is gone."

"I'm still with Mason."

"Not here." She took a sip and rolled her eyes. Her hostility matched Cass', but her attitude was darker. I knew from experience she wasn't afraid to follow up with a threat. She added, "No one stays with their high school sweetheart." She glanced to where Logan was, as he had Kris trapped in a corner, nuzzling her neck. "Half the people are wondering if Logan's your next conquest or if you'll give it up to another guy. Shit. There's already bets on who's going to be in your pants by homecoming."

"I don't believe you."

She laughed and finished her beer in one gulp. She tossed the can into a barrel in the corner and held her hand out. Another beer came down the line, handed from person to person, until it was put in her hand. Sick enjoyment lit up her face as she opened the can. "You might've been accepted, since you got Logan and Jax circling around you in protection, but don't fool yourself. You're not wanted there. You found that out last year because of us. We were up front about it. These hoes," she gestured around the room, "they'll come at you from behind and stab you in the back. Just wait. I'll be standing by, eating popcorn when that happens."

The anger that had been smoldering in my gut since my encounter with Cass erupted in flames. Feeling a hand from behind, I was shoved forward. A brief thought flashed in my mind. I might as well use this chance, so I didn't fight the shove. I let myself fall forward and my fist clipped Natalie on the chin. *Oops.* As she gasped, I tipped her beer on her. I looked back, saw it had been Cass on her way into the kitchen, and reached for her hair. Grabbing a good fistful of it, I yanked her back and shoved her at Natalie. I showed her off, my hand moving up and down as if revealing a prize. I said to Natalie, "Don't blame me. It was this Academite sweetheart."

Cass' eyes rounded, and she struggled against my hold. "I was shoving you, not her."

"You shoved her *into* me." Natalie set her beer on the counter and pushed from the counter. The crowd around her felt the tension. Eyes turned towards us and a hush fell over the crowd.

"I didn't. I'm sorry. It was her."

"I don't give a shit." Natalie sneered at me. Her gaze locked with mine, and I knew she was aware that I had stepped into her all on my own, but she just shook her head.

I grinned. We weren't done. I'd only given her a new toy to chew on for the meantime.

Becky and Amelia were there, staring at Natalie like she was a hyena circling them on a safari.

Good. My jaw firmed at that thought and I started for the kitchen. There was one last crush of people in front of me, but a hand reached through, grabbed my arm, and I was pulled through the crowd. No one stood in the way; they melted to the side. Logan was glaring at me on the other end, Kris tucked behind him. He asked, "What was that about?"

I shrugged. "Same problems. Different day."

Kris didn't pay attention to me, but I was okay with that. I'd met her last year when she had dated Adam and Jeff was sniffing around her, but it seemed that Adam won out. He brought her to the house one night to watch movies, wanting to spend time with Mark, but Logan and Mason had been there too. I couldn't say it was love at first sight since Logan took one look at her and announced that he fucked her, so it was more like love at second sight. Hell. Even with that, I wasn't sure. All I knew is that Logan started dating Kris after that night, and he enjoyed rubbing it in Adam's face that he stole another girl from him. Since then, Adam had been absent from Mark's house—my house too (I was still getting use to calling it that.) Cass mentioned Adam earlier, but if he was here, I was certain he'd stay hidden in the background.

"Same problems? What are you talking about?"

We heard a girl screech. Recognizing it as Cass, I grabbed a beer from the refrigerator and leaned against the counter beside Kris. Logan scowled at the crowd, but turned to me. His eyes were dark and stormy. Kris had been running her hand through his hair, so the curls were gone. He trimmed it short so little ends stuck up instead. As he continued to glare at me, Kris pressed against his chest. Her hand started roaming over it and lifted his shirt. His stomach muscles rippled from her touch, and he sucked in his breath.

I smiled at him.

He expelled a frustrated sigh. "What did you just do?"

"Nothing."

"Logan," Kris murmured, pressing kisses to his neck and around to his mouth.

He moved out of the way and tucked her to the side. His hand was splayed out on her hip, but she was already reaching for him again. A closer look at her revealed she was beyond drunk. She was obliterated. As she tried pawing for his shirt, he shook his head to clear the lust. His scowl appeared again. "Did Natalie do something?"

"Relax, Logan."

His scowl deepened. "No."

I laughed. "I can handle this now. It's not like before with four against one. I know the game. I know the rules of your school. I can take care of myself now."

His head moved back a fraction of an inch. "Really?"

I nodded and opened my beer. It tasted like copper. "Delicious." I smiled anyway.

"Since when do you drink?"

I lifted a shoulder and let it drop. Since Mason was gone. That thought seared through me, but I banked it down. Instead, I said, "Since I'm a senior. Come on. I don't have a meet this week. I can drink, for one night anyway."

Kris managed to evade his hand and wrapped her arms around his waist. He continued to stare at me, studying me. The good-natured Logan was gone. This was the intense Logan, and to be honest, it was one that I hadn't seen much of. When Mason was around, Logan didn't have to worry as much, because Mason took care of things, but he was gone. This year was different, and now Logan had to take care of things.

"I'm here." Heather landed next to us with a huff. Her eyebrows shot up as she inspected Kris, now trying to get her hand inside of Logan's pants. He didn't deter her wandering hands, and he didn't look away from me. As Heather gestured to the crowd, I looked back at him. He was trying to get inside my head like Mason did. He was trying to figure out what was going on with me. Oblivious to our stare-off, she stated, "I'm here two seconds and a chick fight broke out. Talk about that nothing's changed..." She trailed off as she focused us. "Oh."

Logan's jaw clenched.

He was pissed about something. As Kris lifted his shirt and started pressing kisses to his chest, he didn't move. He never broke eye contact.

My jaw hardened, and I raised it. Two could play at this game. What was I doing? I was declaring that something was wrong. Logan wasn't an idiot, nor was he a chicken shit. He would find me later, and he would interrogate me until I confessed, or, I gulped, he'd tell Mason and Mason would get it out of me within seconds.

I dropped the anger, even though I wasn't sure what I was so mad about, and tried to give him a small grin.

His eyes narrowed even more.

"Okay." Heather waved a hand between us. "Not sure what's going on, but I have to pee. Sam, since I'm sure you know this house and all the ways to sneak in and out, why don't you show me to the nearest and most private bathroom we can find?"

I broke the spell and turned away. "Yeah, sure."

"Great." She took my hand and stepped forward, pushing me to the side, forcing Logan to move back a bit. She gave me the space I needed. *What the hell was my problem?* She stared at Logan, but said to me, "So, which way do we go?"

I tugged her backwards. Before we slipped past the refrigerator, she snaked her hand out and grabbed a case of beer. Tucking it against her chest, she turned and followed me, flashing me a smile. "I'm all set. Something tells me we're in need of a girl chat."

I sighed. I had evaded an interrogation from Logan, but I was going to get a different one. As I led her through the hallways and up the stairs, I took her to Mason's room. When she saw the coded lock installed on the outside the door, her eyebrows shot up. I keyed in the code and let us in, saying, "He's not dumb. He knew Logan would eventually have a party or his mom would snoop in here." I gestured to his bathroom. "It's all yours."

"I'm not going to find anything gross and maybe personal in there, am I?"

"No. He mostly stayed with me."

"Gotcha." Putting the beer on his desk, she took a can with her and hollered from inside, "Help yourself. Something's telling me you need to get lit tonight."

I had already had one, but she was right. I took another.

Mason had a couch and love seat on one side of his room. His desk had been custom built into the wall, between two closet doors. His king-sized bed was set in the corner, on a slight pedestal.

I sunk down on one of the couches when Heather came out. She gazed around and whistled. "Shit. It boggles my mind that this is just one of his rooms. He's got like eight hundred, right? His mom's house. His dad's. At college. Yours. Where else?" She pointed to me with her beer can. "That's right, that one penthouse thing you told me he took you to. The lifestyle of the rich and dicks."

"Mason's not a dick."

"Yes, he is." She laughed as she sunk down on his desk chair, straddling it, facing me. "But he's not to you or to anyone he loves, and that's what makes him so damn hot."

I fiddled with the tab on my beer can. I missed him. A wave of longing rolled over me, suffocating me. My throat swelled, and I forgot about Tate's words for a moment. I could feel Mason's arms around me. I could feel his hard chest as I rested my head on it. I could even feel the soft graze of his fingers as he tucked a strand of hair behind my ear, dropping a soft, delicate kiss to my forehead.

Feeling the threat of tears, I shook my head and cleared the yearning. Fuck the three hours driving there, I was ready to throw my purse in the car and head there right now.

"Are you going to tell me, or are you going to make me force it out of you?"

Heather's clear, sober voice was like a bucket of ice water.

"Sam."

I jerked my head up. My fingers were still playing with beer can's tab, and I cleared my throat. "Yeah?"

"Girl," she leaned forward, intense scrutiny on her face, and stated, "you better start talking, or I'm going to drag Logan in here and make him start talking. Either way, I'm getting the truth."

"Why?"

I cursed under my breath as her eyebrows shot up, and she leaned back. "So there is something? Holy shit. What is it?"

I hung my head. Crap. My secret was out. She might as well know all of it before it ate me alive. I looked up, feeling all the fear, all the burden, all the potential destruction these words caused. I said, "Logan's in love with me."

CHAPTER THREE

MASON

I glanced at my phone. It was almost ten and Sam would be calling at eleven. If we left for this party now, I knew I might miss her call. That couldn't happen. Something had been wrong with Sam all summer. I knew she was worried about being apart for a year, but everything would be fine. It was one year. It sucked. Okay, it didn't suck. It was torture at times, but even thinking about her and knowing she was probably with Logan right now, when I was supposed to head to one of Nate's parties, felt like a branding iron to my heart.

Fuck. Whatever. This was what we had to do, but I hated it.

My roommate came back from the shower and glared at me. A towel hung around his neck, and his hands went to his hips. He let the other towel fall. His stomach rolls jiggled as he held back his laughter. "You, man. Matteo doesn't like this. This party, nothing good will come from it."

I showed him my phone. "I'm Skyping with my girlfriend."

Curses came from him as he dove for his towel and disappeared back into the bathroom.

I laughed, threw the phone on the bed, and finished dressing. When he didn't hear any voices, he poked his head back out. His eyes fell to the phone and he scowled. "You a liar, Kade. That wasn't cool."

"Got your fat dick out of my face, didn't it?"

"That's right. Be jealous." He pounded a hand to his chest and swept off his towel again. "It's like the helicopter." His hips started moving, as did his dick, and his white teeth gleamed back at me. He smacked a hand to his bald head as he kept moving his dick in circles. "It goes round and round. All the girls like it. You should try this move. I bet your girl will like it."

Pulling a shirt over my chest, I shook my head. "Sam hasn't complained yet, but I'll keep it in mind."

He grunted and slapped his stomach, making those rolls jiggle again. "It's the only thing that matters, keeping your woman happy. You got a good one?" He didn't wait for my answer and went into his closet. A second later, Matteo came out with a pair of pants, a shirt, a pair of boxers, and socks. As he sat on his bed and began to pull his boxers on, he glanced at me. "Those are some nice threads. You must come from money, Kade."

I scowled. I did, but I didn't want that to define me. "My rich parents didn't pay for these clothes if that's where you're going."

"Oh. Whoa, my dude. I was gonna say that you don't seem like one of those rich pricks." He held his hands in the air, making a show of backing up a step, smirking at me. "I'm messing with you. I can be wack sometimes." He hit himself in the chest.

"Sometimes?"

"Oh ho ho. You funny, man. You funny." He pointed his hand at me and shook his head, laughing as he grabbed his wallet, put two condoms inside, and slid his phone into his pocket. He stood up and spread his arms wide. "How do I look?"

Matteo was tall and large. He had muscles, but some of it was fat. Being an offensive lineman, he needed that. I'd been practicing and rooming with him for three weeks, so I knew he was quick and fierce on the field, but easygoing and a joker off. I was tempted to tell him he looked like one of those rich pricks he was referencing, but I didn't. He wore a white polo over trendy khakis and sneakers that put him in that rich prick category. I knew how much those were, but I didn't want to question it. Where he got his money wasn't my concern. We were still getting to know each other.

"You're good. You hoping to get a few girls?"

"Me?" His eyebrows shot up. He was tan, with white teeth and handsome features. He could. From what I had witnessed around campus, football players at Cain University were like gods. Matteo would have no problem getting a girl, or two, if that's what he wanted. "No, no, no. I'm taken. My girl's meeting me at this party. Speaking of," the scowl he had been wearing when he first dropped his towel reappeared, "we never go to Park Sebastian's frat parties. Why are we making an exception tonight?"

"My best friend pledged. His dad's an alumni." I lifted my chin. "Why's your girl going?"

"Her friends like the frat pricks. She doesn't. She's going because of me." He paused. "You're talking about that dude you were trying to get Coach to let him live in the football house with us?'"

"Yeah." Nate hadn't been happy when he heard the entire house was for football players. He wasn't good enough to make the team, but he'd been fine with that. Nate had known coming into Cain U that he wouldn't be on the team with me. However, when he found out the living situation, he went a different route. "He says they're the best frat to pledge?"

Matteo's scowl deepened. "Because Sebastian's an ass kisser. You're warned, Kade. He's going to try and do you doggie-style. He's been around the game, and he loves football players, especially a football player that's going to the pros. He's like his dad, some senator. They pull people in close until those people aren't useful to them, then they drop 'em."

I followed Matteo, as he led the way to the hallway and down the stairs. A few other players were waiting for us. It was the first night we didn't have practice in the morning. When Nate mentioned the party, I figured I'd go to be supportive. The guys found out and more than a handful wanted to tag along.

When we were on the sidewalk, covering the three blocks to frat row, I asked, "So, how do you know all this?"

"Because he screwed over my best friend last year."

"Yeah?"

"Jamie Satture. They were real good buddies until Jamie got hurt and lost his scholarship. He thought Sebastian would help him out since his fraternity has a lot of money and his father's corporation sponsored the scholarship, but no way, man. That prick dropped him like a one-night stand. Ignored him for the rest of the year. He's bad news, dude. I'd stay away from that one."

It was noted. I wasn't a pushover, but these guys didn't know that. They knew it on the field, but not off. I'd been warned. I knew what I was walking into, and I wasn't happy. Nate was friends with these guys. It'd been a vacation in some ways, being out of Fallen Crest. There were no battles. People weren't plotting to take me down or fighting with my brother or my girlfriend. It'd been me and football. Even Nate had kept away since he was busy with his fraternity. I had a strong hunch that those simple days were about to end. If Sebastian was half as bad as Matteo said, he would not like me. He might think he would, but he'd find out I wasn't one to be manipulated.

Letting out a silent sigh, I grimaced. I didn't want to deal with that battle, but if it came, it came.

The street leading to frat row was packed with cars, which wasn't a surprise. Every road within the campus vicinity rarely had an open parking spot. When we rounded the block, it was evident which one was Nate's house. It was an old house with bricks and green stuff growing up the walls. Greek letters had been carved into the brick above the front door. The lawn had people all over it. The door was open and music blared out from it. As we started across the street, people stopped and watched us. I'd gotten used to anonymity over the last three weeks. Classes hadn't started so no one knew me, but walking with this group of guys, all large and toned, they knew who we were. A group of girls turned to gawk from the patio. Shock filled their gazes and one girl's mouth dropped open. Another dropped her drink.

"Hold up."

A guy separated from a group of guys on the lawn. He disappeared inside, and it wasn't long before another guy came out with him. The second one was taller, as tall as me, but leaner. I grunted. This was Park Sebastian. I could already tell. He was a pretty boy with enough arrogance to fill a blimp. This guy was another Adam Quinn, and at that reminder, I gritted my teeth. The old feeling to rip into Quinn came back to me, but this guy was the new target.

His eyes lingered on Matteo, who lifted his chin in a challenge. Sebastian pressed his lips together, as if holding back a scowl, but walked towards me. His eyebrows furrowed together. I could see it plain as day. He was racking his brain, wondering if we had met already. We had, the day I helped Nate move in, but he hadn't given two shits about me that day, and I hadn't with him. Things were different. My reputation as a wide receiver had been building since I got to school. With my performance on the field and in practice, I wouldn't have been surprised if that had been the real motivation behind Nate's invitation. He hadn't invited me to one all summer. As I stood there and looked right back at Sebastian, I wondered if I was staring at the real reason I'd been invited.

He looked me up and down, holding a cup of beer in his hand.

I didn't stand for this shit at home; I wasn't going to now. "We can leave, if you'd like."

His head snapped back up, and he narrowed his eyes, assessing me once again, but with a different emotion. I had surprised him. Extending his cup towards Matteo, he said, "I'm not in good standing with the football team. No offense, I'm surprised is all."

Matteo shifted on his feet and growled softly.

"My friend is a pledge. He invited me here."

"You?"

It was an unspoken question to find out who I was. I kept quiet. I had no intention of dancing to his tune.

"Mason!" Nate came from the front door and waved a hand. He jogged off the patio and stopped beside Sebastian. "This is my best friend I was telling you about. Mason Kade, this is Park Sebastian. He's the president of our fraternity."

Park started to hold his arm out. I shot Nate a warning look and he stepped in, laughing, as he blocked his president and held his arm out to Matteo instead. "I'm Nate. You're Mason's roommate, right?"

Matteo glanced sideways at me, but shook Nate's hand with reluctance. A corner of my mouth lifted up in a small smirk, and I rounded behind Matteo to stand on the other side of Nate. I was no longer in his president's line of sight. Nate was firmly between us. Reading the situation correctly, Nate waved at the rest of the guys and gestured to the house. "Park said all football players drink for free. Just let the guys manning the kegs know that Nate Monson vouched for you. They'll know what it means, not that five bucks is a lot of money."

The guys headed inside. If I had stood there, Park would have tried to shake my hand again, and I would have ignored it a second time; I wasn't going to shake the guy's hand. Nate knew the awkward situation would've occurred had Park tried to offer his hand again, so to prevent the insult from happening, he flashed Park a grin. "I'm going to show Mason around. We haven't talked much the last few weeks." He pounded my shoulder. "He's been busy with training."

Sebastian stood there, that same frown on his face from before. The other fraternity brother nodded and grinned, waving to me. "Nice to meet you."

"You too."

As soon as we were clear from their hearing range, he muttered, "Fuck, Mason. That didn't take long."

I flashed him a grin. "Yeah. Well, you know me."

He groaned, weaving through the crowd. "You want a drink?"

"No, I'm training."

"Oh." He shook his head. "I didn't even think about that."

"The guys might have a few, but they won't go nuts."

He moved his head in a nod and continued to move through the crowd until we were in the backyard. Guys and girls clapped him on the shoulder, calling out hellos and greetings. Nate said hello to each in return until he found a back table in the corner of the yard. There were a few chairs around it, but we had a private area to watch the party. I nodded. I liked it. As we sat, I noticed people were still watching us.

"Since we're alone right now," Nate started as he sat across from me, "you don't like Park, I'm assuming?"

"He's an asshole."

"You just met him."

"That's all I needed. What's going on with you? I'm not known for getting my reads wrong."

Nate sighed, irritation flashing across his face. Seeing some of the players coming over with their beer, he cursed. "This isn't good."

"Why?"

"Because Park wants to get to know you. His dad gave him the heads-up about you and to make friends with you because of your dad. He asked me about you. I never brought you up to him because I figured the two of you meeting face to face would go how it did." The guys were almost on us, so he hissed, "I don't want a war happening with my fraternity."

"Too late."

He stood, holding my gaze. The guys stopped as they saw the tension. Nate shook his head. "Really? This is for me. You're going to do this?"

"I'm not doing shit." For fuck's sake. This wasn't Fallen Crest. An act of war didn't have to be thrown out there, not yet, anyway. This was on Nate to handle. "I'm here for football and school. That's it. I don't want to get involved with any political social stuff." And that was the problem. That was who Park Sebastian was. Every nerve in my body went on alert when I saw him. Even without Matteo's warning, I would've pegged him the same way. I was surprised Nate hadn't.

He cursed again and stepped back from the table. The guys sat down around it, and Nate shook his head again. "I'll have to figure something out."

"Yeah."

"Fuck, Mason." Nate cocked his head to the side.

I didn't say anything. He should've seen this coming. "When have I ever been friends with guys like that?"

"He knows your dad."

"When has that mattered to me?"

"He knows my dad."

I kept silent. It wasn't my problem. This was his problem, and Nate knew it. He rolled his eyes, raked a hand through his hair, and started to leave. "I gotta take care of this somehow."

He was gone, disappearing through the crowd again.

The guys didn't seemed fazed by our conversation. A few of them were eyeing up the girls, and Matteo grunted at me, nodding his head in approval. "That was smooth, Kade, real smooth."

He had no idea.

He lifted his cup up in the air. "A toast to Kade. I'm thinking this year's going to be epic, on and off the field."

"Hell yeah."

"Cheers!"

"Salute to Kade."

I tuned them out. They raised their cups, did their toasts, and went back to drinking. As we stayed there, most of the guys took off to find girls. Matteo's girlfriend came over with a couple friends, but I tuned their conversations out.

I had only met the guy, but my gut was telling me Park Sebastian was going to be a problem. Nate came over later, less stressed and less sober. I knew this could be a problem with our friendship. Only time would tell. I missed Sam and Logan.

CHAPTER FOUR

SAMANTHA

Heather's eyes got big, but they quickly went back to normal. I caught it, though. She scoffed, her voice sounding strangled, "Huh."

That was it? "You're not surprised?"

"Girl," she started, her voice hoarse. She blinked, cleared her throat, and said in a clearer tone, "I don't think that will shock anyone."

I closed my eyes. This was worse than I thought. If this was her reaction—dear god—that meant it was true. At that thought, my chest grew tight and my heart began pounding. I started sweating and breathing heavy. I was having a panic attack, right here at this party.

Heather had been watching me, and when she saw I was struggling to catch some air, she shot up from her chair. "Christ." She went into the bathroom, and I heard the water running a second later. She came back out with wet washcloths. Wiping one over my forehead, she bent me forward and pushed my head between my knees. She knelt down, patted me on the back, and continued to press the cold washcloth to me. "Breathe, Sam.

Breathe." She began to count in a low calm voice. "One. Two. Three. Four. Five."

I took a breath with each number she said. When she got to sixty, I could breathe naturally again and sat back up.

Heather shook her head and backed away, her eyes wide. As she stumbled against her seat, she plopped down with a thud and pressed the back of her hand to her face. "Holy fuck, Sam. You are pale as a ghost. Shit. The thought of Logan loving you does that to you?"

I didn't want to look in the mirror. Seeing Heather waiting, with concern in her eyes, I opened my mouth. I needed to say something, but I couldn't talk. The lump in my throat constricted all sound from leaving. I closed my mouth and hung my head. What the hell was I going to do?

"You don't..." She started and stopped. "You don't love him back?"

A jolt of pain flashed through me. I raised my tortured eyes to her. I couldn't answer that. No, I didn't want to answer that because I hadn't looked within myself yet.

She watched me, studied me. Whatever she saw in me answered her question, and she nodded. "Okay. I will help you with whatever you need from me. If you need me to play distraction, to use force, to blackmail someone, to burn a house down, I'm down for all that. I'm here for you, for whatever's going to happen." She stopped, hearing herself, and the blood drained from her face. "You have any idea what would happen if this came out? Shit. The world would end. Mason and Logan would want to kill each other."

Renewed pain went through me, but it doubled. It had already felt like a thousand knives were in my stomach, but at that statement, they began slicing through me.

She saw my misery and nodded. "I guess you do."

Exactly.

"Okay. Well," she looked around, fanning herself, "first thing first, you need to get out of here. Logan can't see you like that or he'll be like a dog after a bone. He won't let up until you make up some passable lie to him."

We were headed for the door when she stopped me and turned me to face her. She scanned over my face and cursed. "You need color. We can't even leave without someone seeing you. They'll report to Logan right away." As she was talking, her hands reached up and slapped my cheeks softly. Then pinched them. Still frowning, she bit her lip and continued to talk around it, "They all just want an excuse to run to Logan and this would be a good one." She stopped and asked, "You trust me?"

My eyes widened, but without giving me a moment to brace myself, she reached for the top of my head and pulled me down. I bent over, and she pulled me back up. Feeling blood rush through me, I shook my head to clear some of the hazy spots in my eyes. Heather ran her hands through my hair and fluffed it up, before rubbing my cheeks again. When she stepped back, I felt slightly normal. She nodded. "You look better. I think you'll pass."

She opened the door. We stood beside each other, paused for a moment, and started forward. The hallway was empty. Heather led the way, but when she was going back towards the party, I touched her arm. I pointed the opposite way. "There's a door down there we can slip through."

"Okay." Her voice dropped to a whisper and she paused. She laughed with a half-grin. "Why am I whispering?"

I laughed, and my own normal sound seemed to grate against my ears. "Because we're trying to sneak out, even though we shouldn't feel guilty about doing that."

"You're right." She rolled her shoulders back and lifted her head. "Let's do this, Strattan. We can sneak out like proud ninjas."

I started to laugh, but as we went further down the hallway, a door opened and the laugh died abruptly. Logan was coming out of his room.

Heather saw him at the same time and a savage curse left her.

Hearing her, he glanced up. His eyes narrowed, took us in, and he headed towards us. Shoving his hands in his pockets, his gaze lingered the longest on me before he asked, "What were you guys doing?"

"We had a female chat," Heather spoke up. "What were you doing?"

"Kris passed out. I put her to bed."

"Is your door locked?"

He nodded. "Yeah, I got the same lock that Mason did." His eyebrows bunched forward as he continued to study me. I could feel his suspicion growing and forced myself to keep a mask on my face. Logan couldn't press me. I might not spill what Tate said, what I now knew, but I wouldn't be able to hold back that there was something wrong. He'd be relentless, and it couldn't come out. No matter what. He asked, in a soft voice, "You okay?"

Heather spoke first again, "She's fine. She's missing Mason, *her boyfriend*, that's all."

He turned his dark look to her. "I know who my brother is, and why are you speaking for her?"

"Because I want to. Because I'm spoiling for a fight, Kade, and if you don't want it to be you, you better stand aside."

He didn't move.

She barked, "Now."

He still didn't move. He only lowered his head and narrowed his eyes at her. Glancing at me again, I felt the weight of his gaze. It didn't matter. He knew something was up, and he knew it had nothing to do with the lies Heather had been throwing at him. Logan was like Mason. He could sense through bullshit. Turning so he was facing me directly, he asked, "What's going on? No shit story, tell me what's up."

I closed my eyes; I was caught. I shook my head. "I can't."

"Sam?"

"Logan," there was no way this could happen, "let this go."

He heard the warning in my tone and seemed to reassess me. I never talked to him like this, but this was different terrain for both of us. Mason was always there. Mason was the go-between. Mason was the one we confided in, and now he was gone. Concern and doubt clouded over him and he jerked his head in a nod. Stepping aside, he said in a hurt tone, "Okay. I will."

A pang of guilt went through me. I ignored it and told myself this was for the best. "Thank you."

"You don't have to leave, though. Or do you? Is," he hesitated, still watching me intently, "that the reason you're leaving, whatever is wrong?"

"I..." I turned to Heather. It had been, but now... She shrugged at me. "I guess not."

"Well, in that case, you want to play me and Mark in a game of beer pong?" Logan flashed me a smirk. "Losers lose their shirts."

Heather laughed. "That's not an equal loss. If you lose, you're my beer bitch next weekend." She elbowed me. "Mark'll have to be her bitch at home."

"And if you guys lose?"

She glanced at me, but I shrugged. She said, "What's our punishment?"

I felt his gaze again. Without looking, I knew he wanted to say that I would have to tell him what was wrong, but I glanced up. He saw the warning that flashed in my eyes and said, "You're my beer bitch instead, Jax. How about that?"

"And Sam'll be Mark's bitch at home?"

"Sounds like a good trade."

They were both pretending with their lighthearted banter, but it was camouflage on both ends. I had a problem. Heather knew what it was. Logan wanted to know it. I forced out a laugh. "Since we got those terms decided, let's do this." I headed off, leading the way downstairs. The entire conversation had been awkward, and I knew the game would be too.

When we got downstairs and headed for the ping-pong table, it was a surreal moment for me. The room was filled with people from my past. Natalie and Jasmine were in one corner, drinking and talking with some guys. They both paused when we came into the room, but went back to doing their own thing. Across from them was Cass and her group. They were glaring across the room at the two girls, but I saw fear lurking in Cass' gaze. She was holding an ice bag to her eye, and her lip looked swollen. Her friends were rallied around her as well. Adam was in the background, leaning against the wall with Mark beside him. The two were talking and laughing together. My gaze trailed right in front of Adam, and I saw Becky. She was watching me. There was a hidden emotion in the depths of her eyes, but I didn't want to decipher it. We had sort of made-up. She had been invited to my birthday party, but she'd been absent from my life since. That was fine. I had made a decision to let her and Adam both go. There was always drama involved with the two of them and they kept hurting me, in some manner. When she looked to Heather, I saw the hurt and jealousy on her face.

She thought she had been replaced, but the truth was that Heather had been a true friend. Becky never really had.

Logan stood behind one side of the table and hollered, "Decraw, get your ass over here. Jax and Sam are challenging us."

"WHAT?" Mark pretended to roar back, a wicked grin on his face. He acted insulted, pressing a hand to his chest. "How could this be? This is blasphemy. We are the unconquered gods of beer pong. They dare to threaten our throne?" He left his group of friends in a dramatic flair, as if Logan had hooked him with a fishing line and reeled him in.

"Seriously?" Heather took up position next to me. She shifted on her feet, sticking a hip out and curling her lip up at them. "Can you be more dramatic? Kade challenged us. It wasn't the other way around."

I grinned. Mark had gotten funnier over the summer. He'd been an easygoing guy before, going with the flow, but since Logan decided that Mark would be his new best bud because Mason was gone, the two had become a comedy duo.

Ignoring Heather, Mark jumped and landed with a thud in front of Logan. They pretended to do some type of handshake before sticking their groins out at us. The crowd around us started laughing.

"Anyone else and they would get roasted for being dorks, but since Logan Kade did it, it's the funniest thing they've ever seen." Heather shook her head. She glanced to the sidelines and poked me. "Aren't those two your old BFFs?"

I looked over. Jessica and Lydia were standing by a wall, sipping on their drinks. Two guys were with them, both had their arms around the girls' waists. When they saw I was looking their way, both sucked in their stomachs and stretched their heads, as if trying to look long and sleek.

Heather started laughing. I couldn't hold back my own grin. The old hostility was in their gazes. Lydia turned away after a moment, but Jessica held my stare. She lowered her drink and glared right back. I sighed and murmured, "Yeah, they used to be. That seems so long ago now."

"They're bitches. You're better off."

I hadn't seen Jeff at the party. Scanning the crowd, I ignored the envy from the girls and the interest from some of the guys. A year ago, I'd been an outcast and had to fight for my place at

Mason and Logan's school the semester after that. For once, there was no one planning my demise. Remembering Natalie's veiled threat, I wasn't worried. This year was going to be different. I felt it in my gut. Since Mason was gone, the target wasn't so big on my back. It was still there because of my closeness with Logan, but not as big. It was freeing and that sucked because I knew it was mostly because Mason wasn't there.

"You okay?" Heather had been waiting, watching me.

I nodded. "Yeah."

"Strattan," Logan barked from across the table. He held a ping-pong ball in his hand and gestured to the cups of beer in front of us. "You ready to be our bitches next weekend?"

He was grinning. He looked like the usual carefree Logan that most knew, but I knew part of it was an act. He wouldn't let it go, knowing that something was wrong. It was only a matter of time before he'd get it out of me. I just wasn't ready for that day because when it came out, when I told him that I knew, everything would change. No matter what the truth was, I was scared of losing him and Mason.

He lowered his hand, his grin fading to a small, concerned look.

I shook it off. I couldn't lose them, either one of them. I gave him a reassuring grin and vowed that the truth wouldn't come out. It couldn't. I would be destroyed the day it did.

He lifted his hand again, but the dark concern was still in his eyes. As I watched, he masked it himself and threw the first toss. It landed in the cup right in front of me and without a moment's

44

hesitation, I downed the beer. He could win. I wouldn't care. I was ready to drink all of it that night.

"Well, then." Heather grinned at me. "Looks like Sam's ready to party this year."

I gave her a half-grin, but hung my head at the same time. Mason should've been there. When I looked back up, Logan was studying me. Our gazes collided and he saw the pain in my eyes. Somehow I knew that he understood. He nodded, growing serious for a brief moment. In that one second, we were on the same page. We both missed Mason.

That made everything worse. A burden like I had never felt before was placed on my shoulders. No one could get hurt. It was on me. Tate told me the secret, whether Logan's feelings were true or not, I would shoulder it on my own.

I didn't wait for them to throw again. I grabbed another cup and downed it.

Mark's mouth fell open, but he lifted his arms up in victory. "Keep going, Sam. Mom won't do my laundry so guess what you'll get to do?" He dropped his arms and rubbed his hands together.

I didn't care. My chest and throat were burning. I was willing to do anything to make that sensation go away.

CHAPTER FIVE

MASON

It had been a week since Nate's party, and he called once to have lunch together. Things were different. That was obvious, but I didn't know if it was me or him. I figured it was him since I hadn't changed. I kept to myself and did my own thing. Like right now, most of the team had gone, but I stayed behind. Coach switched my position. I'd been big enough to play lineman in high school, but I wasn't big enough in college. With my speed and still being muscular, just not lineman muscular, he had me as wide receiver now. I had known since the summer he was planning this, and I tried to train a lot during then, but it was different being here. The feeling to play catch-up was weighing me down.

I was running drills when Matteo hollered at me from the sidelines. "Yo, Kade. We be out, man. You sticking around?"

I stopped and wiped the sweat from my forehead so I could see. "Yeah. I'll see you back at the house."

"We're grilling tonight. Grab any food you want grilled up."

"Yeah." When they left, there weren't many others on the field. A few of the assistant coaches were standing in a huddle, talking, but I glanced over and saw my coach watching me.

He changed my position on this team so I needed all the extra training hours I could get. I exploded to cone two, ran around to cone three, passed the second for the fourth cone, and circled back to the second cone. I finished strong going back to the first cone. *Drop your shoulder. Drop your shoulder. Chop your feet, up and down, up and down. Lower the hip. Pivot with your arms.*

When I was done, I repeated it four more times and turned in bounds for twenty yards. I repeated that three times, leaping as high as I could as I covered the distance. After resting for two minutes, I began again with my drills. I kept doing them until some of the lights were shut off.

One of the assistant coaches hollered from across the field, "Go home, Kade. We're closing up."

"Okay." I lifted an arm, but it was too heavy, so I nodded instead. Panting, knowing every inch of me reeked, I headed off to the shower. The locker room was empty except for another player. He was in the weight room and glanced up, but neither of us said anything. We nodded to the other as I went to clean-up. When I left, he was still doing curls.

Walking into the stadium during the day was daunting. This was my dream. I'd been planning to play professional ball since I could remember. Playing for a Division One school was the next step. I was on the doorstep to the professionals. I could taste it. As I left the stadium, a lot of the hallways were dark since the late hour. I got out the doors and headed for the parking lot.

When I stepped off the curb to my vehicle, I noticed there were only a few cars in the lot.

"Mason?"

I stopped when I saw a girl leaning against the far wall of the stadium, and a wave of recognition came over me. Seeing me, she straightened from the wall. She had two friends with her, but they moved farther down. She glanced back to them, and they nodded their encouragement. When she drew closer, I took in the brown hair and dark eyes. The petite frame was the same, but she wasn't the shy high school girl anymore. Dressed in a tight pink shirt and tight jeans like all the other girls at this school, I was surprised to see the confidence in her now.

I grinned. "Marissa."

Her hands lifted to her side. She pressed the back of her hands against them for a second before a smile appeared. She let her arms drop down. Her head was tilted to the side, and as she drew closer, her cheeks grew pink. "Mason." She said my name in a rush.

The confidence *was* there; I saw it appear for a moment. This was the shy girl from high school that I remembered. "Is this a coincidence or..." I studied her friends. They were turned towards each other with their heads bent forward. One was watching me over the other one's shoulders. When she saw me watching them, she jerked back and whispered something to the other. The girl standing with her back to me stiffened. This wasn't a coincidence, but I asked anyway, "Or were you waiting for me?"

"Um." She lifted a hand to scratch her ear. It fell and linked with her other hand, and she lifted up on her tiptoes in a nervous movement. As she rocked back down to her heels, a high-pitched laugh came from her. "This is really embarrassing."

She'd been waiting for me. I had known she was a student at Cain University. She emailed me after she was accepted. I hadn't responded. In fact, I hadn't responded to any of her emails in over a year. She never stopped sending them and because of that, I could understand her embarrassment. Logan told me that I was leading her on after bringing her to the cabin with us. I cut all communication after that, but I'm guessing it hadn't been enough.

I wasn't going to dance around the conversation this time. "Marissa," I started.

She stopped fidgeting. Her gaze jerked to mine and she gulped. She heard the seriousness in my tone, and she held a hand up. "Wait. Mason, wait."

I narrowed my eyes.

She ducked her head down. Her fingers slipped into her pockets, and her hands hung there. "I've been thinking a lot about our friendship over the years."

I didn't have a good feeling about this. "And I think that you started to assume I liked you. I didn't." Her eyes lifted, met mine, and looked away again. Her cheeks grew redder. "Okay, that was a lie. I did like you. I mean, I thought you were my knight in shining armor, the popular guy who became friends with me. I'm nothing. Then the girls started in." She stopped and drew in a ragged breath. Her voice grew thick with emotion as she continued, "You have no idea the things they did."

Regret stabbed at me. "They did the same to Sam."

She still wasn't looking at me. Her hand had been moving back and forth, but she stopped it. All motion froze for a moment. "Your girlfriend?"

"Yeah. She transferred to Public last semester and they tried to do some messed up things to her."

"Like what?"

"Stealing her clothes was the nicest of their pranks, for one." The image of Sam in that hospital bed, her face bruised up, and her body wrapped in bandages flashed in my mind again. It was seared there. I'd never get it out. "They put her in the hospital."

"They did?" She lifted her head again. Her lip trembled. "They never did that to me."

"Sam fought back."

She flinched and looked away. "Oh."

I grimaced. I had insulted her, but that hadn't been my intention. "Look, I'm sorry. That wasn't a shot at you. I was trying to tell you that you weren't the only one who got hurt by Kate and her friends."

A sad laugh came from her. "It wasn't just Kate for me. It was half the school. All the girls hated me. All of them."

"I'm sorry that I didn't stop it."

"I don't know how you could have."

"I could've tried. I did when they were hurting Sam, but I didn't when they were hurting you. I should've stepped in. I'm sorry that I never did. I'm sorry that you had to transfer because of all that shit."

She twisted around. Her friends were watching us. They moved closer when they saw Marissa looking at them. "I have to go." She shook her head, and I could hear the sob in her throat. "I'm sorry, Mason. I have to go."

51

She started for her friends, and they met her half way. Both of them put their arms around her shoulder, and they hurried from the parking lot. They headed down the sidewalk and into the main campus. I watched them for a moment and shrugged. Marissa wasn't my problem anymore. I felt bad about what happened to her and I apologized to her. I meant the apology, and whether she took it or not, that was on her.

*

SAMANTHA

After changing into my running clothes, I headed to the field where everyone was waiting for the coach. The guys had been sent ahead, but we would be running the same course as them. I dropped down to the grass to stretch. When the other girls came out, some of them began stretching like me, but they sat away from me. A burst of laughter sounded from further down the field and everyone looked. A group of girls were coming towards us. Someone groaned a few feet from me, "Juniors. Honestly. Why do we have to run with them?"

I bent over my leg, reaching for my toe. The seniors kept their distance from me, so the juniors wouldn't be a problem. A lot of them were just in awe that I was dating Mason Kade, but I heard my name, "Sam!"

I paused and cursed. Kris was waving at me. Dressed in running pants and a tight top, her hair pulled back in a ponytail, she bounced over to me. Literally bounced. She dropped down next to me. Bringing her feet together in front of her, she cupped them and bent over, but turned to me. She was beaming. "Hey! Did Logan tell you I was joining the team?"

Fuck no. I smiled at her. "He didn't. I didn't know you were a runner?"

"Oh." She shrugged. Her knee was lifted and pressed to her chest as she hugged it for a moment. She did the same with the other one. "I like running. I'm not in your league, but when he found out, he suggested I join the team. I'm new, all for a team spirit, you know."

Still smiling, still forcing it, I commented, "I'm surprised you didn't do cheerleading."

She laughed and spread her legs. She reached for her right ankle, cupped it, and began to lower down over her leg. "Oh, you know, I did think about it. I can be peppy and annoying, I know, but I would've joined to try and make friends. Not to inflate my own balloon, but because I'm dating Logan, I don't have to try at being popular. Being his girlfriend makes a lot of girls super nice to me, if you know what I mean."

My smile widened, and I showed my teeth. "That's funny. They tried to kill me last year."

She chuckled, switched legs, and continued, "Yeah, so there's that. But, to be honest, I doubt my sister would come to see me if I was cheerleading for the football game or something. She'll come to a cross-country meet, though. I know that." She shook her head, wearing a fond smile. "She likes to stalk around in the shadows. She and I are completely different."

"Kris!" One of the girls she walked out with waved. "Come here. I need a partner."

"Oh." Her chuckle faded. "I joined the team to hang out with you, but do you mind if I run with those girls? They're in my grade and the friendships are new. You know how those things are."

My eyes widened. She had expected to run with me? "Uh, that's no problem. I run alone."

"Oh yeah. Logan said something about that. Okay. Good." She hopped to her feet and pretended to punch me in the shoulder. "I'll see you later, if you don't make us eat your dust too early." Without waiting for a response, she went over and dropped next to her group of friends. They moved so they formed a circle, all of them facing each other, and it wasn't long before they were counting out loud at the same time.

The same girl from before groaned again. "Fucking juniors."

I grunted in agreement and went back to stretching. After I finished, I started jogging in place until Coach came out. As he did, everyone stood and he gave us our instructions. It was the same every day. We were told which trail to run, which we always knew because it rotated, and we were told to clock our times when we returned before another stretching period. He looked at me. "Strattan, stay behind a second." He blew his whistle and the girls started off.

I waited until everyone cleared out. "Yeah, Coach?"

"The boys took off ten minutes ago. See if you can take 'em and let me know if they give you a hard time."

"Why?"

He grunted and started walking away. "Because their egos have grown the size of a planet. I need 'em crushed."

"Oh." I grinned. "Will do." I started off. The girls weren't too far ahead, and I was beginning to hit my first stride as I came up to the last ones. I felt the urge to lengthen my stride and lose myself, but I kept it in check as I concentrated on slowly moving up the group. Kris was at the back of the line with her friends. They were still laughing together, but I knew that'd end in another half mile. Kris' cheeks were slightly pink, and she waved as I came up next to her. Giving her a small grin, I continued forward. I wasn't pushing it. I was maintaining my normal pace. It wasn't long before I passed the majority of the girls. There was another group at the front. I'd been running with some of these girls over the last two weeks in August and before school started, so they didn't react when they saw me edging past them. Two more girls were in the lead, but they were staggered, one behind the other. Both of them were seniors and I knew one, Tori, was hoping for a track scholarship. Both wore grim expressions. Their lips were flat. Their shoulders were slightly bent, their head down a tiny bit, and they were breathing easy.

After a few strides, I passed both and the path was clear for me. I had the guys to catch up to. They had a good start on us so I wasn't surprised when it took me almost a mile to catch up. Clearing a hill, I saw their heads go down over the next hill. My blood was pumping, but the sight of them sent a surge through me. This was the ultimate competition, going head to head with the males. Bending forward a bit, I kept my hands loose and continued going down on my heels and pushing off with my toes.

When I began the incline for the second hill, my head went low
and I kept going. They were halfway up another hill as I cleared it.

They were laughing and one glanced back. His eyes widened
when he saw me, then he said something to the others. Their pace
picked up.

I grinned. That would make it sweeter. It took one more hill
until I was neck and neck with the last of them. They were all
glancing at me. The laughter was gone and each wore a somber
expression. Without a word spoken among them, they sped up
again. One guy quickened his speed and the rest followed. I knew
they were running faster than they normally did. It would tire
them out so I waited. I fell behind them, keeping my normal pace.

One glanced at me. A small smirk was on his face, and I knew
they expected me to fall further back. I didn't. I kept on their heels,
out of reach, but close enough to press them ahead. They covered
half a mile and one broke. He fell back. Two of his friends shared a
look. They weren't surprised. I ignored the guy beside me, and it
was four steps before he was behind me as well. Thirty more yards
and another fell behind. I passed him instantly. The last two grew
worried. They cast a look at me. I smiled, yes, I was still there.
They didn't look again. Their breathing was louder. They were
fighting to keep ahead of me. Looking ahead, I saw the main group
of guys. I could feel the surprise from the two in front of me. They
had caught up, but as soon as they realized that, one slowed his
pace. He was winded. A blink of an eye later, he was behind me
like the others. The last one went as well, and I picked up my pace
to close the distance between the other runners and myself. This
time I didn't wait. I bypassed them. I didn't want to deal with any

games. When I cleared them on the side, I ignored the surprise I sensed from them.

I was in front of them and I went back to the center of the trail. There were more ahead of me. We were on a long run that day so I knew I had two miles to go. With that thought and knowing those two miles weren't going to tire me out, I steadied my breathing and increased my speed. My toes pushed off deeper and my shoulders dug forward. The blood was pumping through me. I felt the strength in my legs and imagined the clean lines from my head to my feet. I kept the perfect running posture and grinned. The rush was there. I loved this, possibly more than anything, and when it only took me half a mile to see the next runners, I opened the gate.

I'd been chomping at the bit, holding back, keeping a tight controlled run, but I let loose. I was sprinting and it was seconds before I passed the first guy, the second, and then the third. He was sixty yards ahead of the rest. I covered that without trying. I felt his surprise and ignored him. Swinging in front of him, I moved so there was plenty of space between him and me, but I wanted to make sure I was in the middle. I wanted to make sure he could see right into the back of my head.

One last mile.

I continued sprinting. When I heard him doing the same, I wasn't surprised, but when we saw the field in the distance, I heard his breathing becoming more winded. As I led the way onto the field and to the finish line, I reached over and tapped the clock. That was my time. A few seconds later, I heard him tap his too, but I continued into a light jog around the track. I wanted my muscles loose. He did as well, but he dropped back and reduced his speed dramatically. Everyone did the same. I jogged around the track for another three laps before I dropped into a walk. When my heart rate steadied out, I went over and began stretching.

The guys were on one side of the field. I was in the middle, but I felt their gazes. Glancing over, as I bent and pressed my nose close to my knee, they had varying expressions of hostility. A few were outright glaring. One was seething, his nostrils flaring up, while others were frowning. One of the guys flashed me a smile and gave me a thumbs-up. "Good job, Strattan. You kicked ass."

I turned my head, stretching over the other leg, but I couldn't hold back my smile. It felt good. It felt damn good. I heard someone say, "Am I right to assume Kade helped with your endurance?"

Releasing my leg, I brought my feet together and bent forward, but I looked back over. "What?"

"Kade. He's fast." It was the guy who had been leading that shrugged. "I know he's not a cross country runner, but he's super-fast for his size. Did he teach you tricks or something?"

Another guy barked out a laugh. "Dude, we all know how she got that endurance. I don't think it had anything to do with running."

The one who gave me the thumbs-up shot a disapproving look at his teammates, but the others laughed. Someone added, "No doubt. Kade's the man."

I rolled my eyes and stood as the first of the girls filtered towards us. "I had to deal with petty bitches last semester. Who knew the cross-country guys would become the new catty girls?" I scoffed, walked past them, then turned and extended my middle fingers. "Here's my thumbs-up except to the one in the yellow shorts." He flashed a grin and said, "Hey, thanks." Still walking backwards, I added, "And just to rub it in, I'm going to run home. Be jealous, bitches. Because I can and I know you can't." Giving them a wink, I turned and started a light jog.

I'd have to have Logan or Mark give me a ride back to get my car, but it would be worth it. *So* worth it.

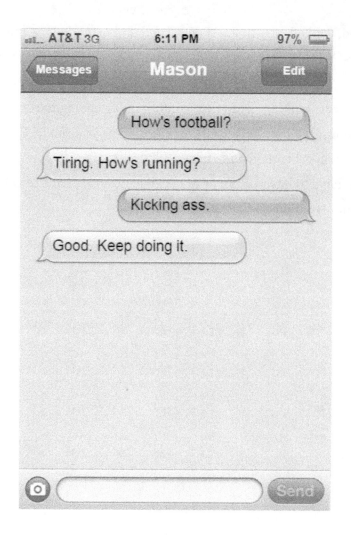

CHAPTER SIX

The next morning, Heather was waiting at my locker for me. She flashed me a quick grin and moved aside so I could open it. As I stowed my bag inside, she said, "Heard you handed a few guys' their asses last night on the run."

I grabbed my book and a couple pencils and pens. "You heard about that? From who?"

"A couple juniors were talking about it when they were coming in." She smirked. "I love people who aren't aware of who else is listening. So did you?"

"Yeah. Coach started me last and told me to smoke the guys. They had a ten minute lead too."

She whistled in appreciation. "God, I love you, woman." A shit-eating grin was on her face.

"I gave them the middle finger when they said I only had endurance because of all the sex Mason and I had."

"Yeah." She glanced around the hallway. A group of cross country guys weren't far away, and her gaze centered on them. Her top lip curved up in a slight sneer. "I heard about that. Precious egos and chauvinist pigs."

I grinned, moving my hip to shut my locker. We began walking to hers since it was closer to our first class. When we passed by the guys, Heather called out, "Hey, Hayes."

A head popped up. It was the guy who'd been in the lead the day before. He had been turned towards his locker, but cast her a puzzled look. "What?" His gaze slid to mine. A small amount of anger stirred in the depths of his eyes.

Heather snorted. We passed by, but she turned around to face them. "Just so you know, if you beat me in calculus, I'm going to tell everyone it's because you like to sew with your mom."

"What?"

"Yeah. Makes no sense, but it makes you look dumb, and I'll feel slightly better." She pointed and winked at the same time. "I grew up next door to you. I know all your secrets and that was virginal compared to what I know about you."

"What?" His eyebrows furrowed together, and he shared identical looks with his friends.

I laughed as we moved around the corner. "The guys didn't even get it."

"It's because they're stupid assholes."

Coming up to her locker, I rested against her neighbor's. "What's up with you? I can handle those guys. Trust me. After Kate, they're a piece of cake."

"Nothing." She shook her head, then paused and closed her eyes. Lifting her hand, she skimmed it down her face. "I need to clear my mind. You're right. You can handle them, but man, I get so angry when guys use sex to belittle a girl."

I grew thoughtful, but before I could say anything, she gave me another grin. This one was more carefree and laid back. She asked, "What'd Logan say when you told him? Or should I ask what'd Logan do when you told him?"

"I didn't."

"You didn't?"

"He was gone all night. I ran home, but he never answered his phone. I was hoping he'd give me a ride to get my car. Mark got the honor instead."

"So much for you being Mark's bitch?" She chuckled, tucking some of her hair behind her ear. She bent down to pick up a book from the bottom of the locker.

"Yeah." The beer pong game had been last weekend. "Although I did do his laundry on Sunday. He wasn't kidding. His entire closet was just dirty clothes. He uses the storage room in the basement for his closet." I grimaced, remembering the smell of dirty boxers and moldy food. "I was tempted to wear a mask over my nose so I wouldn't inhale anything and get sick."

"God forbid, you get sick. Those guys would rejoice on your hospital bed." There was a bite in her voice.

When the first bell went off, we headed towards first period. I threw her a confused glance. "I mean it. Those guys really aren't a big deal."

"I know." She sighed and opened the classroom door. "I just really dislike Hayes. We were friends, but when my mom left, his mom decided we weren't good enough for their family anymore. He agreed and has had a superior attitude ever since. I'm surprised he's never tangled with Mason or Logan. Wait," she stopped and a rueful expression filtered across her face. "I can. He's in cross-country. They're in football. I think he'd piss himself if Logan went after him."

"Who'd piss themselves if I went after them?" Logan had come up behind us. We both jumped, startled, and he chuckled. "Always be aware of your surroundings, Jax. You never know what creeper is stalking up behind you."

"Not long ago you threw your arms around our shoulders and told us we needed shorter skirts."

"And cupcakes," I added.

She nodded and pointed back at me. "What she said. Where'd the love go, Kade? I feel like we need to explore that happy place once again."

He barked out a laugh. As we stopped in the hallway, he moved between us. Hooking an arm around my shoulder, he bent me forward so my head was firmly within his hold and he tugged me into the class. He said over me, "The happy place went away when you got a stick up your ass about my girlfriend." He stopped, patted my head, and added, "And when you started protecting Sam from me." The last was spoken with dead seriousness.

I winced. Shit just got real. Closing my eyes, I could feel the sudden tension come over the room. They'd been talking and laughing, but when he said those words, it acted like a blanket had dropped over everyone.

Logan was tense.

Heather cut out a short laugh. "For real? I'm being a friend."

I felt him take a silent breath. As he let it back out, his body loosened with it. He was forcing himself to relax. "Yeah, well, I call dibs for today. Sam sits with me."

"What?" She started to argue, but I pushed up enough so I could meet her gaze. When she saw me, I shook my head and she got the message. "Fine."

He turned around and led me to the table in the far back. Kicking a chair out, he let go of me and pointed to it. "Sit. You can't avoid me, and you can't say no to your future stepbrother."

He sounded like he was joking, but I caught the heated spark in his gaze. When he dropped next to me and didn't start talking right away, the rest of the classroom began their own conversations again. More than a few kept glancing back, just in case a heated exchange broke out again. Rubbing my neck, I tried to apologize to Heather as she took a seat beside the board. We were next to the window and surrounded by Logan's friends. It wasn't long after that when a group of girls came in. Kris was with them, dressed in a floral skirt, a white tank top, and a jean jacket pulled over it. With pink ballet shoes on, she was ready for a picnic date. Her friends headed to the front two tables in Heather's row and Kris scanned the room for Logan. When she saw me with him, her mouth fell open an inch.

He wasn't paying attention so I hit him with my knee. "What?" I jerked my head to her, and he cursed. "I forgot she was transferring to this class."

"Whatever. Do something quick or you're going to be kissing her ass all week."

He groaned, but got up from the table. "Hey..."

"I'm sorry." She closed her mouth, and her hand jerked out, pointing to me. "I assumed I would sit with you."

"Yeah." His hand lifted to the back of his neck, and he gripped it.

His back was to me, but when he grabbed the back of his neck, it meant he knew he was in trouble and had no idea how to get out of it. I had to laugh. Logan was never at a loss for words, so I stood up and said, "Don't get mad. I made him promise before school started that we'd sit together in a couple classes. I pulled out the sister card."

"Oh."

He twisted around so she couldn't see and mouthed, "Thank you."

I rolled my eyes, then sat back down.

"Okay." Her hands came in front of her and twisted around each other, cradling her book and notebook in her arms. "Well," she scanned the room, "I guess I could sit..."

One of her friends raised her hand. "We have a seat. Come on, Kris. We're more fun than boyfriends. We can gossip."

She laughed. "There is that." Casting another shadowed look at Logan, then me, she started for the front of the classroom. When she passed Heather, my gaze caught hers and her mouth was hanging open. She jerked her hands up and down and mouthed, "W.T.F.?"

I flinched. What the fuck was right. I had an opportunity to avoid Logan. Why hadn't I taken it?

Sitting next to me, he let out a deep sigh of relief. "Thanks, Sam. I had no idea how to back out of that."

I knew. He was family. Secret be damned, he was still family, and I couldn't hide from him. I didn't want to. I pretended to

66

punch him in the arm and said, "What do they say? Bros before hoes? In our case, fam before...females?" I shook my head. "Sorry. I'm not funny."

He laughed, leaned back, and rested his hand on the back of my chair. "Yes, you are, and you're right. Family before all others, right?"

"That sounds better."

"Good." The relieved and jovial look disappeared and his gaze trailed over my shoulder to fix on someone else. It grew dangerous as he said, "You gonna tell me what was said to you at your practice last night?"

I turned and saw the object of his stare. Hayes. He was staring back, but unlike the puzzled look from earlier and the arrogance from yesterday, fear flooded his gaze. He swallowed, his Adam's apple moved up and down, and he turned forward in an abrupt movement. His head went down and his shoulders hunched forward. His table mate cast him a confused look, but didn't say anything.

Logan leaned close and murmured in my ear, "At the first sign of anything, you give me the go. I mean it. I won't be having you getting carted out of another bathroom to the hospital. Can you imagine the beat down I'd get from my brother?"

"I'd imagine it'd be similar to the beat down you'd give to anyone who might *try* to do that again." I stressed the word. "And it won't be a problem. I promise. His ego just got bruised."

"It doesn't matter. Say the word."

I nodded. "I will."

"I mean it."

"I know. I know you do."

"Mason's gone. You're my responsibility."

A surge of warmth spread through me. It gave me hope that maybe it wouldn't matter. If I told him that I knew, he could deny it and we'd laugh it off. Nothing would happen. I wouldn't lose him or Mason. Logan was waiting for my response, watching me intently, and I joked, "What's this shit with me avoiding you? I called you last night. You avoided *my* phone call."

"Sorry." The teacher came in at that moment. As everyone sat up and quieted down for roll call to begin, Logan said to me, "I was having sex most the night."

*

MASON

It was the first week of classes and I had political science with Matteo and Drew. As we went through campus, we drew attention. I was big already, but Matteo was bigger. He was a lineman. He had to be huge, but Drew wasn't a slouch. Some quarterbacks were smaller, but not him. He stood at the same height as us. His shoulders were broad, but he wasn't as filled out as me. He was leaner.

The three of us walked through the quad with our backpacks on and our waters hooked through the straps. People stopped and watched us. They stepped off the sidewalk as we went past, then stepped back on. We heard the whispers behind us and around us.

Matteo's elbow bumped mine, and he nodded his head towards the side. "Those girls are friends with my Georgie."

Drew barked out a laugh. "I still can't get over that your girlfriend's name is Georgie. I've known her for a year, but still. Georgie."

"Her parents call her Georgina, but she hates the name. I tried calling her that when we first started dating, and she wouldn't take my phone calls for a week. I learned real quick." Matteo lifted his hand and hollered, "Ho to the hoes."

A group of six girls were at a picnic table, and unlike most of the rest, they weren't paying attention to us. At his greeting, three of them looked up with snarls at the ready. They were primed for a fight, but when they saw it was Matteo, two rolled their eyes and looked back at their textbooks. The other girls were unfazed. They were either talking or studying, but all of them held a paper coffee cup. The last girl with long black hair, almond eyes, and a clear complexion laughed. She stood up from the table and headed our way. She was dressed in a simple white polo with a pink emblem of a unicorn at the corner and jeans. She was stick thin, and as she walked to us, she was confident. The others around us turned enviable eyes on her, and when she got closer to Matteo, she lifted a fist, pounded it on his chest, and grabbed his shirt. "Come here." She yanked him forward, but he didn't move. He dropped his smirking mouth down on hers.

I glanced to Drew. "This is Georgie?"

He nodded, grinning at the couple. "Yeah. You two didn't meet at the ass' party."

When they broke apart, Drew asked, "Is that Carly over there?"

Georgie turned around, drawing Matteo's arms around her. "Yes, it is, but I'm told to tell you to stay the fuck away from her."

He laughed and pretended to shiver. "Why the hostility?"

Her eyebrow arched high. "Something about a non-phone call after you two hooked up the other night?"

He shrugged, craning his neck to study the table. "We had back to back practices that day. I was wiped out by the time we got home. Trust me, she would've gotten mad at me anyway, saying I wasn't listening to her enough or something." He grimaced, glancing to me. "Chicks. They're all the same. If we don't listen good enough, they get mad. Your girlfriend like that?"

"Nah." I grinned. "I'm the one who has to push Sam to talk."

Drew and Matteo seemed surprised. My roommate broke out laughing. "For real? You're the talker in the relationship?"

"Believe it or not, I am."

Matteo continued to hoot as he slapped his leg. "That's awesome, man. I really have to meet your girlfriend. I know she helped you move in, but that was long ago and you two disappeared right afterwards."

"Speak for yourself." I gestured to Georgie. "It's been over a month, and this is the first time I'm meeting your girlfriend who goes to college *here*."

She tipped her head back, resting it in the nook of Matteo's arm and chest. A low, smooth chuckle came from her. She leaned all her weight against him and crossed one ankle over the other. "That's my fault. I'm in a sorority, and we've been busy with the pledges. The beginning of the year is always the most chaotic. Plus, I have my own room, and no offense to the rest of your house, but being around sweaty, shirtless guys isn't my dream come true. I'm all about my studies, my house, and my man." She straightened up and smacked a hand to Matteo's bicep. It bulged at the touch, and her fingers wrapped around it. The two shared a secretive smile.

I grunted. My roommate might talk a big game, but he was in love with this girl in front of him. Drew was watching them too, but he was patient. It was obvious he'd seen this before.

Breaking their little moment, a radiant smile came over her face, and Georgie gazed around to us. "What class do you guys have?"

Drew answered, "We all have poly sci now."

She flinched, gritting her teeth. "Good luck. Professor Matson is hard core. That's a mixed class, right?"

Matteo seemed happy just to be holding his woman. Drew nodded. "I put it off till this year. Is that a problem?"

"Not if you don't mind dealing with a bunch of eager, stressed-out freshman." Her gaze clicked to mine, and she realized what she had said.

I grinned. "Like me, you mean?"

Her cheeks grew pink, but she smirked at me. "Something tells me you're not like most freshman."

"No way." Matteo shook his head. His arms tightened around her waist, but he lifted one hand to meet my fist in the air. As they touched, he dropped his arm back. "Kade is stone cold cool. He handled Park like he was a baby. It was awesome."

"You knew?"

"I saw that smooth move you and your friend did. You snubbed him, but in a smooth way. I bet he didn't even realize it."

Georgie studied me again. I felt renewed interest from her. She murmured, "My friends like their house. You have a friend there? I know Matt said something about him before."

I nodded. "Nate Monson. His dad pledged there."

"Wait. Kade? James Kade?"

"Yeah."

Her eyebrows shot up. "Your dad pledged there. He's a legend. Didn't he make the Forbes list or something?"

Drew and Matteo grew silent.

I scowled. "My dad's a dipshit. I try to do the opposite of everything he did."

Their shoulders dropped.

"Oh. Still. And didn't he marry into a family who comes from old money too? Like he's the poor one in the marriage?"

"Yeah," I flashed her a hard smile. I don't do personal. "They're divorced and he's now engaged to a psychopath. Again, I do everything opposite of my dad. We don't get along." *Drop it.* I wanted her to get the message without saying it.

Matteo cleared his throat. He gave me an uneasy grin, then patted her on the hip. "We should get going. Lunch later?"

She broke eye contact with me and turned to face her man. They moved to the side as they said their farewells, leaving Drew and I alone. I felt his perusal and sighed. "Yeah?"

He was grinning. It widened at my question and he shook his head. "You really hate your old man, huh?"

"Yeah."

"Me too."

"Yeah?"

"Yeah. He banged three of my girlfriends from my first two years here. The last one was the worst because I actually loved her."

"Shit." I grimaced.

"And he likes to act like he and I are the best of buddies. Your old man know how much you hate him?"

"Yep."

He nodded, a tone of respect in his voice, "You got balls, Kade. I knew you had them before, but that's cool." He pointed to the couple, who were kissing. Their mouths were opened and tongue was being shared. "If we don't break them up, he's going to take her back to the house. He'll skip class for her. The guy is nuts about her."

"What do you suggest?"

"A rough extraction." As soon as the words were out of his mouth, he moved forward. Grabbing Matteo around the shoulders, he propelled him forward, away from Georgie. They protested, but Drew flashed her a grin. "Sorry, Georgie. You two can bang later. We've got a class and your man has to go, or Coach will not be happy with us."

She started for them, but Drew kept moving Matteo forward. I jetted forward, blocking her with my body. She stopped and her mouth fell open. "Hey."

"Sorry." I looked down at her. "Drew's the boss on the field and off. I gotta do what he says." Then I heard Drew call out, "Kade."

I started walking backwards and said again, "Sorry."

Her hands went to her tiny hips and she rolled her eyes. "Whatever. You two are on my shit list for interrupting, but you're lucky I have my own stuff to deal with today." I kept moving after my teammates. She raised a fist in the air, laughing, as she called out, "Do you hear that, Drew? You're victorious for today, but make no mistake. I will prevail. I will make out with my boyfriend one of these days."

A girl with almost white blonde hair came up to her and watched us leave. "For real? He didn't even try to come and talk to me?"

Georgie turned towards her friend, but we were too far away to hear anymore. Matteo didn't say anything. He didn't seem to mind. We went to our classroom in silence again. Walking up behind them on the steps, I sensed the comfort between the two. It reminded me of Logan and me, except Logan would've made a bigger spectacle than those two did back there. At the thought of it, I couldn't wipe a grin from my face. Then we got in the classroom and it faded.

The room was small, packed with chairs with fold-up desks, and the only three that were open next to each other were in the front row. All the chairs were side by side, separated by one aisle down the middle of the room.

Drew turned to us, then looked at the chairs.

Matteo shrugged. "Whatever, man. I'm not getting split up." He plopped down first, taking the middle chair. When we began to sit in the other two, he held up a hand. "Hold on, mofos." Reaching over, he folded his desk up. It wouldn't lay flat. His stomach was in the way so he groaned, but folded it back down. "I had to try."

Drew laughed, took the seat on his right, and folded his desk up. "You can share mine."

"I'm bringing a lap tray with me. I should've remembered from last year."

I took the seat on his left. A girl was beside me. As I brought up my desk, she leaned over so it wouldn't graze her arm and went back to typing on her laptop. It wasn't long before the professor came in, wearing a grey business skirt and a loose buttoned down pink shirt with her hair pulled up in some bun. She paused as she took us in. She was young, probably early thirties. Pressing her lips together in a flat line, she grunted and walked to the aisle between the two groups of desks. There were a bunch of students behind us. All three of us remained silent. We knew we were blocking their view.

The professor moved back so she was right in front of us. She waved a finger in the air. "Something's not going to work here."

Drew shared a grin with us.

Soft laughter filled the room at her statement.

Drew said, "We got in last. What can we do?"

"You three don't have to sit together." She scanned the room. "I see a couple other empty chairs. Gasp. Shudder. The football team might have to sit apart for once."

Drew frowned. "We'd rather not."

"I'm gathering that." Her hand rested on one hip, the other went to scratch behind her ears. "You three are going to have to split up. I won't have nine other students sacrifice seeing the board for your comfort levels."

Matteo grunted. "We're not comfortable, ma'am." He gestured to his desk and let his shoulders fall down. His arms fell against mine and Drew's. He'd been holding himself in, scrunching his shoulders up. "I wouldn't use that word at all."

"Hmm."

A voice from the back spoke up, "We can switch."

Everyone in the room turned to look, but I didn't need to. I recognized that soft, timid voice. It was Marissa.

She added, "My friends and I will sit up front so they can sit back here."

Matteo said, "Miracles do happen. Thank god." Jumping up, he swung his bag to his shoulder and nodded. "Thank you, little Mother Theresas. You will all be blessed in your afterlife and I have no doubt you'll go to the highest heaven."

A few in the room chuckled. The professor wasn't amused. "This is a political science course, not a religious one."

He touched his forehead, his chest, both of his shoulders, then touched his lips. Offering his hands up in the air, he shook his head. "My prayers have been answered again."

Marissa and her friends grabbed all of their books and bags. They came up to the front and stepped aside. Matteo was the first to get to the back row and he plopped down in the farthest corner. He pushed the other desks to the side, giving him more space. Stretching his hands in the air, he folded them behind his head and leaned against the wall. "Wait." He shifted, leaning against the corner of the room. Kicking his feet out, he said, "Much better. Thanks, chicas."

Drew laughed and went next. I followed him. As I went past Marissa, she jerked her gaze away and followed her friends as they sat down. I tensed, but took the last seat beside Drew. We were in the back of the room and the other people in our row had scooted over so we had even more room.

The professor went to the board, and Matteo leaned forward to whisper, "We have to make sure we piss every time we come here. Once I'm back here, Matteo is not moving until class is over. No mofo, no way." He pulled out his water and set it on the desk.

Drew took it down. "Don't drink this until class is almost done. Your bladder's like a girl's. It's barely there."

"You're barely there."

"I remembered your girlfriend saying that to you a few times."

The two shared insults, both unable to hold back their grins at the same time, but I tuned them out. Marissa glanced back over her shoulder. When her eyes caught mine, her face grew red and she ducked back down, facing forward. Her two friends looked also, but they weren't the two that had been with her outside the stadium. Judging from the lack of surprise on their faces, they knew of me and knew of my history with Marissa.

I sat back. I wasn't sure how I felt about that. I wasn't even sure what to think of Marissa anymore either.

CHAPTER SEVEN

SAMANTHA

I'd been right. Coach pulled me from running with the girls and had me start with the guys. After that one day of being smart-asses and getting a chilly reception from everyone in school, they had no choice but to accept me. I'd been running with them for the past two weeks. Since Heather was working and Logan was at his game (which I promised to go to and was running late), I decided to go on a longer run than normal. I hadn't been indulging in my really long runs, the ones that lasted a few hours. When I got home, I stopped outside the back door. The world felt alive to me. Even now, being exhausted, I was more energized than ever.

After stretching, I headed inside and was turning for the basement when I heard my name.

"Sam."

David was standing in the kitchen. He wore his coaching jacket, dress pants, and shoes. A foreboding feeling took root in my stomach. It was Friday night so that meant game night. Glancing at the clock, I saw he only had twenty minutes to get there. I moved from the door and came into the kitchen. "What are you doing here, Dad? You're playing my school tonight. I'm going to be late myself, but you're the coach."

He closed his eyes a moment and nodded to himself.

I waited, but the interest turned to alarm. Something was wrong. "Dad?"

"Um." He shoved his hands into his pockets, and his head went down. "I have something to tell you."

"Something so important that you're going to be late for your game?" I glanced around. "Is Malinda and Mark here?"

"No." He shook his head. "It's you and me. Mark's warming up, and Malinda's already there with her friends. They don't know I'm here."

A lump was in the back of my throat. No one knew. "Is it Mom?" *Did I care?* All the turmoil and pain she caused came back to me. I hadn't thought about her in a long time. I didn't want to either. I gritted my teeth. "Is she getting out?"

"No, Sam. It's," he faltered for a beat, "it's your father."

"What?"

"Garrett. Your biological father."

"Did something happen? Is he okay?"

"He's here, Sam."

"Um." I shook my head and laughed. "I heard you wrong. Right?"

"You heard me right." His head came up and he caught my gaze. His small smile turned sad. "Your father moved to town. He and his wife are both here."

"This is joke." It wasn't funny.

"He came for you, Sam. He wants to form a relationship with you. He said things are good with his wife again. He called me a few months ago and told me his plan. That was before you moved in and things got better between us. I wasn't sure when the right time would be to tell you and the summer got away from me." He closed his eyes and hung his head once more. "I'm so sorry, Samantha. I've been waiting to tell you during a weekend you were going to see Mason. I know you're planning on leaving tomorrow."

My thoughts were going in all directions. I shook my head. "Don't say what I think you're going to say."

"You went on a run, but I know that you'll go to a party tonight with Logan and Mark and," he broke off, his voice full of emotion. He cleared his throat before continuing, "I know how the rumor mill works. They're coming to the game tonight. People will notice. Someone will tell you. I needed to be the one to tell you first."

"They're here? Like, actually here?"

He nodded. "I'm so sorry, Sam. I should've told you as soon as I knew, but I didn't know for sure if they were coming. I didn't want to alarm you and them not come."

"You're sure they're coming?"

"He called me this afternoon. They bought a house. They both have jobs here."

"Where?" A buzzing sound was in my head. I couldn't shake it off. I had to know the places to avoid. "Where?"

"She's a chef at the country club, and he was added as a partner with a law firm in town." When he saw my panic, his voice trailed off. "What can I do to help you?"

"Nothing." Shit, shit, shit...I glanced at the clock again. It was 6:30. I had a three hour drive. I could be at Mason's before ten. "I have to go."

"Wait."

I turned and headed for the stairs. "Go, Dad. Go to your game!" As I turned for my room, he came to the top of the stairs and hollered down, "Are you okay, honey? I can tell him to stay away. Do you want me to do that?"

"NO." I reached for my door, but it wouldn't open. Fucking shit shit shit. I stopped, closed my eyes, and sucked in some air. I needed to think clearly. Breathing out, I tried to calm myself. The door handle. I needed to turn the stupid door handle.

"Sam?" He started down the stairs.

"Just go, Dad. I'll be fine."

"But where are you going?"

"I need a minute. I'll be fine." My voice was hoarse. He could hear my panic so I brought it down. "I'm fine. Honestly. Go to your game. This isn't worth missing your own game, Dad."

"Are you sure?" He was at the bottom of the stairs.

I shut my door. As he got there, standing right outside of my door, I locked it. It turned in the next moment. He would've come in. My knees grew unsteady and I fell on my bed.

"Samantha," his voice was muffled through the door, "you don't sound okay."

I wasn't. "I'm going to see Mason."

He grew silent. After a moment, he asked, "I thought you were going in the morning with Logan and Kris?"

"I'm going tonight."

"Oh." He sounded disappointed. "Sam, listen. Please. I will call him. I will tell him not to go to the game and that it's too soon for you. Don't travel at night. Wait till tomorrow. Go with Logan. Fallen Crest Public and Fallen Crest Academy are playing against each other tonight. He'd want you to watch. I know it's important to him."

"I know what game it is." Closing my eyes tightly, I bent over and caught my head in my hands. My elbows rested on my knees, and my pulse was pounding. He was hurt. Why did my dad sound hurt? My biological dad was in town. I didn't want to deal with that. "I'll be fine, Dad. I promise. I just have to...figure stuff out."

"Okay. Well, call me if you need anything. Please, Sam." He sounded so exhausted. "I'll call Garrett and tell him to back off. We can figure this out at your pace." He paused. I heard the scrape of his hand against the door. "I love you, honey."

I nodded and said, "I love you."

I stayed there, just waiting until I calmed enough to drive, but everything he said filtered in. Mason was at college. He wasn't here. I couldn't run to him for everything, and going with Logan and Kris in the morning was the smart thing to do. Pushing back the old panic that had kept me company for so long, I went to shower before I could change my mind. It didn't take me long to dress. Pulling on jeans and a tee shirt, I was out the door within fifteen minutes. I didn't think. I didn't allow myself to dwell on anything. I just drove, and when I pulled into the parking lot by the school, I felt some of the anxiety rising.

No. I shook my head. Closing my eyes, I imagined a lever being pushed down, shoving my anxiety down with it. It left my head clear. I waited to let it sink in and felt better a moment later. I didn't want to waste time so I took off through the cars before the anxiety came back up.

While weaving through the cars and the last little bit of a crowd that lingered outside the ticket booth, I braided my hair. When it was my turn to pay, Natalie stared back at me. A scowl formed on her face and she had a smug smile. "Well, well. If I don't let you in, something tells me your stepbrother's going to be upset with you."

Irritation rose in me. "Give me a ticket or I'm leaving money with the first teacher I see and going through anyway."

I stared her down. We both knew who they'd believe.

She rolled her eyes. "Five bucks."

I put it on the counter and she gave me a ticket. As I took it, I asked, "How'd you end up back there in the first place?"

"Fucking detention. We're still paying for beating your ass last year." There was no remorse in her tone and the girl next to her froze. She glanced sideways as if fearful another beat down would happen. Natalie mused, "We'll be doing this shit and anything else the superintendent wants us to do until we graduate. Those were the terms or we would've faced legal charges and expulsion." She chewed her lip, studying me. "I'm starting to think legal charges wouldn't have been that bad."

I grinned. Natalie was harmless to me now. I felt it. There wasn't any heat behind her words. I could feel how empty they were. "We could go another round? Maybe it'd lessen your sentence, although, think about all the fines you would've had to pay."

"Yeah, that sucks."

She rolled her eyes. "Go. Stop torturing me. My life's already pathetic as it is with me behind this table."

I laughed and headed towards the football field. A large crowd spilled out from two sets of bleachers. There was one on either side of the field and enough people lingered at the end of them to form one large crowd that circled the south end of the entire field. Fallen Crest Academy fans mingled with Fallen Crest Public fans. It was a sea of red and black mixed with the occasional neutral normal clothing. I didn't want to run into any of the Fallen Crest Academy Elite so I hightailed it to the FCP bleachers. When I got there, it was packed.

I hadn't counted on that. I thought there would've been a few empty spots. I was missing Heather. She would've waved someone over and voila, we would've had a perfect seat.

"Sam!"

I instantly groaned, but couldn't ignore Kris. She stood from the far end in the student section and was standing in the second row. The first three seemed reserved for the most popular people in school. She was second row. That meant she already had higher status than I ever would, if I'd been social. With her hair split and woven into two side French braids, she waved at me, holding an extra sized liquid cup in the other, gesturing beside her. She yelled, "Come on. I saved you a seat."

Uh...I had no choice. Trying to smile at her, I walked past the entire bleacher and stepped up to her row. The girls in her row stood up and filed out without a single complaint. My eyebrows shot up. I'd been prepared to look like an ass as I stumbled over everyone. They continued to watch the game and waited until I went in.

"Hi!" Kris' eyes were lit up. Her free hand grasped mine and she pulled me down to the seat. The others filed back in. The one next to me was one of the most popular girls in Kris' grade. From what I could recall, most of them were on the drill team. Kris patted my arm and her smile stretched wider. "Logan told me you'd probably be late because you were running. He was right, huh? Tabitha," she leaned across me and said, "when you guys come back from your routine, you know what to bring."

The girl gave her a thin smile. "We know. It's not our first rodeo."

Kris giggled, falling back into me. That was when I got the first whiff of booze. "Whoa. When did you start?"

She pointed to Tabitha and her cheeks got redder, along with the tip of her nose. "We had a few in the bathroom."

Tabitha gave her another cold smile, but Kris just clutched my arm. "You were so much fun at that one party. You should drink with us more often, Sam. Yeah." Her eyes lit up again and her mouth fell open, like she had the most wonderful idea in the world. "That'd be amazing. Let's both get drunk."

"Uh..."

"Oh, come on. Logan will take care of us, and you'll see your man tomorrow. You have no worries, none whatsoever." She bent over, giggling into her lap.

I asked Tabitha, "Did you slip her anything else?"

She shrugged. "Just a good dose of Jack Daniels, not what you're suggesting."

"Why are you the Ice Queen and she's Giggling Rudolph?"

She lifted another shoulder. "Because she insisted on drinking a third of the bottle. That's on her, not me. We have a few during the game, but we have to get to the party. That's when we only do shots and nothing else. We're not stupid."

I gritted my teeth. "You're stupid for talking to me like that."

She opened her mouth, a hot retort on the tip of her tongue, but she caught the warning in my gaze. She closed her mouth and shook her head. "I don't know what you're problem is. We didn't do anything. We like Kris, unlike you."

I grunted. That was fair. Turning my back, I patted Kris on the arm. "Okay. You might want some coffee at halftime or Logan will be putting you into bed before he goes and parties after the game."

She grimaced. "Oh my god. You're right." A pained expression came over her face. "No more, Jackie, not until the party anyway." She sighed and rested her forehead against my shoulder. Her hand reached for my hand. "I'm so glad we became friends. You're not stuck-up like I thought you might be. Anyone else in your position would have the head of a Uranus."

Really? *That* planet? Catching a small grin from Tabitha, who must've overheard, I shook my head. "Okay. Let's keep that one between us."

"I think you're so cool."

"Yep." I was not commenting on that one. "Let's watch the game."

"Okay."

For the most part, Kris tried to watch. When Logan scored, she stood up because everyone was standing up. When FCA punted, she stood up again. I tugged her down, and she started another giggling fit. She clamped her hands over her mouth and whispered in my ear for everyone else to hear. "It's so weird for me because I dated the one quarterback and now I'm with the other quarterback."

"You dated the second string quarterback also."

She gasped. "I did. I forgot about Jeff. I shouldn't have. He's a sweetie."

I gave her a dark look. "You know a different Jeff than I do."

"That's right. You dated him too. Wait." She cocked her head to the side. "He cheated on you. He didn't cheat on me, but I didn't really *date* date him. We hung out. It was like the before-dating, before being a couple. Does that make sense? That's what Adam and I did. And I didn't sleep with them. I only fooled around with them." She groaned. "A year before that, I probably would've slept with them, but Charlie yelled at me enough. She said I used guys to make myself feel loved." Her voice tapered off and her eyebrows slowly lowered together. Her head went down as well. "She said it's because our dad left us and I compensated—"

BUZZ!

It was halftime. I grabbed her arm. "Let's continue this in a bit. I have to get some water." The girl in front of me stood up and I saw my opportunity. Slipping over her seat, and instead of fighting the crowd for the stairs on the side, I grabbed the lowest bar and slid my body underneath it. Landing on the grass, in front of the bleachers, I ran alongside them until I could slip around the fence that kept the crowd from going onto the field.

The teams were still milling off the field, and I was almost to them when the last of the Fallen Crest Public team stepped off the track field. I figured Logan and my dad were both ahead, so I started to cross their path for the concession stand. I didn't really need a water, I just didn't want to get pulled into Kris' story. Just hearing the small amount of pain with her first words, I knew there was a ton more. I had my own trauma to deal with. I didn't want to start feeling sorry for Logan's girlfriend.

I heard: "She said that, David?"

"It's too soon, Garrett. I'm sorry I didn't catch you in time."

"No, no. I forgot my phone in the car and you wouldn't have Sharon's..."

They kept talking, but I couldn't hear what they were saying. All the anxiety from before blasted up, exploding into my chest and throat, filling me with dread, like I was about to witness a car accident and saw it coming. I knew to avoid it, but I couldn't. As that registered with me, my head turned and I saw them. They were standing off to the side. David's head was bent down, his hands on his hips. A clipboard was in one of his hands and he was chewing on his whistle at the same time. Garrett stood over him. His features were as chiseled as I remembered from the last time I saw him, but his hair seemed whiter. I continued to study him and laughed softly to myself.

They looked at me. David straightened abruptly and Garrett moved back a step.

I laughed again, shaking my head. "For some reason, I imagined you in a business suit. That makes no sense. It's a football game. I suppose you only wear those when you're working, being a big hotshot lawyer..." My mind was spinning and

I stopped. My throat was dry. I'd been going to get water, that's right.

"Sam—" David started.

Garrett stepped around him. His eyes were glued to my face. He said, "It's because the last time you saw me I was in a business suit."

"That's right." I could picture it again. "You hugged me and never came back."

"Sam," David said again.

I shook my head. "It's halftime and you're the coach. Go, Dad. I'll be fine." I waved at Garrett. "Damage done. He's here. I've seen him." I swallowed over a lump in my throat. "I'll deal with it."

He looked between us, then shook his head. His shoulders slumped down and he murmured, "All right. I love you, Samantha. Just remember that."

"Got it." Lifting my hands, both of my thumbs shot up. "Two thumbs-up, Dad. That's what you get for this whole thing. Well done. Way to prepare me and way to not follow through with what you promised. He's here anyway."

David opened his mouth. "Sam—"

"Go, David." Garrett's hand came down on his shoulder. "She lashes out when she's hurting. She gets that from me."

I don't.

David said. "She doesn't, not all the time."

A bubble of laughter was coming up. I could feel it making its way from my stomach, gliding past my chest, slipping around the lump in my throat; my mouth opened and it pealed out. As they heard me, they stopped. I bent over. More laughter kept coming. I couldn't stop it, and I didn't want to. Kris had the right idea. Get drunk. Not deal with things. That seemed to be working for her. She was popular. She had friends. She was liked. I sighed, the laughter subsided, but it was on an anguished note. Even I cringed as I heard it with my own ears. I lifted a hand to them, letting it fall back to my side right away. "Look at you two. One thinks he knows me and the other...oh my god. This is a comedy skit. Why was I panicking at the thought of seeing you? This is the best entertainment I could get. You both think you know me when only one of you was around, but you both left. Now you're both back. Fuck," I grunted. My eyes started to water and I flicked the tears away. "You're both a riot."

My stomach rolled over and I shook my head. "Go away. I don't want to deal with either of you."

"Sam?"

Turning, the voice was like music to my ears. Logan was standing there. He was holding his helmet with his dark hair sweaty, sticking up in clumps. His cheeks were smudged with black paint, dirt, and sweat. He had mud and grass stains all over his uniform.

"What are you doing? You have halftime."

"I was told to come out here." He walked forward, then saw David and Garrett. "Fuck."

Exactly.

In one motion, his arm reached out for me and I went to him. I didn't huddle there. I stood tall, but I moved into the shelter of him for a moment. One damn second, and as I did, he rested his hand lightly on my back. His body was rock solid, and I heard a growl in his voice that started deep in his throat. "What the hell's going on?"

"Logan." David sounded exhausted.

I started laughing again. "I have to go."

I started to step back, but he kept me anchored to him. His head craned to see me. "Sam? Stay. No."

I shook my head and pushed off from his chest. "No. I'm going to see Mason." Mason made me feel better. He always had. He always would. "I'm going to see him."

"Sam—"

I started off down the field, towards the opening in the gate. Then I saw Natalie. She was standing there with the money box in her hands. Of course. They took tickets until half-time. A voice in my head said that, like I was adding what two plus two was. That was ridiculous. What was wrong with me?

She rolled her eyes. "My god, could you be more dramatic? I don't even know what the situation is, but I know the signs. Samantha Strattan, there she goes. Always fucking running." She gestured to Logan. "He left his locker room to be your protector, but that's not good enough for you. You're running away to Mason. Grow up. Like I said, find your balls and start flashing them around—"

I saw red. My eyes narrowed and I lowered my head, as if I was going to charge her. "You want me to find my balls?"

Natalie grunted. She dropped the money box, kicked it to someone on the sidelines, and smirked back at me. "I'd love to get a taste. Bring it on, Strattan. I don't need my friends to back me up. I can take you on all by myself."

Memories of being in that bathroom last year, of being hit, how I crawled away from them, and how they dragged me back dredged back up in my throat. A flash of white covered my vision. White hot fury. It was then my mind checked out.

I wanted to do damage, like the damage they did to me.

I lunged for her, but an arm wrapped around my waist. I was yanked backwards.

"No!" I didn't need to see who was holding me. It was Logan. He set me on my feet, then adjusted his hold so I was thrown over his shoulder before I could move away. He began walking from the field and down to the parking lot.

I ignored the stunned looks on both my dads and the crowd that had formed. Natalie was glaring at me as Logan crossed the parking lot and went inside the school. He dropped me on my feet and pointed in my face. "You stay here. I mean it."

"No—"

"SAMANTHA!"

My mouth shut. I moved back into the wall.

He let out a ragged sound. "God. Just stay. I have a coach who's pissed at me. Wait ten fucking minutes." He didn't wait for a reply, he swept into the locker room. As the door opened, I heard his coach yelling, "Are you ready—" The door closed and I was left alone in the hallway. The rest of the hallways were in the dark and there were only two lights on in the entrance, for both teams to enter their own locker rooms.

I sunk down to the floor and pulled out my phone. I needed Mason.

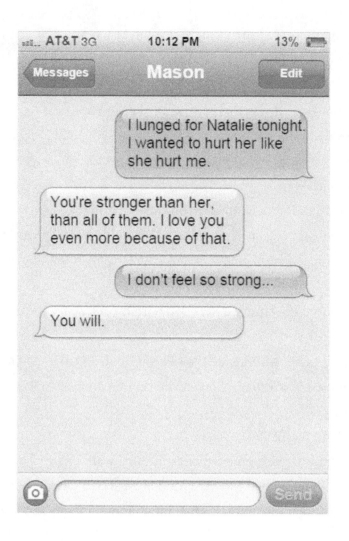

CHAPTER EIGHT

"Sam?"

The sound of his voice was enough. I felt myself calming down. "Hey." Hearing loud music and an announcer on his end, I asked, "Where are you?"

"I'm at a restaurant with the team. They're doing some grill thing. The guys flip food in the air and tap their cups. It's not my thing, but Matt seems to live for it."

I grinned. "How is your roommate?"

"Sam." Suddenly all the background noises disappeared and I could hear his voice clearer. I also heard the concern in it. "What's going on? You don't call this early."

"My dad is here."

There was silence before he asked, "You don't mean David?"

"No."

"Where are you right now?"

Sudden cheering and clapping came from inside the locker room, followed by a thunderous sound. I said, "I'm in the hallway outside the locker room. Logan brought me in here. I was at the game when I saw him. Mason..." Gripping the phone tighter, my feet slid back and I pulled my knees tight to my chest, resting my forehead on them. "I didn't even know. David knew, but didn't tell me until today."

"Is he there for a visit?"

"To stay."

He sighed. "I'm sorry, Sam."

"I'll be fine." As I said it, I knew it was true. I knew I was overreacting.

"No, I meant that I'm sorry I'm not there."

"Oh." Hearing the raw emotion in his voice from over the phone, a warm feeling flooded me. A little tingle started and it continued to spread. "Why does that make everything better?"

He laughed. "There's nothing I can say over the phone that'll help, but if I was there, I would just be with you. I know that helps me, when you're standing next to me."

"I don't like this long-distance thing." Pressing the phone even tighter to me, I wanted to reach through it. I wanted to feel his arms around me. Right now, the phone was my closest connection to him. "And you did help me."

Another softer laugh. "It's for a year, just one year, and then you'll be here."

"Yeah."

There was another moment of silence before he asked, "Are you okay otherwise?"

No. "Yes." Hearing the team cheering again, I knew they were coming outside, and I lifted my head. "I will be. I promise."

"Okay. I can hear them in the background."

"Yeah." God, there was so much I wanted to say. The phone wasn't enough. His presence would've been. He should've been there, right with me, alongside of me. He wasn't, though. "I love you."

"I love you back." He seemed to hesitate, and then added, "Be strong, Sam."

My breath caught in my throat.

He said, "You already are, but don't be afraid of it. Be you, who you are on the inside. You won't lose anything." He paused again. "You won't lose anyone."

The door burst open and the first of the football players took off past me, shoving open the doors back for the field. As they went by, their sounds deafening, I said into the phone, "I will. I am. I love you." I thought I heard him say the same and a second later the call was disconnected. Logan broke off from the line of players and stood next to me. I held my hand out, he caught it, and pulled me to my feet. His gaze fell to the phone still gripped in my hand. My knuckles were white around it.

He asked, "Mase?"

I nodded. The emotion was choking me, but it was the good kind of emotion. I wiped a tear away.

He threw an arm around my shoulder and turned for the door. "Come on. Stop being a sniveling, crying mess—" I elbowed him in the side and he chuckled, "—and come cheer me on. I'm awesome, Sam. Have you not gotten the memo recently? It's supposed to go out every Friday morning with Twitter alerts. #Logansawesomenooneforgetit." He flashed me a crooked grin. "I'm going to make shirts. Yours can say Kade Crew on the back of it. How about that? But no family discount. Sorry. I'm a cheap bastard."

I laughed. It felt good to laugh. As we started through the cars, I saw them. Garrett and a woman were coming down the path in our direction. They were watching the players run by them, making sure to stay out of the way. As the last of the players ran past them, they turned and saw us. Only a few yards separated us.

Logan dropped his arm and moved forward a step. I touched the back of his arm and shook my head. Reversing our positions, I was the one in front by a small inch. Two parked cars were between us and them, but I could see they were holding hands. This was his wife. He had left and not come back because of this woman. Their shared history was the span of my entire life. It was then that I realized I'd been jealous of her. I met my father, thought he would be around, and lost him to her. It took him a year to return.

There were questions. There were emotions, and I didn't want to deal with them.

As if sensing my decision, Garrett led the woman around the opposite side of the cars. Logan's coaches were behind us and one said, "Kade, get your ass with the team." They moved around us. Logan remained at my side. As they moved further up the hill, he called out again, "Logan! Now."

I didn't say anything, but I pushed Logan ahead.

"You sure?"

I nodded. I was still watching Garrett. They paused when the coach spoke, but his head went back down as he led her away. They began angling further away, moving through all the cars, until they were on the sidewalk next to the school.

Logan had gone ahead. I was the only one in the parking lot and I couldn't stop watching them. Even after he was out of eyesight and turned to follow the sidewalk around the other side of the school, I still stood there.

It hit me. My dad really was back.

*

MASON

"Dudette."

Grinning, I turned. Matteo had left the table and was in the doorway of the lobby, pounding his chest. With a wide smirk, he pounded his chest again and grabbed his pectoral, jiggling it. He winked. "Like that? There's more to come."

I shook my head. He'd already had too much sake. "My girl called."

He grunted. "She's still coming this weekend, right?"

"Should be here before the game."

"Good. I want to meet her. Georgie and I will be at her place all weekend." He puckered his lips out and lifted a hand, pretending to make out with himself. "You two can get it on. All. Weekend. Long."

He stopped, waited for a reaction from me, and I gave him a smirk of my own. I had every intention of enjoying Sam this weekend. Even the thought of feeling her again was getting me hard.

Matteo burst out laughing. "You're a too-cool type of guy, Kade."

I shrugged. "Why don't we stop talking about my girl and head back to the festivities." I clapped a hand on his shoulder. "It's your birthday, brotha. How crazy are you getting tonight?"

He sighed. "Not as crazy as I'd like."

"That's why you're going out tomorrow night after the game too."

"Yeah." He pursed his lips together. "Why aren't you coming again?"

Because Nate's fraternity was having another party, and he wanted Logan and Sam to go. Knowing the history with my roommate and Nate's fraternity, I only shrugged. "We'll do a stop-over. I told Sam she'd meet you since you didn't get to when they helped me move."

"Yeah. True." He nodded as we started back to the main room. "I intend to spend the rest of my birthday weekend between Georgie's legs. That girl is like paradise. One touch and I'm salivating like I'm in a damn desert."

"Ah," a voice spoke from behind us, and we turned. Park Sebastian had come into the waiting room of the restaurant, dressed in a tuxedo. A girl wearing a red, slinky dress was perched on his arm, and he hustled her inside, towards us. As he did, she lifted a hand and caught a tendril of hair in her finger. Twisting it around, she gave me a seductive smile. Her lipstick matched her red dress. Park didn't seem to care about his date as he scanned Matteo and me up and down. As the room filled with more of his fraternity brothers, he said, "Enjoying a quiet dinner before the big game tomorrow?"

Matteo grunted, showed him his teeth, and lumbered back into the main room. As he walked by me, he said, "Sorry, brotha. I'm out. I want to keep my birthday buzz."

"Understandable." I clapped him again on the arm before he left.

Park tilted his head to the side, and his eyes narrowed. "He's never going to not-hate me, is he?"

Glancing through the room, trying to find Nate, I murmured, "Well, you did screw over his best friend." As I said those words, my best friend finally came into the room. Nate's eyes widened and he began to push his way to us. As he did, I murmured, "Speaking of best friends..." When he moved around the last of the crowd, Nate's date came with him, and my tone trailed off. Marissa was with Nate. Seeing my attention, her cheeks pinked and her head turned to the floor. The hand she was holding onto Nate's arm with tightened, her fingers digging into his tuxedo jacket. Her other hand readjusted a strap from her dress as it slipped off her shoulder.

"Hey." Nate flashed me a grin. He pulled Marissa forward a step. "I totally forgot Marissa was coming to Cain U. Did you remember?"

"Yeah." Marissa still wasn't looking at me. "We ran into each other the other day, and she's in a class with me."

"That's awesome." Park moved forward too. His date was behind him, closed out because Nate had adjusted so he was slightly in front of her. It was a small circle of Nate, Park, myself, and Marissa who was looking at the wall. Park seemed eager.

"Another high school friend." His eyes fixed on her with a keen look in them. "I'll have to get to know you better."

Nate shared a look with me. I was fighting from rolling my eyes, and Marissa looked ready to disappear into the floor.

Nate said quickly, "Hey, so, Logan and Sam are coming tomorrow night, right?"

Marissa's head jerked back around. Both her and Park focused on me.

I nodded. "Yeah. You going to the game?"

"Yeah, I'm going—"

Park interrupted, "A bunch of our brothers are going. Who's Logan and Sam?"

I had no intention of telling him and started to tell him *that* when Nate forced out a laugh. "Uh, yeah. I guess Park and some others are going with me. I'll send Logan a text. We can meet up at the end or something."

I nodded. That sounded fine with me, but Park asked again, "No way. These are more friends of yours? They can sit with us. We have a private box. Lots of food and booze." He winked at me. "If your friends are into that. I know you're not a big drinker yourself." He swung his head to Marissa. "How about you..."

My irritation level had been on a good, slow burn with the conversation, but seeing that Park didn't know Marissa's name switched the level to slightly amused. Marissa shot him a glare, and Nate seemed to be holding back his own laughter. Park forced out a small laugh. "I'm sorry. I must've forgotten your name."

"We were never introduced."

At her soft retort, Nate and I shared a grin. Some of the old Marissa was still there. She could be feisty at times.

"That's right. We were all in such a hurry to get to the restaurant." Unfazed, Park drew his date closer to his side, bringing her into the circle. She lifted her head and looked down her nose at Marissa, whose shoulders pinched together. Her size seemed to shrink, and she took a step backwards. Park ran his hand up and down his date's arm. He said to me, "I don't know how long your group will stick around, but head over to our table at the end. We're all going to a formal banquet for the fraternity after this. This is our dinner. It's an exclusive thing, just for the brothers and their dates, but you're welcome to join. Just you, though." He glanced over my shoulder. His fraternity brothers started to move around us and into the restaurant, but I knew he was focused on Matteo's table. "We can find you a date, if you'd like. That'll be no problem for a guy like you."

My grin chilled.

"You can call me, if you decide to join us." Nate lifted his eyebrows, giving me the unspoken message to hold back. I rolled my eyes and leaned back on my heels. Fine. I'd play silent for now, but the asshole needed to stop insulting me. Offering up a girl for me when I had Sam—I took that as a big fucking insult. Nate propelled Marissa forward. "Park, they have our table ready for us. We should go. Mase," he halted, seeing the glare I had fixed on Park. He cleared his throat. "Uh, call me later."

He moved forward, but Park held back. I turned. I wasn't going to wait around for a private chat with the douche. As I began to follow the end of his group, waiting until I could veer off to my table, someone brushed against my arm, giving me a good graze of a breast. Glancing to the side, I saw Park's date. She shot me a secretive smile before she turned to follow Park, who was always watching me. When he saw my look, he shot his eyebrow up in question, and I had a feeling he wouldn't have minded if I wanted his date. He winked at me, but turned and ducked into a private room before he saw my real reaction.

When I got to Matteo and took my seat again, he asked, "What'd Park Sebasstian want?"

I grunted and took a good swig of my sake. "The guy's going to be a pain in the ass, isn't he?"

"He's got a man boner for you. Big time."

I sighed. I had hoped not to make enemies so soon, but that time was coming faster than I thought. I shrugged. I'd have to deal with him sooner than later.

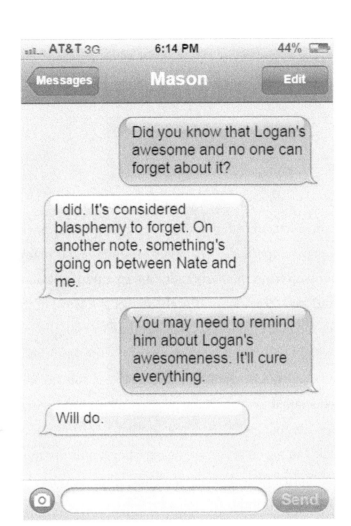

CHAPTER NINE

SAMANTHA

The next morning, I headed across the street with my backpack on and a big paper cup filled with coffee. Malinda had it ready for me when I came up from the basement. She gestured to it on the counter and said, "I know your night sucked." A wave of thanks rolled over me and I grinned at her, heading to grab the coffee, but she intercepted me. "Hold up there, honey." She wrapped her arms around me and rocked back and forth. As she did, she murmured against my ear, "I am so sorry about last night. You must've felt ambushed." Giving me another tight squeeze, she pulled back, but gazed at me as she kept her hands on my shoulders. "Your father doesn't think and when he does, he's got Analise still in his mind, chirping away, and he freezes sometimes. It's not an excuse. He should've dealt with Garrett way before last night. I'm sorry you went through that."

Her embrace had been warm and welcoming. As she continued to hold me, a tear came to her eye. This was going into the territory of loving motherhood. It was foreign to me. I gave her a small smile. "I'll be fine. I have to deal." I eased out of her hold and grabbed the coffee. Lifting it, I added, "Thanks for this."

She nodded, heading back to the sink where she'd been doing dishes. "You go and have a good time. I know you've been missing Mason like crazy."

I had turned, headed for the front door, but glanced back at her words. She gave me a small wave, looking over her shoulder at me. "Have fun, Samantha." It was said softly, but she meant it. There was something else in her tone. Sadness? It sent alarms off in me. I was uncomfortable. She was sad for me. I nodded again at her. I felt stupid. What was I supposed to say here?

"SAM!"

Hearing Logan yell from the street, I laughed. Some of the awkwardness left me. "I'll call you later?"

At the warmth that surged in her eyes, I assumed that'd been the right thing to say. Another tear slipped from her and she brushed it aside. "You do that."

"SAM! You butt-munch, get out here."

I started to laugh, but Malinda rolled her eyes and yelled back at him, "BUTT-MUNCH? YOU YELL AT MY DAUGHTER AGAIN, I'LL SHOW YOU A REAL BUTT-MUNCH! I'll take one big-ass bite out of *your* ass, and it won't be the feel-good type of bite, you hear me?"

My eyes went wide and there was a beat of silence before we heard Logan laughing. "Oh god. I have nothing to come back with." He raised his voice, "You WON, Malinda. You hear that? This one time. The butt-munching mother has won."

She grumbled, but she was still grinning. She said, "Go, Sam. I'm good. And yes, please call tonight."

I nodded. When I went outside, Mark had slowed his car next to Logan's. Cass was next to him, a smug, satisfied smirk on her lips. The sight of her should've made my smile dim, but it didn't. *Malinda's daughter*. Hearing her call me her daughter hadn't sent panic racing through me. I had liked it, a lot.

Mark was closest to me. Cass had her window rolled up, but as I rounded their car to Logan's, Mark stuck his head out of his window. "I forgot you were going to see Mason this weekend."

"Yeah." Tossing my bag into the backseat, I went to the passenger door and opened it, but I didn't get in. I rested my arms on the top of his car. "Where are you going?"

Mark pointed to the house. "Mom said she was cooking breakfast." He cursed. "Your dad's at a football conference today. Now you're gone. She planned this thing."

"Planned what?"

He grimaced, glanced at Cass, but turned before she caught his look. "Mom asked me to bring *her*."

Logan pealed with laughter.

"What are you..." It clicked. Malinda wanted to see Cass with only Mark around. I laughed. "Sucks to be you."

He glowered. "Crap. I should turn around before she sees me. I can make up some excuse—"

"Mark." Malinda had opened the front door. A towel was in her hand and she waved it at him. "I see you. No running away. Get your butt in here." When Cass looked at her, Malinda's smile turned sweet. "You too, Cassandra."

Logan choked on a laugh. "Run, Mark. Run for your lives. She just threatened to take a bite out of my ass, and she likes me." He lifted an eyebrow, taunting him further, "Guess what she'll do to her." He leaned down, a smirk on his face. "And she doesn't even like you, Cass."

Cass scowled, but she caught herself before she said anything. Logan was Logan Fucking Kade. She knew better.

Logan's smirk grew, and he stepped back from the car, leaned against his, and folded his arms over his chest. "Yeah. Malinda's going to eat you alive."

Mark looked worried. He cursed again and hit the steering wheel. "Whatever. Let's get this over with." He jerked his head to us. "Have fun guys. I am officially envious of your road trip." He sighed. "All right. Here we go."

As his car eased forward and turned into the driveway, Logan turned around and opened his door. He stopped, his gaze met mine, and we both stood for a moment. The cockiness fled and he gave me a tentative smile. "Her daughter, huh?"

I bobbed my head up and down with a giddy smile. "She said it." I didn't have to tell him I liked it. He could tell.

He murmured, "That's good."

We both got inside and I looked down at my lap. It was two words—her daughter—but those were two words that would've sent me running for hours six months ago. "She didn't even think about it, Logan. She just said it."

"She's good for you."

Yeah. For my father too.

We didn't talk, even when Logan stopped at Quickie's to get gas. He got out, filled the tank, and we both went inside. I wanted more coffee. Grabbing water and soda, Logan took my coffee from me to the register and paid for everything. I didn't fight it. I'd pay the next time. Once we were back in the car, we went to pick up Kris.

When we got to Mason's campus, there wasn't enough time to find him before the game. When Logan headed inside to help Kris with her bags, I stayed in the car, but heard raised voices. A battle between Logan and her sister set us back four hours. Her sister didn't want Kris to go. Logan did and he won, of course, but we were supposed to have been there before noon. Mason said the team ate and went to the locker room a couple hours before the game. As it was, we were late getting into the game. Cain University wasn't a small college. Their stadium was massive and just getting to our seats was a workout. A lot of people stood in the aisles and in the stairways. We sat down just as the second quarter started. After the third touchdown by the Wolves, the crowd no longer sat in their seats. Everyone remained on their feet, and the adrenalin from the team swept through the stands.

The fans were invigorated.

Everyone's voice was hoarse as they cheered on the team, but not mine. Since we arrived, I had barely paid attention to the game. I was riveted by the sight of Mason. Watching him jog back to the sidelines, my throat went dry. The need for him grew and an ache started between my legs.

I needed his touch. It had become like oxygen to me.

"You think Logan loves me?"

It was the question and nightmare that had been haunting me for three months. I closed my eyes. My glow from earlier had faded long ago. It wasn't the time to think of this. Mason was within touching distance. This was about him. That question had been pushed to the back of my mind.

"Or is it too soon?"

"What?" I glanced over at Logan's girlfriend. Kris. She had asked that question. It hadn't been in my mind. Relief swept through me, but I realized her second question and looked to the seat on her other side. It was empty. "Where'd Logan go?"

She sighed and bit down on her bottom lip before her head jerked down. She was twisting her hands together. "He went to find Nate. I guess he finally texted him, but do you think he loves me?" Her head bounced back up. A hopeful look was in her gaze. "It's too soon. I know it is. I'm stupid for asking."

"Uh..." I had no idea what to say. "It's been two months?"

"Yeah." Her thin shoulders lifted up and down. "We've been official for two months, but we hooked up a month before that." She paused as she began biting the inside of her cheek. "When did Mason tell you?"

My eyes got even bigger. I didn't talk about Mason. I barely talked about him to Logan and Heather. "Um." What did I say? Kris was pretty with wheat-blonde hair and striking green eyes, but she was nice. She was genuinely nice, which is why I knew so many guys had been after her. "We...um..."

She let out a hurt sigh. "He should've said it by now. That's what you're saying, isn't it?"

"No, not at all."

She shook her head. "No, I got it. I bet you and Mason knew right away. Logan hasn't said a word like that. He hasn't even said he likes me. Since the beginning, it's been about needing me, wanting me, having me. I know he feels lust for me." She pretended to shiver. "The chemistry was amazing, but it's died down over the last few weeks."

She continued, "He's amazing. I've heard all the girls talking, you know. They all want him, and I know I've been so lucky. I was talking to some of the girls from the team. They said Logan's never had a girlfriend, except for that one girl. Candy said Tate was trash anyway. He only had one-night stands, but they think he loves me." She paused and added, "Jessica and Lydia said the same thing too."

"Jessica and Lydia?" I hadn't known she was friends with my two ex-best friends.

"Yeah. I went to Cass' party last week. I talked with them for a bit. I've heard nasty things about Jessica, but she's been nice to me."

"You went with Logan?"

How had I not known about this? If Logan had gone to an Elite party, especially hers, I would've heard about it.

"No." She grinned. "Not at all. I didn't even bring it up to him, but I heard he dated Miranda too."

"That was only for a month."

"I thought Cass would be jealous of me, but she seems happy with your brother."

My eyes got big and I stiffened. My brother? A low growl started in the bottom of my throat. Mark wasn't my brother, not yet.

"Those two were meant for each other." She sighed, sounding wistful. "Sometimes I think I might have that with Logan. He can be so loving and thoughtful at times, but at other times, it's like I'm not even in the room."

I pressed my hands to my forehead. A headache was forming, and I could tell it wouldn't be leaving anytime soon.

She sighed again. "I just don't know what to do. I feel like I'm losing him. Hearing all the stories about him, I guess I should've been prepared for this. Cass told me—"

"Who aren't you friends with?" I snapped.

She stopped as her eyes got big. "Uh, we're not super tight. I mean, Adam's friends with her and we hung out a bunch last year so..."

I saw the fear in her eyes and reined myself in. She was listing off so many ghosts from my past. Transferring to Fallen Crest Public should've put a stop to her connections to them, but I realized that it hadn't. They were friends with Mark, and they were friends with her. I wanted to groan. They were still so close to me.

"Should I not be friends with her?"

It took me another moment to comprehend who Kris was talking about. Cass. "No, no. I'm sorry for reacting. I don't have good memories from that place."

"Oh." She frowned. "I'm sorry."

"It doesn't matter." I gave her a smile. "Really. I'm sorry how I reacted."

She went back to twisting her hands together. "No one talks about you over there."

Really?

She added in a rush, as if she were confessing something, "I was really confused when I saw you at the party last year. I was with Jeff and he told me that you guys dated, but I had no idea that Adam Quinn wanted to date you, and I had been hanging out with him too. I found out you were close to Mason and Logan Kade. I mean, I heard about them my first day at FCA, but no one mentioned you." She lifted her head up and down as she said that word, "I found out your dad was the football coach at FCA aaaand you're living with Mark Decraw." A nervous giggle slipped from her. "For someone that I had never heard about, you're connected to a ton of people." She snuck a timid look at me. "I've been scared to talk to you about that. I'm glad I did."

I wanted to curse. "You're saying that Miranda and her friends never talked about me?"

"Well," she hesitated, "they have said some things, but nothing good and I didn't put two and two together until Adam and I went to Mark's and all of you guys were there too. I don't really listen to the bad stuff. That's been done to me at my old school. A lot of the girls were jealous because some of the guys liked me."

"Give it time. I'm sure the same thing will happen at Fallen Crest Public too."

She flinched as if I slapped her.

I grimaced. "Sorry. You're friendly. Maybe it won't happen to you."

A relieved look came over her, and her shoulders dropped. "I'm very careful, especially since dating Logan. I've noticed a big difference. People are more cautious around me and some of them are fake. Some kiss my ass. You can just tell, you know?"

She was giving me a look as if we were friends, as if we were allies.

It was then that I saw why Adam, Jeff, and Logan liked her, and why even Jessica and Lydia were being nice to her. She was new. She hadn't been stabbed in the back by anyone—yet—and she didn't know how vicious people could be.

She was refreshing, for them. Not me. I glanced around. *Was Logan coming back?*

"It's fourth and fifty-seven," the announcer said over the stadium.

Glancing at the field, I saw Mason on the sidelines. He was ready to go back in for the next play and I waited. The team was setting up to punt, and he was flagged in. I looked at the scoreboard; it was the fourth quarter, and there were two minutes left in the game. The score was twenty-eight to three, a sure win for the Wolves.

"Where did you say Logan went?"

She shrugged. "I think he went to find Nate. I guess he sent him a text or something, saying he was in the stands somewhere. He'll be back before the game is over. So, can I ask you a question?"

I tensed. What did that mean?

"Why isn't Nate on the team? From what everyone's been saying about him, Mason, and Logan, I thought he'd be playing with Mason. He's not."

"Oh. No. Nate's not good enough." I hesitated. The truth was that Logan wasn't even good enough. Division One football was too competitive. It was a stepping stone before the National Football League.

The ball was punted and the punt returner caught it. He started forward; two guys from the opposing team were coming at him, but were blocked by Mason. He rammed into one guy, sending him to the ground, pivoted on his heel and wrapped both arms around the second guy. He threw him onto the ground, falling on top of him as his teammate soared past him.

"Shit, what a tackle. That's a freshman?" someone from behind us muttered.

His friend commented, "Roster says Mason Kade."

"Where'd he come from?"

"School's few hours away, but his stats are good."

Pride swelled through me, but it wasn't anything new.

Kris' phone buzzed at that moment. A soft grin came to her as she read the text, then she showed it to me. It was from Logan.

With Nate in the back. By the 23rd door. Tell Sam. Staying back here with Nate and his friends.

"Come on." I wasn't waiting any longer. "Let's go find them."

It didn't take long to spot them. Nate and his friends stood out. They had congregated against a wall, but were garnering a bunch of attention. The girls in front of the concession stand across from them giggled together and whispered behind their hands as I passed them. There were other groups of girls to the side, also eyeing the guys. A sense of déjà vu came over me. It felt like my first week at Fallen Crest Public all over again, but it was Nate getting all the attention this time.

I scanned the group. "Where's Logan?"

Nate jerked his head to the side. "Pissing." He broke out in a big grin after that and pulled me in for a hug. "Good seeing you. It's been too long."

I laughed, but I had to admit it felt good.

"Hi, Nate."

Remembering Kris, I stepped back. Nate gave her a brief grin and waved, and I saw the hurt settle in her gaze.

"Hey. Kris, right?"

I caught the wink he sent me. Oh, yes. Nate pretended to forget her name. He was subtly putting her back in her place. She wasn't in the Fearsome Foursome, or whatever we were when it was just Logan, Nate, Mason, and myself. A wave of gratitude came over me. I saw Logan heading our way at that moment.

"Yes, hi." Her voice had dipped down, but Logan wrapped his arm around her shoulder and pulled her tight into his side. He scanned the group. "So, we won?"

The buzzer went off inside the arena, and I grinned. "Guess so."

"Nate." One of his friends stepped forward, a broad grin on his face. He was tall, over six feet by a few inches, with sandy-brown hair and crystal blue eyes. He looked like he had stepped from the brochure for an Ivy League school. "Are you going to introduce us to your friends?"

Nate was silent for a moment and paused, giving me a questioning look. I glanced to Logan and knew he noticed the change. The air shifted. We both studied Nate, who forced out a polite laugh. "Uh, yeah. Logan, Sam, this is Park. He lives in my fraternity house with me."

"Hi." I knew Mason didn't like this guy so I assumed Nate wouldn't have brought him to the game. Sharing another look with Logan, I saw he was thinking the same thing.

Nate's head moved down an inch. His entire demeanor shifted so he came across as more self-conscious. "Mason said the plan was to come to our party tonight?"

Logan slowly nodded. "Yeah. That's the plan." He was studying Nate's friends more, his eyes lingering on Park longer than it was polite.

"Well, we'll see you guys there." Nate moved forward. His friends took the cue and began to leave. Park flashed us a smile and lifted his hand. He started to say something, but Nate clapped him on the shoulder and shook his head. His friend frowned, but heeded the warning. He turned and followed behind the rest of the fraternity brothers. Nate was the only one who lingered behind.

He shot a meaningful look at Kris, and Logan got the message. He turned to her, "Hey, babe?"

"Yeah?" Her head jerked to his.

"Maybe you should go to the bathroom? The drive to the restaurant might take a long time with traffic after the game."

"I should be fine. We have to wait for Mason, right? I can go then."

"You and Logan are going to the restaurant. I'm the only one who's going to be waiting for Mason."

"Oh."

Logan shook his head at me, but patted her on the arm. "Why don't you go now? Nate needs to talk about something private anyway."

"Oh." Her eyes widened as she snuck a look at Nate, who gave her a tight-lipped grin. "Okay. I'll wait over there when I get back."

As she hurried away, there was a brief moment of silence between us. Nate glanced from Logan to me. We were waiting to see what Logan's reaction was going to be, but Logan turned to me and narrowed his eyes. I tensed, was it coming? But he only shook his head and said to Nate, "So what's going on? Mason told us you wanted to network, but with that douchebag? Why are you in a fart house?"

"Not that it's any of your business, but Mason lives in the football house. All his roommates are on the team and that means all his friends are going to be his teammates. I'm not on the team. Branching out isn't a bad idea for me."

Logan grunted. "It's a piss poor idea, and you know it."

Nate sighed, shaking his head. "Look. Whatever. Mason said you guys are going to dinner and then coming to my fart's," he grimaced, "frat's party? Is that the plan?"

A gleam appeared in Logan's eye. I knew that look. Logan wanted to fight. I murmured, "You sure you want us there?"

"Yeah." Nate gentled his tone. "It'll be nice to have you guys all there."

"What about douchebag?" Logan jerked his head in the direction the fraternity brothers had gone. "He's not going to like us. You know that."

"Just," Nate sounded so wary, "come for me. Okay?"

"Yeah. We'll come." Logan's glower deepened. "But I'm not kissing any ass tonight."

Nate grimaced. "Try to be nice."

Logan kept quiet, and that was the best answer Nate was going to get. Nate lifted a hand and said he'd see us at the party. I waited until he had disappeared into the crowd before I asked, "What are you planning?"

"I'm going to piss his friend off."

With the dark intent brewing in his gaze, I knew Logan was going to make enemies that night. I shrugged. It was going to happen. I flashed him a grin. "Looks like we're getting a head start for next year."

He grunted in response before we sat back and waited for Kris and Mason.

CHAPTER TEN

MASON

"Hey, man." Drew came over and propped a hand on the top shelf of my locker. He had showered and dressed in jeans and a Cain University shirt. "I heard your woman's in town."

I narrowed my eyes and bent to grab my own shirt. Pulling it on, I asked, "Yeah?"

He ran a hand through his hair and bent over so he could see in my mirror. As he fixed his hair, he said, "A bunch of us are going downtown for Matteo's birthday. He can let loose tonight. He mentioned that you're going to a frat party tonight?"

"Yeah." I watched as he moved his head at all angles to inspect his hair. When he saw a clump that was pressed flat, he bit his lip and lifted his hands to tug them apart. Logan did this shit. He had cut his hair so it was shorter, but there was enough for him to spike it like my quarterback. I kept mine in a crew cut. I didn't want to waste time, and Sam seemed to like it. Good enough for me. As he moved to a new clump of hair, I told him, "You know my best friend is there. He wants to show the house off to my brother more than anything. I doubt we'll stay late."

"I'm surprised you're going. Matteo told me you're a no-nonsense guy. I would've thought Park Sebasstian would be road kill to you." His fingers pulled apart two hairs that were sticking up. He rubbed them so they stuck up even higher, then nodded to himself. He turned to face me again and smirked, but when he saw the no-nonsense expression on my face, his smirk fell flat.

I said, "I'll deal with anyone who tries to mess with me."

His eyes narrowed and studied mine. He nodded. "Sounds good." He pounded me on the shoulder. "We're at Cliché tonight. Just ask for the Cain U footballer's private box. They'll show you the way." He turned to go, but paused. "A lot of the guys from the team go there."

"What are you talking about?"

"Don't worry about age. They worked out a deal with one of the captains a long time ago. They don't serve 'alcohol' to minors." As he used his fingers for air quotes, I assumed that meant we could get alcohol just fine if we wanted. He added, "And don't feel weird. A lot of the guys bring their wives too, you know, the guys in serious relationships like you."

I grunted. "Yeah, okay. We might swing by. My brother would probably like the club."

"Sounds good, man. Have fun with the wife and kids."

As soon as Drew moved away, Matteo lumbered over to me. He had showered, but he only managed to get his pants on. Still shirtless, he was rubbing lotion over his chest as he said, "You coming out tonight?"

"I think so." I jerked my head in Drew's direction. "The wife comments, are those veiled insults?"

"What?" My roommate's eyes got big, and he glanced where Drew was talking to two senior players. "No, man. If it is, I'll be pissed. They call Georgie my wife too. That's what they call the serious relationships."

"So there's no shade with that?" I wanted to make sure. Drew had been smirking, but I knew he was still on an adrenalin high from the win. He threw four touchdowns, but I wasn't going to stand and be laughed at without hitting back.

"No, no, no." Matteo seemed taken aback. His hand paused in rubbing the lotion, but he started again a moment later. "They want us to be wifed-up. Girls can mean problems for the single guys. Hook-ups sometimes become baby-mommas. Some of that shit happens on purpose. You know how it is. They want the guys to have wives. They're more stable. Those girls are rocks for some of us. I know Georgie is for me. If I step out of line, she smacks me back in, and I regret it for the rest of my life."

I grinned, easing up a bit. "Good to know."

"How about you?" He sat down on my bench. "You don't talk too much about your woman, but you guys talk every night."

"Me and Sam?" I grunted. "I guess I'm the rock."

"She doesn't smack you around if you step out of line?"

I didn't step out of line. I never wanted to. Shrugging, I commented while I saw my phone buzzing, "No. We don't really fight that much." I read the text and saw it was from Logan. **Get your ass out here. Mine is hungry and wanting sweet relief, if you know what I mean. Serious, tho. Get out here. Sam won't look away from the hallway you said you'd be coming from.**

I typed back: **Coming.** I said to Matteo, "I need to go. Happy birthday and I'll see you later tonight."

"Yeah, I want to meet your woman. She didn't stop by earlier."

I began backpedaling and lifted my arms up in a shrug. "They were late. Logan said there was some fight, but they're here now." As I moved through the main open area of the gym, I raised my voice and lifted a hand, "Happy birthday to Matteo! May your dick be tired tomorrow morning."

"You douche," Matteo called after me, laughing.

The guys who were still in the locker room called out their own cheers for him, and as I went out the door, I knew my roommate was soaking up all the attention

It didn't take long to walk from the locker room to where I knew Logan and Sam were waiting. I came up the side stairs, and when I opened the door, I noticed the stadium had cleared out. Going past some offices and conference rooms, I turned and saw them at the end of the hallway. The walkway was huge. Sam and Logan looked like ants compared to the massive posts around them. One of them jerked upright from a wall.

I grinned, waving. It was Sam. Fuck, it'd been too damn long. She broke into a run, and I walked faster. Her eyes were wide, her mouth opened, and there was no hesitation. She threw herself at me. Grabbing a hold of her, I turned and pressed her against the wall. My legs were unsteady, from the game and seeing her, and I needed more balance. Closing my eyes, I pressed a kiss to her forehead and hugged her. She hugged me back.

Home. That's what Sam was to me.

Moving to her ear, I whispered, "It feels good to hold you again."

She clasped onto me tighter and wrapped her legs around my waist. When she didn't respond, I knew she couldn't. I wanted to kiss her, but she was pressed into my chest and her head went to my shoulder so I stopped thinking and just held her. I'd forgotten how perfectly she fit with me.

I needed time with just her.

Logan had walked closer, but he saw my look and nodded. Reaching behind him, he took his girl's hand and said something in her ear. When he led her out the door, I knew he had given us some privacy. I wasn't going to waste any time. Sliding my hands under Sam's ass, I stood from the wall and her legs tightened in response.

"Mason?"

I turned for one of those conference rooms. Locking the door, hitting the lights off, I pushed her against the wall again. Her legs fell so she was standing on her own, and she gazed up at me in confusion. I cupped the back of her head and slammed my lips down on hers.

Fuck. She tasted good.

Her hands lifted and bunched my shirt collar in her fists. When I started to lift up again, she pulled me back down, taking command. It wasn't long before my hand was inside her shirt, nudging underneath her bra. I was two seconds from opening her jeans and shoving mine down when I remembered these rooms had cameras.

FUCK!

Ripping my mouth from hers, I rested my forehead against hers. I wanted to be between her legs, feel her body underneath mine, writhing as I moved inside her, slow and steady and harder, as we both forgot where one began and one ended.

She whispered, panting, "Can we please take a separate car from them?" Her hand went to my pants and began kneading the bulge there.

I laughed, turning into her neck. Kissing her, I murmured, "I think we'll have to. God, I've missed you." I couldn't stop myself. I lifted her in my arms again, hoisting her high so her legs wrapped back around my waist, so she could look down at me. Her eyes were dark with lust, glazed over from it, and she let out one of those small sighs of frustration.

Her hand lifted, and she ran her fingers through my hair, cupping my cheek. She smiled down at me. I saw the love and warmth, but I paused as I saw more. There was misery and pure agony. Something was wrong and I didn't think it was just from our separation. I bit my tongue. I wanted to question her, push her buttons so she spilled what was wrong, but that wouldn't work anymore for us. Sam needed to tell me on her own.

My own pain sliced through me. There was distance between us, physical and emotional. My hand lifted and I rubbed a thumb over her lips, lingering over the bottom. I murmured, "I know something's wrong."

She stilled.

I never looked away from her. "I can't push you to talk anymore, Sam. You have to tell me on your own. This won't work otherwise."

A tear formed and, biting her lip, she jerked her head in a nod. Some of her hair fell forward to block her face, and I tucked it behind her ear, my hand lingering there. I began to make circles on her cheek with my thumb. It was a loving gesture, and my god, I loved this girl. Feeling a surge of that emotion go through me, it pushed the pain away. We'd be fine. We'd have to be.

I let her back down to the floor, but kept her in my arms. Resting my chin on the top of her head, her arms slid around my chest, and she burrowed into me again. I asked, "Will you tell me what's wrong?"

I felt her nodding against my shoulder.

This was important. The urgency of it coursed through, me and I tipped her head back up. Our eyes collided and held. "I mean it, Sam. You have to tell me. This shit is work. We both have to put into it. No running."

"I won't." A small grin tugged at the corner of her mouth, and she cupped my face in her hands. "I promise. I won't."

"What's wrong?" Because I knew there was something going on. "Is this about your dad?" No... That didn't feel right. It was something else.

She hesitated.

"Sam."

She shook her head. "You know me and my family. Terrifying. But no, I just..." She faded and glanced away.

I bit back my words. I wanted to make her tell me, but Matteo's words stayed with me. His woman smacked him back into place when he faltered. Sam didn't do that for me. It hurt to acknowledge that. We needed to have that. I hadn't known how bothered I had been when he said those words, but it did. Sam rarely put me in my place.

"Sam," I whispered.

"I know. There is something, but I'm not ready to talk about it." She held my gaze, and I saw she meant what she was saying. She added, "I will tell you, but not yet."

"You will?"

She nodded. A small tear slipped out and trailed down her cheek. She ignored it. "I love you so much."

I nodded, then pulled her back to me. Her head tipped back and her lips raised for mine. I brushed mine against them. I wanted to make love to her that night. I wanted to show her that everything would be fine, that she could tell me anything, but I also just wanted to hold her and not let go. Feeling all that, I applied more pressure to the kiss, and she sighed from contentment.

It was later, much later, when we finally left that room and headed down to the parking lot. I was grateful Logan gave us that moment of privacy. It was needed. When Sam was gone, there wasn't just literal distance between us. It was like we were on the same page, but there was a tear between us. Seeing her again helped to mend that tear. We were on the same page again. She felt like home again.

My hand tightened around hers. She squeezed back.

When we got to Logan's car, Logan threw his arms around us, separating us again. I shot her a grin when she stepped back. I clasped my arms around him. "Hey, man."

Logan pounded me twice on the back before letting go. A wide grin stretched over his face. "I feel hornier than a dog who almost got his balls snipped off. Shit, man. Your face is gorgeous. Have you always been this fine specimen?"

I laughed, shoving him away. "Hump your woman, not your brother."

It felt good to have him there. It felt good to have them both there. Logan threw his head back, grabbing for his woman's hand again. He continued smirking at me. "Dinner? I know I'm starving."

And then a party and booze. I knew that was where Logan was going, but I shook my head as I grabbed for Sam's hand again. "Change of plans. Let's hit the frat place first, and briefly." I paused. Logan narrowed his eyes and a spark flashed for a second. There was a story there, but he slid his eyes to his girlfriend and gave me a small shake of his head. Message received. I'd ask later, so I added, "And my roommate wants to meet you guys."

"Matt?"

"Matteo. It's his birthday this weekend. We had a dinner last night, but he was tame." He sat on my bed later in the evening for a 'serious' talk about Park Sebastian. The talk never started. Matteo declared that he was hot and started taking his clothes off. I went to the bathroom and when I came back, he was spread eagle on my bed, naked. Too much sake had him snoring loud enough to wake the two rooms on both sides of us. I corrected myself, "I think he was tame last night. I've got a feeling tonight will be a night to remember with him."

"Where's he at?"

"They're at Cliché."

Logan's girlfriend jerked forward, clinging to my brother's arm with both hands.

"What?"

"Did you say Cliché?"

"Yeah."

Logan glanced to her. "What?"

"That's the hottest club here. Oh my god. We're going there?"

Sam sighed beside me.

Logan prodded, "Have you been there?"

Her lips pressed tight and she shook her head, but a squeal left her.

"All right," I continued. She'd been annoying this summer, but as she started bobbing up and down and more squeals left her, I held back the usual blast I might've given someone in the past. Logan liked her. I had to deal with it.

"Sorry." Her cheeks were red. "We used to live not far from here, and I know it's *the* place to go. Charlie used to go there a ton, but she's forbidden me to ever step foot inside." She started clapping. "I'm so excited."

Logan was grinning at her. "And this is why your sister hates me."

"I don't care." She began waving her hands instead. "I'm so excited. You guys have no idea. This place is epic."

"Well, whatever." Her hands fell down at my abrupt tone. I ignored how she jumped back a step, and said to Logan, "The birthday party's there. I figured we'd go. Nate can show off his house to you guys, and we can head there after?"

131

"Sounds good to me." Logan's tone turned predator-like. He shared a look with Sam, who didn't say a word. When she saw that I caught the brief exchange, she gave me a slight nod and slanted her eyes towards Logan's girlfriend.

I got the message so I said, "Give me a ride to my car? We can head to your hotel, switch it up, and take one car?"

"Sounds good to me."

We piled into the car and left for where my car was parked, clear on the other side of the stadium. On the drive to Logan and his girlfriend's hotel, Sam told me what had happened between Logan, Park, and also Nate. I wasn't surprised. The guy was a dick, but I also knew that I might need to watch Logan a little more than I had planned.

I waited in the parking lot as Logan and his girlfriend went to check in. They took their bags up to the room, and Sam put her bags in my car. She was standing next to me when Logan came back out. Seeing that he was alone, I didn't waste time.

"Sam told me what happened with Park."

Logan sneered. "That guy's a dick."

"I know."

"He needs to be brought down."

"Not by you and not tonight."

Logan's head reared back an inch. "Say what? He's a fight waiting to happen. The guy's a creep about you."

"I know, but I'm going to handle it, and I'm going to do it on my timetable." Logan snorted. He began to turn away, but I caught his arm. He looked back, reassessing me. I told him, "I mean it. You get to leave. I don't. This is my world, and I'll handle him when I have to. Right now, I don't have to. All he's doing is kissing ass."

"Whatever. Yeah. Fine."

"I mean it, Logan."

"I know." He gentled his tone. "I mean it. I know. I'll bite my fucking, no-nonsense, butt-muncher tongue tonight. It's your call. I'll follow your lead."

I relaxed, slightly. "Butt-muncher?"

He flashed me a grin, his eyes darted to Sam's, and he shrugged. "You see. That's what happens when you get all big and old and move away to a Division One school. You miss out on inside jokes, like what a butt-muncher is."

His girlfriend came out of the hotel and headed our way. I glanced at Sam. She rolled her eyes. "It's really not that funny—"

"Ah," Logan cut her off. "But it's our funny. It's Fallen Crest funny." He pretended to sneer at me. "And you'll never know."

His girlfriend got to us, threw her arms around Logan's neck, and the two kissed. I punched him in the arm and he broke it off to glare at me. "Yes?"

"Keys, asshole." I flashed him a grin. "You get backseat, bitch."

Handing the keys over, he pressed them into my hand harder than necessary. Yeah, he got my slight insult. My grin grew as I got behind the steering wheel. Sam sat next to me, and the two gropers slid into the back. I turned the car around and headed for Nate's fraternity house.

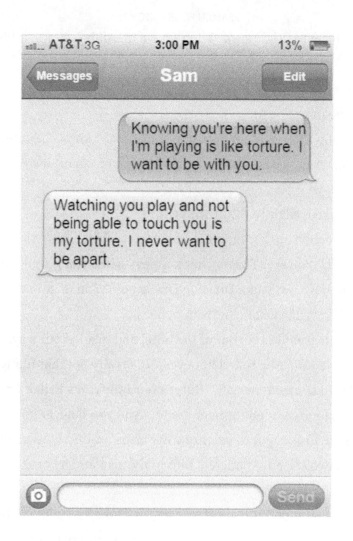

CHAPTER ELEVEN

When we got to the fraternity house, Nate met us at the door. He gave me a slight frown. "I thought you were doing dinner first?"

"Change of plans."

"Oh." He continued to frown. "Okay." A quick smile covered his face and he reached behind him. Tossing a beer to Logan, he said, "Help yourself. I figured you wanted to release some stress this weekend?" A second beer was handed to Logan's girlfriend. She took it and her eyes lit up like Nate had given her a hundred dollars.

The girl was weird.

Logan laughed, throwing his arm around her shoulders. He jerked his chin up, saying to Nate, "Forget the bullshit about who you're bunking with, you're a good man to me." He glanced sideways at me as he added, "I'm all about staying out of trouble, you know."

I grinned, but Nate narrowed his eyes. "Uh. Okay." He turned to me. "Anything I should know about?"

"We might not stay long."

"Yeah." A knowing look came over him. "I figured."

Logan snorted, opened his beer, and took a swallow. As he finished, he gestured the beer to me. "Mase wants to put off the battles for as long as possible, but we all know his tolerance for ass kissers. He's got none. Do him a favor, Nate, stop bringing your buddies around him."

"Oh god," Sam groaned beside me.

Logan's girlfriend squeaked and moved an inch behind the group. Logan was riled up. He wanted to fight. Sam saw it too and we shared a look. It was going to happen.

Nate just sighed.

Catching Logan's gaze, I looked pointedly at his girlfriend. I wanted to talk, but not in front of her. He rolled his eyes, but got the message. "Kris?"

"Yeah?"

"You said you wanted to go to the bathroom." With a hand behind her back, he propelled her further inside the house. "Maybe Nate can show you where it is?"

That was his signal. He didn't want Nate to be a part of our talk. And Nate got it. His nostril's flared, his jaw clenched, but he forced out a polite smile. "Of course. I'll take you to my own bathroom. It's clean and private."

"Oh good."

His hand replaced Logan's on her back and he guided her forward, but shot Logan a dark look over his shoulder. Logan lifted his beer in a salute.

I snorted.

Sam began to move to the side of the patio, but I shook my head. "No."

Gesturing to the window right next to it, Logan added, "You have no idea what they can hear."

"Oh. Okay."

I led the way off the patio, to a corner of the yard. A few people had gathered outside, but they weren't paying any attention to us. I looked at my brother. "What's got you worked up? Did you really hate Sebastian that much?" He was annoying, but damn, a bug could be squashed easily. Logan's reaction didn't make sense.

He shook his head. "Whatever. I'll be nice. No worries."

I glanced at Sam. "Something else happen that I don't know about?"

Logan snorted. "Like she'd answer that truthfully."

My alarms shot up and studying Sam, I caught the glare she sent his way. Her lips pressed tight, and she shook her head, turning away. She'd been present with me. I felt her. But Sam could slip away. Her mind would leave the room, thinking about other things, shutting her emotions off, but I knew it was because of Analise. Being raised by a monster like that would leave scars, deep scars, but I had felt her just now. She'd been present. She'd been real. She'd been raw.

She was gone again. Her walls were back up. I touched her elbow, tugging her to me. "Hey. What's going on?"

She began to shake her head when Logan muttered, "Shocker." She stopped, and her glare got colder.

I looked between the two of them. "What the hell is going on?" They were involved in a heated stand-off.

Sam crossed her arms over her chest, but one of her hands broke free. She gestured to Logan. "Ask him. We were fine this morning and now he's ready to rip into the world. The guy was an ass, but Mason's right. He wasn't that bad."

Logan rolled his eyes. "Maybe I'm just sick of the bullshit and lies going on. Something is obviously going on with you, and you won't say a word about it to me. This," his finger moved in a circle between the three of us, "is a joke. I'm in Fallen Crest, but it's like I'm a stranger to you. Coming here, and—" He stopped and cursed. "Whatever. I'm fine. I'm sorry." He sent me an apologetic look. "Sam's been distant as hell since you left. I have to fight with my girlfriend's sister just so I can see her. We went five rounds today. That's why we're late. Seeing Nate with that douchebag. What the hell, man? It's like he doesn't even want to be friends with you anymore. That pisses me the fuck off. I just want to punch someone."

Sam wasn't letting him in. I grunted in response. I could relate. There were times her wall was up to me and it hurt like hell to break through it, but I couldn't do anything about it. As for the rest... "Nate wants to branch out and make new friends. I don't blame him. My friends are going to be my teammates. I'm not too interested in making new friends up here."

"Still." Logan cursed again, then downed the rest of his beer. When it was empty, he crushed it and left to toss it in a garbage can by the house. Nate and Logan's girlfriend came back onto the patio. Both wore uncertain expressions and Logan's whole demeanor changed. He'd been tense and wanted to rip into someone, but as she stepped outside, his shoulders went back, his head lifted, and I knew he stuffed all that down. As she laughed at something Nate said, she went to Logan and he wrapped his arms around her legs, lifting her in the air and whirling her in a circle.

She laughed, hitting at his shoulder, but Logan moved her further away from everyone.

That was on purpose. When he set her back down, he met my gaze. I knew he wanted to leave and turning, I caught the knowing look on Nate's face again. He headed off the patio and approached us. He skimmed a look at where Logan remained, and said to me, "You're going?"

"It's for the best."

"Logan's in a mood?"

I didn't answer. I wasn't going to throw Logan under the bus. Nate knew I wouldn't and he didn't wait for a reply. He said to Sam, "It was good seeing you for a little bit. I wanted to show you the alumni room. My dad's picture is in there." He nodded towards me. "So is his. It's kinda cool to see all the history."

"Yeah."

I grinned. I couldn't stop it. Sam had been silent most of the time, but that one word told us all how uncomfortable she was. As my hand touched the small of her back, I felt how tense she was. Maybe I needed to push more and find out what was wrong? I knew it was bothering Logan as well.

Distracting me, Nate said, "Park wanted me to invite you to a dinner we're doing at the end of the month. I promised him I would invite you. Some of the alumni are coming back, including my dad."

We both knew I wouldn't go. I didn't even respond. "I'm sure we'll go out for breakfast or lunch tomorrow. Did you want to come?"

"That sounds good," Nate said.

"Okay."

"Bye, Nate."

"See ya, Sam."

Logan had gone ahead for the car. When we got to the sidewalk and before we got to the car, I asked Sam, "You've been distant with Logan?"

She stiffened again, then jerked her shoulder up in an abrupt shrug. "It's nothing. I mean, it's me doing my thing, but it's nothing."

I pulled her to a stop. "I'm not hearing that it's nothing." There was more. I heard the undertone of anguish in her voice.

She closed her eyes and her forehead went to my chest. Her shoulders lifted again and fell back down as her hands rested on my waist. She murmured, "It's hard. You're not there and..." Her head tipped back. Her eyes were swimming with unshed tears. "Being close to Logan makes me miss you even more. If I shut him out, I shut out that pain. Sometimes."

My thumb went to her chin. Moving it back and forth in a comforting motion, my own emotion rising in me. "It's a year and then you'll both be here." But it didn't matter. My reassurance fell on deaf ears. I could tell because I felt it too. We were family and the family was torn apart. Drawing her into my arms, I rested my chin on the top of her head and held her. That's all I wanted, for only a moment. No matter what we did, the truth was that I was a three hour drive away. Logan was with Helen and Sam was living with another family, again. My hand swept down her back and she burrowed even closer to me. I dropped another kiss to her head.

We stayed like that, for a few seconds, before Logan honked the horn at us.

I lifted my hand, not moving away from Sam, and gave him my middle finger. His laughter pealed out a second later and I glanced over, grinning. He flicked me off right back, then hollered, "Let's go. You two can get it on tonight. I want to party with my brother."

Sam stepped back, grinning ruefully. "He switched from wanting to fight to wanting to party."

Lacing our hands together, I started for the car. "You know Logan. He never changes."

We shared a grin because only the Threesome Fearsome, what Logan called us, really knew the real Logan. He'd want to stir shit up before the end of the night. That was just him.

*

SAMANTHA

My hand never left Mason's. When we went inside the club—as Kris squealed, gushing over everything, the walls included—we were led to a private area. When we got there, I felt overstimulated. There was so much to take in. The club was huge, like a smaller version of the football stadium. The private booth or box, I wasn't sure what it could be called, wasn't a private booth or box. It was a private everything. We had our own floor with its own dance floor, set above the main dance floor. The DJ booth was attached to our floor, set in a corner so the crowd below could see him. When he began a new beat, they went crazy, waving their arms and pounding on the floor.

It was nuts. I'd never seen anything like this.

Dry ice filled the room with white smoke. When the DJ would raise his arms, a burst of white smoke would shoot out over the floor. It raised and covered the front of our floor as well. Neon lights flashed all over, and I had to cover my eyes so I could adjust before a headache came on. There was a bar when we first entered the club, then another bar at the end of the hallway going to the private floor, a third at the top of the stairs, and four more set up all around us.

I touched Mason's arm and he leaned down for me. "Is your entire football team here?"

"Uh." He scanned the room and nodded. "Looks like." He flashed me a grin. "Matteo's birthday is a big deal. The team loves him."

I could see that. There were people everywhere. A group of guys stood in a circle by the dance floor. They were sipping their drinks, talking, and watching the girls dancing. And the girls knew it. They'd smile over at them, move more seductively, and the guys would smirk back at them. There was an area filled with couches on the other side of the room. Again, a group of guys sat there, leaning forward with their elbows on their knees or lounging back, but it was obvious they were involved in a big discussion. Scattered around them, on the outskirts, were a few couples. A guy and girl had paired off. A few of the girls were straddling their guys and they were kissing, and I skimmed over the couches near us. There were more couples, but these were holding hands, talking, laughing, or just sitting beside each other.

Feeling Mason's hand curve over my hip, a surge of warmth and pride went through me. This was his world. All these people had the best clothes. I'd been around wealthy people. I grew up going to Fallen Crest Academy. The average student came from a home who made $250,000 a year. Living with Mason and Logan, they were even wealthier than that, but I had never been intimidated by their money. I was now, and I had no idea why. Standing in this room, seeing the flashy clothes, the athletic bodies of all the guys, I felt apprehensive. My hand rested on top of Mason's, and I left it there.

He glanced down, a small question in his eyes, as he pulled me closer. "You okay?"

I forced myself to nod, but my neck was stiff. "Yeah." *Just don't go anywhere.* Hearing my own inner thought, icy fear plunged my insides. I was losing Mason. I felt it.

Breathe, Samantha. Breathe. Run. Keep going. That'd been my mantra for so long.

My eyelids lifted and I skimmed over Logan. His arms were wrapped around Kris from behind. She was pointing around the room and his head was moved down beside hers. As she said something, he nodded and kissed the side of her neck.

"Sam."

Jerking out of my thoughts, I forced my hand to loosen around Mason's. I had been clenching onto him so tight, that I saw an imprint of my hand over his now. Instead of rubbing his hand so the blood could flow back into it, he lifted it to my chin and tipped my head back. He peered down into my eyes. A memory of when I first moved in with them flashed in my mind. He always could see inside me. My palms started sweating and a grin cracked over my lips.

"What?"

"I forgot what it felt like when you do that."

"Do what?" A grin teased at the corner of his mouth, but he continued to look at me.

This was Mason. I was front and center to him. Always. "You can see inside me. No one else can do that."

He nodded.

I started to look away, but he caught me and lifted my chin again. Moving so he was directly on top of me, his forehead rested gently against mine and his nose grazed against my nose, resting there. His chest lifted, tension filled him, and he let it all out. His body relaxed. His finger softened and began to caress my skin, then he murmured, "I can see inside you because I'm in there. You let me in." His thumb rested against my cheek. He cupped the side of my face. "You always let me in and I knew, even when you first moved in, that you didn't let anyone in. If I don't tell you every day that I'm honored for that privilege, then I'm a fool. Because I am very honored." He tilted my head back, raised my lips, and held his just over mine. They teased me, resting there, but not pressing against mine. "I love you so much, Sam. You're in me too, just so you know. You can see inside me."

As he murmured those words, something broke off and fell deep in my gut. I knew Logan loved me, and I was keeping that a secret. Shame, guilt, and disgust all swept together. Feeling a tear coming, I didn't want him to see that. He would press me. I wasn't ready to face that yet so I surged up on my feet, grabbed a hold of his face with both hands, and pressed my lips to his.

I was starving for him. Tasting my need, Mason wrapped his arms around my waist, lifting me off my feet and moving us. The sounds from the club grew muffled and the lights dimmed. We were in a room. It was only us, no light, no one else. He opened his mouth over mine.

Answering my desperation with his own, he lifted me higher and I crawled up his body. My legs wound around his waist, clenching tightly. His hand slid under my shirt, grasping onto my breast. It wasn't enough. Moving so I could get a better angle, my mouth opened over his and I felt his tongue slide inside me and brush against mine. It was a delicious rub, and I whimpered, needing more. I would always need more with him. My hands fell to his jeans. I wanted him in me, all the way in, but his hands brushed mine aside.

My legs tightened around him in protest. I rubbed my chest against his and tried again.

He blocked me, but his hand wedged inside my jeans, and his fingers plunged inside me.

I gasped, feeling the rush of pleasure.

Mason nipped at my bottom lip while his fingers plunged in and out. He wasn't being gentle. As his fingers kept thrusting, I was paralyzed from the sensations. They were building, and they were overwhelming. I tried moving my hand to him, wanting to give him pleasure as well, but his fingers kept going in and out.

God. It was coming.

My head fell back to rest against the wall. As my climax was nearing, I gasped and arched my back. Mason's head fell to my exposed throat. He kissed me there as his fingers continued their onslaught. A groan built from deep in my throat. As it began to slip out, Mason kept going, but he covered my mouth with his.

A scream erupted out of me, muffled by his lips, as I hurdled over the edge.

He held me as the tremors ripped through me. When they had faded and I could walk, my legs slid down from around his waist to the ground. Still holding me, he brushed a hand over my forehead, smoothing my hair and tucking a few strands behind my ears. He leaned down, and his lips grazed over mine in a soft kiss. "No matter what's going on inside you, I'm here. I always will be." He pressed another kiss to my forehead. "I love you."

My hands grabbed and fisted his shirt. I loved him too. God, I loved him. The entire act of what he did was beautiful, loving, and tender all at the same time. I didn't deserve him.

"Sam?"

"I love you too, and I don't deserve you." *Just tell him. Get it over with. Let the chips fall where they lay.* I was screaming at myself, but I silenced that voice. "When we get home…" I was going to make it up to him. I was going to love him how he just loved me.

A cloud of confusion appeared over him, but as he read the promises in me, it cleared and a small grin showed again. He bent down and I closed my eyes, waiting for the feel of his lips again—

"Tell me you're not boning in a club?" A loud voice broke the moment. The door opened wider, letting in the neon lights and booming music. A silhouette of a large guy stood inside the doorway, and he flung his arms up. "I'm staying at a sorority house for you, man. This is supposed to happen at home. Do you not appreciate the sacrifice I'm making for you?" His hands cupped together, and he shook them at us. "Sorority chicks. Vanilla scented everything, even their forks smell like mocha and sweat pea. Pink shit everywhere. Bowls of ice cream. Boobs flashing all over the place. It's hell, Mason, and you're in here getting it on?"

He made a sound of disgust, shook his head, and turned to leave. "What I do, my roommate, and you don't appreciate it."

Mason chuckled. His hands finished zipping me up, one of his slid into mine, and he pulled me out of the small room. A group had congregated in the center of the floor. Other guys, I assumed they were also football players from their large sizes, stood with Logan and Kris. His arm was around her shoulders, and he grinned wickedly at us.

When he caught my eye, one of his eyebrows curved up.

I rolled my eyes.

Logan started laughing. "This is what I lived with for a year. They're rabbits, man."

Mason pulled me closer to his side, then gestured to the guy who had interrupted us. "Sam, this is Matteo. My roommate. Matt," he indicated Logan, "this is my brother and my girlfriend."

Matteo was intimidating. He was bald, tan, and large. He stood as tall as Mason, but he was twice his weight. He was wearing a sleeveless shirt and jeans and I saw the muscle definition. He wasn't all muscle, but I could tell he was a powerful lineman. His dark eyes flashed and a wide grin appeared as he raked me up and down. He harrumphed and nodded. "Yep. I can see the obsession." He jerked a thumb in Mason's direction. "Your man is obsessed with you. He don't talk. He's not all frou frou with his emotions, but a brotha knows." He turned to Mason. "She's a good one. I can tell."

"I know."

Matteo went to Logan's side and threw an arm around his shoulder. His hand patted the arm that Logan had around Kris. "You can be obsessed with your woman. Me, I'm obsessed with your brother. You didn't prepare me for him, man. What were you thinking?"

Mason frowned slightly. "What are you talking about?"

Matteo's smile widened. He pounded his chest and pounded Logan's chest. "There's a soul brotha connection here. You should've told me I'd be meeting one of my kindred."

"Oh my god." Mason laughed. "Why am I not surprised the two of you are already friends?"

Logan winked. "And guess what? He hates Park Sebastian as much as me."

"See." Matteo's head bobbed up and down with an approving grin. "Soul brotha connection. SBC. That's what I'm calling it."

Logan jerked his chin up at Mason. "And you're not included. You're not a SBC-er. That sucks for you."

A couple of the guys in the group started laughing. One, who was leaner than the rest but just as tall, shook his head. He had brown hair, long enough for him to gel it up into small spikes. He had dark eyes, high cheekbones, and a soft face that gave him a young, pretty boy look. He said to Mason, "Your brother and your roommate are in love with each other."

Mason grinned at the guy. His hand moved to a loop in my jean's waistline. His finger went through it, anchoring me to him. "I'm seeing that."

Matteo and Logan had stopped listening. They turned to each other and both held the other's head in their hands. They began moving up and down, as if participating in a dance/football huddle together. They began chanting. When I heard it, I started laughing.

"S-B-C." With each letter, they moved up and down. "S-B-C." They began saying it faster and faster. The rest of the group started in, shaking their fists in the air. When it was so fast, sounding like only one loud word, Logan and Matteo threw their arms in the air, making the sound of an explosion. The other guys did the same.

Logan stepped back, grinning like crazy, but Matteo danced around. He jumped, planted his feet on the ground, and began shaking his fists in the air, pumping his arms like he was a machine, and he went faster and faster until his arms were a blur. The guys formed a circle around him, bringing their fists down in the air as they began their own chant, "Cain. Cain. Cain."

A battle cry came from Matteo and he jumped in the middle of the circle. He stayed in the same spot, but jumped so he was facing north, then south, then west. He went all the way around, his arms still going, the guys making the same chant, until finally he seemed to combust. His head tipped back, his arms shook in the air, and the rest of the guys flung their hands up at the same time. They were all saying, "Cain U. Cain U. Cain U. Cain U."

The pretty boy guy moved into the circle. He lifted a hand. As he did, the group fell silent. All their hands lifted in sync with the leader. They were waiting, watching him, and as he brought his hand down, they slammed theirs down on top of his. One last cheer erupted from them, "Cain U conquers you!"

The rest of the room, including the staff at the bar, joined in and the sound was deafening. The school pride was unmistakable.

Mason leaned close to me. "This is our chant before we run out of the locker room. We start it right when we step on the field, and at the end, the stadium joins in with the last line and we run out." His eyes were sparkling. "It's an adrenalin rush."

I nodded, but I had no words. The unity and tradition was strong. I had felt it at the game, but I felt it even more now. These football players were gods here. My hand curved under Mason's and our fingers laced together. He was one of them. Everything fell away.

I was proud to be at his side.

I want to take you home, bend you over, and come home. That's what you are to me, Sam. Home. I love you.

You're home to me too. And yes, please. I'd love to come as well... Fuck, I love you, Mason.

CHAPTER TWELVE

When I woke up, Mason was gone. The door to his bathroom was open so I knew he wasn't in there. A rumbling began in my stomach and I laid back down. I didn't want to move. The whole night had been a lot to take in. We had stayed at the club for a few hours. It had been nice to meet all of his teammates. I could tell they already respected Mason, and his roommate adored him. It was obvious. Grinning, I remembered the look of brotherly love Matteo had given Mason when we said our goodbyes. The big lineman had been drunk, and his girlfriend told me later that he was glowing because he was so happy about meeting Logan, but I could tell that his supposed soul brotha connection wasn't only with Logan. It was with Mason as well. When we left the nightclub, Logan and Kris had stayed, but the guy who led the chant (Mason formally introduced him later as Drew) reassured us that he'd make sure Logan would get a cab.

"Morning." Mason came through the door with a cup of coffee in one hand and a toasted bagel on a plate in the other. He put both on the stand beside the bed and sat next to me. The bed dipped under his weight. "You sleep good?"

"Mmmm, more than good." His finger trailed up my arm, and I closed my eyes. A feeling of contentment filled me. As his finger went to my shoulder, I rolled to my side, and he went down my other arm. Images of the night came to me, once we had gotten to his room. I felt a stirring between my legs again. We had spent the rest of the night making love. "What time is it?"

"It's eleven in the morning."

We had slept four hours. I grinned up at him. "Aren't you tired?"

"Nope." He grinned. "Not a bit. You?"

I shook my head. "I should be." But I wasn't.

We shared a look, then I began tugging him down to me as his phone went off. Groaning, I flipped onto my back as he went to answer it. "Logan." He paused, twisted to see me, and I sat up. "Yeah, yeah. We can do that." He paused again, his eyes narrowing. "You sure? Okay. I'll call him."

When he hung up, I asked, "What'd he want?"

Mason came back over and sat beside me, his phone in hand. As he pressed two buttons and lifted the phone to his ear again, he rested his hand on my leg. "He wants to meet for brunch. He wants Nate to come too."

"Oh." I chuckled. "I'm surprised he didn't ask for your roommate too."

"He did. Hey, Nate." His voice lifted. "Logan called. He's up for brunch. Do you want to come?" Another pause. "Sounds good. I was thinking the diner on campus." He laughed. "Yeah, okay. See you."

I waited as I assumed he was texting Logan where to go. When he tossed the phone to the nightstand, I asked, "When do we have to leave?"

His grin turned predatory and his eyes darkened. One of his hands slid under my back as the other went up my leg, under the covers, until it found my core. One touch, that was all it took and I was already panting. Moving so he was positioned above me, holding himself upright so his weight wasn't on me, Mason gazed down at me.

The corner of my mouth tugged up. I loved when he was in this position. Sliding my hands up over his shoulders, his neck, the sides of his face, and into his hair, I whispered, "I love you."

The lust darkened even more in his gaze. His head tilted to the side as my hand fell to his cheek. He moved into my touch, closing his eyes, then lowered himself so he was just lightly resting on me. The other side of my mouth lifted up. This was another position I loved as well. My leg curved up around his waist and I pressed him into me. Enough foreplay. I was already wet. Sensing my urgency, he moved up again, but grabbed my leg and clamped it there, still wound around his waist. As he readjusted, my body adjusted with his. Pressing a kiss to my throat, he moved even further up and I shoved down his pants.

He was in me within seconds. As he pushed inside, I gasped from the sensations. He whispered against my throat, "I love you too."

He began moving and our hands found each other. He held them above my head, against the headboard as he kept thrusting. I ceased thinking. I never wanted this to stop.

*

The plan was to head back with Logan and Kris after brunch, which turned into lunch, so Mason had my bag on his shoulder as we cut through campus. When I asked why he picked that diner, his reasoning was to show Logan and me as much of the campus as possible. I grinned at that. "You mean the front lawn of a frat house and Cliché nightclub wasn't academic enough? We didn't get the whole experience?"

Mason laughed, then shrugged. "The frat stuff probably is. I don't know about the club, but," he gestured to the tall buildings around us as we headed through a quad, "this is what college is like. I walk through here every day." We were coming up to a large black glass building. As we drew closer, I saw faint shadows from inside, where people were, but the place looked like a nightclub as well.

I raised an eyebrow. "This is the diner?"

"Yeah." He reached for the door. I went first and his hand settled on the small of my back. "The team eats here during the day; it's got a buffet, including a salad bar, so you can get whatever you like."

"You had me at buffet." But the salad bar sounded good too.

Mason paid for both of us right away. "Yo." Logan waved from a corner booth. It curved into the wall and could sit eight people comfortably. Kris was sitting right next to Logan, squished beside him. His hand was under the table, as were hers. Her shoulders were also hunched forward and pinched together, like she was trying to appear as small as she could get. There were bags under her eyes, and she seemed pale. Her hair had been pulled back into a messy ponytail.

I grinned. She was hung-over. Logan, on the other hand, was beaming. He continued to wave until we scooted in with him.

Mason slid next to Logan, and I took the end. There was enough room so we didn't have to move all the way in, and remained at the edge of the booth.

Logan asked, "Nate coming..." His question faded as his gaze went over our shoulders. His eyes widened, and his mouth moved into a silent O.

Mason looked first. The exhaustion from Kris was contagious. Some of my own seeped in and I was too lazy to turn all the way around. I felt Mason tense—he wouldn't have tensed if it was only Nate—so I turned to look, and I saw her. She was tiny. She had her brown hair pulled up in a high ponytail. Unlike Kris', which looked cute and messy, this girl's was sleek and pristine. Her hair was long too, falling past her shoulders. Two things caught my attention more than anything. One, she was holding Nate's hand. No, correction, she had a death grip on his hand with both of hers, and two, her gaze was glued to Mason's, like she feared his reaction.

Logan muttered, "As far as twists come, this one sucks balls." He shot a glare at Nate and muttered, "I thought the mantra was no dumb shits allowed?"

"Logan!"

Tate's voice came back to me. *"Has he told you that Marissa's going to Cain University too?"* It clicked, and it felt like an anchor dropped inside me. This was Marissa, and no, Mason never told me. I snuck a glance at him from the corner of my eye. He wasn't looking at me. His jaw was clenched, and his eyebrows furrowed together.

I barely remembered her from the one time I almost met her. Mason had kept her away from everyone, myself included, but things were different now. I was closer to him. She was not anymore. As they stopped at the end of the table and stood there, their hesitation was obvious. I couldn't ignore the flicker of jealousy in me.

Marissa was here. She could be in the same room as him whenever she wanted, within a few minutes. I could not. That alone had my teeth grinding, and I shot Mason another look. He hadn't told me she was here.

He was studying me this time. The jealousy morphed into anger, and my eyes narrowed at him. We would talk. That was a promise from me to him, and I caught a wary look flash over his face. Oh yes, he got the message loud and clear. Leaning back in the seat, I decided I wasn't going to say a damned thing. This was Mason's rodeo. I was going to sit back, watch the fireworks, and set off some of my own when I got him alone later.

Marissa was watching me, biting her lip. One of her hands released her grip on Nate's wrist and tugged down the bottom of her shirt. She was overdressed, wearing a pink sweater, a lacy, white camisole underneath, and a jean miniskirt. I had on a pair of jeans and Mason's black shirt. It engulfed me, but it was comfortable and smelled like him.

I won. Hands down.

Kris was studying her too. She looked her up and down and glanced down at her own outfit, a hooded sweatshirt and pink sweatpants with a big sequined heart stitched onto one of her pant legs. A soft curse left her and she tucked some of her hair behind her ear, then tried to smooth out the rest. When she realized Logan was still staring, heatedly, across the table, her hand fell back to her lap and her shoulders lifted in a shrug. She settled back like I had and glanced at me. A faint grin was shared between us, and at that moment, we were allies.

I laughed to myself. I hadn't seen that one coming. We turned, as one, and regarded Marissa again. Her eyes got even bigger at the new attention, and she moved back a step, still holding onto Nate's wrist. He pulled her forward, gesturing to the booth. "I brought a friend."

"Really?" Logan grunted.

Nate paused and turned to me since I was on the edge. I wasn't moving. Seeing that, he guided Marissa to the other side and she scooted in beside Kris. The two girls glanced at each other again. Kris pressed her lips together and gave her a brief smile. Marissa's hand flicked back up to her face. A strand of her hair was already behind her ear. She untucked it, then tucked it back in place as she bit her lip. Finally, she lifted her head and turned towards us.

She was openly staring at Mason.

Everyone was quiet. It was a matter of seconds before Logan jerked forward. The bomb was about to be detonated.

He waved a finger between Nate and Marissa and smirked. "When'd you two start to bone?" Marissa shrunk down and Nate straightened. He opened his mouth, but Logan held his finger back up, silencing him. A wicked grin came over him and he slowly turned his finger until it was pointing right at Mason. "Because if this is the beginning of a budding romance, you're already losing, Nate. Her doe eyes are trying to drink Mason up. If she was a dog, she'd be humping his leg by now." He grinned at her. "No slipping under the table, Marissa."

"Logan!" Nate glared at him. "Shut the fuck up." He said to Mason, "Marissa's your friend. I thought she'd be welcomed. You going to let him bully her?"

Mason was quiet. I felt his attention more on me, but I refused to look at him.

Logan was, though. He laughed. "I'm serious, Nate. Are you two dating? That'd make more sense as to why she's here. If so, I'll shut my trap, but if you're not, what are you thinking? No offense, Marissa," he warned, which meant he was about to offend her, "but you're a psycho. Mason told you to take a hike last year, and you're still emailing him. If you're a student here, I don't believe for a second that's a coincidence. I know you're tight with Tate. She did the whole redemption tour when she left Fallen Crest. She knew. She would've told you."

"Logan." Mason shifted forward. At his movement, Logan quieted and everyone waited. "Stop." He said to Nate next, "This *is* a little awkward. You know that."

Nate rolled his eyes. "Like insulting one of my fraternity brothers and friends? That's awkward too."

Oh—what? I reared back; everyone jerked at that. Logan let out a surprised sound. "That's a better twist. Let's duke this shit out." He leaned forward, his elbows rested on the table, and he swung his head, looking from one end of the table to the other. Mason and Nate were involved in a heated stare.

Mason's eyes narrowed. "That's what this is about?" His tone was soft, too soft. A shiver went down my back.

"Yeah."

Nate wasn't backing down. Mason shook his head and gestured to her. "This wasn't the right move for that."

"Why?" Nate clipped out, jerking his hand at me. "Because you haven't told Sam about Marissa? Because you should've by now, you know. You afraid your moment of dishonesty will affect your precious twosome?"

Logan held up a hand. "I'd like to interject." He gestured from Mason, me, and himself. "We're better known as the Threesome Fearsome."

"Logan," Mason said, shooting him a look.

Logan moved his finger in a circling motion, going down, whistling as he made the motion. He grinned. "That's the sound of the Fearsome Foursome going down the drain."

"Logan!"

He held his hands up. "I'm done," he said to Mason. "Carry on, my brotha."

A cry came from Marissa and she turned, trying to shove out of the booth, but Nate was blocking her. He didn't register what she wanted, he was still glaring across the table, so another whimper left her and she began pounding on his arm harder.

Logan cleared his throat. Nate looked over and Logan pointed to Marissa. "Heads-up."

"Oh." He stood up and Marissa shot out of the booth. She took off. She didn't wave or say anything. She didn't look at anyone, even Mason. Pressing a sleeved hand to her face, she ran, and we watched as she went through the doors and down the sidewalk.

"That was a good exit. I haven't seen one like that in a while."

160

"Logan."

"What?" He lifted his shoulders. He said to Mason, "I was speaking the truth. I don't like her. I've never liked her."

Nate made an exasperated sound. "You guys don't change. Nothing changes."

Logan's eyebrows raised. "What are you talking about? That was a douche move on your end and you know it. You should think about what you're actually mad about. You're mad at Mason because he doesn't like someone you like? When's that a rule for us? We don't like people all the time, and we've never forced anyone down someone else's throat. And this is Mason. You know how he is. Don't twist that stick up your ass and name it Mason when it should be named Sebastian Dickstick."

Nate had quieted, but he sighed. "You didn't have to be so aggressive with her."

"Maybe." Logan rolled his eyes. "I'll give that to you, but maybe not. She's still weird, Nate. You can't deny that. She always had some weird fascination with Mason, and it's still there. It took me two seconds to see it, but why haven't you? Or you don't give a fuck? That's a better question. Who are you friends with because you're not acting like ours."

Nate had no response. He stood there as his shoulders drooped down.

Mason asked, "You done?"

Logan held his hands up. "I'm done. For real." He gestured to Nate. "He's all yours."

"Mason," Nate started, but he stopped.

Mason nudged my leg and I stood. He stood behind me and like that, Logan and Kris did the same. Those two started for the door. As they went by, Logan said, "We'll be in the parking lot on the left."

I nodded and held back. Mason waited until they were out of earshot. Nate looked ready to fight, but he didn't. Growling, he opened his mouth, closed it, opened it again, and closed it once more. Lifting a fisted hand, he pressed it against his cheek, softly, before shaking his head. He turned to Mason. "I'm sorry. Fuck. Logan's right. I'm sorry, Mase."

"Yeah." His hand came to rest on my back again. "We can talk later."

It was time to go, and it was time for my own fireworks show. Walking in front of Mason, I glanced up over my shoulder at him. He met my look, but didn't say anything. Neither did I, but I was going to. I wasn't the only one with a secret.

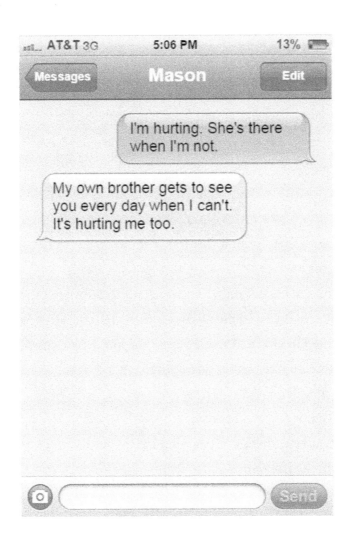

CHAPTER THIRTEEN

"Sam, stop."

I was headed to the parking lot, but Mason tapped my arm and gestured to the coat room. It was abandoned and after I passed him, going in first, he shut the door behind us. He didn't say anything for a while.

I shook my head. I didn't know what I felt. I wasn't the jealous type, but he hadn't told me about Marissa. He should've, and when he continued to frown at me, I figured he knew that as well.

A headache was forming, so I lifted a hand to rub my forehead. "Are you going to talk?"

"I have no idea what to say."

"Point taken." I started past him again, but he caught my arm and swung me back around.

"Sam, wait." He touched the other side of my hip, gently, and continued to hold me in front of him. His eyes rolled upwards and I wanted to snort. He was looking for what to say. He said, "I should've told you."

I pulled away, but only moved back a step. "Yeah."

"I'm sorry."

Folding my arms over my chest, I waited. "Yeah?"

He looked in pain. His eyebrows furrowed together and his mouth strained to one side. A hand lifted to scratch his chin. For once, Mason wasn't in control. He seemed at a loss for words. He lifted his hands in a helpless motion. "I have no idea what to say. Shit. I'm a horrible boyfriend."

The tension began to lift inside me. He was being genuine.

He added, "She emailed me last spring and told me she got in. I meant to tell you, but I forgot. It was during the whole Kate ordeal. I was more worried about you, and it slipped my mind. I'm sorry. I should've remembered and I should've told you."

"You knew she was here before today?" He hadn't looked surprised to see her when she walked in.

His eyes closed, his nose wrinkled, and he cursed. "Yes. I did."

I lifted an eyebrow, waiting.

"It's weird. This whole thing is just weird. I don't know how to explain it."

"How many times have you seen her?"

"A few," he admitted.

"A few?"

"Yeah." He grimaced. "The first time was outside the stadium. I was going home after practice, and she was in the parking lot. It was...odd. I honestly don't know what to say. She used to like me—"

"She still does."

He nodded, running a hand over his face. "—and I was going to deal with it. Right then and there. I really was, but she beat me to it. She told me she used to like me, but she doesn't anymore. I apologized for not helping her when we were sophomores, when the girls were picking on her, and she took off."

This was so confusing. Something wasn't right and I opened my mouth to tell him.

He beat me to it. Mason lifted a hand, halting my words. "There's no friendship with Marissa. Honest to god. There's not. I meant to tell her that, but she ran off. I don't know if she could sense what I was going to tell her and didn't want to hear it or what. I have no idea." Okay. I started to say something again, but Mason touched my arm. "Hold on. Let me tell you all of it."

There was more?

His eyes narrowed, watching me warily as he said, "She's in one of my classes."

What?!

"I've never once talked to her in there. She sits with her friends. I sit with mine. There's been no interaction at all. Then," he hesitated, raking his gaze over my face, "Friday night, the guys and I went to a birthday thing for Matteo. Nate and his fraternity came in. Marissa was with Nate. She was his date."

"And she came with him today."

"Yeah."

I shook my head. "What the hell is going on with Nate? Why didn't you tell me any of this? I should've known." My finger jabbed at his chest, poking him. "You should've told me."

"I know." He caught my finger and held it there, pressing my whole hand against him. I felt his heart racing. "I'm so goddamn sorry. I really am. I should've told you the first night. I meant to. I've just been," he shook his head, "things are different. I'm scrambling. I don't have you and Logan. This year is just..."

"...different." I sighed. Things were changing. I went to him and slid my arms around him, pressing against his chest. He was stiff at first, then relaxed as his arms wrapped around me in return. He tightened his hold, and it wasn't just me hugging him for comfort. He was hugging me back. The knots were back in me, stretching wider and wider inside me, but I didn't think they would go away for a long time. We were in a different chapter of our lives.

"Sam?" He tilted my head up and peered down at me. His thumb brushed a tear from my cheek. "You okay? I am sorry."

"I know. I am." Things were changing. "You're my anchor and you're not there and she's here and I didn't hear about it until today. It doesn't sit well. It doesn't make me feel good."

A swift curse left him and he rested his forehead on mine. His thumb rested on my cheek. "I am so sorry. I mean it."

I believed him. "Yeah." But it didn't make it hurt any less.

"Yo—oh. Sorry!"

Twisting around, we saw the tail end of Logan as he left the room. Once the door was shut, he said from the other side, "Sam, your phone is off or you're not answering. Your dad called me. He wants to talk to you about something."

Mason asked me, "What's that about?"

I shrugged. "If I were to guess, Garrett."

"We haven't talked about him yet."

"I know." I stepped back, and as soon as his hands left me, I missed his touch.

"I am sorry, Sam. I really am."

I shook my head. "No. That wasn't...never mind. I don't know if I should be worried. I'm not. Maybe I should, but I'm not. You not telling me she was here bothers me." Tate had. He hadn't. That was an extra kick in the gut. "Tate told me that Marissa was coming here. I should've asked you about it, but I didn't."

"Wait. What?"

"Yeah." I lifted a shoulder up and let it drop. "I should've asked you. I shouldn't have waited to see if you would tell me or not." But even as I said that, I was the liar this time. I hadn't told him about Tate because I didn't want him asking more questions, about what else she had said. Biting my lip, I waited to see if he would do that.

"Tate? When did you talk to Tate?"

"At Manny's. You guys left to prank some of the Fallen Crest Academy people. She showed up to talk to Heather about something, and I was there." I felt a pang of regret slice through me. "I didn't believe her. I thought she was making it up, trying to cause problems with you and me, so I didn't want to give her the satisfaction. I didn't say anything."

"Did she say anything else?"

That Logan is in love with me. "No."

"Oh." He crushed me against his chest again. His arms wrapped tight around me once more, and his shoulders lifted with tension. "Tate's such a bitch. I should've told you immediately. This is all my fault."

No. No, it wasn't. It's mine too, but I can't find the voice to tell him that, so, feeling like a coward, I pulled away. My hands rested on his chest, feeling the strength of his heartbeat underneath them. He was so warm, so strong. I just wanted to bury myself against him again. Life would be so much simpler if I never had to leave his side.

Knock. "Sam?"

Hearing Logan again, we pulled away. Mason skimmed a hand down my arm and slipped it into mine. We had an entire year to get through.

"What?"

Mason must've sensed my thoughts.

"I was just thinking that we have to talk more."

He grinned and I saw the love in it. Lifting my hand to his mouth, he pressed a kiss there and murmured, against my knuckles, "I love you, Samantha."

Choking on a sob, I whispered back, "I love you too."

When we went to the hallway, Logan was outside the doorway, leaning against the wall, a small scowl on his face. He straightened from the wall and handed the phone to me. David's name was on the screen. Logan shrugged. "I didn't know what to say. He doesn't usually call me. If it's not an emergency, I'm really sorry. But he says it is."

I lifted the phone to my ear. "David?"

"Honey." He sounded relieved. "Oh good. I didn't know if I would get ahold of you in time."

"We're about to leave. What's going on?"

"Nothing too important, but I wanted to let you know that Malinda is headed out of town tonight. She and some of her friends are going to Vegas for a couple nights. I won't be home when you get there. I have to head out of town for a football meeting so it'll be just you and Mark. His girlfriend might be there too. I'll head back as soon as I can. I'm really sorry, Sam. I meant to be home when you got there. I wanted to talk more about Garrett, and I was hoping to have some father/daughter time."

"Oh."

He waited a beat, then asked, "Is that okay? I can cancel. I could reschedule for another weekend, but—"

I gripped the phone tighter, pressing it harder to my ear. "No." I hadn't gotten a phone call like this in so long. "That's fine, Dad. I'll be fine. I'll just do homework or hang out with Logan."

"Okay. How's your time with Mason? No, don't answer that. I'll ask later tonight. Maybe we can still get a movie in. I'll hurry and try to get home as soon as possible."

"Okay." My throat was raw. "Sounds good. Thank you."

He chuckled. "You don't have to thank me, Sam. I'm being your parent. This is what we do."

Yeah. That's what they did, and it felt good. I wanted to thank him again, but silenced the words. This was what normal parents did. This was a normal type of relationship. I was becoming normal.

"Bye, Dad. Love you."

"Love you too. Safe travels home. Say hello to Mason for me."

"Sure." Ending the call, I turned. Both Logan and Mason were watching me with expectant looks. As I handed the phone back to Logan, I grinned, feeling silly at the same time. "He didn't want me to come home and not know what was going on. He was telling me his plans for today."

Logan narrowed his eyes.

Mason softened, holding my bag for me.

"What? Like he was giving you an order or something? WTF, man?"

"No," I told Logan, "he just didn't want me to come home and not know where everyone was, and speaking of, you're coming with me to the house. Malinda and David are gone so that means Cass will be there. I could use some back-up to deal with her."

He didn't look happy, but murmured, "Done deal."

Mason glanced at his brother and rolled his eyes. "David's just trying to be a good dad." He nudged him with his elbow. "Stop analyzing it. The guy's trying."

"I'm thinking about what this means for us." He pointed to all of us. "We're her family. He's moving in on our territory. How will that change things?"

"It won't." I glanced to Mason. "Nothing changes for you either. You're still sleeping in my room when you come home on breaks."

"Breaks." Logan laughed as we all began moving towards the door. He clapped Mason on the shoulder. "No offense, but I hope I don't see you for the holidays. Your team has to rock it. Keep playing. Keep winning and get to the championship game, brother."

"I'm a freshman." Mason leaned over me and held the door open. As I ducked under his arm, his other hand rested on my back. It felt good having it there. As we stepped outside, he said to Logan, "I've got three more years after this year. I'm not too stressed about it."

Logan snorted. He ran a hand through his hair, held it up, and waved across the street. Kris waved back from the front seat of the car. He laughed. "I'm not thinking about you. I'm thinking of my other brotha. My SBC-er. Matteo's heart would be broken. That cannot happen. You realize that, right? Don't break my soul brotha's heart, or I'll break yours." At the end, he extended his middle finger and poked Mason in the chest. "I have to look out for my soul brotha."

In a swift movement, Mason caught the finger and pretended to yank it backwards, like he would break it off.

Logan laughed, pulled his hand free, then rolled his eyes. "Whatever." He threw his arms around Mason, pounded him on the back, and pressed a quick kiss to his cheek.

Mason groaned, but didn't fight it. "Really?"

"Love you, brother." Logan took my bag from Mason and darted across the street. Turning back around, he pointed at us. "Say your goodbyes, again, but hurry." Patting his stomach, he flashed a grin. "I'm starving. We need to hit up a drive-thru fast. Sam, hurry it up."

"Please," I shouted at him.

"Please," he added, giving me a thumbs-up sign.

Mason turned to face me squarely, tugging me close again. "Call me tonight."

"I will."

"I love you." His thumb went to my bottom lip and rested there.

I closed my eyes, feeling the tenderness in that small touch. It warmed me, casting so many other worries away, but I couldn't ignore the nagging voice in my head. I couldn't be hurt that he had withheld information from me when I was doing the same thing. I needed to tell him. I did. And I would, but not now. My stomach clenched. I couldn't, not yet. Instead, I said, "I love you too."

His lips touched mine, such a soft graze, sending a tingle through me. I fell in love with him all over again. The smallest of touches from him went the farthest distance with me. A rush of love swept through me, and as I pulled away and headed across the street to Logan's car, a tear slipped free. I let it go. Getting into the backseat, I didn't look away from Mason, even after Logan and Kris both waved and Logan turned out of the lot.

I moved in my seat so I could keep watching him. He had recharged me, until the next time I saw him, but damn, I knew being with him wouldn't come soon enough. After Logan turned at a stoplight and I couldn't see Mason anymore, I moved back around and slumped down in my seat.

I was quiet the entire ride home.

Logan dropped Kris off first, but I overheard their plans. She was going to go to his house later to do homework. When we left and parked the car outside my house, he invited me over as well. I declined. I wanted to be alone and that meant a good long run for me. I didn't want to think about things, not then.

When I went inside, I heard Mark studying with Cass, so after tossing everything in my room, I changed and headed out for a run. I needed to clear my head.

After running to Manny's, Brandon told me that Heather was spending time with Channing; the two were on a date. Turning around, I headed back home, but I didn't want to go inside so I stretched outside and circled the house to the porch swing on the front patio. I had taken blankets out there one night. It had become my new sitting place.

"Samantha?"

David was coming up the driveway carrying two take-out bags. He paused before coming up the two steps to the patio. He held the takeout up. "I forgot to get a movie, but I remembered dinner." Putting the food on the small table next to the swing, he eased himself down to sit beside me. "Why are you out here?"

At that moment, the light switched on inside behind us and I glanced over my shoulder. Mark and Cass had come up from the basement to the kitchen. He opened the fridge as she, holding back a grin, slid across the floor to hip check him. Mark flashed a smile and rounded on her, letting the fridge door shut. As his hands found her waist, he lifted her on the counter. A husky laugh came from her, and she rested her arms over his shoulders as her legs slid up and down the backs of his legs. Murmuring something, he bent forward and nuzzled her neck. Her eyes widened in response, and he tugged her closer, putting his mouth to hers.

David had twisted so he could see what I was looking at. A slight frown marred his face, his eyebrows burrowed forward, and his lips pressed tight together. He turned back around. Scratching at his ear, he caught my perusal of him and lifted a helpless shoulder. "He's not my son. I have no idea what to say in these moments. Is that okay? Should I allow him to do that?" He twisted around again and bit down on his lip. He began chewing on it as he murmured, "I mean, they're not doing anything. They're making out." He pretended to shudder, giving me a small grin. "You never did that growing up. I was never concerned about Jeff.

You could barely stand to let him in the house, much less your bedroom." He shook his head. "Then all that went down with your mother, and I lost the right to say anything. You were with Mason Kade. Granted," he gave me a sideways look, "Mason Kade is a normal parent's worst nightmare, but that year, I was thankful for him in some ways. After seeing the two of you together and having him check me, your father, I knew he'd protect you against Analise. I was thankful for that." He looked back once more.

Mark had moved to the table and laid Cass down on it. She tipped her head back and arched her neck for him, as he began trailing kisses down her throat. Her hands cradled him, and she moaned when he moved further down, tugging up her shirt so her bra was exposed.

Feeling a laugh coming up, I stuffed it down. This was entertainment. I didn't want to interrupt it.

"Oh, dear." David tugged at his collar. "What should I do?"

I couldn't hold it in. Laughter pealed out of me, but when they paused and glanced towards the living room window, I ducked down. David let out a small chuckle and ducked down beside me. We were both hiding, and he whispered to me, "I should interrupt them. They should stop doing that there."

David lifted his eyebrows at me in a silent question. I shook my head. I wasn't the parent. Realizing what I had just thought, the amusement faded. David was the parent. His phone call earlier had reminded me of that.

He must've caught the change in me because he asked, "What?"

"Nothing."

David covered my hand with his. "Tell me what's going on with you? I know you've been coming out here a lot lately."

One corner of my mouth lifted in a halfhearted grin. I let it drop, though. I didn't want to talk about Mason, so I said, "It's hard being in there sometimes."

"Why?"

"Come on, Dad." Giving him a wry grin, I rolled my eyes. "Our house was tense. Everyone walked around on egg shells. Mom could blow up at any second. And that was when it was peaceful." Then the explosion would happen. It always happened. "The screaming. Things flying. The yelling. The crying. The threats of leaving and divorcing you. There were the times she actually did leave." My throat was dry as I swallowed. "Going from that house, to the Kades where I knew nothing would last. Everything was fake with Analise. She was a ticking time bomb. I always knew she would go off, and I would wait for it. Being here," I shrugged again, "it's so silent, but no one's walking around on thin ice. I haven't heard anyone fight yet. There's been yelling, but it's usually Malinda yelling at Mark not to be late or to come eat, or she's yelling at Logan for some reason. It's so..."

David supplied, "Healthy?"

"...eerie." I flashed him a grin. "But yeah, healthy. I keep waiting for the other shoe to drop, when everything good stops again."

"Oh, Samantha." He patted my arm. "It's not going to. Your mother was sick—"

I gave him a dark look. "And evil."

"That too, but Malinda is a completely different person. She's loving. She's warm. She's—"

I patted his arm this time. "I know. I love Malinda. I really do. I'm not saying anything bad. I'm just not used to this," gesturing inside the house and around us, "world. When's the shit going to hit the fan?"

"Well, I don't think it's going to happen how you think." He was watching me intensely. "I'm sorry about Garrett."

And the other shoe just dropped. "Yeah."

"He called. He'd like to have dinner with you, if that's okay with you? I know I said earlier that I wanted to discuss this." He sighed loudly.

I laughed shortly. "Why do I feel like running again?"

"I think you should do it."

"Run?"

"No, you know what I'm talking about. I think you should have dinner with Garrett."

"Why?" My voice grew louder. I looked at him as if he'd grown a second head. "You want me to have a relationship with him? He came here, made a lot of promises, and took off. For a year." I shook my head. My voice got even louder. "I mean, hello. Look at you. What if I love him more than you? Aren't you thinking things like that? What if I want a relationship with him, and I don't need you anymore?"

David was shaking his head as he stood. His hand was held out, as if to calm me. I realized with a jerk that I was standing. *When had that happened?* Then he said, "Of course I'm thinking those things, but that's selfish of me. Yes, I just got you back, and yes, I'm trying to mend things with you too, but he's your father. He left to make things right with his wife and he's back. He's trying with his daughter. Analise kept you from him. You can't fault him for that."

I turned. I wanted to run, but I gritted my teeth. Balling my hands into fists, I looked back to him.

When he saw I wasn't going, he lowered his hand. "Samantha, you have more family on his side. Have you thought about that?"

What?

"Yeah. I didn't think you had." His voice was so soft, like his heart was breaking. "He has an entire family that wants to meet you. Cousins. Grandparents. Analise had no one. Her parents, who knows who her parents were. They abandoned her at an early age, and she never grew healthy attachments with anyone else. You may never know what relatives you have on her side, but you can with Garrett."

"I don't care." But I did.

"You've met my family, but, because of your mother, that relationship is strained too. Garrett's family is your blood." His voice dipped to a firm level, "I'm not saying welcome him back with open arms, but you can set the boundaries for what you're comfortable with."

"Like what?"

"Like," he glanced around and gestured to the house, "have him and his wife come here. We'll have a big dinner, all of us." He gritted his teeth. "Logan too. That'll be interesting, but yeah. Have him come here. Get to know him on your territory, and you ask him questions instead of him getting to ask you questions. We'll be there to enforce the rules if you want." An abrupt laugh ripped from him. "I have no doubt Logan will enjoy enforcing any rule, just by himself."

"Yeah." *Was I really going to do this?* I heard myself saying, "Okay. Yeah. That's a good idea."

"Do you want me to make the plans?"

I nodded. "You call him." When he stood and grabbed the take-out bags, I stopped him. "But I pick the night."

"That's fair enough." He gave me a reassuring look. "I don't think anything bad is going to happen anymore. I really don't, Samantha."

As he went inside, I felt my phone buzzing and pulled it out. Mason was calling. Realizing the irony from my father's parting words, I answered and headed down the street. I didn't want to walk past Cass and Mark, and I didn't want David overhearing our conversation.

"Hey," I answered.

"Hey yourself."

At the sound of his voice, the world righted again, and the knot that was always there started to loosen.

CHAPTER FOURTEEN

Closing my locker, I was heading to cross country practice Thursday when Logan came up behind me and threw his arm around my shoulder. He hooked it around my neck and pulled me so I was walking sideways as he kept going straight. He flashed me a smile. "Hey there, sister dear."

I rolled my eyes, but grinned back. Hitting him in the chest, I asked, "What are you doing?"

"Did you hear the news?"

"That you're awesome? That's old. Duh."

He stopped and people streamed around us. No one complained about our abrupt stop, but this was Logan. No one complained about anything that had to do with him. If they did, they made sure he couldn't hear it. Since we had come back from seeing Mason, the old joking side of him had returned. Everyone took notice. He'd been serious before the trip, more serious than people expected from him, but when someone yelled out from behind us, "Coming up, Kade!" he raised his hand, palm upwards, by his head and one of his friends slapped it with his own, moving past us without breaking stride. Logan never broke eye contact with me. His only reaction was when his smile turned into a cocky smirk. He raised an eyebrow. "You're being funny, Strattan? I'm pretty sure you need to take a class before coming into my arena of awesomeness."

He winked and held his hand out to me.

I glanced at it. "What's that?" As soon as the words left me, I knew I didn't want to know.

He looked at it, back at me, and raised his hand higher. "It's for you to pay the fee. No one enters Logan's Arena of Awesomeness without paying my interest rate. Don't worry. It's only sex percent." He paused and waited.

I got it, grunted, and began moving down the hallway for the lockers. "Seriously, Logan."

He hurried back to my side and threw his arm around my shoulder again. "Get it? Sex percent?"

I didn't look at him, but I could imagine the wide smile on his face, waiting for some reaction from me. My reaction was an elbow to his gut. He grunted, but laughed at the same time. "You think Mason would kick my ass if I enforced that? Huh, huh?" Wiggling his eyebrows, he grabbed my elbow and pulled me to a halt before I disappeared into the women's locker room. "Our coach is going to be late. I've got time."

Placing a hand to his chest, I moved him back a step. "Sure."

His eyes got wide. "Are you serious?"

I grinned at the person coming up behind him. "Your boyfriend just threatened to make me have sex with him."

He barked out a laugh and he smiled at Kris. Holding onto her bag, she narrowed her eyes, as she studied both of us with her lips pursed together.

"Hey there, girlfriend. You have time to step into Logan's Arena of Awesomeness for five minutes?"

"What?"

Another laugh ripped out of him. "Nothing." He started for the men's locker room, but turned around and pretended to shoot both of us with his fingers. "Catch you two later."

A stream of guys were moving behind him into the locker room. One of them threw his arm around Logan's neck, bent him over, and pretended to tighten his arm in a chokehold. Logan was dragged inside, but it wasn't long before a roar of laughter filtered from the room into the hallway.

Kris sighed. "My boyfriend can be really weird."

"Yep."

Turning as one, we both went into our locker room.

Once we got inside, we parted ways. She went to her locker, surrounded with her friends, and I went to mine in the back row. Coach had kept me running with the guys who were sent off first so I hurried into my running clothes, grabbed my iPod, and was heading out the door when one of the team captains came in. She was standing in the doorway and said, "Hold up, Strattan. Girls are going first today."

"Really?"

She nodded. "Yeah, he wanted me to spread the word." Cupping her hands around her mouth, she yelled, "GIRLS, GET YOUR ASSES MOVING! WE'RE RUNNING FIRST!"

There was silence for a split second and then the room filled with shrieks. A couple girls came around to the door. "What?"

She motioned for them to hurry up. "Come on. The guys are running with the football team so we have to take off first. We're all doing the same trail."

"Shit," one girl said. "They're going to lap us."

"Exactly. Let's go. I don't want to hear the crap they'll give us if they lap us." She glanced at me. "Sorry, Sam. You're supposed to wait fifteen minutes before going, but you could stretch with us if you want?" She didn't wait for a response and headed back out.

The other girl had darted back to her locker and told the rest what was going on. It wasn't long before everyone was in a frenzy. Lockers were slammed shut as the girls got dressed in record time, and I stepped back, pressed against the wall, as the girls ran past me. Kris was one of the last. She paused before pushing through the door. "You're running with the guy's team *and* the football team?"

"I guess."

"I don't know if I should be jealous or sympathetic." She started through the door, but tossed over her shoulder, "I'll settle with, 'don't trip my boyfriend.'"

The door shut behind her, and I muttered to myself, "Why the hell would I do that?" I shook my head and cleared my thoughts. It didn't matter who I was running with. The guys had calmed down eventually and I had been incorporated as one of their own. I wasn't nervous about running with them and the whole football team. That would be an adventure, one I planned on having them eat my dust. I was going to run faster than normal. I was itching to go on a long run, all by myself, and had been holding back. Coach wanted the majority of my running with the guys, so I didn't go on the long ones by myself, as much.

After using the bathroom and grabbing a second bottle of water, I started out. The girls should've taken off by now. When I went outside, the lawn was covered with guys. There must've been thirty of them. The entire football team was spread out, all stretching, and I saw the cross country team in one corner, looking at the players with something akin to disgust. Hayes caught my eye and waved me over, but Logan intercepted me a few feet from them.

"Sam." He patted the ground next to him. His knee was pulled up and his leg was over his other leg. He leaned forward, stretching his back. "Sit. We get to run together."

Hayes stood from the ground. "She's running with us."

Logan looked up. His slight grin had faded as a dark, ominous expression replaced it. "We're running with you too."

Hayes hesitated, but lifted his chin an inch. "No, you guys are running behind us. If you start off in front of us, you're only going to impede our times. Be considerate. There's no way you guys can keep up with us."

Eric Hayes was tall and thin. He had a perfect body for running, which he knew. A handful of football players filled in behind Logan, and it looked like a smaller version of Goliath being challenged by David. Logan was lean, but he was muscular. His friends and teammates behind him were bigger. They were not only built to run, but to chase down their prey. As they heard the condescending tone in Hayes's voice, their nostrils flared, and I imagined the entire cross country guy's team just became their prey.

There were dark promises in Logan's gaze, but he only smiled. "Sure." He waved his hand in front of him. "Show us the way. We'll let you guys go first."

Hayes started forward, but caught himself. His eyes narrowed and he glanced at me. Nope. I wasn't giving him any reaction. He had dug his own grave. People knew not to cross Logan.

Logan moved forward. "Sam's running with us."

Hayes snorted. "She runs with us."

Good god. This was on repeat. "What route does Coach want us to go?"

"The scenic route."

My shock was immediate. That was the trail that went the whole way around Fallen Crest. It even went on a ridge that looked over the back of Fallen Crest Academy and their football field. I grunted. If this was just the beginning, I didn't want to know what drama might happen when they saw my dad's football team practicing. I did the calculations in my head and knew we'd be hitting that hill during the middle of their practice.

I started forward.

"Where are you going?" Hayes asked me, his voice strained.

I cast him a grimace. "I'm leaving. I'm starting before all of you guys." I gave Logan a quick grin, but saw that he didn't care. His eyes were still fixed on Hayes.

I shook my head and started off, hitting my timer to begin my run. I wanted to get a little ahead of the guys because I had a feeling the football team would be bearing down hard on the cross country team. Logan didn't take to being insulted. Even if the distance was longer than they ran, I knew their football team did runs like ours for conditioning. I just didn't think Hayes knew that, and as I started off on the path, I chuckled to myself. He was going to learn.

I took it easy at first, warming up. My first intention had been to press hard today, but after seeing the show of testosterone between the guys, I was going to do the opposite. I was going to take my time. They would lap me, which they did. The cross country team was pushing harder than they ever had, but the football team wasn't far behind. The difference between the teams was that Logan's group could only run like this one day. Hayes and the rest would be winded from going so fast, but they'd be able to do the same route tomorrow.

After the third mile, the football team had slowed and began to separate. Even as I began to pass them up, I knew I wouldn't find Logan until later. He'd keep up with Hayes, just to piss him off, or he would try. It was mile five when I passed the girl's team. I imagined they were annoyed at first, but by the time I got to them they were all smiles. I didn't blame them. I remembered running with Mason. It was exhilarating. He was a primal specimen of hotness. Mason. Running. I fought against pushing him down on the trail at least twenty times.

I noticed Kris ahead. She wasn't running with her friends. Instead, she had paired off with two football players. I didn't know their names, but I recognized them and remembered they were juniors. They weren't friends with Logan, I assumed, as one guy kept falling back to check out Kris' ass.

When I passed them, I glanced over, caught Kris' gaze, and didn't look away. She swallowed and looked down to the ground. I moved on, but before I went over a hill and fell out of eyesight, I looked back once more. She had separated from the two guys, but they didn't seem to mind. Their gazes were trained on her ass with smirks lingering over their faces.

Well, shit. What was I supposed to do about that? *Nothing*, my inner voice piped up. Shaking my head, shoving everything out, I kicked forward with more speed than I had anticipated. The need to push harder was back. Gritting my teeth, I let it loose. My legs lengthened their stride. I held my hands loose so those muscles wouldn't be exerted, and my head ducked down a little bit.

It wasn't long before I lapped all of the football team. Skimming over the last two guys, I recognized one of Logan's friends, Derek, and he gestured ahead. Nothing was said, but I got the drift. Logan was still ahead. I sprinted over four more hills before the trees began to change.

Fallen Crest Academy had planted spruce, pine, and redwoods around the campus. The redwoods were still young, but they towered over the running path. I kept going ahead. I was approaching the ridge that overlooked my old school, and the closer I got, I popped my earbuds out and listened. I was right. I could hear shouts and grunts ahead. The sound of shoulder pads smashing into each other came next, along with a thudding sound. I didn't expect to see anyone on the trail, but as I came around the last bend, some of the cross country guys were there. They had stopped and were watching the team below. Logan and another guy stood at the end.

I had to laugh. The paradigm from Logan and his teammate versus the cross country guys was almost comical. Their shoulders were broad. Their shirts had been abandoned and tucked into their waistbands. With arms resting on their hips, their backs were covered in sweat, but their muscles looked finely sculpted. If Mason had been there, he would've perfected the image of male hotness.

"Stop checking me out, Strattan." A grin teased the corner of Logan's mouth. "You're practically family." He waited a beat. "You'll turn me on."

I rolled my eyes and slowed to stand beside him. Eric lifted his head. I felt the weight of his gaze for a moment, but ignored it. Nodding to the football field below us, I asked, "Are you guys ogling my old team? Or just need an excuse for a breather?"

We weren't too high up and, as if hearing me, they glanced up from below. Two of the players paused, then said something to another two. Those looked up and they spoke to another group. That group looked up. A ripple effect spread over the whole field until the coaches realized their players weren't paying attention. One of the coaches left their huddle and moved to get a better view of us.

It was my dad.

Logan chuckled. "He must love me so much by now."

I sighed. "Not quite." Lifting a hand in a wave, I called down, "Hi, Dad."

One hand went to his hip, holding his clipboard, and the other went to his forehead, shielding his eyes from the sun. "Sam? What are you doing?"

The guys to my left looked over to us. Hayes kept shifting back and forth on his heels. His hand kept fidgeting with his shirt and I knew he was darting looks at us too. Logan rolled his shoulders back, propped one on my shoulder, and leaned against me. He waved down. "We're scouting the competition. What do you think, Mr. Strattan?"

Even from our distance, I could see my dad wasn't happy. He pointed up to us with the clipboard. "It's Coach Strattan to you, Logan."

His arm fell from my shoulder, and he straightened next to me. "Yes, sir, Coach Strattan." His tone lost some of the amusement, and I bit down on my lip. My dad had just put Logan in his place, but I had no idea how or what place it was. I just knew Logan reacted to the bark from him.

Catching my reaction, Logan cursed and rolled his eyes. "Why's your dad all puss and shoes at home and Mr. Hardass on the field?"

"He's a coach." I flashed him a grin. "Which he just reminded you of."

"Shut up." But Logan couldn't hide his half-grin. "I think I got a chubby for your dad. Don't tell Mason. He'll think I'm cheating on him."

"Hey, Logan." His friend suddenly shifted to the side, his back turning towards us, facing the path coming from the right.

The cross country guys moved to see down the path and a few of them cursed. They looked to Hayes, "What do we do?"

Hayes looked to us. I didn't move, but Logan rounded the side to stand next to his friend. As he moved, I got a glimpse ahead. A few of the Fallen Crest Academy players were coming up the side hill, heading our way. They were dressed in shirts, shorts, and their shoulder pads, but a few had black streaks on their face, giving them an intimidating air.

Logan said, "Okay. That's far enough. Stop, drop your pads, because it's hammer time."

Someone snorted. "Fuck off."

The team stiffened, but a wide grin escaped me. That was Mark. Moving so I could see better, I noticed that Adam had remained on the field, and I was glad. Only a handful had come with Mark to see us. I circled out to stand on Logan's free side. As I did, I asked, "What are you doing up here?"

Logan added, "Mark, I was introduced to a Soul Brotha this past weekend. Do you know what that is?"

"Say what?"

"A Soul Brotha. It's a connection. I have a fellow SBC-er and," Logan gestured to him, "I think you are one too."

"Oh no." I groaned.

Logan laughed. "Don't hate, my little Sammy cupcake."

"Your what?"

Pointing to Mark, he continued, "You can't deny the love between your future stepbrother and your other future stepbrother." He pointed to himself. "We're all one big happy family. Soul Brotha Connection. It makes sense."

The corners of Hayes's mouth were turned downwards. I could imagine he thought Logan had grown two heads. I rolled my eyes. "You're so weird lately."

Mark laughed. "Did he get laid right before practice?"

I started to say no, then realized I had no idea. "Did you?"

"Logan's Arena of Awesomeness has no closing time. It's open twenty four seven."

I said to Mark, "He got his dose of Mason. I think he missed him more than he realized."

Logan opened his mouth, but I elbowed him. "Don't even go there." His mouth closed.

Mark grinned. "Your dad sent us up here." He scanned the rest of the group. "We were thinking that since our best guy was out of the game the other week, and if the rest of your team was up here, we could scrimmage." He nodded towards Logan. "We think you guys got lucky before."

"Today?" Logan scratched his head and glanced behind us. The other guys hadn't appeared yet. "We're still spanking these guys' asses here."

Hayes snorted, puffing out his chest. "Speak for yourself. You're holding on by a thread."

Logan shot him a look, his eyes glittering in the sunlight. Or evil mirth. "Whatever. Once I get a hold of a thread, I don't let go. Ask Quinn down there. I like to make people pay if they hurt someone I love."

Gone was the joker and hello to the fighter. Mark shot me a questioning look, but I shook my head. I didn't want to get into it. Clearing my throat, I asked, "Would you do a challenge somewhere else? Or maybe another time? These guys are doing a conditioning run today."

"Sure—" Mark started to say.

Logan interrupted, "Tomorrow night. We have a game, but they leave the lights on. We can scrimmage then."

"Wait. With everyone? Full uniform?"

"Just the guys. A friendly thing." Logan's tone did not indicate friendliness.

Mark glanced at me and his teammates. None of them said a word, and Mark shrugged. "Sure, but I have to warn you, like I said before, our best player couldn't play last time. We might be like a whole new team with him."

Logan's eyes lit up. A slow grin spread over his face. "I'll look forward to that."

Mark and his teammates left, and it wasn't long before Hayes took off with the rest of the cross country guys. Logan's friend remained behind, but he stood at a distance from us, waiting for Logan to start running again.

Logan looked at me.

I looked at him.

He liked to fight. He liked to cause havoc and that side of him had been dormant for a while. I saw it in him again. It was like it had been awakened, a prowling tiger that was getting tired of its cage. That's when I realized the Roussou pranks had served a purpose for him, an outlet, and he needed a new outlet.

I sighed. "Don't hurt Mark."

A flash of irritation heated up his eyes, but he smirked at me. "Not Mark, but there are others on that team who have hurt me." He paused a beat. "Hurt you."

"That's over."

He shook his head. "Not true. Those beasts always linger. They're always there, waiting to get out." Then he turned and started off. When he saw I wasn't running with him, he paused and glanced back at me, running in place.

I didn't move.

He shrugged and took off down the trail alone.

I was starting to wonder what beast was inside Logan, and why hadn't I realized it was there until now.

CHAPTER FIFTEEN

"Okay." Heather stuffed her hands in her jean pockets. The wind whipped her hair around, but she let it go. Her eyes flashed at me with irritation. "What are we doing here?" She gestured to the football field.

I laughed. "A challenge was thrown out and Logan pounced on it. I think he's restless because he doesn't have Roussou to rival with. He's turned to my old school." I didn't share my other theory, that a darker beast had been awakened inside him.

She nodded, skimming an eye over the group of guys who stood in a huddle on the fifty yard line. It was Friday night. We had been there five hours earlier for an official game, but the lights were still on like Logan said they would be. Heather murmured, "This is ridiculous. There's a reason Mason didn't go to your school, because your team sucked. Ours dominated. They're going to kill those guys."

"I know." I watched Mark, Adam, and their friends gather together, away from the FCP group, and shook my head. Even though Mason was gone, and he had been the star player, the new group of seniors still looked primed and ready to tear into the FCA group. The guys from Fallen Crest Public School were bigger and meaner. They were tougher. That was the bottom line. The guys from my old school were leaner and nervous. "Mark's an idiot."

"How did this happen again?"

"Logan's team ran with the cross country team yesterday. Their coach was gone so they were doing conditioning with us. Our trail went over a hill by my old school, they were having football practice, and one thing led to another."

Heather groaned. "This is all about the size of their dicks, which of course correlates with their precious egos. They're all idiots."

"Pretty much." Watching them, I saw the hesitation on Mark's face. The rest of the guys kept glancing towards Logan's group. Their wariness was evident.

"So who's the new guy?" Heather craned her neck to get a better view.

I stiffened.

She caught my reaction. "What?"

"How'd you know about a new guy? Mark mentioned him earlier, but you..." I failed to follow the connecting dots. This was from left field.

She grimaced. "Channing talks about him all the time. FCA doesn't play Roussou, but he said their new guy is all anyone is talking about. He's some big star from another school or conference or whatever football terms they use."

A sense of dread began to take root in me. The more she talked, the more I knew Logan might have a surprise in store for him.

At that moment, Mark yelled to someone on the sidelines. "Cass! Where is he?"

"I don't know. He's coming," she shouted back.

Heather turned and cursed. "How did I miss them?" Cass and her friends were in their own group, standing on the sidelines further down from us. "Those are the bitches from your old school, right?"

"Yeah."

"Where's the girlfriend?"

"At home with her sister."

A few of the drill team girls from FCP were on the other side of Heather and me. A couple of them exchanged insults with Cass, which I was relieved about. They seemed focused on each other and not on me. I was getting a break. That was before Heather got there. Both groups were aware of Heather, who screamed sex just by walking. When she saw Cass watching her, Heather puffed up her chest and spread her arms out. "What?"

Cass narrowed her eyes and her lip curled up, but she turned away. Then she felt in her pocket and pulled out her phone. "Mark! He's here."

Everyone looked towards the parking lot. A car had pulled up and turned off its lights. It wasn't long before a guy was jogging to the field.

"This is the new super stud?"

I shrugged. "I guess." I turned to watch, but was distracted when Logan headed to us. When he got near, I saw the concern in his gaze. "What's wrong?"

"Can you hold my phone in case Kris calls? She's been off lately, and I don't want to miss her call."

Heather started laughing. "You're on the field, ready to cream Sam's old school, and you're worried about your girlfriend?"

"Yeah." He shot her a dark look. "These posers are nothing. This is already handled, and yes, I'm worried about Kris. She's been weird lately."

"Where's your phone?"

He gestured to his bag that was on the ground beside me. "Front pocket. Thanks, Sam."

I nodded.

"KADE! LET'S GO!" Mark yelled.

I heard how smug he sounded and glanced over at him. The new guy had joined their group, and they closed ranks, forming a tight circle. Mark waved at us. "You're being consoled by a bunch of girls because you're scared?" He scoffed. "I would be too!"

Logan yelled back, "I know what drawer you keep your panties in."

"Come on, Kade!"

I yelled back, "Shut it, Marcus."

Heather said, "Oh, whoa."

Mark laughed again. "Bring it, Sam! I know where you sleep."

"Goes both ways, buddy."

Logan started laughing. He shook his head and placed his hand on my shoulder. "I'm going to destroy them. The cockier they are, the more fun it is for us." He started back to them, but said to me, "Don't forget my phone."

"What is with him and this girl?" Heather's eyebrows bunched forward together. "I'm starting to think he actually cares about her."

I shook my head, but made sure to grab his phone. Stuffing it in my pocket, I shrugged. "He does care about her. What makes you think he doesn't?"

She gave me a pointed look.

Oh yeah. I'd forgotten for a brief moment.

I gave her a tight smile, feeling a weight settle back on my shoulders. "Let's just cheer them on."

"Yeah, yeah." She rolled her eyes and turned back to the football field. They didn't have their full teams and no one was wearing uniforms, but as they lined up across from each other and as Adam began the count, I was surprised at the fierceness rippling from both sides.

"This is all in good fun, right?"

Heather barked out a laugh. "Nothing's friendly when it comes to guys and their egos. Besides, Mason's gone and everyone's going to challenge Logan to see if he can hold the throne by himself."

The ball was snapped and Adam fell back, ready to throw. There was no one open so he looked to run. I looked down the field and saw Logan. He was running alongside a blocker. Both of them were going towards Adam. His blocker took out an FCA lineman. Logan ducked around the stretched arm and sprinted for Adam. It was only those two.

This was supposed to be friendly, but Logan squared down, tucking his shoulder in place. Adam didn't see him until the last second. He tried to evade him, but it was too late. Logan got him square in the front. He wrapped his arms around him and threw him down. It was a fair tackle, but it was so quick. Everyone was silent for a moment.

Logan was the quarterback. Tackling had been Mason's forte, but no one could deny it; it was an outstanding move. Even Adam was startled by it. When everyone remained silent, Logan smirked, turned, and pointed at Mark. He said, "That's one. I'm going to be counting these all night, Decraw." His shoulders rolled back and he raised his chin in a cocky challenge before heading back to his group. "All fucking night, Decraw."

"I thought Logan hated Adam? What's with him and Mark?"

"Nothing." I was still stunned by Logan's swiftness. "This is what they do at home. They love riling each other up, but that tackle was meant for Adam for a reason. Logan still hates him."

"There are others on that team who have hurt me, hurt you." Logan's words floated in my memory, almost haunting me, and a dark shiver went through me.

Heather grunted and gestured to the field. "Okay. I thought it was weird before, but that guy won't stop staring at you."

"What guy?"

"The new guy. When you yelled at Mark before, he whipped around. Right after he saw you, he looked like he'd seen a ghost. I thought it was weird, but whatever. He's new, but he's still staring at you. You know him?"

Looking for the new guy, I started to say, "I've never met him..." My gaze collided with dark eyes, dark tousled hair, square jaw, and the start of a smile on his face. My voice trailed off. My mouth hung open. I did know him. I knew him too well. "Shit."

Heather glanced at me. "Who is he?"

Someone I never wanted to see again. I shook my head. "I have to go."

"What?" She whipped around and followed me as I hurried from the field. Logan's phone was clutched in my hand, but Heather grabbed my arm and pulled me to a stop once we were closer to the parking lot. "Wait." She pressed Logan's bag against my chest. "What the hell is going on? For real. You have to tell me."

No. I couldn't.

She sighed and her hands rested on her hips. "Sam, come on. This is you and me. You told me about Logan. Tell me about this guy, whoever he is. I can tell he is *someone* to you."

"Oh my god." I pressed my fingers to my forehead and tried to rub the headache away. "This is a nightmare."

"Apparently." She took my hands, pulled them down, and got in my face. "Spill it, woman."

I couldn't believe I was going to say this. "His name is Jackson Sallaway. He's my ex's cousin."

"Okay." She scratched her head. "That's not the dramatic answer I was expecting, but okay. I guess?"

"No, you don't get it."

"Yeah, following you on that one."

"I lost my virginity to him."

"OH." She moved back a step, both eyebrows arched high. "For real?"

I nodded.

"Whoa. I wasn't expecting that answer."

"And Mark's right. He's an amazing player."

202

"Logan just kicked his ass."

I shook my head. "Jackson was on the other side of the line, but I know him. He watches and studies the players. He looks for all the weaknesses and once he has everything figured out, he exploits those weaknesses."

"Is he as good as Mason?"

"No." I was being honest. "But he's been watched by scouts for years. That's how I met him. I went to a football tournament with Jeff to watch his 'superstar' cousin one weekend."

"And how did this de-virginizing occur?"

I hated even thinking about it. "Jeff was being an ass. I caught him hitting on a bunch of girls. We were at a party so I went the other way and got drunk. Jackson showed up. He was nice. He was good-looking—"

"He's still good-looking. Quinn's got competition for the golden boy of FCA, by the way."

I shrugged and hugged myself, warding off the bad memories. "Anyway, one thing led to another."

"You were drunk and slept with him?"

I nodded. "I know. I'm an idiot."

"Was he drunk?"

"I think so, but it wasn't like that. It was just...it was a mistake. I cheated on Jeff. I was wracked with guilt for the longest time, well, until my mom left David and we moved in with Mason and Logan. Once that happened, I didn't think about him anymore." I swallowed, pushing down the regret that surged up again. "I know Jeff is an ass or was an ass, but I expected better of myself. I didn't think I would ever cheat and I did."

"Did you ever talk to him about it?"

"No. He fell asleep and I left. I called my dad and made him come and pick me up. Jeff never said anything about it. I remember thinking he was being nice about me ditching him, but he probably cheated on me that weekend anyway. God," I groaned, "what a mess."

She stuck out her bottom lip and pulled me in for a hug. "Oh, Sam." She began to rock me back and forth in a soothing motion. "You're human. You make mistakes and you probably cheated because your ex was an asshole. I doubt he made you feel loved."

"Sam."

I tensed, hearing him, but I didn't look right away. Heather kept me in her hug. She asked, "What do you want me to do?"

This wasn't something I wanted to deal with, but I knew Mason would say to deal with it. Nip it in the bud and get it moving. I tried to calm my nerves, and told her, "Stall Logan. I don't want him to know about this."

"He will." She pulled back, but her hands lingered on my shoulders. "You know that."

I did. "Just stall that from happening."

"On it." She moved her head in a nod. Her hands fell from my shoulders, and she saluted me with two fingers, a smirk already appearing. "I'll probably get in a fight with him. It's the best stall tactic I got right now." She started backpedaling. "Just be ready for the fireworks. It's not going to be pretty." As she went past Jackson, she gave him a swift pat on the back. "You have no idea what you're about to step into, but I have to admire your balls. You must have a cement pair."

When she turned and walked the rest of the way back to the football field, an impish grin appeared on his face. He ran his hand through his hair, messing it up again. I had to laugh. Putting up with Jeff for years, Jackson had seemed like a god to me. He had a leaner build back then, and with his dark eyes, friendly grin, and high cheekbones, he had a soft look to him. It appealed to me, and I saw that he still had that same look. He was pretty.

I noted, "You've put on some muscle."

"Yeah." He shrugged and stretched his arms across his chest. "My coach said I had to when he switched my position last year. It worked for me." Biting his lip, he moved closer to me and stopped a few feet away. He gestured to the field behind him. "I told the guys I was going to call Jeff and see if he wanted to play."

"Are you?"

He laughed. "No. Jeff wouldn't play anyway. He quit the team. I don't know if you knew that."

I didn't, and I didn't care. I couldn't stop looking at him. The memories from that night came back to me; how his hand rested on my knee and I turned into him. How he placed his other hand on my shoulder, drawing me closer for a hug. That was all we did, at first. I pushed the memories away. "Why are you here, Jackson?"

His eyes widened an inch, then he laughed. "My parents are going through a divorce. My mom wanted to move close to her sister, and so we're here."

"But the football program? Jeff told me that you were scouted."

"I was. I already committed to a school. It's a soft commitment, but yeah. I know FCA doesn't have that great of a program. Still. I like your dad. I have a lot of respect for him, and my last coach speaks highly of him. He says your dad has been turning the program around, so this year might not be too bad."

So he was staying. That meant he was going to be popular. He had the looks. He was friendly, nice, and it was only a matter of time before he started coming to Mark's house.

I murmured, "I see."

His eyes scanned over my face, and he laughed softly. "You're not happy about the move?"

"It doesn't matter."

"You know," I tensed, hearing his tone turn serious, "this doesn't have to be awkward. I can see that you've got a whole new life. Jeff said you transferred last year and something about a new boyfriend." He pointed to the field again. "Is it Logan Kade back there? I've heard of him, just didn't know you were attached to him."

I shook my head. "No. I'm dating Logan's brother."

"Ah. Gotcha. I've heard of him, you know." His head moved up and down in a slow nod. "Mason Kade. He's a big deal."

"Yeah, he is." My tone hardened. "He's better than you."

A short laugh came from him. "You're more honest than you were before." He grinned. "I approve. I always thought my cousin was an ass to you."

"He was."

"Yeah..." He glanced to the ground and bit his lip again.

I almost rolled my eyes. Jeff did the same thing when he was nervous. I guessed it was a family trait. "Look," I cleared my throat. I was all business. "This doesn't have to be awkward."

"You're right."

"We had sex. It was one time."

"You're right." He moved back a step. The nervous behavior stopped, and he raked a hand through his hair. "It's good to see you. I think it was nice to catch up since we did run into each other. I'm not a big partier so we probably won't run into each other at parties."

"I live with Mark."

"What?"

"Mark Decraw. I live with him. My dad is with his mom, and I'm living with my dad, so that means that I live with Mark. Just thought you should know, in case you come over to hang out with Mark sometime."

"Oh." Realization appeared in his gaze. "Yeah. Got it. Okay. Good to know, in case that ever comes up."

"It will. His mom likes to be a mom to everybody, so I'm sure you'll be invited to the house sometime."

"Okay." His head bobbed up and down. "And when I get that invitation, should I..." He paused, waiting for my answer. "Accept it...?"

"I don't care."

"...or don't accept?" He nodded again. "Okay. That sounds like another plan. I'm glad that's cleared up as well."

"Yeah."

"Yeah."

We stood and stared at each other.

"Okay." He jerked a thumb to the field. "I'll be going back there."

"Okay." I would be staying right where I was.

Then we heard, "Screw you, Jax! What the hell is your problem with my girlfriend, and where the fuck did Sam go?!"

This was going to be a long night.

CHAPTER SIXTEEN

MASON

Nate and I hadn't talked since Sam and Logan's visit. I kept to myself and my teammates. Football. My team. School. That was my life besides my nightly phone calls with Sam and talking with Logan every few days. When I went to class, I never looked in Marissa's direction. She was a non-factor. I meant what I had said. There was no friendship between us. The only awkwardness that happened was when we had been paired to be in a small group together. There were three others so our group presentation meetings were strictly business for me. We met in the library, and if the conversation steered towards hanging out, going for a beer, or hobbies, I brought them back to the assignment.

We were in the library again, and it was our last meeting. Matteo and Drew were coming to meet me. All three of us were going to find a study room on the third floor and lock ourselves in to study for our exam. And, as I thought of them, I glanced to the clock on the wall. They were supposed to be here by now. Irritation grew in me. This meeting was supposed to have been done thirty minutes ago, but they were still discussing who was going to present the bibliography.

I leaned over and grabbed the paper from the other guy. "I'll do it." They were quiet, and I leveled all of them with a hard look, gathering my books. "Are we done? Everything's set to go?"

"Uh." The guy's Adam's apple bobbed up and down. He tugged at his collar, stretching his trendy polo from his neck, and shrugged. "I guess. Yeah?" He looked to the others, but they weren't saying anything. Marissa's head was down, avoiding my gaze. The two other girls in the group looked dumbfounded. The redhead recovered first. She was interested in me. I had known the second our group was formed. Her shirt was lowered, her skirt was raised, and she kept flipping her damn hair over her shoulder. Some girls did that when they were uncomfortable, but not this one. This girl barely touched her books. Now, her finger went right to her lip, and she pulled on it.

I wasn't an idiot, and I never engaged. Averting my eyes and not talking to her were the only tactics I used. Other times I would've been an asshole, telling her straight out that it wasn't going to happen, but sometimes that backfired. The girl would come on to me harder. So again, like all the other times, I ignored her and glanced at the last girl. Unlike the redhead, this one seemed more like the old Marissa. Her brown hair was frizzy. She kept taking her glasses off and pinching the top of her nose. Her sweater was too baggy for her. When her elbows went to the table, her sleeves kept falling down and she would tug them back into place.

She sat right next to Marissa. Comparing her to the new Marissa, who was wearing a tight pink shirt and leggings that looked like jeans, almost made me miss the old Marissa.

The redhead asked, "Are you in a hurry to leave?"

I turned to her. She was rubbing her lips together. "Yeah. I need to study. Are we done here?"

Her eye twitched, and she stopped rubbing her lips together. "I don't know." She glanced to the guy beside me. "I was thinking of having everyone over for dinner? Are you guys interested? We can celebrate being done with our presentation?"

The guy's leg jerked under the table, and he immediately grabbed for his crotch. He was too excited. Under her knowing gaze, he swallowed again. His hand moved to his leg and he flattened his palm out, stopping his leg from jumping so much. "That sounds cool."

His voice trembled, but he caught it, cleared his throat, and covered it with a smooth, "I don't know how long I can stay, though." He glanced at me from the corner of his eye.

I tried hard not to react. He was a buck thirty. My leg had more muscle than he had in his entire body, but the guy wanted to bang the redhead. *Good luck, buddy.* They both looked at me, and I saw everyone around the table was waiting for my response.

"No." I scowled.

Marissa bit out a laugh. "Why am I not surprised?"

I lifted an eyebrow. This was new.

She waited, then shook her head as another laugh came out. "You don't even give a shit, do you? You aren't even going to ask me what that means."

"I already know." *Where was this going?* "I'm an asshole. You know that."

The redhead's eyes got big. "You know each other?"

"No." Marissa kept shaking her head. She sounded sad. "We really don't."

My eyes narrowed. I'd been patient with her, but that was gone. I didn't like dealing with head games, and I was starting to think that was Marissa's new forte. "What do you want, Marissa?"

She stiffened, but her eyes went to mine. A small glimmer of fear appeared there. "What do you mean?"

"You waited for me outside the stadium for what? To tell me you didn't like me, then you're in my class and there's no conversation between us. You go out with Nate and his fraternity and then show up for lunch with my brother and my girlfriend. Now we're in a group together, there's no small talk from you, and this? You're throwing attitude at me? Why? Have I summed this up enough for you, or do you want me to keep going?" I leveled her with a hard stare. "I don't like chicks who are passive aggressive and I really don't like chicks who try to mind-fuck someone. Be straight, tell me what you want, and I'll give you a straight up answer."

I already knew she wouldn't like being put on the spot like that.

"Whoa," the redhead murmured, leaning back in her chair. The others seemed like they wanted to disappear, but Marissa kept staring back at me.

"Forget this." Shoving back her chair, she grabbed her books and left. Storming off seemed too dramatic for her. She just, left.

No one said a word for a moment, but I didn't care. I started gathering my books together as well. Taking it as a cue, yellow polo dude took off and the junior Marissa look-alike wasn't far behind him. I lingered; Matteo and Drew should be coming soon. I saw the redhead was still standing by the table. I glanced up. "Yeah?"

"You're an asshole."

"I said that."

"But you're right. From the sounds of it, she doesn't want to hear 'no' from you, and that's all you're going to give her." Pressing her lips together, she pushed them out like she was going to kiss something, and tilted her head to the side. She grinned. "Girlfriend, huh? How faithful are you?"

I didn't bat an eye before answering, "I made out with one other girl while I was with my girlfriend."

Excitement filled her eyes.

"I was setting her up to take the fall *for* my girlfriend. Some other asshole wanted to hurt someone I cared about." Seeing Matteo and Drew come through the doors, I stood. "I gave him someone else that I gave no shits about."

The excitement vanished immediately. Her shoulders dropped, and she gave me a cold look instead. "Wow. You really are an ass."

I shrugged. I'd own it. I walked past her.

*

SAMANTHA

Logan wanted to fight. I could tell.

The football challenge was scrapped. Heather's tactic had been so successful the two declared an all-out war. She was carted off the field, giving him the middle finger, yelling that he was too controlling over me while Logan looked a mix of confused and enraged. The drill team hadn't wanted to leave. They hated Heather, so of course they wanted to hear her demise happen. Anyone who went against Logan would see that end, but it'd be different this time. As soon as Heather was carried past me, she gave me a small wave and called out, "Please do damage control. I love you."

I sighed, nodded, and pressed my hands to my temple. It wasn't long until Logan tore off the field, after her. Unlike Heather, none of his friends were holding him back, so I swung my arm out and caught him around the chest. Logan kept going, but so did I. I used his momentum and let my body follow through. I was lifted up and latched onto his back.

"Sam!" he growled, but stopped walking.

When he glanced up and tried to dislodge me, I waited, holding onto him tight until I saw Heather get into her car. When her headlights turned on, I let go. My body slid down his.

"Stop, Logan."

He wasn't moving, but I put my hands on his shoulders and stood in front of him. As I did, he continued to glower at me and crossed his arms over his chest. Then he said, "I'm getting sick of Jax's problem with Kris. My relationship is none of her business. What's her problem? I'm not boning her. We joke about it, but, man, I like Channing. I'd never do that to him."

"Or to Kris."

"That's a given." He rolled his eyes.

It was at that moment when everyone else decided to leave. A few of the drill team said their goodbyes to Logan. A couple touched his arm and gave him seductive grins, but he just jerked his head in a nod to them. I caught their disappointment before they moved forward. The words party and drunk were tossed around before they climbed into their cars and zoomed off. By this time, most of the Fallen Crest Academy crowd had left as well, but I stiffened. Mark and Jackson were still there, so was Cass, draped all over Mark. Some of Logan's friends lingered as well, and they stopped beside us. Everyone was waiting for what Logan had to say next.

Mark grinned. "Didn't take you for a sore loser, Kade." His head lifted and he rolled his shoulders back, a smirk appearing over his mouth. "Not that I'm surprised." He clasped a hand on Jackson's shoulder and pulled him forward. "You've met our secret weapon. You're lucky you guys aren't playing us again this year."

Adam joined the group. A bag was thrown over his shoulder, and he paused, glancing at me first, before skimming over Logan and Mark. Logan tensed, but his jaw only clenched shut. Adam said to Mark, "Is there a party in the plan for tonight?"

"Logan," Derek spoke up behind us.

Logan nodded. "Derek's throwing a party. You guys can come."

Adam stiffened. His eyes jerked back to mine, and I knew he was thinking about the past. He had steered clear of me for so long, and there was still tension between us; it filled the air. I saw Jackson looking from Adam to me. His eyes fell to the hand Logan had placed on my side. I hadn't realized he was touching me, but I let it go. There was so much bad blood between Logan and Adam.

A thought occurred to me: *Was that the real reason Kris wasn't there? Because Logan had stolen Kris from Adam?*

Adam never replied to Logan's invitation.

Logan laughed. "She won't be there, if that's what you're worried about."

His hand tightened on my side, and Adam saw that motion too. The problem wasn't Kris. It was me. Adam had stopped pursuing me, and I had ended our friendship long ago. That history needed to be left alone, but this was Logan. He was protecting me. Still.

"You're such an ass, Kade." Adam's words were quiet, but they were clearly spoken.

"I'm the ass? You think I don't know about your phone calls and text messages?"

Oh. Not me. This was all about Kris. Relief flooded me, and my shoulder sagged from the sudden release of tension. A small grin appeared on Jackson's face as he noticed it. A warm feeling went through me, and I remembered why I used to like him so much. He'd been kind when I needed it.

Adam scoffed, distracting me. "Kris and I are still friends. You need to deal with that."

"Right. Friends. That's what you said you wanted from Sam too."

No, no, no. I didn't want to get pulled into this.

Adam glanced at me, but clenched his jaw again. "Sam and I are no longer friends, thanks to you and your brother."

Oh shit. I closed my eyes. Logan was going to blast him, and I shot Mark a pointed look. He could step in. Anytime now.

Seeing my look, Mark narrowed his eyes, and I gestured between Logan and Adam. His eyes got big as understanding dawned. He cleared his throat. "Uh, hey guys. The party sounds awesome. We'll spread the word. Derek, you're on 54th, right?"

"Yeah. Two blocks from your house."

"Sounds good." Mark grabbed Adam and turned him towards the parking lot. He began pushing him forward and waved at us over his shoulder. "We'll see you guys there."

Derek said, "Bring beer. I don't know if I can score a keg tonight."

"Will do." Mark kept directing Adam ahead. Cass trailed behind them, but she paused, turned half way back to us, and narrowed her eyes at me.

What'd I do?

Then she glanced at Jackson, and a cold feeling spread through me. She must've caught our shared look. Oh hell. I had no doubt that she'd twist that somehow, but I rolled my eyes. She could try. The only person who needed to know about Jackson was Mason. I'd have to tell him as soon as possible.

"Cass doesn't like you much, huh?"

I bit down on my lip, hearing Jackson's question.

Logan turned to him. "You're the new kid?"

"Yeah. We didn't formally meet." Jackson held his hand out. "Jackson Sallaway."

Logan glanced at me. "Sallaway?"

"He's Jeff's cousin."

"Your ex?"

I nodded. "Yeah."

He gestured between Jackson and myself. "So you two know each other?"

Jackson glanced at me, and I braced myself. Logan couldn't know. I wasn't ready to tell him who Jackson was and, as if he could read my thoughts, Jackson said, "Just a tiny bit. My cousin brought her to a game a long time ago." He nodded to me. "It was nice meeting you. I don't know if I ever told you that. I thought you were a good person for putting up with my cousin."

He had covered for me. I snorted, my knees suddenly shaky. "Yeah. Jeff's a good friend, but a horrible boyfriend."

Jackson grinned, laughing. The sound was so genuine.

Logan's eyes narrowed at him and asked, "Are you coming to the party tonight?"

His laughter stopped, and his eyes flicked to mine. "Um..." He looked towards the parking lot. "Everyone left, huh? I'm not a big partier. Who usually shows up to those?"

"Everyone."

I stepped back as Derek moved forward.

Jackson lifted a hand, rested it against the side of his face, and shrugged. "Sure." His finger indicated Logan, Derek, and their other friend. "You three are your team's captains?"

Derek started to answer him, but Logan urged me forward. Apparently, we were leaving. As we did, Logan tossed over his shoulder, "We'll see you guys there. I have to try and sneak my girlfriend out of the house."

Derek laughed. "Quinn's going to love that."

Logan ignored him, his hand still on my side, as he directed me to the car and to the passenger door. I frowned as he opened it for me, and when I got inside, I waited until he went to his door. When he opened it and got into his seat, I asked, "What's going on with you?" I jerked my hand back and pointed to the door. "Since when do you open doors for me, and two, I thought you said Kris wasn't going?"

He lifted a shoulder. His shoulders were so rigid. "I don't know, Sam. Okay? I was trying to be nice. I won't, if that's your deal."

Taken aback, I didn't comment. Holy shit. Where did this side of Logan come from?

He cursed. His hand dropped from the steering wheel and his car remained idle. "I'm sorry. I'm being an ass to you, and you don't deserve that. Quinn started texting Kris a bunch, and she's been responding. It's pissing me off."

"Oh."

"She's my girlfriend. She shouldn't be talking to him. She knows how I feel about him, but she won't stop. She keeps saying they're just friends." He grunted. "Fuck friends, that's what Quinn wants." He glanced to me, seemingly hesitant. "I haven't said anything to you. I know you've got your own stuff, with Mason gone and your dad here again. Again, I'm sorry for being an ass."

He hadn't picked up anything about Jackson. I felt like I had just bypassed a bomb exploding. "It's no problem. You and Kris are you and Kris. For what it's worth, I don't think she'd ever cheat on you, if that's what you're worried about."

He cursed again and hit his hand against the wheel. "I don't fucking know what I'm worried about. I feel like this whole year is off, you know?" He sounded haunted. "Is it just me? Is it because Mason's not here?"

He was looking for an answer. I lifted both my shoulders up and let them fall. I didn't have one for him. "I miss him too."

"Yeah," he said softly. "Maybe that's just it." He groaned, raking a hand through his hair, letting it rub over his face before dropping it to his lap. "It's just, it's Quinn, you know? I hate that loser. Anything she gives him makes me feel like crap. Any time she texts him or smiles at him or takes his phone call, the douche thinks he's winning her over me. I hate this shit. I hate relationships." He grinned at me. "I think Tate messed me up for every girl."

"Just talk to Kris. She told me that she used to sleep with guys to feel loved, something about having daddy issues. If she's talking to another guy, maybe it's those old issues rearing up, and she's just not handling them. I don't know." I reached over and squeezed his hand. "For what it's worth, she's crazy about you. I know she is."

He turned his hand over so his palm rested against mine. He sighed, lacing his fingers with mine. "Thanks, Sam. You're right. I'll just talk to her first." His eyes narrowed, and his hand tightened around mine. "Then I'll kick his ass."

CHAPTER SEVENTEEN

I had Logan drop me off at home. He went to the party, but I never heard if there had been any drama or not. Mark was still sleeping when I got up the next morning and headed for a shift at Manny's. As I got to the little diner, I breathed in the smell of grease, dirt, dust, and sweat. The front door was open, and I could hear yelling, mixed with a fast country song from inside. Opening the screen door, I noticed a group of guys huddled around the bar. The top of Brandon's head was visible as a bottle was tossed in the air. When I didn't hear glass shattering, I assumed he was doing his usual bartending show. When I moved past the bar for the back employee room, he saw me from the side of the group. In mid-pour, he flashed me a smile. "The prodigal sister has returned."

I grinned. "Still dreaming about being in *Cocktail*?

"You know it." He winked at me. Finishing the pour, he slid the glass to its customer and held his hand towards me. "Hold up, Sam."

I paused, but glanced around with my uniform in hand. There were two other servers that I didn't recognize, along with Rosa and Frank, who was doing the dishes. When Brandon finished putting the money in the register, I asked him, "Where's Heather?" It wasn't normal to have five servers on a shift.

"That's what I wanted to let you know. She's at Channing's. Rosa's filling in for her."

"Oh." I was disappointed. It's why I had picked up the shift, to work with her. "Okay. I'm still on till nine tonight?"

"Yeah, that's the other thing. Our numbers are down, so we don't need you today. I'm sorry, Sam. I was supposed to call you and let you know."

Double oh.

He grimaced. "I got slammed, or I would've called you earlier. I am sorry."

"So you're saying I have a free day?"

"Go find Logan and get drunk." He paused and then added, "Road trip to see Mason?"

I laughed, but I was considering it. I turned back and was headed outside when someone stepped forward. The screen door hit him in the head. "I'm sorry—" I started, but stopped when I saw who it was.

Jackson.

He had taken off his sunglasses and rubbed his forehead as he squinted to see me. "Sam?" He held his sunglasses up. "Apparently I need more than these. That sun is blinding. I didn't see you at all."

"I hit you. I'm sorry."

"I'm good." Giving me a grin, he turned and looked around us. He scanned the parking lot, the patio, and leaned around me to see inside the diner. "Are you here with someone?"

I held up my uniform. "I work here."

"You do? I've been eating here for the last three weeks."

"I work here," I paused, "randomly. I don't have that much time with cross country. You know, with school too."

"Ah. Yes." His hand lingered on the side of his face as he gazed down at me. "Jeff used to talk about you running all the time. You still run?"

"Yeah."

He laughed and shook his head, rolling his eyes. "Jeff always bitched about you running. He tried to tell me that's why he cheated on you, because you ran all the time."

"What?"

"What?"

He said... "You and Jeff talked about him cheating?"

"Yeah—" The screen door opened again as three guys left Manny's. Jackson glanced around, then gestured to a table and chairs in the corner. "Can we just...do you want to...I don't know. Could we talk...a little? After what happened and last night, I feel like we should talk. Maybe for some closure or something."

"Yeah." That sounded good. He was right. Closure. As he sat down, I sat across from him.

I stared.

He stared back.

This was going wonderfully. "So..."

At the same time, he said, "Yeah, so—" He laughed. "Man. This is awkward, huh?"

"Little bit." I curled my hands together on my lap. "It's probably me. I don't socialize much. I don't have to. Pretty much everyone knows me by now."

A keen look came into his eyes, and he leaned forward, propping his elbows on the table. "Yeah. Jeff said when you guys broke up, it wasn't long before you were with Mason Kade. Since

I've been here, I can tell that probably sent some shockwaves through school, huh?"

"You could say that." I grinned. "Things are fine, for the most part."

"That's good." His head bobbed up and down. His smile never left his face. "And your boyfriend is at Cain U?"

"Do you know that because of the gossip or—"

He shook his head. "Football. It's known where the big recruits go. Signing day and all."

"Signing day?"

"Yeah…" He trailed off. "He would've committed then, well officially committed."

"Oh."

"You didn't know?"

I shook my head. "Mason never said anything."

He scratched his ear and tilted his head to the side. "I think he only had his mom and some old guy there. Yeah. I'm sure of that. It's televised…" I felt like I'd been punched in the chest. His eyes widened. "And you didn't know that either." He glanced down to the table. "I was going to say it's weird that his brother wasn't there or I would've recognized Logan." His voice quieted. "Signing day's a big deal too…I'm not being helpful, am I?"

Signing day. Helen and another guy had been there. It was televised. My jaw clenched. More things Mason had kept from me.

"Sam?"

He said that so softly, so tentatively, I wanted to melt. Feeling my throat choke up, my fingers pressed into my palms, and I willed all the weakness to go away. I wanted to scream, but I

226

didn't. As I forced everything down, I gave Jackson another smile and brushed that damn little tear away. I wasn't weak. I wasn't going to act like it anymore.

I forced out, "What were you saying?"

"I'm sorry," he said, an extra layer of earnestness in his eyes. He leaned forward again. "It's always February fourth. Maybe something was going on, and he didn't want to bother yo..." He trailed off again. A look of concern came into his eyes as he noticed that I winced.

That was around the time I was in the hospital. Mason hadn't said a word.

"I didn't want to talk to cause problems. I'm sorry."

I shook my head. "No, it's fine." *Change of topic, please.* "So your parents are getting a divorce?"

He winced, gritting his teeth at the same time. Lifting a hand to run it through his hair, he blew out a puff of air. His shoulders slumped down, and he started to pick at the tablecloth with his fingers. "Yeah. Uh. My dad kicked us out."

I frowned.

"Not me, but he kicked my mom out. He can be a huge asshole."

"It must run in the family." Memories of Jeff flashed in my mind.

"Yeah. It does, but this is what I wanted to tell you." His tone dropped to a serious note, and he lifted his head. When his eyes found mine, I saw an intensity in them. "I didn't set out to sleep with you that night. I'm sorry if it came across like that. I'd been drinking. My parents were having problems, and I wasn't a real nice guy that year at school. I was kinda like my cousin. I was a whore, but anyway, I didn't mean for anything to happen. I want you to know that. You were just so nice, and you were hurting. I knew Jeff had done something to upset you and we hugged and ..."

I swallowed over the knot in my throat. "I'm aware of what happened that night."

"I liked you."

"What?"

"I liked you, before that night. Jeff showed me your picture, and he talked about you a lot. Regardless of how he treated you, I know my cousin loved you, but yeah. I think I started to crush on you because of what he'd say and then I met you in person, and you were more, you know? So I just wanted you to know that I wasn't using you or anything. I would've dated you too, or pursued dating you, but you disappeared the next morning, and Jeff told me later you two were trying to make it work." A shadow crossed his features. "I thought maybe I'd leave you alone after that."

My mouth was slightly open as I listened to what he was saying. I never expected to hear that. *He liked me?* Because I had no idea how to respond, I snorted. "Jeff did not love me. No matter what you say. He had been screwing one of my best friends for two years."

"He did?" A flash of anger appeared in his gaze.

I straightened, taken aback. "I'm over it. Trust me, things got better for me." And with all the talking about Jeff... "Where *is* Jeff? I haven't seen him since this summer." A small buzzing sensation was in my stomach from Jackson's explanation. I should address it, but I had no idea what to say. I wasn't sure if I even wanted to talk about what would've happened if he had pursued me. It didn't matter. It was in the past.

He leaned back, rolling his eyes. "My cousin has a girlfriend."

A grin tugged at the corner of my mouth. "Why am I not surprised?"

"Yeah." He was grinning too and propped his hand up, shaking a finger in the air. "His new girlfriend is a serious Christian."

"What?" Bombs exploded. "Jeff's with a Christian? Manwhore Jeff?"

Jackson nodded, a smile stretched from ear to ear as he laughed. "I know. Can you believe that? And get this, he's not been around because on the weekends, he goes to a wilderness camp with her."

My eyeballs were going to fall out. I couldn't believe this.

He added, "They do bible studies, bonfires, singing. All of that."

"Sex?"

He kept laughing. "Oh, they're having sex. Jeff said she's changed him and strengthened his faith, but the sex is his influence on her. He said he can only be so much of a saint, you know." Jackson kept laughing, and he shook his head. "Man, I laughed so hard when he told me he's in love with this girl. I never thought it would last."

"How long have they been together?"

"I think they're going on three months."

"Wow." I was stunned. "That would explain why he hasn't gone to any parties."

"Nope. He said he's been praying. They do lots of praying."

"Good for him."

"Yeah." His grin faded a bit, and his laughter changed to a soft chuckle. "This has been nice."

"This?"

He gestured from me to him. "This. Talking to you. It was so easy to talk to you that night. I wasn't used to that. I'm usually shy around girls."

"I thought you said you were a manwhore that year?" But I agreed with him. It was easy to talk to him.

He chuckled again, stretching an arm up to rub the back of his neck. "Talking and having sex are two different things." He flashed me a grin. "Sometimes being a football star comes in handy. I'm sure Mason and Logan have that effect. They're like gods around here."

"Yeah, they are."

Memories of when I first moved in with them came back to me. Going to eat with Mason and him getting free food. He had been given free beer at the gas station a few times. So many girls. They had all wanted him. I'd almost forgotten what that limelight was like. He was gone, and all that attention went with him. Now, I was only Sam.

"Sam?"

I glanced up and realized Jackson had been watching me, waiting. "Sorry." I shook my head, clearing my thoughts. "I was just remembering when I first started dating Mason. It was hard to get used to, but now it's different."

"What do you mean?"

I glanced up. He seemed genuinely interested, but not like others would have been. Other people would've wanted to know about Mason or Logan. It was different with Jackson, and I knew that he would understand.

I heard myself asking before I realized what I was saying, "How do you handle the attention?" I flushed. I had no idea what I was asking. "I'm sorry. I don't know where that came from." I started to stand from my chair. "I should go—"

"I don't."

His words stopped me, and I slowly sat back down. "What do you mean?"

His tone was so soft. "I don't handle it. I meant it when I said that I'm shy around girls. You're different, Sam. You don't have an agenda. You're not trying to use me for anything. Hell, I don't even think you want to talk to me, but I like it." He waved his hand over his face. "I'm not dumb. I know I'm good looking, and I'm good at football. I might have a future there; I'm not sure yet. I know I'm playing in college, but that's all I know. Girls are already looking at me with dollar signs in their eyes." He looked away, but raised his eyes again.

He was looking at me, but it was different. I felt a sudden tension go through me. It was like he was seeing through me. No one looked at me like that except Mason. My fingers curled around the sides of my chair, and I bit down on my lip. I wasn't sure what he was going to say.

"I've never met Mason, but Logan seems comfortable with the attention."

My fingers relaxed, and I leaned back in my chair. Feeling myself nodding, I replied, "He is. I think he's so used to it that he doesn't even realize it's there half the time."

"What's your boyfriend like?"

"What do you mean?"

"How does he handle everything? I mean, he's gotta be huge at his college already. His name's all over ESPN when they talk about Cain U."

I shrugged. "He's fine. I don't know. He said his focus is school, football, and me." A small grin escaped me. "Mason's like Logan. I don't think he knows anything different."

"Yeah. That's how he seems, from what I've seen and heard about him."

"Yeah."

"Then there's all the girls. Aren't they vicious?"

I laughed. "They have been. Not to Logan's girlfriend, though. They seem to love her." I barely talked to anyone except Mason, Logan, and Heather, but I was opening up to him. I was telling him things that I was just becoming aware of myself. Kris had been welcomed with open arms when she transferred, but they had attacked me. I was jealous of her. I was jealous of how easy her transition had been.

Jackson murmured, "But that's because they were jealous of you. I mean, Mason's a big deal. It must've been nuts with him here. I can't imagine. I've heard people talk about Logan and his girlfriend. I might be a guy, but I can tell that a lot of girls think they're going to break up sooner rather than later. I know how girls work. They're just being patient, biding their time."

"Maybe." I shook my head. "This conversation's been weird." I stood.

He laughed and stood with me. "But nice. It was nice talking to you again."

Going to the step that led down to the parking lot, Jackson went with me. "I thought you were going to eat?"

He shrugged. "I don't know. The idea of going in there and sitting at a table with a bunch of people from school isn't real tempting." His gaze lingered on me. "It feels empty for some reason."

A van was parked right next to my car, and as we crossed the parking lot, a guy hurried out of Manny's and darted around us. He got into the van and started the engine. I was about to step forward, but Jackson touched my arm and pulled me back. He was watching the van and a second later, the driver reversed out of his parking spot, going right into the path that I would've been in. Without casting a look to us, he swung his front end around and gunned the engine, spitting up dirt from his tires.

I would've gotten hit. My mouth opened. I was about to say thank you, but the words caught in my throat.

Logan was standing on the other side of my car.

My eyes rounded.

He was looking at where the van had gone. His features were scrunched up, a scowl was on his face, and he looked back. As he did, his eyes met mine briefly, then fell to the hand that Jackson still had on my arm. Guilt flooded me. I jerked over a step. Jackson's hand fell down and he turned to me, his eyebrows furrowing forward for a slight second, and he saw where I was looking. As he did, he moved back a step.

An accusing look appeared on Logan's face, and he pressed his lips in a flat line.

Everything happened in a split second, from the van leaving, to Logan seeing Jackson's hand on my arm. I had reacted, but it was a bad reaction. I wasn't doing anything wrong. I didn't know why I reacted how I did, but it was too late. Logan started for us and I swallowed. This could get interesting.

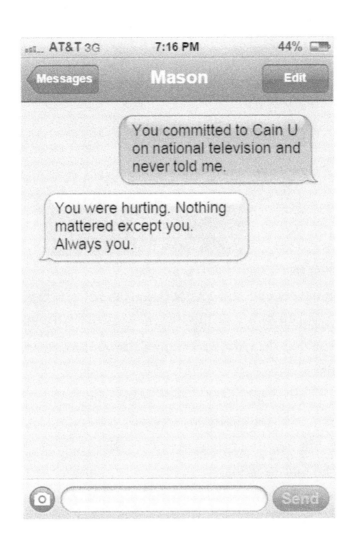

CHAPTER EIGHTEEN

"Oh look." He tilted his head to the side, pushed his hands into his pockets, and gave us a cheeky grin. "It's the happy couple. Out for brunch?"

This might get worse than I imagined. "Logan." I caught the glare he sent to Jackson. "This is not that."

"Yeah, not giving a shit what it doesn't look like. I'm giving a shit about what it does look like." Turning so he was facing Jackson squarely, he narrowed his eyes. "Who the fuck are you?"

"I'm Jac—"

"I know your name, Jackass. I'm asking who you *think* you are." He moved a step closer, his eyes narrowed into slits. "She's dating my brother. Don't come here and take advantage of her because she's nice and lonely."

Heat surged to my cheeks, and my head went down. *Lonely?* I was missing Mason, but to hear it said out loud was embarrassing.

"I wasn't. I didn't." Jackson shifted towards me. "Sam?"

I shook my head. I hadn't told Mason yet, and I wasn't going to tell Logan first. "Stop it, Logan. I told you last night. I know Jackson. We were talking about Jeff. My ex. His cousin. Remember him? He worshiped you last year."

Logan rolled his eyes, but didn't say anything. When he shot me a look, I knew he was saving it for when Jackson left. I sighed on the inside. Oh joy for that conversation. As if sensing the same thing, Jackson said, "Well. I suppose I should go. It was nice running into you, Sam." He jerked his head in a nod. "Kade."

"Jackass." Logan nodded back, his reply monotone.

Pausing, Jackson glanced back at me, then pressed his mouth in a flat line and lifted his hand in a small wave. "See ya, Sam."

We waited as he went to his car and pulled out of the lot. As soon as it turned onto the road, Logan gave me an incredulous look. "Sam? What the fuck?"

"We have history." I shut him up with that.

"What?"

I cursed at myself. *Why had I said that?* "Look, he was nice to me one night when Jeff was being his usual asshole self. You don't have to worry about anything. Trust me. I'm not even friends with him, but I'm not going to ignore him."

He snorted. "You've been smelling Malinda's perfume too much. It's gotten in your head if you think that guy doesn't want, at least, friendship." He pointed to where Jackson left. "He wants *way* more than friendship."

"Logan," I didn't want to argue, "what are you doing here?"

He lifted a shoulder. "Okay. That's my cue to let it drop, but I'm telling you. That guy's going to be 'around' a lot more than you think." He lifted his fingers to form quotations in the air. "And I know the dude knew you worked today. Mark told me he was asking about you at the party last night."

"Really?"

"Really." He gestured to Manny's. "I came to hackle you while you worked. You're not working?"

"They don't need me today."

237

"I see. Is Jax in there?"

I shook my head. "She's with Channing." And because I remembered that I hadn't squared things away from last night, I added, "Hey, don't give her a hard time the next time you see her."

"What do you mean?"

"About last night. She was stalling you. I wanted to talk to Jack—"

"Jackass."

I kept going, "—son last night. She doesn't have a problem with Kris. She was just having my back last night."

I expected a smartass response back, something derogatory about Heather, or maybe a cocky remark about Kris. I got silence instead. "What's wrong?"

Logan continued to stare at me, long and hard. He was dressed in a long-sleeve shirt. A slight breeze sped past us, plastering his shirt against his torso, but he didn't move. He continued to stare at me. His dark hair moved in the sudden rush of air. He kept staring. His hands slid back into his jean pockets, outlining his lean frame and broad shoulders.

"Logan?"

He murmured, his voice low and grave, "There's about three things wrong with your last statement."

My mouth went dry. *Oh shit.*

He moved closer one step. His hands remained in his pockets, and he looked down his nose at me. He would've been intimidating to anyone else. I wasn't anyone else. I was family. Holding my breath, I waited to see what he was going to throw at me.

He lifted a finger. "One. You lied to me."

"I didn't."

A second finger uncurled up. "Two. You had someone else lie to me."

I kept quiet and just waited for him to finish.

A third finger. "Three. Someone else was in the know, not me."

"Logan—"

"*Not* me," he repeated, a flash of anger filling his eyes. "Not me, Sam. You put Heather above me. We're family. You shouldn't put anyone above me except Mason." He shook his head, so slowly. "I know you're dealing with something, and I've tried being patient. Mase keeps telling me to be patient, but it's starting to piss me off. If we're no longer family, maybe you should let me fucking know."

"Logan—" The word cut off in my throat. He shook his head and turned away. "Logan."

Instead of answering, he went to his Escalade.

"Logan!"

He didn't answer. He got inside and pulled out of the parking lot within seconds.

Well...fuck me.

*

MASON

A week later

"Kade." Drew signaled to get my attention, but I barely heard him. I couldn't hear much except the music. We were at Cliché, on the private football floor. A huge group had congregated to celebrate the end of exams. There were others from school, and I recognized a couple girls from our class, but I was there for only one reason. I needed to make sure my roommate didn't get too plastered. Ten a.m. practice was going to come too damn early.

Drew waved again, mouthing my name once more, so I slid out of the booth and rounded it on the other side. As I sat down next to him, I watched Matteo dance. He wore a white, unbuttoned shirt. His bare chest was solid muscle, but his stomach ended with a fat roll hanging over his jeans. Grinning, sweat rolling down his face, he rubbed a brisk hand over his bald head. He placed one hand on his hip, pointed at us, and yelled, "FOR YOU, GUYS!" With his hand still raised to us, he took a dramatic step, turning so his ass was facing us. With his hand up, he started pointing at the others around him, keeping in rhythm with the music. At the same time, the deejay suddenly switched the song. Loud bass slammed through the speakers. It sent a wave of energy through the crowd and everyone started dancing harder. As this happened, Matteo glanced over his shoulder at us, winked, and bent low. His ass stayed up, and he began twerking.

"Oh my god." Drew looked down. His shoulders lifted as he began laughing, shaking his head at the same time. "Only Matteo."

"Mason!" Matteo yelled again. He had moved closer to us. A small ring of people continued to surround him, but there was an opening for us. "Roommate pay per view." As he shouted each word, his ass twerked up and down. The bass in the song changed again, speeding up, and Matteo stopped shouting. He kept going, matching the fast pace of the song.

"We do not need to see this."

I grinned. "Just be glad we're getting the back end view."

Drew tucked his chin to his chest and bent over the table. His shoulders shook even more. When he kept laughing, I frowned. A tray had been placed on the table with ten shot glasses. All of them had been emptied. There were a few other empty glasses next to them. I was about to ask how much he had when Matteo lumbered over to us, panting.

"Guys." He bumped the table with his hip, tipping over a few of those glasses. Matteo had no clue. He slapped a hand on his knee, bending over so his face was close to ours. Some of his sweat splashed off his arm onto us.

"Ew." Drew leaned back, as much as possible, pressing against the booth. "Matty, back up." He ran a hand down his arm and flicked some of the sweat off. He glanced at me, but I flashed him a grin and tugged at my long sleeve.

He groaned. "I get too hot if I wear those."

Matteo was looking between us, his head moving back and forth, like he was watching a tennis match. I turned to him, and when he sensed the small conversation was over, his eyes lit up. "Okay. I have an idea."

"No." Drew and I spoke at the same time.

Matteo paused, looked at both of us, and said again, "I have an idea."

"No." We spoke again.

"What?"

Drew rolled his eyes. "You're plastered. Any idea you have right now, we're not doing. It's going to be a stupid idea."

"It's an awesome idea." His eyebrows were arched high, and his eyeballs seemed to be bulging out. His entire face was animated.

"We have practice tomorrow morning. Are you going to live long enough to get there?"

"No," he said to me, and turned to Drew. "So about my plan—"

Drew pointed at me. "He's saying no. I'm saying no. Fuck, Matty." He ran a hand over his face and let it drop to his lap with a thud. "I'm wasted, and I'm more sober than you. This is a problem."

"I have an idea—"

"NO!" Drew and I shouted, speaking as one.

Matteo paused, his eyes skirted back and forth, and he opened his mouth. I groaned. He was going to say the same damn thing. Drew jerked forward and pointed at the dance floor, "Hey, look!"

Matteo whipped around, a permanent grin on his face.

As he was turned, Drew tapped my arm. "We need to get him out of here." He stopped, held up a finger for me to wait. "We need to get me out of here too. Coach is going to kill me tomorrow."

Matteo was still looking for what Drew had pointed at.

"Coach is going to kill all of us." I grabbed Matteo's arm, prepared to drag him with us, whether he wanted to leave or not.

"Not you." Drew stood with me and fell behind me. "You're sober. Thank god you came with us. We don't need any press recording us trying to hail down a cab. Matty would flash his tits and if that wouldn't work, I'm sure he would've performed a strip show."

I started to laugh, but Matteo whipped his hand backwards and slapped me.

"Hey!" That fucker hurt.

He was still looking ahead of us. His hand came back, his fingers spread to deliver another slap. He said, "Hey, hey, hey." He reached farther, trying to hit my face.

I dodged, stepping back into Drew. My elbow got him in the gut, and he doubled over. Matteo's hand was still flailing around. Grabbing it, I yanked him back. He looked up at me, still grinning, and pointed with his free hand. "It's that chick you did a presentation with."

Letting go of Matteo, so he didn't fall but couldn't hit me again, I scanned the dance floor and saw Marissa in the middle. Her head was back. Her eyes were closed. Her hair was let down. It touched the small of her back as she held her arms in the air. A guy was grinding against her. His hands were holding her hips, and as she kept dancing, he eyed her rack. Wearing a tiny tank top and a short skirt, he was getting a good view. As I watched, one of his hands slid around her hip to cup her rear end. He grabbed a good handful, and a smirk etched over his face.

"Wasn't she mad at you or something?"

I did a double take at Matteo. "How are you this drunk and still remember shit like that?"

He shrugged, grinning. "Steel trap." He tapped his head.

The presentation had gone fine, but Marissa refused to talk to me when we met right before class. Matteo and Drew had been there, waiting for me to go in, so they had caught the tension between us. I was surprised others hadn't. The entire class had walked past us. When Marissa turned her back to me, it had gotten a few raised eyebrows.

I looked for the others from the group. The redhead had talked to Drew after our exam so I knew that's how they got invited, but I didn't see her or the other two. "Is she alone?"

Matteo grunted. "She doesn't look alone." The guy still had his hand on her ass, but he leaned forward and kissed her exposed neck.

Marissa didn't react. She kept raising her hands in the air, pumping her fist to the music. The deejay started a new song, bleeding the songs together so the beat slowed. So did Marissa's hands and she paused. As the beat built, speeding up and getting louder, everyone waited. Then the beat exploded and another wave of energy went over the crowd. Marissa reacted, jumping up and down in a frenzied motion. The guy leaned back, just holding onto her hips to keep her close.

Drew said over my shoulder, "Dude. She's clueless. She doesn't even know that guy is there."

A growl came from me, and I pushed Matteo forward.

He said, "Hey."

I kept propelling him forward, using him to break through the crowd. I said over my shoulder to Drew, "Stay close. Watch the crowd to see if any girls react when we get to her. She might be here with a friend."

He nodded.

When we got to them, the guy looked up. They did a double take at the sight of Matteo and grinned, waving at him. Matteo said, "Hi, douchebag. Release the wench."

"What?"

I rolled my eyes, stepping around Matteo. When the douchebag saw me, saw the scowl on my face, his hands lifted in surrender. "Oh whoa. I thought she was single. I swear."

I grabbed Marissa's arm, but she kept dancing. I said to him, "She's wasted. She doesn't even know if she's single. Get lost before I decide to find out who you are and kick your ass later."

His eyes got big, and he was gone in an instant.

"Marissa." I pulled her closer. "Hey."

One of her eyes opened, peeking at me. "Huh?"

The smell of alcohol singed my nostrils, and I moved so I could yell into her ear, "Who are you here with?"

Giggling, she stopped dancing and rested a hand on my chest. She lifted her shoulder up and cringed. "That tickles."

Drew moved closer. We were beginning to attract attention. I lifted an eyebrow, silently asking if he noticed anyone. He shook his head and said, "She might be alone. I have no idea."

Matteo started dancing next to us. When he began moving away, Drew grabbed his arm, anchoring him in place.

"Marissa, do you have your phone on you?" I couldn't see any pockets on her skirt, and she didn't have a purse with her. I said to Drew, "She has to have friends here."

"Yeah, but if she does, they're not around." He was skimming the crowd. "I'm not seeing anyone I even recognize. How did all these people get invited? We're the only football players here."

Matteo bumped into us.

I jerked my head at him. "Take a guess."

Drew groaned. "Yep. It's time for us to go home." He focused on Marissa. "What do we do with her?"

"I have no fucking clue. I would call Nate to see if he knew where she lived, but I don't have my phone."

"Why don't you have your phone?"

"We came here straight from class. I left it at home, thinking we'd go back to the house before coming here."

He nodded, then lifted his shoulders in a shrug. "Well, she can come with us? I'll sleep on the couch. She can have my room. It's a single."

The thought of Marissa sleeping at my house didn't sit well with me, but I had no other choice. I grimaced. "All right. Let's head home." My hand curled tighter on Marissa's arm, and I yelled in her ear, "Last time. Are any of your friends here?"

A fresh wave of giggling sputtered out of her and she shook her head. "No," she said. "I don't have any friends. Not even you. You used to be my friend." She poked my chest. "We're no longer friends." The laughter subsided, and her tone turned sad. "I wish we were still friends."

Drew heard her and an alarmed look flashed over his face. "She's going to start crying. Let me take her."

I nodded, released her, and took hold of Matteo. Drew leaned close to her ear. I assumed that he was telling her who he was, even though it wouldn't have mattered. She was too drunk to care. On that note, I slapped a hand on Matteo's back. "Time to head home, buddy."

He jerked his head in a nod, leaned forward, bunched his shoulders so he looked fierce, and began to lead us out of there.

CHAPTER NINETEEN

SAMANTHA

Logan was distant during the entire week and people took notice. Heather asked what had happened. I didn't want to talk about it. He'd been right. Since Mason left, I had pulled away from him. The Threesome Fearsome was down to a Twosome Fearsome, but with different players. I'd been so worried about losing my family because of Logan's feelings for me that I'd been the one to jeopardize it. Because of that, I had kept to myself for the week.

It was Friday night, the football team had won, so of course, that meant a party. This time one of Logan's friends was throwing the party. When I pulled onto the road by the house, I parked towards the end. I didn't want to be boxed in. As I started walking towards the house, more cars passed me to park closer to the house. I glimpsed at some of the drivers and knew it was going to be a big party. Fallen Crest Academites had been invited; I recognized a few of the people. As I got to the house, I realized there were more people there than I had thought. The house was packed. There was barely any walking space. I started to wedge myself through two big guys, both with their backs to me. Suddenly, from behind me, someone shouted, "OUT OF THE WAY! KEG COMING THROUGH!"

I was pushed to the side, ramming against two people. One cried out in pain, then a growl sounded close to my ear. "You bitch! Get off me." I was shoved back. Time slowed, and I knew what was going to happen.

I turned, seeing some of Logan's friends headed right towards me. They weren't looking ahead. Their faces were straining as they pushed the keg on a dolly, and it was coming fast. People had scattered and I had a brief thought that they must've done this before. I closed my eyes. I was still in the air from being shoved back. I couldn't do anything. I was going to get hit, so I braced myself. At the last second, someone grabbed me and yanked me the other way.

A rush of air slammed into my chest, but I pressed against whoever was holding me, flattening myself as much as possible. The guys barreled past me. A litany of curses followed them. "Watch where you're fucking going!"

Someone yelled, "You almost hit someone. She would've been wiped out."

The rush of relief left me weak, and I turned to thank whoever had saved me. Natalie. Her lips were pressed tight together, the ends curved down, and a dead look was in her eyes. She shoved me away from her and shook her head. "You got your ass kicked last year. If I knew a keg could've done it, we would've saved the trouble. Honestly, Sam, you suck. You almost got laid out."

"Thank you." I blinked a couple times. I had no idea what else to say. I blurted out, "Why?"

Her mouth opened into a snarl, then she stopped. "I have no idea. I don't even like you." She lifted a fist between us. "You attacked me at the football game."

"You attacked me during a basketball game."

She paused.

I waited, and my eyes narrowed.

She shrugged. "I'm tired of fighting your ass."

My eyebrow arched at that one. "You're tired? Try being me. That's all I've done since I transferred to your school."

"Whatever. Whine about it. You're through the hazing." She started around me and threw over her shoulder, "You're one of us now, Sam. Christ. I need a beer." She shoved through the crowd, and a surreal feeling came over me.

I shook my head. I had no idea what had just happened and reminded myself why I was there. *To talk to Logan. Make things right.* So I headed off again and searched through the house. He wasn't in any of the rooms. When I was going through a screened-in porch, I glanced to the side and noticed someone huddled in a chair in the far corner. A beer was open next to him, and he had a sweatshirt on, the hood pulled up to cover his face. I stopped. I knew that guy. Taking a step closer, I asked, "Jackson?"

He turned. His hood slipped back an inch, revealing his face. The ends of his mouth were strained, and there were bags underneath his eyes.

"What are you doing there?"

He sat up. His leg had been resting on the chair across from him, but he removed it and I sat down. He cast a wary look behind me and into the house. "I forgot how much I don't like parties."

"Why'd you come?"

He flinched, picking up his beer. It was still full, but he took a little sip and grimaced after he swallowed it. "It's better than being home." He lifted a shoulder up in a shrug. "A bunch of the guys invited me and wouldn't take no for an answer, so I came. I figure I could hide until I go home in a few hours."

"Stuff with your mom?"

"Something like that." His eyes narrowed, as if a different thought came to him. He leaned forward, resting his elbows on his knees. "Hey, listen. I lied to you."

"What?"

"Yeah. Last weekend. I knew you worked there. It's why I went. I'd never been to that place before, but I didn't stalk you for a creepy reason or anything. I just wanted to talk about that night, you know, with us."

"I know."

"Your boy came up to me. He told me to stay away from you." Lifting his hands, as if surrendering, he leaned back in his chair. "I'll be honest. I'd date you, Sam. I'd do it in a heartbeat if you were single, but no shade here. I'm not trying to manipulate you or anything. No tricking. Nothing like that. I really did just want to clear the air."

"My boy?"

He gestured outside to the backyard. "Logan Kade."

"He told you to stay away from me?"

"Yeah. Look," he shook his head, "it wasn't in a bad way. He was actually nice about it, but I could tell that he wanted to rip my head off. I don't want to cause problems. I had kinda hoped we could be friends, but like I said, no problem. Since I am interested in you, he's right. I'll stay away."

Jackson was interested in me? He said he would've pursued me before, and he was saying the same thing again. There was a ball of tension in my stomach. The more he talked, the deeper it dug down. Jackson was different than Mason or Logan. He understood the shadows, how comfortable it could be there. That was a foreign concept to Mason and Logan. I sighed, rubbing a hand over my face. Jackson had been easy to talk to the night he took my virginity, and he still was. That hadn't gone away, even though I had been ripped apart with guilt over cheating on Jeff. Now he was here and a different part of me was coming back.

"Jackson, you're fine. You don't have to worry about Logan."

"Yeah?"

"Yeah." I didn't know what I meant when I said that, but Jackson was like me. If he had pursued me, I would've dated him, but I couldn't think about that. Things would've been different, maybe. I would've been with him instead of Jeff when my mom left David for James Kade. For a split second, I envisioned that year if I had been dating Jackson, then the memories of that time came back to me. Mason watching me in the kitchen. Seeing me in the dark when Logan had no clue. The day he made me a sandwich and never said a word about it. All the tension I felt around him. The night Logan went to a party, and Mason stayed home with me. Then the cabin, being with him. I hadn't been able to fight my feelings for him.

No. It wouldn't have been different. I just would've cheated on Jackson.

Jackson was watching me. He asked, "What's wrong?"

I stood and spoke softly, "When you told me last week that you were interested, a part of me had wished that you had pursued it. I was miserable with your cousin, and I hope that you would've treated me better, but hearing this, I thought about it again. I was so sad with Jeff. You would've been a break, just a brief one to take away some of that pain." My head moved in the slightest shake. "It wouldn't have lasted. I remember that year, when I moved in with Mason, and even if I had been with you, I would still have ended up with him. I love Mason so much. Being away from him is hard and Logan's right. I'm lonely. I'm hurting. I miss Mason, but nothing would've changed. No matter what path I'm on, all roads lead to him. They always will."

Jackson nodded and murmured, "I hope he realizes what he's got with you."

The corners of my lips tugged, forming a small grin. "He does. I think I'm the one who doesn't realize it sometimes."

He lifted his beer and tipped it towards me. "It was nice being considered a maybe-friend for a little while."

My grin grew. "Yeah." *Logan. Making things right.* I groaned. That was the real reason I was there. "He's outside?"

"Logan?"

I nodded.

He gestured to the backyard. "He and his friends are by the campfire, holding court."

"What do you mean?"

"Just go and see for yourself. You'll understand."

I turned for the last screen door. Pausing, as I was about to push it open, I said, "It was nice to talk to you. It was nice seeing you again."

"You too."

I pushed open the screen door, and as it shut behind me, I heard from him again, "You too, Sam."

The backyard was packed as well. Bean bags were being tossed on one side. Another group was hitting a volleyball over a badminton net and laughing when the ball wouldn't go over. The garage had its doors lifted. Light flooded out from it, illuminating the front of the garage. A basketball hoop was attached to the top and a couple of guys were holding beers in one hand, shooting a basketball with the other. People stood in groups all around, laughing, drinking, flirting, telling stories. I walked around, looking for a campfire, but it wasn't until I circled to the other side of the garage that I saw the flame. It was set back in the farthest corner of the backyard and a ring of people had formed around it, but they stood away, standing sideways so they could talk to their friends, but the closer I got, I saw they were sneaking looks at the campfire.

I realized why. Log benches were set around the fire, lined with guys, but there was no laughter coming from that group. Varying intense expressions were on all of them and no girls were there. The girls were in the groups standing away from the campfire, but still looking over at them every few minutes. An exclusive feel filled the air. It intensified the closer I got, until I was standing at the edge of the groups. I, too, couldn't look away from the guys around the campfire.

Jackson said they were holding court. I understood. Even if I didn't know Logan and saw him sitting there, I would know these guys were the top of the hierarchy. Confidence filled their shoulders, and as they spoke, it was heard in their voices as well. Even though they weren't doing anything, they commanded attention from everyone surrounding them. More than few girls casted lustful looks to them. Some of the guys standing on the outskirts shifted on their feet and glanced around. Their hands gripped their beer cans tight before shoving a hand into their pocket. They shifted again, finally striking a cocky pose to cover any insecurity they had shown.

"You want another, Kade?" A guy stood from the log he was sitting on.

People shifted, watching as he said something else to his campfire comrades, then he was joined by another guy. Both lifted their legs, stepping over their benches and moved towards the groups surrounding them. The crowd shifted, automatically letting them through. As they passed by, they didn't notice me.

In that moment, I felt like Jackson. I felt like I was in the shadows, not being seen, like I had before Mason and Logan came into my life. I felt the old loneliness settle back on my shoulders, weighing me down. A couple girls turned to me. They nudged each other, all moving so they could scan me up and down. I looked down at the ground, trying to hide a smile. The sense of anonymity was gone. It had been there for a split second, but I was recognized again. I let out a sigh. Being invisible and visible had pros and cons to it, but it didn't matter.

Stepping forward, I rolled my shoulders back and raised my chin. Being in the limelight was how Mason and Logan lived. That meant that's where I would be with them. As I moved closer, Logan's friends saw my approach. Nothing was said to each other. They all stood and left, leaving Logan alone. As I got there, he glanced up. He had been sitting with his back to everyone. He said, "I figured it was you." He gestured to the empty benches. "They wouldn't have left for anyone else."

I lifted my leg to climb over and sat next to him. My back was turned to everyone else too. "Even Kris?"

"Even Kris." His head lowered and he closed his eyes. His shoulders dropped slightly. His hand was on his leg and it turned, opening.

He was hurting.

I didn't think; my arm lifted and my hand slid into his. His hand wrapped around mine. He tightened the hold, our fingers laced together, and I squeezed.

He gave me a half-grin. "What's this for?"

"For messing up. For being self-absorbed." I bit down on my lip. "Because you're hurting and that makes me hurt too."

He closed his eyes. His head moved lower and his chest jerked up. A second later, he said, "Thank you, Sam." His voice was hoarse. He squeezed my hand back. "Thank you."

"I'm sorry."

He nodded. "I know." He lifted his arm, our hands still joined, and laid it across my shoulders. He pulled me into his side. His head bobbed down to rest on my free shoulder, his face right next to mine. He murmured, "I needed this."

"Me too."

"Mason left, and I lost him and you." His eyes moved so he was watching me from the corner of his eye. "Are you back?"

"I'm back." I nodded, grazing my cheek against his. "I promise."

"Good." His body had been tense, but as he said that word, all of it left him. He relaxed next to me, his arm sagging. It would've slipped off, but I kept my hold on his hand and tugged it back into place. We shared a grin and readjusted. I burrowed closer to his side and he propped his arm further over me, nearly blanketing me so our hands rested close to my lap. His head moved, against the top of mine, and he turned, pressing a soft kiss to my temple. He murmured, "I've missed you."

I had missed him too, more than I realized. Regret filtered through me, but Tate's words came back to me: *Logan's in love with you.* I hadn't tried to distance myself from Logan. I tried to distance myself from those words, but they came back. They were going to haunt me forever. I had to accept it.

"Sam?"

I moved an inch over so I could see him. "Yeah?"

"What's been going on with you?"

Nerves sparked up in my stomach. A feeling of doom settled in my chest, but I had to tell him something. I had to let go of one of the secrets. "You know that Jackson guy?"

"Yeah?" He tensed against me.

"I don't know if Mason ever told you, but I slept with another guy before him."

"That guy?"

"He was my first, and I never saw him again until last Friday night."

"For real?"

"Yeah."

"Oh, man." He pulled me back to his side. "I'm sorry. I should've backed off. That's why he went to see you." The corner of his mouth dipped down. "I told him to stay the fuck away from you, or I was going to find his closest female relative and bang the hell out of her."

Oh, god. Only Logan. "Well, you don't have to."

He grinned. "I wasn't quiet either. I think people heard."

"He said you were nice about it."

"I wasn't. I was an asshole."

"He's not a factor. It's nice not to regret that night, but it's over. Jackson's not going to be a part of my life." I lifted my eyes to hold his again. "You and Mason are."

"Threesome Fearsome again?"

I nodded. "Threesome Fearsome going strong."

"Damn straight." He flicked the corner of my lip, grinning at me. "I love you, little sister."

"Little?" I straightened up, moving so I could turn around and face him squarely. Our hands let go and his arm slipped down my back, resting behind me. I wrinkled my nose. "I believe I'm older than you."

He shrugged. "Age doesn't matter. It's what's in here." He touched his chest.

"Your heart?"

259

"My lungs. They're stronger than yours. I'm in better shape. That's what's important." His grin stretched from ear to ear.

"Oh, god." I punched him in the side and rolled my eyes. "But I'm older and wiser."

"Not true." Still grinning, he tugged me back and wrapped his arm around me. He moved so he was hugging me from the side. His forehead lowered to rest on my shoulder. He glanced up at me from the corner of his eye. "Thank you for telling me about Jackson."

"Yeah." I shot him a dark look. "Do not tell Mason. I want to tell him myself."

"I promise. When are you going to tell him?"

"Tonight."

"Tonight?"

I nodded. "I'm leaving after this."

He lifted his head from my shoulder. A serious expression came over his face. "You're driving there?"

"I wanted to come and make things right with you, then go to see him. I'm going to stay there for the weekend."

He nodded. "Mason trusts you. You don't need to be nervous."

I knew that. Giving him a soft smile, I lifted my hand. Forming it into a fist, I pretended to hit his chin. The corner of his mouth lifted as he held my gaze. I asked, "Are you and Kris having problems?"

A storm passed in his eyes. Hesitating, his chest lifted, and he answered, "Yes."

"I'm sorry."

"Me too." He shook his head, closed his eyes, and when they opened again, a mischievous look had replaced the sadness. Wrapping his arms around me, he stood and swept me up with him. I was tossed over his shoulder. He climbed over the bench, smacked my rear, and yelled out, "Derek! Do you have a pool?"

"No!" I started kicking. "Logan, put me down."

He started forward. The crowd moved aside for him. Smiles started to spread around the backyard. His friends had moved to the basketball court. When we got there, they noticed the change in his attitude, and just like that, like a switch had been flipped, the party atmosphere went up a notch. It was all because of Logan. He seemed to infect everyone.

As he kept laughing, I felt the reverberations through his body as he moved me around. "Huh? Huh? Want to get wet, Sam?" His head straightened, and he hollered across the backyard, "What about it, Derek? If you don't have a pool, please tell me you have a large tub."

I should've been fighting more, but I couldn't. Logan's excitement was even affecting me. I had a feeling that I'd be trying to dry off on the drive to see Mason.

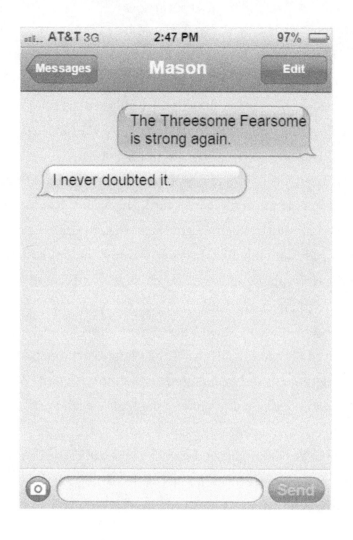

CHAPTER TWENTY

It was dark, nearing one in the morning, when I got to Mason's house. I called, but he never responded so I was relieved to see the living room lights on when I headed for the front door. Instead of ringing the doorbell, I knocked softly. Mason told me earlier they had practice in the morning, but that it was exam week too, so he didn't know if people would be sleeping or staying out to party. When the door swung open, I recognized their quarterback.

He squinted at me, rubbing the side of his face. He pulled the door so it was only a fraction of an inch open. His head poked around the frame. "Who are you?"

"I'm Samantha, Mason Kade's girlfriend. You're Drew, right? We met a few weeks ago."

At the mention of 'girlfriend', his eyes got big and he stepped back from the door. Still holding it open with a hand, he tilted his head to the side.

I flushed. He was looking at me like I was an alien. "Is there a problem? Do you have rules that I can't be here?"

"You're Kade's girlfriend?"

"You don't remember me?"

"No offense, but when his girlfriend was here, I only saw her for an hour. Mason kept her all to himself, not that I could blame him." He skimmed me up and down. "You sure you're her?"

I crossed my arms over my chest. *What'd he mean by that?* "Yes."

"Girls show up all the time and say they're so and so's girlfriend. Kade's serious about his girlfriend so if I let you in and he throws you out, don't be surprised."

"Well, I am his girlfriend and thank you?" This conversation was weird. "I don't know what to say to that."

He shrugged, stepped back, and opened the door wider. "Your funeral, lady, if you aren't who you say you are." He gestured up the stairs. "He's probably still awake. We just got back an hour ago. Second door on the right."

I stepped inside. Shooting him a dark look, I said, "It's the third door on the left."

He flashed me a grin. "Ah. So you have been here before."

"Whose door is the second on the right?"

"Mine." He was beaming. As I stepped past him, heading for the stairs, I smelled alcohol on his breath. Things were making sense. He laughed to himself, saying, "It would've been awkward if you had gone to my room." Then he shut the door, locked it, and went to the living room.

I paused, right before going upstairs. He plopped down on the couch, pulled a blanket over him, and burrowed face first into the cushions. He mumbled, "Hit the lights, would you? They're right there."

I skimmed the wall. "Where?" I saw nothing.

"Right there." His voice was becoming drowsy. "Left wall."

I glanced to the right instead and there they were. Flipping them off, I saw a small light upstairs, so I could still see. When I started up, I heard him mumble, "Thank you."

The light was off in Mason's room, and hearing loud snoring from inside, I left it off. Tiptoeing in, I went to the direction of Mason's bed and felt for the bedcovers. Before I could wake him, a hand snaked out and grabbed onto my wrist. With a cement-like hold on me, I was pushed in the direction of the hallway. Mason got up from the bed, looming large over me. He never made a sound. For a moment, my heart paused, and a chill went down my spine. Once we were in the hallway, he shut the door and pushed me against the wall, still holding onto my arm. The little light illuminated the side of his face, and I could see the fury in his eyes. His mouth was pressed in a flat line. His jaw clenched, and he rasped out, "What the fuck are you doing?"

The air was held trapped in my throat. I couldn't talk for a second, then I whispered, "Mason?"

His eyes narrowed.

I waited a beat.

His hand abruptly dropped mine, and he stepped back. "Sam?"

"Yeah." My heart slammed back into pace, pounding against my chest. "Holy shit. Who did you think I would be?"

A door opened from across the hallway. A girl stood there in a tight shirt and skirt, wiping her mouth. Her hair looked like she had just run her fingers through it. She started out to the hallway, saw us, and jerked back. Her eyes widened and her mouth dropped open. She went back into the room and slammed the door shut.

It took one second. That's all I needed before I knew who she was. Marissa. Even thinking that name was like a punch in my gut. I looked at Mason, leaned back against the wall, and crossed my arms over my chest. "What the *fuck* is Marissa doing here?"

He ran a hand over his face and cursed. "She was wasted at Cliché."

"She's not wasted now." My blood was starting to boil. "I want her gone."

He held his hands up, backing away. "I'll take care of it. Promise." Pausing in front of that door, he glanced over his shoulder.

"I'm not leaving."

"I know. I just..." A small grin appeared and he raked his gaze over my face, lingering on my lips. "I'm happy you're here."

Oh fuck. My blood went down to a simmer at the look in his eyes. I rolled my eyes. "I want her gone, Mason."

"I know. I know." He knocked on the door and braced his hand against the doorframe. As he did, his back muscles bunched together and my mouth went dry. I skimmed down his back, to his lean waist, and saw the boxers he was still wearing. They were black and molded to his ass. I wet my lips. An ache started between my legs, and I pressed them together. It'd been too long since I felt him, since he held me in his arms, since I felt his lips against my skin. I closed my eyes shut. He was getting ready to kick her out of the house, and all I wanted to do was jump him. Leaning back against the wall, I moved my hand to touch the plaster. The cool feel of it helped some reality sink in, only a tiny bit.

266

He knocked again. "Marissa?"

Waves of longing and yearning crashed down on me. I blinked, shaking my head. I heard her say through the door, "Is Sam still there?"

Wait. Here came the anger, tangling with need to feel him inside me. Mason lifted his head, looked at me, and paused. His gaze met mine, and he saw the tornado whirling in me. His eyebrows lifted, and he straightened from the wall. "You okay?"

I tried to shake my head. I couldn't talk, and my neck muscles were stiff. My chin moved just slightly. I choked out, "Leave her."

He nodded, reaching out to me. As his hand touched my arm, I shivered. His thumb rubbed over my skin, and I bit down on my lip. A groan escaped me. As it did, as I tried to swallow it, I couldn't look away from him. He was having the same reaction. As he heard my groan, his eyes darkened and he went back to watching my lips. Pulling me to him, he bent his forehead to mine, and murmured, "My roommate's in there."

I shook my head. I didn't care, and losing the will over my own body, I pressed against him. He was hard. Feeling the bulge, my eyes closed. I moved against him, pressed my hips into his, and rubbed against him.

"Sam." His voice was hoarse. "Shit. Okay." Taking my hand, we went back into his room and through it to the bathroom. Once inside, he lifted me onto the counter and shut the door. It was locked and he hit the switch so the fan turned on.

I shook my head. That wouldn't be loud enough.

Groaning, he peeled away from me and went to the shower. It was turned on at full force, and he came back to me. I watched him, my mouth open, dry, and my heart pounded. I just wanted him in me. I wanted to feel his body pressed over mine as he moved in and out.

He stood in front of me, and his eyes drank me in with a stark look of need. I swallowed and began panting. I spread my legs, beckoning him, but his gaze trailed over me, down my front, lingering on my breasts, dropping to my waist. A look of fierce concentration came over him and his chest lifted. Holding still, his hand went to my leg. He grabbed hold of me, then moved between my legs. I started to wind them around him, but he shook his head. Gazing at my lips, he said, "No." His hand lifted to my bottom lip, his eyes smoldering. He bent forward, his breath a caress over my skin as he said, "I love you so goddamn much."

Reaching up, I grabbed the back of his head. My fingers fisted chunks of his hair, and I said, "Fuck me."

A tender expression came over him, but he grinned and leaned down to touch his lips to mine. I sighed at the feel of them, just there, resting on mine. I waited, but he didn't apply pressure. I needed that pressure, so I pressed up against him. I felt Mason holding back. *Fuck that.* My other hand grabbed the front of his boxers and I yanked him to me, scooting myself forward at the same time. We were pressed so tight together, he was almost in me. He was pressing right at my opening. I grinded against him, panting into his mouth.

He was trembling. His hand was still bracing himself against the counter. I ripped my mouth away.

His eyes were trained on my lips. His other hand ran down the side of my face, sweeping over my cheek, then my throat. It trailed all the way down until it rested between my breasts. "This, Sam. This is mine. This is what you have of mine too." A look of love swept over him, filling his eyes, and he softened. I froze as that look raced through me, taking the world away. It was me and him. Right then. Right there. The emotion so damn thick in me, I murmured, "Mason."

He shook his head, his forehead resting against mine. "You, Sam. I love you. Only you. When I'm not with you, I survive. When I'm with you, I live."

"Mason." Tears were running down my face. "I love you so goddamn much too."

He nodded, touched his lips to mine again, and bent down to slide his hands underneath me. I was picked up from the counter and taken into the shower. He backed me up against the wall, still holding me upright, but it didn't matter. My legs were wound so tight around him, I wasn't going to fall. Running my hands over him, over his jaw, over his shoulders, down his chest, then back up to his face again, I opened my mouth to his. His tongue slid inside, meeting mine, and the kisses turned into a battle: who was commanding who. I growled as his tongue brushed mine, sending a heated frenzy through me.

My jeans were unzipped. His boxers were shoved down and kicked off. He took my hand, pressed it against the shower wall, and slid inside me.

I gasped, arching my back and exposing my throat. His mouth fell to lick there, and he began to move.

As he kept thrusting, I moved with him. We were moving as one, just wanting to feel the other, needing to feel the other, and right before I came, he nipped at my throat, then lifted his head back and met my gaze. We watched each other, seeing the release in our eyes. There was an explosion. A guttural groan came from him—no me. It was coming from me. Mason held me still, he wouldn't look away, as I shook in his arms. When I was done, he dropped his head back down. His lips pressed against mine, and he breathed into me. "I love you."

"I love you too."

*

After drying off, I looked up at Mason. I didn't want to talk. Love and so many other emotions were still with me, choking me, and he seemed to understand. He came to me, then bent and lifted me in the air. He carried me to his bed. As he reached to shut off the bathroom light, Matteo flipped over in his bed and mumbled from under the covers, "A shower, huh, brotha?"

Mason stiffened, but flipped the switch. The room went back to darkness and he replied, "Yeah."

"That's good...good for you." His voice trailed off and a loud snore came next.

Ducking his head to my neck, I felt him laughing and bit down on my lip so my own didn't slip out. Mason shook his head, but crossed the room to his bed. The covers were pulled back, and he set me down. I moved to one side and felt the bed dip under his weight as he sidled up behind me. A second later, he wrapped his arms around me and I closed my eyes. A deep satisfaction resounded throughout me, replacing all the anxiety and worries from before. For that moment, for that night, I knew I wouldn't have to be concerned about anything.

He brushed his lips to my neck. "I love you. Thank you for coming."

Feeling tears threatening to spill, I squeezed his arm. "I love you too."

Then we went to sleep.

When I woke up, Mason was gone and a note was left on his nightstand. **Practice, then home. Coffee downstairs. Some of the other players' girlfriends are around. They can help if you need anything. Love you. Mason**

After getting dressed, I snuck downstairs for coffee and a bottle of water, then went back up to his room. Before I went inside, I glanced over my shoulder to where she had been. The memory of Marissa came back to me and I wrinkled my nose. Mason hadn't explained what she was doing here, but I wasn't stupid. He thought that I was her when I first came in. The fact that he'd been prepared for that possibility, of her sneaking into his bed, didn't sit well with me, but today was going to be a day of other confessions. I needed to tell him about Jackson.

I wanted to groan and bang my head against his desk. I called Logan instead.

It rang three times before he picked up, "Sam?"

"Hi."

I grimaced. I had said it so stiffly, he would know something was wrong.

"What's wrong?"

And he did. I let out a sigh, closed my eyes, and rubbed at the top of my nose. "She was here last night."

"Who was?"

I didn't get a second to tell him before he exploded, "Are you fucking kidding me? Marissa? He didn't tell me that."

"Yeah." I was miserable, then the rest clicked in. "Wait? You talked to Mason already?"

"He called to ask if something had happened. We didn't talk long, but he never said anything about Marissa."

"What did he say?"

"That was it really. He called and asked, 'Did something happen? Sam's here.' My response was, 'No.' I didn't say anything about Jackson because you told me not to; although, he won't care. Then someone yelled his name and he hung up. That was the conversation."

"Oh."

"Why was she there?"

"He didn't tell me yet. We," my cheeks grew warm, "didn't get too much talking done last night."

"Oh." He laughed. "Gotta love that my sister called me because she was too busy banging my brother to get an explanation about his stalker. That's my new Twitter handle."

"Logan," I rolled my eyes, "you're not helping."

He had been laughing, but grew serious. "Oh come on, Sam. If she was there, she did something to get there. Since you're not calling all butt-hurt, and you already told me you and Mason were getting it on—if you're literally butt-hurt, I don't want to know— I'm assuming she wasn't in his bed?"

"No. Across the hall." *He thought that I'd been her.* "Should I be worried about her?"

"Worried that Mason will cheat on you? Do you really need my response? I'm warning you. It'll be sarcastic, witty, and somehow referring to your ass hurting again."

I gripped my phone tighter. "You could've just said no."

"No."

"Okay."

"You might need to worry about her doing something crazy. The girl's got something loose in her head. Mason never saw it. I think because she was so in love with him, but never tried to get anything from him. That's my theory. He didn't have a high opinion of any female at that time."

Hearing a beep, I glanced at the screen and saw a call from him. I said to Logan, "I have to go."

"Hey."

"Yeah?"

"Thanks for calling me."

"What?"

"You called me, right? That means you called me before Heather. Once you talk about something, you usually let it go. You're not like other girls and talk about it over and over again." His voice quieted. "Thank you."

He sounded so grateful that I felt another tear at my eye. I brushed it away and murmured, "I'll talk to you later."

"Eh, about that..."

I glanced at the screen and saw that Mason had ended the call. Hearing the change from Logan, I sat up slowly. Growing concerned, I asked, "What did you do?"

"Yeah. Mason and I talked about one other thing before. I didn't tell you because I wanted to know why you called."

Why did a feeling of doom settle back on my chest? "What?"

"Kris and I are coming up for dinner."

CHAPTER TWENTY-ONE

MASON

Marissa was gone by the time I was dressed and heading out. There was no note. When I went downstairs, no one remembered seeing her leave. I didn't question it. Marissa wasn't my problem, but I knew Sam would worry, so when I got back from practice, we went to my room. Matteo said he would stay at his girlfriend's again, so I knew we wouldn't be interrupted. I needed this time with Sam. I needed to make things right.

I glanced at my watch. We had an hour before meeting Logan and Kris at the restaurant.

My throat was thick as I started, "I'm sorry, Sam." I'd been so happy to see her last night that Marissa had been an afterthought, but looking at it through her point of view, I was ashamed. I should've taken Marissa to a hotel, not the house. "I need to explain why she was here in the first place. I will apologize profusely for it because I screwed up. She shouldn't have been here, and I should've been thinking about you first the entire time." I started with the facts. "She was wasted at the club. She had no phone, no purse. She wasn't answering questions. We couldn't find any of her friends, and I forgot my phone at home. I couldn't call Nate, who would've known where she lived. Drew offered his room for her and that was it. A guy was all over her. If we had left her, I'm sure she would've been raped by him. But having said all that, she should've never been brought into this house. I wasn't thinking. Drew was drunk. Matteo was twerking against everything. The car door. A street light. Our mail box. Marissa started to cry that we weren't friends. I wasn't thinking. I'm so sorry."

If I'd been her, if I had come to her house and found Quinn in the hallway, I wouldn't have handled it like her. I would've wanted to hurt him and probably would've, regardless of the circumstances. Sam was everything to me. Any guy that tried to threaten that, threaten our relationship, and I saw red. Even thinking about his past antics sent a fierce wave of anger through me. I protected Sam. That was my job, and I had failed last night.

"You thought I was her."

"I did." *Fuck.* "I couldn't tell how drunk she was, but I know she has feelings for me. It was in the back of my mind that she might've tried to sneak in. I'm really sorry, Sam. I really am. Then you came in, and I saw red. I was mad at her for you. If that makes any sense. I was mad that she would dare try to come in when she knows I'm with you, when she knows how much I love you." I grimaced, remembering how rough I had been as I grabbed her arm and pushed her into the hallway. "Are you okay? I grabbed you too hard last night."

She nodded. "I'm fine. You didn't. You were..." Her head hung down. "You were rough because you thought I was her. Thank you." She looked back up, raw emotion swimming in her eyes.

"Jeff never would've done that for me, but you do. You always take care of me."

But I hadn't. Not last night.

"She didn't look drunk when she opened the door." She looked up, searing me with the agony in her eyes. "She looked tired, but not drunk. Drew said you got in an hour before I got there. If she was that wasted, she wouldn't have sobered up that quick."

I sighed, sitting on the bed. "I know."

She shook her head, blinking for a moment, and for that brief moment I couldn't see the pain she was in. When she opened them again, it was there. It hit me like a ton of bricks. I was a part of that. I had hurt Sam. Gritting my teeth, my hands curled into fists. I hated that. I hated any pain she might endure and knowing I had contributed to it, even if it hadn't been intentional, gutted me.

She murmured, "Am I supposed to worry about her? Is she going to try something else? Logan said she's crazy."

"She was a friend to me when I didn't like the female gender. I felt like they wanted to use me, use Logan, use my dad. Marissa was a friend that showed me not all girls want to use someone for something. I haven't wanted to deal with her, with this crush she has on me, because I cared about her."

Sam frowned.

I held my hand up, seeing she was going to say something. I said softly, "I don't care about her now. I'm not friends with her. I hate thinking that last night was a set-up, that somehow she worked everything so she was brought here, but I can't rule out that possibility."

"Have you talked to her?" She looked back down at her lap. Her hand started to pick at imaginary lint on her pants. She did that when she was nervous or couldn't deal with the pain inside her.

"No." I waited a beat. "Do you want me to?" Marissa was nothing to me, but she kept popping up, and she was becoming a problem. I would do what Sam wanted. This wasn't about me or Marissa's feelings. This was about what Sam wanted me to do. It was all about how to make her my first priority, remember that she was my first priority. When she didn't answer, I prodded, "Sam?"

"I don't know what to say. I hate that she's here. I trust you, but I don't trust her." She cringed and pressed her fingers to her forehead, rubbing at a headache. "She just won't go away. Why won't she go away? I don't know what to think about last night. She came to that lunch, then she's in your hallway, and you're apologizing for not dealing with that."

Hearing the misery in her voice sealed it for me. Marissa was done. Sam would never be exposed to her again, and it was my job to make sure it didn't happen. If I had to, I would make Marissa hate me. Maybe then she'd stay away.

I knelt in front of her. My hands went to her legs, felt how stiff they were, and I cursed inside. "Hey."

She gazed down at me. Raw hurt was in there. I helped put it there. I couldn't talk for a moment, but said, "I'm sorry. I'll make sure she goes away. I promise."

The relief was evident. Her head bobbed up and down in a weak nod. A different look came across her features, and she stiffened. Her shoulders lifted, staying there. "I have to tell you something."

Logan told me about the douchebag. He gave me warning that another guy was sniffing around Sam, but that was it. As soon as Logan said that to me, I knew it was the real reason Sam was here. She hated keeping secrets, so this must've been eating away at her. I nodded. "Go ahead."

"It's about that guy I told you about, the guy who took my virginity."

My insides tensed. Even her saying that, made me want to hunt him down and punch him. I didn't know much about the guy she had lost her virginity to, but I wasn't dumb. I knew she regretted it. A part of me relaxed at the same time, though. The usual condemnation that she had whenever she had spoken about him wasn't there. I still heard the nervousness, and that made me even more wary.

Trying to sound casual, I murmured, "Yeah?"

"He's here. I mean, he's in Fallen Crest."

Fucker.

Looking back to her lap, she rushed out, "His name is Jackson; he's Jeff's cousin. I cheated on Jeff with him, once, a few months before we broke up. I never talked to him after that, but he recently moved to Fallen Crest. His parents are going through a divorce. He's going to school at FCA. He's," her tone softened, more hesitant, "he's a big football star."

"Jackson?" *What was her ex's last name?*

"Jackson Sallaway."

The name registered. "He plays tight-end? He was at Cequate High School?" Shit. He was good.

"There's nothing there."

I felt her eyes on me, and for once, I was the one not looking at her. Yeah, she was right. There wasn't anything there because if there had been, that guy would be fucked. I shook my head, cursing to myself. Even if I wanted to kick his ass, I wouldn't have. Sallaway's reputation was a good one. He was a decent guy. He didn't mess with other guys' girls, and he wasn't cocky.

I gritted my teeth. "He's good-looking? His nickname is Pretty."

She laughed, but it stopped immediately on a high-pitched tone. "Yeah."

I groaned. "That makes it worse."

"He's not you."

A hollow laugh came from me. "I'm aware. He's there and I'm here."

She stood, a determined glint in her eyes as she approached me. Her chin was set. I had to laugh. Sam was going to make me feel better. She was going to reassure me, whisper how much she loved me, and tell me how great of a guy I was. I already knew these things. I didn't need her to remind me because in the end, she'd still be leaving. He'd be there and I'd remain here. My stomach was already in knots, but I lifted my head and waited for her to stand in front of me. As she did, my hands went to her hips. Hers cupped my face and she whispered, her eyes so goddamn loving, "No one will ever be you. All roads lead to you, Mason. No one else matters because I'm always going towards you."

I nodded, feeling the graze from her fingers over my skin. "I know." I tugged her onto my lap, and as she was going to sit sideways, I lifted her and pulled her legs so she was straddling me instead. I could feel her heart racing and the tension in her body. She was trying to reassure me, but I could tell this was scaring the shit out of her.

Running my hand up her back, slipping it under her shirt, I watched her. This was one of my favorite moments, when I would touch her and could watch her reaction. Her eyelids dropped, and she relaxed. I slid my hand further up her back, slipping it under her bra, and pulling it towards her front, under her arm. Feeling her breast, it was warm and solid. I cupped it, my thumb rubbing over the nipple. As I did, Sam squirmed like she always does. Her legs surged against mine, pushing into me, and she leaned forward into my hand. Her neck tilted to the side, as if granting me access there.

I leaned forward and kissed her neck. We had thirty minutes. I was going to enjoy every minute of it and make sure Jackson Sallaway was a very distant memory for her.

*

SAMANTHA

"I don't think Mason likes me."

We were in the women's bathroom when Kris shared that with me.

Mason had made love to me before we left for the restaurant. He'd been possessive and a little rough, but I enjoyed it. Even thinking about it brought back a rush of memories. I was growing heated and ducked my head, hoping Kris hadn't witnessed my red face.

She sighed. "Oh my god. It's true, isn't it?"

I looked up. She stopped fixing her hair and turned, biting her lip and wringing her hands together. Her puppy dog-like eyes were fixed on mine, and it was obvious that her feelings were hurt. She added, "I haven't done anything wrong. I don't think. And I always say hi to him. I try to talk to him, but he just looks at me and walks away or says something to someone else, like I haven't even spoken. I have no idea what I've done wrong."

Oh boy. "Um." I had no idea what to say. Mason was an ass at times. "Have you talked to Logan about it?"

She nodded. "Yeah, but he doesn't say much. He changes the subject or leaves like Mason does." A soft groan came from her. "We've been having problems. I'm sure you've noticed. I mean, everyone has. I don't even know how to talk to Logan sometimes."

"The last girlfriend Logan had really hurt him. She came onto Mason one night, and he might be standoffish to you because he doesn't want the same thing to happen again."

Her eyes lit up with hope. "You think that's it?"

No, but I wasn't going to tell her that. If Mason had one inkling she might come onto him, he would share that tidbit with Logan immediately. The only redeeming fact I could think was that Mason wasn't being mean. He just wanted nothing to do with her.

283

I smiled at her. "It's just the four of us tonight, so see how the rest of the evening goes?"

"Yeah, you're right." She nodded to herself and turned for the door, squaring her shoulders back like she was going into battle. "Let's do this." A determined expression came over her. Her eyebrows furrowed, her lips pressed together, and she raised her chin up. She was on a mission.

As we walked back to the table, I caught a glimpse of Mason and Logan with their heads together. I could see the intensity in their expressions from across the restaurant. When we got closer, they didn't stop their conversation. Logan was saying, "I don't agree with you. We should call Nate tonight, go over there, and deal with this. I'm coming to this same school next year. I don't want to come in the middle of a battle. It's fucked up that you guys haven't squashed this."

Mason flashed him a grin and rubbed my shoulder when I sat next to him. He said to his brother, "We can't go and bomb their cars. These guys don't fight like that. The situation isn't a situation. And I will squash this with Nate, for the Marissa incident."

"That's bullshit."

Mason's eyes narrowed. "What's up your ass? You've been in a mood since you showed up."

"Nothing." Logan's scowl deepened, and he moved his chair back. "I have to go to the bathroom."

Kris spoke up, "He's mad at me. We had a fight on the way here."

Mason and I shared a look. I had no idea what to say to that.

Mason nodded. "Okay."

Her forehead wrinkled and her lips were pressed together, like she couldn't decide something. Then she nodded to herself and rested her hands on the table. She looked right at Mason. "Why don't you like me?"

Oh, shit.

Mason lounged back in his chair. His hand had been rubbing my shoulder, but stopped. "What?" He looked at me.

I told him, "She's not talking to me."

He scowled, but it was gone instantly. "Excuse me?"

Kris's throat moved up and down as she swallowed. Her hand lifted from her lap, shaking, and she laid it down on the table, spreading her fingers wide as if she could calm herself that way. "I have not done anything to you. I've been polite and even friendly, but you act as if I'm not here. I would like to know why you don't like me." She paused a beat. "Please. Is this why Logan and I are having problems? Do I need your approval to date your brother?"

"You already are dating."

"I meant for the next level, where we're more serious."

He glanced at me. I shrugged. This was on him to handle. He turned back and settled all of the weight of his gaze on her. I had been on the receiving end from one of those looks from him, before I knew he loved me. When she grasped onto the tablecloth and her hands fell into her lap with a thud, I could sympathize with her.

He said, "I can give you my honest answer, but I will warn you. You won't like it, and it will hurt your feelings." He waited before adding, "Do you still want my answer?"

"Yes." She raised that tiny chin again. "I do." I could see fear lurking in the depths of her eyes. Pain flashed in there as well, but it was moved aside, and her shoulders rolled back once again.

"I don't dislike you. I don't like you either. I'm sorry if I come across as rude. I don't intend to be, but I just don't think about you."

"What do you mean?"

"You don't matter to me."

She sucked in her breath, and the blood drained from her face.

Mason added, "Your relationship with Logan won't last. It's only a matter of time before he decides to dump you and you know that. I can see it in you. I don't know why you're kidding yourself. You're just lying to yourself and the longer you do, the more you're allowing yourself to be hurt by him."

"You have no idea—" she started, snarling at him.

He shook his head, stopping her. He softened his tone. "I'm not saying this to hurt you. I am sorry if that's what you think, but I know my brother."

She began to shake her head as tears started to fall. "You don't know this. You can't..." Her voice trailed off and doubt clouded over her face. Her head dropped until her chin tucked against her chest. From my seat at the table, I could see tears dripping onto her hands. She never brushed them away as they fell steadily.

Mason glanced at me, a small frown on his face. He said, "I know you love my brother, but he doesn't love you."

Her shoulders lifted, and she inhaled a sobbing breath.

He added, "I think you know that too."

"Excuse me," she choked out and rushed from the table.

"Kris—"

Mason grabbed my hand and held me back. "Don't."

"You broke her, Mason. Let me go after her."

"No. Let her go. It's the best thing for her."

"She's hurting—"

"Yes, she is, but if you go after her, you'll end up saying something to give her false hope, whether you mean to or not. Logan doesn't love her. You know that. I know that. Logan knows it, and she does too. Let her deal with this on her own. She'll be stronger because of it."

I sat back down. Maybe he was right.

Logan came back at that moment. He scanned the table. "Where's Kris?"

Mason never faltered. He never looked away. He spoke clearly, "She asked me why I didn't like her."

Logan froze. "You didn't. Oh, god. Mase, tell me you didn't."

"So I told her."

"Oh my god." Logan's hand flew up, and he pressed his palm to his forehead. "For real? Why? Shit, Mason. Why? That's not on you to tell her." He shook his head and raked his hand through his hair. "Look, I have to find Kris and see if I can do something to make this better."

When he rushed from the restaurant, an alien feeling settled over me. This was off; Logan's reaction wasn't normal. I turned to Mason, still stunned at what had happened. "You basically ended his relationship, and he wasn't even mad at you." I shook my head. "That's not normal. Why didn't he get mad? Why didn't he do anything?"

"He went after her."

"To make it better. That's what he said, but..." I looked towards the front of the restaurant where Logan had gone, but didn't see him. I blinked, still in shock. "Why did you answer her like that?"

We were attracting attention. There hadn't been any raised voices or angry movements, but I felt the audience growing. Head after head had turned in our direction. Mason saw them too and cursed. He gestured to the door with his head. "Can we finish this outside?"

As I followed him, a foreboding sensation grew in me. When he led me down the street, then around a corner for more privacy, almost all of me had stopped feeling. I said again, "Why did you answer her like that?"

"Because she asked me."

"Why didn't you lie to her? You knew it would hurt her."

"Because she wanted to know the truth."

It sounded so simple coming from him, but I couldn't get over the surreal feeling of this situation. "You broke them up. Why did you do that? You just caused pain for them."

His eyes narrowed, and he shook his head. He looked puzzled. "Because it's the truth, Sam. Logan doesn't love her. She knows that, and she asked me because it was time for her to hear it. You don't seek out an answer unless you actually want to hear it. She's not dumb. She knew what she was going to get when she asked."

"You hurt them, though." I couldn't get past that. A tightness had settled in my chest, burrowing deeper and deeper. "If you hadn't said anything, they'd be still together. She wouldn't have left crying. Logan wouldn't have chased after her. I mean, even if they get back together, this will still be between them."

"He doesn't love her." Mason shook his head, slowly, as he gazed at me. "Why is this bothering you so much?"

A bitter laugh gurgled up from my throat. *Why was this bothering me?* "You could've held your words and no one would've gotten hurt. That relationship is done, but if you'd just kept quiet, everything would've been fine."

"Sam." He started for me.

I moved away. My voice rose. "I mean, this is their relationship. That's his girlfriend. It's gone because of a few words from you; you destroyed them."

Tate's voice haunted me. *"Logan's in love with you."* I closed my eyes as that thought screamed in my head. *I could destroy everything. I could destroy us.*

"Sam." Mason was shaking his head as he took another step towards me. Concern flashed in his eyes. "She loves him and he doesn't return the feeling. That's not fair to her to remain in that relationship. She asked me for a reason. She wanted to know the truth, and I'm guessing that she didn't have the heart to hear it from him."

"But how do you know?"

"I've known since the beginning."

I sucked in my breath. "Have you guys talked about it? I mean, what other stuff do you talk about? How do you even have those conversations with each other?"

"I know Logan. I know when he's in love, and I know when he's using a girl for a distraction."

Oh god. My heart skipped a beat. I shook my head. This was my nightmare coming true. The real truth was right there. I felt it lingering beside us, and he was so close to it. One step and he'd stumble on it, and he'd know. I was holding my tears back. The truth would be out.

I shook my head. I couldn't lose him. I couldn't lose Logan either. "Mason," I whispered, my voice hoarse. It was there, on the tip of my tongue. But I stopped myself. I couldn't lose him.

"Sam?"

"Nothing."

His shoulders lifted in a silent breath and I turned away. His hand touched my arm, and I turned into him at the gentle touch. He pulled me in, his arm moving around me, his other smoothing back my hair, falling to cup the side of my face. His thumb moved back and forth on my cheek in a comforting motion, and he pressed a soft kiss to my forehead. His lips brushing my skin and his breath warming me, he whispered, "I love you."

I clasped onto him and I nodded. I couldn't talk.

He whispered again, "I won't push you, but I know something else is wrong, other than Sallaway. You can tell me whenever you want, but I love you. I'm not going anywhere, not unless you want me to." His chest lifted and stayed there, suspended on his last word, until I burrowed to get even closer to him. His chest fell, as if he'd been scared for a moment.

I couldn't do it. I couldn't say a word. I held on tighter to him.

Logan called when we were in Mason's Escalade. He and Kris were at the hotel, and they'd be going back tonight. Mason asked, "Is there anything we can do?"

I waited, but I never heard Logan's response. Mason put his phone away and told me, "He's not mad, but they're talking. Kris called her sister, and she demanded Kris be taken back or she was coming to get her." He gave me a halfhearted grin. "The sister sounds like a handful."

I nodded. "She doesn't like Logan."

Mason laughed, but it was halfhearted as well. The conversation was dropped after that. When we got to the house, he held my hand and led me upstairs. After changing, I slid into bed and sighed from contentment as Mason pulled me into his chest. We didn't talk. We didn't do anything. We just held each other. I remained awake, but I never moved. I wanted to savor this feeling. I never wanted it to go away.

CHAPTER TWENTY-TWO

Logan and Kris didn't break up. I didn't ask how he pulled that off, and he never told me. However, things didn't go back to normal for them. Everyone knew the happy couple was no longer the happy couple. Even the girls in cross country steered clear from asking questions about Logan, and I knew they used to love gushing about him. As the season was winding down, our coach had the girls and boys run together. Everyone was pushing themselves because of it. It was no longer a competition against each other, but a competition against ourselves. As it was, more people began running alone and without the cliques. Almost every practice ended the same, I ended first with Hayes behind me. We were getting close to the state meets, where college scouts would come to recruit. I already had a scholarship, but I wanted one to Cain University. That scout was going to be there. I qualified to run, but the entire team did as well. Our last practice was grueling. We had two days of rest, but everyone was pushing themselves to their maximum limit. When Hayes came up to me after everyone had finished and were stretching, I wasn't surprised when he asked if I would do another run with him.

We were supposed to rest, but I knew he was concerned. He hadn't gotten as much attention with scouts as I had so I nodded, and we started off again. We didn't talk. We didn't need to. If I lengthened my stride, he did too. If I picked up my pace a half second, he matched mine. He was using me to make himself better. When I realized that, I threw him and grin and really let loose. I held back during practices, but if he wanted to really get better, I was going to put him through the wringer. Switching off the normal running path, I took him to my favorite one. We sailed past Quickie's and up to the hills. By this time, I had almost every part of that path memorized; I didn't think as I avoided rocks and big branches. Hearing Hayes curse behind me, I glanced back and saw that he was on the ground.

Panting, I went back. "What's," breath, "wrong?"

"I almost tripped." He scowled at me. "Is that why you brought me here? To injure me?" He stood up and brushed dirt off his running tights. "You must really hate me. I was hoping to get recruited too."

I rolled my eyes. Six months ago his words might've stung. They bounced off me. "Chill, buddy. If you want to go against the best, you have to go where the best goes." I spread my arms out and began jogging backwards. Giving him a cocky grin, I said, "I'm the best and this is where I run my best. Get your ass up and let's go. If you can't keep up, then slow down. I didn't put those rocks there. If you don't see them, that's on you. You didn't have to follow me."

"You're arrogant."

"No." I took off, and threw over my shoulder, "I'm the best. I'm just confident." I took off and it wasn't long before I heard him behind me.

He never caught up to me, but he stayed within viewing distance. When we got back to the school, Hayes looked like a puddle of bones. I wasn't sure if he could keep standing, but to be honest, my legs were like jelly too.

There were no cars in the parking lot and no one was in the locker room, so I collected my bag and keys. Hayes had done the same. He was heading out the door as I came out. Seeing me, he held it open and fell in line with me.

"Uh." He cleared his throat.

I lifted an eyebrow, and as we got to my car first, I turned and waited.

He was so stiff. "Thank you. I know I'm an asshole. It's just pretty fucking humbling when a girl comes on the team and kicks my ass. You're good, Stratten. You're really good. Thank you for running with me."

"Are you being sentimental?"

The wind had picked up, brushing over us both. Both of us reeked and were covered in sweat; my hair never moved an inch. It stayed in its high ponytail.

He shrugged, looking away. "I hated you for half the season, but now that we're almost done, I can say that I am glad you were on the team. You made us better. The entire team wouldn't have gone to state if you hadn't pushed us."

"I did?"

"You did. Trust me, just by being you and making us eat your dust. You helped us. You helped me."

"Rest, Hayes. You're delirious from the running today." The side of my lip curved up in a grin. "You'll get a scholarship. Just pretend you're running against me."

"That might help actually."

"You're back to being an ass. The world feels right again." Opening my door, I got inside and leaned out the window, "See you tomorrow, Hayes. We had a nice moment."

He groaned, heading towards his truck.

I started the engine, and as I passed by him, I shouted, "Let's not do that again." I pulled out of the lot and headed home. When I got there, I saw Mark's and Cass' cars in the driveway. The euphoria from a great run had started to dwindle, and I knew what I'd be walking into if I went inside. I didn't want to go in there. Garrett had been calling every night. To be fair to my biological father so he couldn't be accused of keeping me away, David relayed the messages to me, but I knew I wasn't getting all of them. The pressure to see him was building up, but I didn't want to be worn down. When I asked Mason for his advice, he told me to say, 'fuck you and the horse you rode in on.' The last couple times, as David was apologizing for another message from Garrett, I finally snapped and relayed Mason's words. A big grin came over my dad, and he gave the message back. It hadn't worked. Garrett kept calling. It was by accident that I found out that David hadn't been telling me how much Garrett had been calling. They had to put the phone on silent in the evenings. That tidbit slipped out when Malinda was explaining to Mark why Cass should only call him on the landline. It hadn't made sense to me, but Mark knew instantly. He laughed and said, "Good one, Mom. I know that phone's silenced in the evening because of Sam's other dad. No, thank you. Cass will keep calling my cell phone."

He left, and I heard Malinda mutter from the stairs, "Not if I stop paying for that phone. It'll take you a year to figure out that it doesn't work anymore." She grunted. "Food for thought."

I went to the front of the house and sat on the porch swing. I didn't want to hear another message. I wasn't ready. I was still there when Helen came stomping from her house, across the street, and up our sidewalk. She was wearing a beautiful gown. It was light blue and matched her eyes perfectly. Like always, her hair was pinned up in a sleek bun. She had a hand resting on her neck, holding down the pearls so they wouldn't bounce. She wasn't looking up. She was watching where she walked and paused, one hand holding up her dress, so she wouldn't trip or tear it, as she stepped onto our stoop. As she let it drop, she lifted her head and saw me.

Her eyes widened and her head reared back an inch. "Oh, Samantha. I didn't see you there."

I lifted a hand in a careless wave. "Yep. Saw that. Sitting here." I let my hand drop back down with a thud.

Her eyes narrowed. "What's wrong with you?" she rushed out, like it was an afterthought, not really caring about the answer. She craned her head so she could look inside the house again, through the door's windows. I knew who she was looking for.

"Logan's not here."

She looked back at me. Her gaze swept me up and down. "Are you sure? You look like you were running. We both know that could take hours with you."

I said, dully, "He's on a date with Kris."

"Kris?"

I gave her a second look. "His girlfriend."

Her eyebrows lifted. "Logan has a girlfriend?"

"Good god," I muttered.

"What's she like?" Helen left the door and moved towards me. Her hand went back to holding onto her precious pearls.

I shrugged. "Peppy. Little. A cute, pixy-like girl."

She paled. The corners of her lips curved down. "She sounds dreadful. Wait. Was she over the other morning?"

I nodded.

"Gracious, I had no idea he had taken her as a girlfriend."

I gave her a sweet smile. "I think he loves her." I wanted to watch her squirm.

"He does?" She tried to hold back a shudder.

I nodded. "He asked me about home pregnancy tests last week too."

She froze, then drew to her fullest height, and rolled her eyes. "Har, har, Samantha. You're so funny. You've been spending too much time with Logan, you know. That's something he would've said." Her lips pressed together, and she let out a sigh. "What's your problem? You look like I used to during my first marriage."

"I'll take that as an insult."

She waved me off and moved so she was leaning against the post. After making sure her dress wouldn't stain, she fixed her steely gaze on me again. I had a flash of Mason staring me down before we started dating.

She lifted her hand and made a circling motion. "Okay. Get on with it. What's your problem?"

"Why do you care?"

"I don't, but my son does." She grimaced. "Both my sons care about you. So tell me. Out with it. What's going on with you?"

"You know," I mused, a sense of not giving a shit surged up in me, "any other adult and I'd want to know your angle. There's always one, but with you it's so clear cut."

Her eyes narrowed.

"You're either being honest with me," I paused and saw a deep frown come over her face, "or you're going to use this against me in the hopes that Mason will dump me or Logan will stop caring about me."

She shook her head. "No." She rolled her eyes again. "I'm a realist. I would love to take credit that I have that much pull with either of my sons, but I don't. You know that. I know that. We just need to move on with how it is."

Had she given up on Mason leaving me?

As if reading my thoughts, she waved a hand at me. "Oh, don't worry. If I see a chance, I'm jumping on it. You know I feel Mason deserves better than you, and Logan," she grimaced, and her body produced a mock tremor, "we both know how Logan is. Mason pretends to take into account what I say. I know he doesn't, but he gives me the slight respect of appearing as if he does. Logan, well, Logan is Logan. The world might be a better place if he learned how to be fake once in a while. He doesn't have the patience or time to pretend, even for his mother." She leaned forward, her lips pressed tight together. "I'm not an idiot, Samantha. Mason loves you. I know he'll never stop, and it's the same with Logan. So, again, what's your problem? I need to turn over a new leaf at some point. I might as well start now."

I had to give her points for honesty. "My dad's in town."

She was silent for a moment. "I assume, since we're on David's porch, that you're referring to your biological father. Garrett? He's in town?"

I nodded. "I know your history. I don't give a shit that he used to bone you."

She leaned back. "As you shouldn't. I'm sorry, Samantha."

I looked to her, surprised at the honesty in her tone. She gave me a tight grin in return and nodded, saying, "I mean it. I do. Garrett abandoned you when you thought you were given a new family member. I'm not completely insensitive. I'm aware who your mother is, what she has done to you, and that David seemingly abandoned you as well. Your whole world was ripped upside down, and it's being pieced back together." She closed her eyes and her hands tightened around the pearls resting against her neck. "Something similar happened to me in my life, but not to the same degree. I'm not a fool. I understand why you cling to my sons as much as you do. They were the family that replaced the one you lost."

Hell had frozen over. Helen was sympathetic to my plight. "Do I need to check your purse? You don't have a dagger to stab me with, after being so nice, do you?"

She scoffed. "Fool girl. An enemy isn't always an enemy. Sometimes, in the rare moments, we can be the greatest ally."

I continued to stare at her with my eyebrows lifted.

"You're right. Don't listen to me. I'm sympathetic because I used to love Garrett myself. I understand how his abandonment must feel." She paused and then murmured, as if talking to herself,

"I'm so sorry, though. For a child in your situation, it must be terrifying to let someone in."

A limousine slowed outside her house and pulled into her driveway. She wasn't watching so I pointed across the road. "I think your ride showed up."

All sympathy vanished and she stood from the post. Straightening her dress, she let out an annoyed sound. "Please tell Logan that I will be gone this weekend. I've been trying to talk to him all week, but he keeps leaving the room before I can get a full sentence out. It's irritating." She glanced over her shoulder, and her features softened for a moment. "I suppose I'll see if this pans out." The softness left her and she turned to me. As if remembering that I was the enemy, clear distaste flickered in the depths of her eyes. Her top lip lifted in a sneer. "Please pass along my message to my son." She left, sweeping her dress up and hurrying down the sidewalk and road in record time for someone in heels as high as hers. She moved past the gate leading to her house so I couldn't see who got out of the car, but I heard a low murmur of conversation. It was only a moment before the car door shut and the limousine's brake lights turned on. It reversed and headed off.

It was the next morning when I relayed the message.

Logan met me on the street as I headed outside with Mark. He gestured to me. "Ride with me. You don't have practice today, right?"

I shook my head. "Nope, but I have a shift at Manny's."

"You can take the car for your shift, and I'll make Derek drive me there after practice."

"Okay." I headed over and waved to Mark. "See you later."

Instead of answering me, Mark went to the driver's side of his car and opened the door. He didn't get inside, he just stood there. After another moment, he glanced back, and stuck his butt out a little more. Logan winked at me, then went and smacked him on the ass. The two laughed, but didn't say anything. When Logan got inside his Escalade, I shook my head. "You two are very weird. Do I need to be worried you might be my future brother-in-law? Or future stepbrother-in-law? Whatever. That's so messed up."

Pulling out to the street, he leaned out his window and gave Mark the middle finger. Mark's car had pulled away, going the opposite direction, but a second later, we saw him stick his middle finger up as well. He held it high as he went up a hill and over.

I was done trying to figure them out.

Logan flashed me a grin. "I love your other future stepbrother."

"I'm sure you do."

He laughed and yawned. "Are you nervous?"

"For?"

"Sam."

I sighed. "Yeah." The state meet was in two days. In two mornings, I would be driving there instead of school. I wanted to throw up.

"I'm going."

"What?"

"I want to be there. It's a big deal, right?"

"I mean, I already have a scholarship. I have a back-up if I don't get one from Cain."

"Yeah, but the Cain U scout is going to be there." He'd been laughing seconds ago. Now he was so serious. "That's a big deal, Sam. Why are you downplaying it?"

My stomach decided it didn't like my breakfast. I pressed a hand there, trying to soothe my nerves. "Because if I don't get it, I don't know what I'm going to do." The Escalade rolled to a stop at a light, and I looked over. Logan met my gaze. His seriousness wasn't faked. It was real. He was thinking about me, worried about me, and I could see the support from him. He was right there, seeing how scared I was. I murmured, "I have to get a scholarship to go there. If I don't..."

"You will." He reached over and took my hand. The light turned green and we started forward. Logan squeezed my hand. "I'll be there for the whole thing. Whatever you need, you tell me. I'll be your running bitch. I'll give you a radio and you can call me any moment. I'll come running. I'll do whatever. If you want an inspirational poem, call me Logan Angelou. If you want music to warm you up, I'm the new Beastie Boy. Whatever you want."

"Thanks Logan." The ball of tension was still there, but I had to admit it had lessened by the time we got to school. It wasn't until then that he let go of my hand.

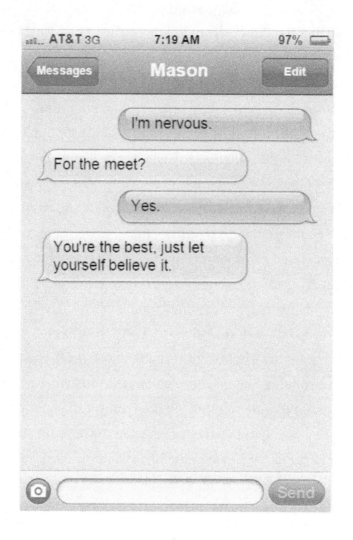

CHAPTER TWENTY-THREE

MASON

The conversation with Nate had been put off long enough, so I headed to his fraternity house. I knew it might end ugly, but I was done with being patient. We had made a deal going into college. I was about football and school. He was about networking and branching out. That was fine with me as long as he didn't assume I would go along for the ride. I was tired of social drama. I was tired of fighting. I was tired of worrying about my girlfriend getting hurt. My intention with college was to keep my head down and to keep moving forward. Then he fucked it up. He wanted me to be friends with his friends. No. That wasn't the deal. After he brought Marissa to that lunch, I knew it was Nate's way of giving me the middle finger. He declared his side in that one move, and it wasn't with me.

The street was full of cars when I got to the house. As I found a spot and headed towards the house, I heard cheering from the backyard. Rounding the side of the house, I saw a large crowd had formed behind it.

A loud horn sounded and the crowd erupted in cheers. They flung their fists in the air. A few guys dumped their cups over their head, drenching themselves in beer. They let out a primal sounding cry as they shook their heads in a frenzy.

"Ladies...and the rest of you ladies," a voice boomed through a microphone, "we are here for the Rival Revelry Rally because we are going to what?"

The arms shot up in the air again and a collective sound went out, "Revel!"

"That's right, folks and Greek brothers! We may be in rival houses, but under the system, under the national blanket of our fellow houses, we are all brothers at heart. Am I right?"

I started through the crowd. As I did, I could see a guy standing on a platform set above the crowd. With his last question, he held the microphone to the crowd, and they yelled back, "No!"

He brought the microphone back and asked again, smirking, "What was that?"

"No. No. No," the crowd chanted.

"No what?"

"No to brothers!" The crowd yelled out their responses at different moments, but the guy next to me grumbled, "I'm not saying I'm a brother to those Alpha Omega's. No fucking way. Is Dusty nuts?"

His friend elbowed him in the side. "Just go with him. You know he's leading to something big."

"No way."

Dusty gripped the microphone, bringing to his mouth once again. "All right, ladies and gents. If you're not Greek brothers at heart, then what are you?"

"RIVALS!"

The sound was loud and yelled with such force, the air switched. It'd been light and fun, but a deeper feeling came over the group. It was intense. When I glimpsed the fierce determination in a couple of the guys' faces, I knew there was a history between Nate's fraternity and this other one.

"YOU'RE RIGHT! WE'RE RIVALS AND WE'RE GOING TO REVEL AND WE'RE GOING TO RALLY TONIGHT. AREN'T WE?" Dusty shouted into his microphone.

"HELL YEAH, WE ARE!"

A chant started, "RIVAL. REVEL. RALLY. RIVAL. REVEL. RALLY." It kept going, but I ignored it, skimming the crowd. I saw Nate on the back porch and started for him.

"AND GO! FIGHT, YOU MOTHERFUCKERS!" A whistle sounded, and the cheering intensified. People began pounding their feet. I turned back, startled at the ferocity that had come over everyone, and saw two guys had started to circle each other below the platform. One threw a punch and the other countered.

The two houses kept going crazy.

They were having their own boxing match. Stepping around the last group, I covered the two steps to the patio. Nate had seen me. He was standing in a corner, tucked in the back with his brothers. He made no move to meet me. With lawn chairs between us, a couch, plus his friends, I couldn't get any closer. I lifted my hands up in a questioning gesture. His chest lifted, fell back down, and a reluctant expression came over him. He said something to the guy closest to him. They moved and he was able to get out to me. As he did, I stepped back. We didn't say a word as he led the way inside. We didn't go to a room. He went to the front of the house. After the door shut behind us, a loud cry came from the back of the house.

I grinned. "You guys volunteer to go in the ring?"

Nate rolled his eyes, shaking his head. "No. It depends on the match. This one went to the best fighter in the house. When we fight each other, you're picked if you lose at a different competition. All part of hazing."

He sat on a chair, and I leaned against the railing. "You guys are still hazing?"

"Yep. It's pretty much all year."

"I see." I didn't ask how it had been for him. There were red marks on his neck. A couple bruises had appeared over his cheek, and his eye was swollen. I ran a hand over my hair and gestured to his. "They made you cut your hair?"

"Yeah." He grimaced.

It was short, almost as short as mine. Nate kept his black hair longer than mine, enough so he could spike it when he wanted the badass look. From his reaction, I was guessing the haircut hadn't been his choice.

"Look, I'm sorry I brought Marissa to the lunch," he said abruptly. Kicking out his leg, he rested it on the railing a few feet from me. His chin lowered to his chest, and he looked straight ahead. The corners of mouth were strained. "I fucked up. Again. I was pissed at you about Park. I like him. He's a big fucking deal with my fraternity, and this is important to me."

"What's important to you?"

"This." He gestured around him. "All of this and you're fucking with it."

"How?"

"Because." His feet kicked off the railing and he jerked forward. His elbows slammed down onto his knees, but he still didn't look at me. "You just are. I mean, would it kill you to be friends with Park? He's not a bad guy."

"To you."

"What?" A wary look filtered over his features.

"He's not a bad guy to you."

"What does that mean?"

"He doesn't give a shit about me. He gives a shit about what I can give him. I'm not stupid. He was good friends with a teammate last year. That teammate got injured and couldn't play on the team anymore. Guess what happened?"

Nate shook his head. "No. No way. Park said he had nothing to do with it. He said it was preposterous that the guy even came to him." He looked up, a cloud of denial and disbelief hanging over him. "Park's got connections, but for him to expect him to do that? He's not god. He can't work miracles."

"The scholarship was given to him by Park's dad."

As I said that, I waited. Nate's eyes narrowed, but he started shaking his head. "No. No way. I mean, that's an ass move."

"Exactly."

He stood slowly, his eyebrows bunched together, but he kept shaking his head. "I can't believe that. I mean, why wouldn't he help them? That just makes Park look like an ass. There's more to it. There's gotta be."

Did it matter? I shook my head. "I'm not here to convince you the guy is an asshole. I'm here to tell you that I don't have to be friends with him. I told you that to give you a clue that this guy doesn't walk on gold-rimmed clouds. He's just a guy and you're here, pissed at me, your best friend, because I'm not friends with him. Since when do we hold each other to friendship contracts? You've never had to be friends with mine. Shit. Half the time you and Logan don't get along. I'm not forcing my brother down your throat. That's on you. If you don't like him, you don't like him."

He was still fighting what I was saying. A small amount of irritation built in me. I didn't need to plead my case. Nate was breaking the deal we made. I was pleading my side as a consideration to him, to our friendship, but this was beginning to piss me off. My eyes narrowed.

"Fuck it." I stood from the railing. "I don't have to be friends with your friends. That's the bottom fucking line. If that's an issue with you, we're done as friends. I won't be controlled and manipulated. It's an insult every goddamn time your buddy tries to manipulate me. I've held back. I've held back a lot, but if he keeps it up, that's it. My time of not fighting is over. It'll be game on after that."

Nate's lips curved up in a snarl. "Why are you like this? Why can't you just be friends—"

"Because I won't be fucking used or controlled." I got in his face, stepping close. "I had enough of that crap growing up with my parents. No more. After my dad screwed our family, I vowed to be done with these games. Park," I tapped the side of Nate's head, "got in there. This isn't you. You kept screwing Parker when I wanted a freeze-out. I didn't push, and that was for someone's safety. That was agreed upon by all the guys, but you broke it. Even then I never gave you this fucking ultimatum."

"No, Mason." Nate backed up. He kept shaking his head. The cloud of denial was a fully enclosed wall. It slammed down between us, and when he took another step back, I knew I couldn't break through it. He was gone. Park Seba*ss*tian had taken my best friend from me. "This is insane. I'm just asking you to be friendly with him. That's all."

My jaw clenched, and I felt as if a nerve had been hit one too many times. "If that's all you think it is, he's brainwashed you a lot more than I realized." It was pointless trying to talk to him. I needed to move onto the second matter at hand. "What's up with you and Marissa?"

"What?"

"Marissa. What are you doing with her?"

"Nothing. Why?" He had a hand on the side of his face, as if he was still pondering something, but it fell back down to his side. His head straightened and he focused on me more clearly. "Don't tell me you're interested in her."

"No, but she's causing problems for me and Sam. I don't want to deal with her again. Keep her away from me."

A spark of anger lit up his face, and his mouth tightened. "So you're giving me orders? I thought that's what you said Park was doing. He can't, but you can?"

My eyes were almost slits. The ball of anger spread, moving up from my stomach. It was in my chest, but it was still rising. "I know you're friendly with her. You took her as a date to that dinner. I don't know what her agenda is with me, but I know she's got one. *If* you see her," I emphasized that word, "tell her to stay away from me. It's never going to happen. The sooner she accepts that, the sooner she can move on and maybe fuck you."

My own anger mirrored his features. His eyes snapped to attention and his shoulders shifted back, readying for a fight. Nate moved closer to me this time. "Excuse me?" He lowered his voice.

So did I. "You heard me."

I was waiting. The crowd was cheering from the backyard, but we were about to have our own fight in the front. There was no announcer, no microphone, no audience for us. Nate had gone into that world where he needed those things. Attention. Power. Control. That's what he wanted. I didn't need any of it. His eyes shifted to the left and I knew he was going to throw a punch.

His arm lifted. So did mine. I blocked his right arm with my left, then reared back with my own right and let it go. My fist slammed into his face. It happened, as if in slow motion. We were standing so close together. Neither of us stepped back, but as I made contact with his face, I could see his skin rippling from the force of my hit.

He dropped. His body went to the ground, and at that same moment, another burst of cheers went up from behind the house. I knelt, checked to make sure he was breathing. He was. I'd only knocked him out. I turned, stepped over him, and left.

Now I knew. That friendship was over.

Fucking hell.

*

SAMANTHA

It was morning.

Every tendon in my body was stretched tight. I had perpetual butterflies in my stomach. It felt like they were on speed, whipping back and forth. When the first gun sounded, it was our alert to head for the starting lines. As I did, my legs were almost numb. I couldn't feel them, just the nerves inside me. I looked to the sidelines.

David, Malinda, Mark, Logan, and Heather all waved back at me. Mason had a game that afternoon. He couldn't make it, but he had called last night and this morning. There'd been ten text messages from him the last time I checked my phone. All were filled with good lucks and reassurance that everything would work out no matter what. It was easy for him to say; he was already at Cain University.

I was being irrational. He was there. I wasn't. I needed to get there. It was on me. This was my job.

People were yelling out good luck to me. I heard my name being cheered, but it all faded. My eyes were trained on the referee holding his hand in the air. I waited. Everyone waited, and the more I focused on him, the more my nerves faded away.

The horn sounded, and he dropped his arm in a dramatic motion.

We were off.

The front of the group started off. I had been placed in the middle. It never took long for the groups to scatter. I waited again. Because of the press from the other runners, I couldn't start out at my normal pace. I was itching to go, though. It was taking everything in me to keep from veering to the edge of the crowd and putting distance between me and them, but some girls spread out, and it took only a few more paces before I was able to stretch my legs.

I could see the front runners. They were going hard, but this meet meant everything to some of us. It meant my future.

"Don't hold back, Strattan." My coach had pulled me aside when everyone left the bus earlier.

I'd been confused. "What are you talking about?"

Eric Hayes got off the bus, followed by two more guys. They all glanced at us as they went, but Coach waited until they were out of hearing distance. He lowered his voice, "I know you, Strattan. You hold back automatically. Don't. Not here. You go as hard as you can. Most girls might lose their momentum in the second half, some don't. Some go faster the last half, but you go strong the whole time. I know you run on your own still."

"Only sometimes."

"It doesn't matter. I've known. This is your run. Run today as if you'll never run again. You got it? You can take state. You could even go to nationals. Run your ass off. That's all I'm telling you." He pointed to my head. "Turn that off and just go."

"Okay." I could do this. "I will, Coach."

"Good." He clapped me on the shoulder. "Do what you need to do. I'll see you at the finish line."

With that said, I set my internal speedometer to full force. Once I did this, I knew this was how I would go the whole way. I didn't pay attention to who I was passing. I didn't look to the sides as people were lining up ahead, trying to keep up with me. It wasn't long until I realized I was alone. Either I was in first or the girls who *were* in first were too far ahead of me.

I wasn't running against them. I was running against myself.

The first marker was set up. I soared past it. The second had a small group of people. My eyes were focused, but I caught movement from the corner of my eye. They were waving their arms. I heard the yelling, but it was muffled. I rounded for the third. This time, a larger group was there. Someone was running to get there, to be there when I went past it.

"Sam!"

That was Logan. A small tear came to me, but it flew off my cheek. I kept going.

The fourth marker had more people.

The fifth doubled in size.

The sixth and seventh were the same. As I flew past, I realized they were there for me. I heard my name clear as day, but it didn't slow me down. I didn't let it distract me.

I remembered Mason's last text as I cleared a hill and started down it: **Run your ass off. Run to me. All roads, Sam. I'll be there.**

I had one more marker. A referee was supposed to be at each one of them, but I didn't remember seeing him. I wasn't seeing anyone. The finish line wasn't far and I wasn't tired yet. My legs stretched wider. I envisioned everything in my mind. My heels dug into the ground. My muscles bunched, pulling me forward with my momentum, and my toes went next. I pushed off from them, sending myself forward into another sprint. Over and over again. I could go faster. I saw the end and the large crowd that had formed, waiting on me.

I soared over it and my head went back. My chest was gasping. That had been the fastest run of my life. I wanted to keep going, but I forced myself to stop. As I did, people ran at me.

"Sam!"

That was Logan. I turned to him, a wide smile on my face, and saw Mason instead. He was standing in the middle of the crowd, a proud look on his face. I registered that he was wearing Cain U athletic clothes, a warm-up jacket and pants. They hugged his form, accentuating his muscular build and lean waist. His pants rode low on his hips. He looked good enough to jump. I met his gaze. I couldn't look away. His eyes were lit up with love.

I didn't think. I leapt for him. My legs wrapped around his waist, and I clung to him as my arms went around his neck. I didn't think he would be there and he was. I wasn't going to question it. I was just going to revel in it.

"Okay. Where's the sharing means you're caring?" Logan held his arms out. "I'm right here. I care too."

Mason started to let me go, but I clung tighter to him, pressing my face into the crook of his neck and shoulder. He wrapped his arms around me once more, and his hand splayed out over my back as he rocked me back and forth. For a moment, just one more moment, it was only him and me. I breathed him in, remembering what it had felt like as he pressed me down on the bed. With him inside me, holding me, kissing me.

He was home.

"Logan." He cleared his throat. "Standing right here. The two love-tweeties can get alone time later. Still wanting to share some caring here."

Laughing, I lifted my head.

Logan patted his chest and spread his arms wider. "Sam, you just kicked major record ass today. I'm still willing to be your bitch, but I want a hug."

Before I could unwind my legs from Mason's waist, I was transferred from him to Logan. "Oh!" My legs dropped to the ground and Logan lifted me back up. His arms were tight around my back as he whirled me in a circle. When he set me back down, he leaned back and grinned down at me. A stupid happy look was on his face and he shook his head. "I'm so fucking proud of you. You have no idea."

"We all are." Malinda was next. She pulled me in for a hug. Then David. Heather. Mark was last, and it was an awkward hug. There was no body contact. His arms lifted up and around me, then he patted me on the back and moved away as soon as it was done. From a safe distance, he nodded. "You did really good."

I laughed. I had to. "They're not going to hurt you for hugging me." I pointed to Mason and Logan, and realized Logan was gone. "Logan?"

Mason was looking past my shoulder, and I turned to follow his gaze. He was greeting Kris, who looked ready to fall down. Her hair was soaked with sweat. After he hugged and kissed her, he handed her a water bottle.

"Uh." Mason stepped forward. He sent an apologetic smile to Malinda and David, his gaze sweeping over everyone as he touched my elbow. Applying pressure, he guided me away from the group again. "I have to head back right away."

"That's right. You play today, don't you?"

He nodded. "I do. It was nice seeing everyone."

Malinda held her arms out and shook her head. "Oh no, you big muscular football hottie. Get that tight ass over here. I am the mama bear and I want a hug. I don't get to see you that much anymore." Instead of waiting for Mason, she lifted his arms and wrapped hers around him. They were standing close so I heard her whisper, "David's relieved you're not going to be around for Christmas break, you know with the slumber parties, but not me." She moved back, brushed a tear away, and cupped the side of his face. "You're just so handsome. I miss you, and I know Sam does too. Everyday."

Mason's gaze met mine. I let him see the truth in her words. Having him there made everything right.

Seeing the look, Malinda made a crooning sound. Her other hand lifted to cup the side of my face. She was holding us in the palm of her hands, looking back and forth between us. "You two will go the distance. I just know it. Neither of you need to worry. True love always survives. It's supposed to." She patted us both on the cheek and groaned. "I just love you both so much, and on that note, I will step back. You two love-tweeties, as Logan called you, need some time alone. It was so nice seeing you again, Mason. I'll invest in a teleporting machine. I think everyone would be happier with that invention."

He laughed. "Yeah, that would be nice."

"Okay." She turned, waving as she did. "Love you and drive safe."

"Malinda," David called, "leave them be."

"Mom," Mark groaned.

I glanced to Heather who was waiting beside Mark. She gave me a two finger salute. I wasn't sure what that meant, but assumed it wasn't bad as she watched Logan and Kris. A small smirk was starting to form on her face when I looked back to Mason.

He was waiting for me. He sighed and pulled me close for another hug. He had to go. That's what he was saying. When his chest tightened and he lifted his head, I knew he was going to say something. I shook my head. No talking. Not now. Just us. That's all I wanted.

But when he pulled back and dropped a soft kiss to my lips, it wasn't enough. It was never enough. As he headed for his car, the feeling of victory dimmed a little bit.

"Sam!"

I turned and hugged the rest of my teammates as they came over the finish line.

CHAPTER TWENTY-FOUR

MASON

I was heading for the locker room when a guy passed me. A second later, I heard, "Kade?"

Turning around, I asked, "Yeah?"

He was wearing a Cain U athletic jacket, so he was on staff. I glanced to the clipboard in his hands, but couldn't place him. He was my height, over six feet, with a trim build and tan complexion. A whistle hung from around his neck. He was probably in his forties, his dark hair was combed to the side with grey on the sides. He pointed at me, a phone cupped into his palm. "Mason Kade. Wide receiver on the football team."

"Yes, sir."

He patted his chest, still holding his phone. "I'm Douglas Montgomery. I just got off the phone with a buddy of mine. He's at the state cross country meet, and he mentioned that he could've sworn he just saw you there."

"Yes, sir. I was there."

"That's an hour away."

I nodded. I was aware because I was late getting into my uniform. The buzz from the stadium was loud and parking had been a nightmare. It was the first game of playoffs. Everyone was ramped up more than normal and this guy, whoever he was, was going to make me even more late. "Yes, sir. My girlfriend ran today. I wanted to be there for her."

"Your girlfriend?" He eyes narrowed and he tilted his head to the side. His hand lifted, rubbing his chin. "You're from Fallen Crest, right? My buddy was going to watch a girl from there. Which one was your girlfriend?"

Hearing his question, I was filled with pride. I tried to hold back a smile, but I couldn't. I said, "The one that won."

"Really?"

"Yes, sir."

"WHERE THE FUCK IS KADE?!"

Hearing my coach, I gestured behind me. "I need to go or I won't be seeing any playing time. It was nice meeting you."

"Yeah, yeah." A keen look came over him and he held his hand out. "It was nice meeting you." After shaking hands, he patted me on the shoulder. "You're going to go far. I can tell. Maybe your girl too. How about that, huh?"

"KADE HAS THIRTY SECONDS TO GET HIS BEE-HIND IN THIS LOCKER ROOM—"

"I'm sorry, but I really have to go." And with that abrupt statement, I sprinted and crashed through the locker room door. Once inside, I ducked my head down and ran through the team. They had already formed a circle in the middle of the room, all in uniform, all raring to go. Even though I just got there, I felt the nervous excitement from the guys. "I'm here. I'm here. Sorry, Coach."

"Get your gear on, and you will be giving me a damned good excuse why you're late."

I nodded. He meant after the game. He had already taken his spot in the middle of the room with his coach's jacket on and his whistle in hand. He never used it, but he liked to swing it around for his speeches. I caught the look in his eyes. He was primed and ready to go.

As I dropped my bag and started changing, Drew patted me on the back. He leaned in close and whispered, "Did she win?"

I nodded, not saying a word. Coach was still watching me. Matteo started to lean in close, from the other side, but Coach pointed at him. "Swallow your words, Robards."

Matteo scooted away. "Swallowing, Coach."

"This is team time." As he said those last two words, he pointed at the floor. His hand moved up and down in an abrupt motion. "Team. Time. Not social time. Not time to ask how his girlfriend did. Team. Time. My time. Mine."

He swept his gaze around the room, waiting, watching. That one gesture changed the feel of the room. There'd been nerves, some jokes, but as our coach lifted his chin, everything settled in the room. As he started his speech, I finished getting my uniform on and slowly sat down between Drew and Matteo.

"Gentlemen," he looked at each person, holding their gazes for a beat before moving onto the next person, "this is the first game of the playoffs. This is the game that when we go out there, we either win or we lose. If we win, we keep going. You keep doing your jobs. If you lose, we're done for the season." He shook his head, taking off his hat. As he did, he rubbed a hand over his hair before putting the hat back into place. "For the veteran players, you know how I get during playoffs. I don't believe this is the last game. It's the next game. It's the next win. We keep going. We always keep going. Sometimes we go all the way and sometimes we don't. That's fine. You can go home, rest, and enjoy the off season. You've had a good season so far, but the playoffs..." His voice was soft, but everyone could hear him. Everyone was so still. "The playoffs is where we make our season great. That's my job. My job is to keep you going, to remind you how great we can be as a team, that there's a reason our stadium fills up every game." He pointed out the door. "Do you hear that?" He paused and the buzz from the crowd filtered into the room. "That's our fans. Those are your fans. We love them. We're grateful to them, but we're not here for them. You're here for you. We aren't playing against the other team. We're playing against ourselves. Each game, to do better. Be better. Each game, play as if we're six down, thirty yards to go, and we're at fourth down. It's the next play that'll make or break the game for you. Fourth down. That's our mindset. Every play, we go hard. Every play, you strive to be perfect. Every play is fourth down. You got that?"

No one said a word. No one looked around. We were all focused on him.

"How are we playing?" he asked us.

As one, we answered, "Fourth Down?"

"How?" he raised his voice.

"Fourth Down!"

"HOW?" He cupped the backs of his ears. "I WANT TO FUCKING HEAR YOU!"

The other coaches waved their arms in the air. "Stand up!"

"Get to your feet!"

We stood. The ones who were kneeling clambered up and as we did, Coach jumped up on a chair. He yelled, his hands around his mouth, "HOW ARE WE PLAYING?"

"FOURTH DOWN!"

"HOW?"

"FOURTH DOWN!"

"I WANT TO HEAR YOU SAY IT ONE MORE TIME!" He jumped off the chair and the assistant coaches started clapping their hands. They started to chant, "Fourth Down. Fourth Down. Fourth Down."

Matteo was intense. He was waiting next to me, cheering with the group, but he was watching our coach. When he nodded at Matteo, it started. Matteo jumped into the middle of the circle and started bobbing up and down. They were still chanting Fourth down, but it was going to change. Any second. The adrenalin was coursing through me. In this moment, we were one. We were going out there. We were going to conquer, and Coach was right. It was us against ourselves. To be better. To be the best. To be perfect. Every single word he said resonated through me. It resonated through all of us. We were proud to be at Cain U. We were going to keep being proud. Matteo tipped his head back and let out a battle cry.

Everyone started banging their helmets against the lockers. Those in the middle stomped their feet and Matteo started the next chant.

"Cain U. Cain U. Cain U."

We kept going, kept banging our helmets, but there was another section. Drew would lead us out and we would keep chanting as we ran out of the locker room and onto the field. We were just waiting. It would be any moment. The longer he waited, the higher our adrenalin grew.

He stepped forward. He was the signal. Everyone turned. We fell in line, single file, and started from the locker room. He led us out, taking over as the leader for the chant. Matteo fell in line behind me. We stopped banging our helmets. Instead, they were held at the waist by both hands. Our heads went down and our shoulders hunched forward. It was a sign of respect to those who followed Cain U's traditions. We entered the stadium like this every time, like gladiators going out to fight. As we jogged out like that, each assistant patted us on the shoulder, giving us their approval.

We ran down the hallway, our feet a constant clattering sound against the floor, echoing around us. We could hear the crowd in the stadium. Music, cheering, announcements. We kept chanting the whole time. It was this moment that I savored the most, when the crowd heard us coming. As they did, the volume dipped for one second. There was a slight pause and a cheer erupted. They started cheering with us and it would spread through the entire stadium.

Cain U.

Cain U.

Cain U.

Drew paused at the threshold. He held his helmet up and started ahead. We didn't jog. We ran out. The crowd stood and waited with their hands lifted. Drew waited on the field, and still in single file, we ran around him to form a circle. His helmet was still in the air. Then he brought it down and we finished the chant. Everyone did.

"Cain U, conquers you!"

After that, it was time to play football.

*

SAMANTHA

The state meet was a two hour drive from Fallen Crest. With most away meets, we traveled together on a bus and were allowed to get a ride home with family afterwards. But since this was the last meet, Coach wanted everyone to travel back together on the bus. We were a team on the way there. He wanted us to keep that unity on the way home, at least for this last time. After showering and changing, everyone agreed to a celebratory pizza stop.

I was in the back of the bus with my headphones on as we headed to the pizza place. Logan had texted earlier. He was going to meet us there, but I knew Malinda, David, and Mark had gone home. Mark needed to get back for some reason, but Malinda made sure that it was okay with me if they skipped the pizza stop. I was fine with it. I had to admit that I was still glowing from the win, the medal that was hanging around my neck, and the talk a Cain U scout had with me. He wanted to talk later in the month about a scholarship. When he found out that I ran track too, the talk was scheduled for the next week. All of those things, plus seeing Mason there and knowing Logan was waiting to eat with us, I was on cloud nine.

"Kris! Woman! My god."

Hearing that shriek, I lifted my gaze. Kris was three seats up and bent over, whispering to one her friends. Judging from the wide eyes, sly smile, and red face on both of them, I wondered what they were talking about, but I saw the giddiness on Kris' face. She seemed happy. In fact, the entire team was in a good mood. A few runners hadn't placed, but as a whole, the entire team got medals.

"Shut up," Kris laughed, hitting her friend on the arm. "Shh." Before bending back down, she shot me a look. Our gazes collided and the laughter stopped abruptly. Guilt flashed in her eyes, then she looked away and jerked her head down again.

I hadn't asked Logan about their relationship. They were still having problems, which magnified after it came out that he didn't love her, but Logan had been spending a lot of his time with her. Or, at least, I had assumed. He wasn't home and he wasn't at my house. I couldn't stop myself. I was happy. I wanted to make sure Logan was happy too, so I took my phone out and sent him a text.

What's going on with you and Kris?

There was a slight pause, and my phone buzzed back. **Still screwing. Why?**

Snorting, I rolled my eyes. **Are you guys still good?**

You never ask. Why now?

I'm worried.

Why? Something I should know?

Why are you not answering the question?

328

Why don't you tell me when you and Mason have problems?

I groaned, but he was right. **Sorry. Just concerned.**

I'm at the pizza place. We can talk later.

I frowned. **Okay...**

There was another long pause. I wasn't sure how to take his last text. If they'd been better, he would've said they were humping like rabbits. He didn't say that. My phone buzzed once again. **Let's just talk later. You sure you have to ride home on that bus?**

Coach said I did.

What if you missed the bus after eating?

That never happens.

I'll pay someone to say you're there.

Laughing, I shrugged. **Sounds fine with me.**

Awesome. Okay. I just ordered pizza for you guys. Tell the coach. You guys have a private room in the basement.

Thanks. I will. I put my phone away just as the bus pulled into the parking lot. As soon as everyone had gotten off, I relayed Logan's message to the coach, who nodded and asked, "Did he already pay—never mind. I'm going in there to pay before that kid does. Don't have these problems with normal kids."

I didn't know what he meant by that. When I went inside, the front lobby was full. Everyone was waiting around so I slipped to the side and headed for the bathroom. When I was in there, the door opened again and Kris' friend from the bus was giggling. She shrieked, "He's here, Kris! What are you going to do?"

The sink was turned on, but I heard Kris respond, "So is Logan. It's awkward."

I'd been about to flush, but I caught myself. Pulling my hand away, I held still. I was in the back stall so they couldn't see my feet unless they looked.

"Wait." Kris abruptly turned the water off. "Are we alone?"

"Yeah, yeah." Her friend yawned. "No one else came in here. We're good. So," her voice rose from excitement, "what are you going to do?"

Kris sighed. "I have no idea. I always get myself in these situations."

"You've been spending almost every night with the guy. Isn't that what you said? He's always at your house?"

"He is, but we're studying. Nothing's been going on. I'm still with Logan."

Her friend snorted. "Logan Kade who doesn't love you. I mean, my god, Kris. Mason Kade is the one who broke that bubble for you. Wait. Let me swoon here for moment. Fucking hell. Mason told you that. That's like real and intense. I'd die to have him talk to me like that. Just to be that close. He was always so standoffish and exclusive, you know. He'd only talk to his friends and Strattan. Ugh. Don't even get me started on Strattan."

"I like Sam." Kris sounded tense. "She's been through a lot. Leave her alone, and no, it wasn't wonderful being told by my boyfriend's brother that my boyfriend doesn't love me. Mason's gorgeous, but he's scary. At least to me."

"Yeah, but that's over. You got a new boy toy, right? Are you going to break up with Logan tonight?"

She let out a sigh. "I don't know if I'm going to break up with Logan. Things with me and AJ are just friends. I still love Logan."

"Who doesn't love you." I could imagine her friend rolling her eyes. "Come on, Kris. You look like a fool. The longer you stay with him, people are going to look down on you."

"No one knows he doesn't love me."

"Yeah, right. Everyone knows."

"What are you talking about?"

"It's pretty obvious that he never loved you. Look," she dropped her voice, making it softer, "I'm being a friend when I say this, but you were never taken seriously. We know when Logan loves someone. He loved Tate, and sorry to be the bearer of bad news, but most people think he loves Sam too."

"What?" A guttural groan came from Kris. "Sam's like family to him."

"There's been distance between them this year, which makes sense. He's got a girlfriend, but trust me, he definitely loves her, whether it's as family or something more, but it's there. Both of them love her." She groaned. "The bitch doesn't know how lucky she's got it, and when you and Logan break up, he's going to be all over her. Trust me. You won't be defending her when that happens."

Every word Kris' friend said felt like a knife stabbing into me. Tate's words came back to me, and I pressed my hands over my ears. I didn't know if it was to block Kris and her friend out or block Tate's words from haunting me. Biting down on my lip, I shook my head. Silence. I tried to calm the storm unleashed in me, but it didn't matter.

"Logan's in love with you. Now you have to deal with it."

Tate's words slammed back, full force, and they almost drowned out what Kris and her friend were saying.

I tried to clear my thoughts and strained to hear when her friend added, "Look, you need to prepare yourself. You have to end things with Logan. You're free pussy to him. It's why he's keeping you around, but he doesn't love you. As your friend, I'm telling you that you look like a fool."

Logan loves you.

STOP! I screamed in my head and it worked. For a split second, the storm went away, and I could hear someone softly sobbing from inside the bathroom. Kris was crying.

She said, "You're being really hurtful, Jen."

"No. I'm preparing you. You should also be prepared that Logan's going to sleep around. That's how he's been the last two years, until you. He's going to go back to it and everyone at school will go nuts. Girls don't think right when it comes to Logan. They just want to jump him. They don't care about the consequences."

Gritting my teeth, I decided I couldn't hear any more. I flushed the toilet, ignored the shocked gasps, and walked out. Kris' friend was Jen Conly. I shouldn't have been surprised. She was the top 'it' girl in their grade. Kris turned away, pressing into the towel dispensers. If she could've walked through them, I had no doubt she would've. As I washed my hands, I held Jen's gaze the entire time. I was cold, angry, and wanted to rip into her. I let her see, but she didn't look away. She held my gaze, swallowed nervously, but lifted her chin.

I smirked and held my hand out for a paper towel. Kris pulled two out and handed them to me. As I dried my hands, I shook my head. "Shame on you."

"Sam," Kris started.

I talked over her, "You're pressuring her into breaking up with Logan, and I'm betting that you'll be one of those girls all over him the second she does."

Kris sucked in some air. "Jen?"

Her friend didn't look away from me. As I had spoken, a cockiness came over her. A defiant look entered her eyes and she lifted a shoulder. "So what? You can't deny it. Logan Kade is fucking hot. Yeah. I probably would screw him if I had the chance, but I'm not going to lie to myself. He's not coming to me for a relationship. He never would. I'm not going to waste my time and have feelings for him, but he's Logan Fucking Kade. I wouldn't turn down a screw with him. It's more like a status thing, especially when he's going to be messed up after getting dumped."

"Oh, god." Kris choked back a sob, then rushed from the bathroom.

As the door swung shut, I lifted a finger and waved it back and forth in the air. "Tsk, tsk. That wasn't a very friendly thing to do."

She rolled her eyes and shook her head. "No, it wasn't, but my job was to break them up. I think I just did that."

"I hope, for your sake, that she tells him exactly what happened in here."

"She won't," Jen taunted me, her eyes darkening. "Same reason you won't either. I know Tate. We were neighbors before she moved, and we got caught up when she came here last year. I

333

know everything you know, and I also know that you haven't said a word about Logan being in love with you. There's a reason. I know that's why you tried to distance yourself from him too. No, no. You're not going to say anything to him and neither will Kris." She gave me a bright, beaming smile, and went around me to open the door. "Oh, and the other reason she won't say a word is because she knows it's true. You didn't see the look in her eyes when I said those words to her. It was priceless."

"You're such a bitch."

"Yeah, but I'm not a dumb bitch like Kris. I'm helping her out in the long run. She won't be so naïve anymore, and hey, she might develop some claws of her own." She skimmed me up and down. "Lord knows you had to."

I hated her, and I hated the fact that she was right.

She left and the door started to swing shut behind her, but I caught it. I wasn't the type to go after someone, but this girl deserved it. I was going to obliterate this junior.

CHAPTER TWENTY-FIVE

Kris was gone. She wasn't in the lobby, neither was her 'friend,' but Logan was. He was leaning against a far wall with his hands in his pockets. His shoulders were hunched over, giving his lean physique an even leaner look. His lips were pressed together, as if he was pondering something, and one of his feet was hooked over, resting across the other foot. He wore jeans that rode low on his hips, pressed even lower because his hands were in the pockets, pushing them down, and his shirt hugged his chest and stomach. It had ridden up, exposing an inch of his flat muscles underneath. He must've ran a hand through his hair because it was messed up, sticking out all over, but on Logan, it gave him a cute and adorable look that mixed with the always dangerous and dark vibe he gave off at times.

I stopped and sighed. Kris' friend said Logan Fucking Kade and seeing how he was waiting for me, drawing attention from the staff and the other customers in the room—even some of the older women—the name fit him.

He saw me and the pondering look switched to a grin. He stayed there, against the wall, and as I headed towards him, he held up one arm. I stopped right in front of him, but he shook his head. "Nope." He caught my arm and pulled me in, his arm fitting around me. He was strong and warm pressed next to me. I needed to find that Jen girl, but for a moment, I leaned into him.

No matter what, he was family. Kris had been told, and it was only a matter of time until the truth came out. Even thinking about it, made my stomach clench with nerves, but a part of me was just waiting for it to happen. Secrets never stayed secret, and for once, I was going to hold Logan and Mason to their promise. No matter what happened, we were family. They had better not leave me.

"You okay?" He tightened his arm around me, looking down at me.

"Yeah." But it was time. I started to pull away when I heard a whispered gasp from behind me. "Oh my god."

My heart dropped. Kris. Stepping completely away from Logan, I tried to prepare myself for what I was going to see in her eyes, but as I met her bleak blue ones, I couldn't have prepared myself for the torment in them.

She had a hand pressed to her mouth. "It's true, isn't it?"

Logan straightened from the wall. "What are you talking about?"

"You and her."

I swallowed. This was going to get bad. "Kris," I started, stepping towards her.

She scooted back, shaking her head. "No. Stay away from me. It's true, isn't it?"

"No." But it was. "It's not."

"Yes it is." She jerked her head up and down.

Logan started for her, lifting his hand out to her. "Kris? What's going on?"

She darted out of his reach. "You and her. It's true."

"What?"

I glanced around. We were drawing a crowd. A head popped up from the stairs that led to the basement. Hayes came up, followed by a bunch of others. I didn't know where Kris' friend was, but she was probably hiding. I had every intention of hunting her down later.

"Kris, stop it." I moved forward, taking charge. "It's not true. Don't listen to your friend. She was trying to mess with your head. She even admitted she'd try to sleep with Logan too. She just wants you to break up with him. That's what that whole thing was about."

"WHAT?" Logan whipped around to me, then to her. "You're breaking up with me?"

"No." Kris was crying. Both of her hands were balled into fists, and they were pressed against her mouth. She kept shaking her head. Her shoulders started jerking up and down from the sobs coming out of her. "That's not all. It's true. Sam, just admit it too. I can see it in you. I saw it in you before. You believe it too."

I closed my eyes and looked away. I couldn't admit to it, not here, not like this. I whispered without thinking, "I didn't think you had caught on to that."

"Caught on to what? What the fuck is going on?"

"Logan." Kris dropped her hands. Her face was a patchwork of white and red spots. Her mouth was red from where her hands had been pressed against it. She swallowed some of her tears and wiped the rest from her face. "Do you lo—"

"I picked the best fucking time to get pizza EVER!"

Oh no. I recognized that voice. It had been in my head the whole year.

Right in the doorway was Tate, the root of my ass pain. With a beaming smile on her face, her long blonde hair hanging loose over her shoulders, and wide eyes as she took in the scene, Logan's ex-girlfriend looked ready to climax. She shook her head. "My god. Is this what I think it is?" She checked her phone. "My old neighbor texted earlier that you'd be here, but I didn't think my timing could be any better. This is a gift handed down from heaven."

Oh hell. Even wearing a baggy white shirt that hung down to mid-thigh and jeans that were so tight they looked like leggings, she still looked like a model. Her jeans were ripped at her knees, but it looked stylish. Little tiny black shoes completed the look.

The guys agreed with me. I swear I saw drool forming in the corner of Hayes' mouth. I glanced sideways to Logan. His eyebrows were bunched together, a wrinkle in his forehead appeared, and he just seemed confused.

"Tate? What are you doing here?"

"Getting my rocks off right now." Her gaze swept the room once again. "This is so amazing."

Kris turned to Logan when he said Tate's name, and it clicked. Her mouth fell open. "This is your ex? You loved *her*?"

Tate closed her mouth, but it was pressed in a firm grin. Even her dimples were showing and laughter spilled from her tightened lips. "Oh, honey. I'm not the one you need to worry about."

No, no, no. I already knew, even before she rested her gaze on me, what Tate was going to say.

She was enjoying this too much. I heard, "You need to worry about little Strattan right there. Logan doesn't love me. Oh no. I screwed that up, but this chick, she's got it going." Her voice was clearer, and I opened my eyes to see she had moved forward a few steps. "A little birdie told me that you haven't let out the secret. Can't say I blame you. Why mess up a good thing with one brother? I mean, Mason's gone. You and the other brother can get *your* rocks off too, if you know what I mean."

She laughed. She wouldn't stop laughing. The sound sickened me.

"What. The. Fuck. Is going on?" Logan was gritting his teeth, turning to me, then back to Tate and Kris. "Tate, what the hell are you doing here?"

"Oh no." She waved a finger at him. "This is my town, Logan. I go to school here. You don't have any right to say that to me, to make me feel like I'm trespassing. It's you this time. I get to flip it on you and make you feel unwelcome. My town."

"I don't fucking care."

She reared her head back, flipped her hair over her shoulder, and her hand fell to her hip. "Well, you should, because this whole thing is about you." She circled the room with her hand. "This is all about you or should I say about how you fee—"

Kris cut her off. "Do you love Sam?"

Tate shot her dark look.

Kris placed both her hands on her hips and stuck her chin out at her. She said to Tate, "How do you like that? You didn't get to say it." She muttered, "Bitch."

It was a small victory for Kris, and one for Logan even though he didn't know it. Tate had been rubbing her paws together. She'd been so happy to be able to deliver the news, and even though I heard it coming, I couldn't talk. I was frozen, but I glanced at Kris. I tried to thank her for interrupting. Those words should've been spoken by me, but I hadn't said them. I held it in too long. I didn't know if I ever would have said Tate's words, but they were out. And they hadn't been delivered to Logan by someone who only wanted to harm us. Even then, as Kris nodded at me, I knew she still cared about him.

I turned to Logan. He was right next to me, but he was radiating tension. His jaw was clenched tight, his shoulders were rigid, and he was staring down at me, heatedly.

He was furious.

"Cat got your tong—"

"Shut the fuck up." He turned to her, his eyes flashing in warning.

Tate fell back a step. Her own eyes widened again. "Whoa."

"This is from you?" He was still looking at Tate.

"Wha—what do you mean?" A wary expression came over her features.

"This." He pointed at me, Kris, and our audience. "Did you do all this?"

She shot a hesitant look at the crowd, but shook her head. "Not them."

"Kris?" He was still interrogating Tate.

"Yes."

"How?" he commanded, the word coming from deep in his throat.

She heeded it. "My neighbor is one of her friends."

"She's not," Kris added. "Not anymore."

341

"Not my neighbor?"

Kris rolled her eyes. "Not my friend. She's my enemy."

"Oh." A cloud of confusion settled over Tate, but she just shrugged and looked back at Logan. "Whether or not it's true, you need to know that I told Sam last summer. It was my last goodbye present."

Logan seared her with a dark look.

She stopped, her chin trembled a little, but she swallowed. Her head lifted again, and she smoothed out her shirt. "I went to Manny's to say goodbye to Heather. Sam was there and I couldn't keep the truth to myself any longer."

"Truth." Logan snorted. He raked a hand through his hair. "You don't have any idea what the truth is. You wanted to mess with us. That's the truth. Stop lying to yourself, Tate." He cursed. "And I thought you changed last year. All this bullshit about making amends, turning over a new leaf, trying to make things right."

"I was," she shot back. "I fucked up. I wanted to try with you again. You're the best guy I had and lost. That's on me, but let's be real here. I'm not a saint. I mean, come on. I had no shot. You should've been honest with me right away."

"What?"

"You strung me along. Used me for sex—"

"Stop, Tate." His voice dropped back down. He was keeping himself calm, but the level of hate in his eyes gave me an indication of his true feelings. "I never lied to you. I never said we'd date. I told you we wouldn't. You still came onto me, and it wasn't one time. I told you over and over again, but you kept coming. You're the one who called me. I never called you first."

"Stop it."

He laughed. "The tides have turned. You keep throwing out the truth. I'm going to throw out the real truth. Now you want me to shut up?" He waved at our audience, who still hadn't moved. "The truth, Tate, is that none of these people give a shit about you. They're up here to watch some shit storm go down in front of them. They're eating popcorn, enjoying this show." He jabbed his hand in the air, his finger pointing at her. "You gave this to them. You. Not me. Not Sam. Or Kris. You did, coming in here and acting like you're too good to be in the gutter."

"Logan," she whispered. Her head hung down.

He jerked forward a step, stopped himself, and looked back at me. I was burned by his look. He was still furious, no. He was enraged. Another shit storm was coming our way. Logan was holding it in. That was going to be between him and me.

He shook his head, still looking at me, but moved back around to focus on Tate. "The truth is that you're still in there. You're not out. You never left the gutter. You're the same girl who came onto my brother when the guy who loved her was next door. Mason wanted to throw you out of the house naked that night. I wish he had. I wish our dad hadn't stopped him."

She'd been crumbling, but it switched. The fight came back to her and she reared back, her eyes seething. "Okay, here's the real truth. I hate that bitch behind you." She stabbed in the air, pointing at me. "But I hate your brother even more because he didn't need to hurt me the way he did."

"Mason hurt you because you hurt me. Don't you get that?"

She kept going, as if he hadn't talked, "And I hate you because I still love you and I'll never have you. There's the real ugly truth, right there for you. But everything else, I *have* changed. I did make things right with Marissa. I meant that when I said it. I'm her friend. I have been for years and I wanted to come back and see if I could get my other friend back, but because of her," everyone knew she meant me, "there's no hope in that. Heather acts like I'm dirt underneath her feet."

"You brought that on yourself. No one else did this. Stop fucking with my family." Logan turned to Kris. His voice softened, "I'm sorry you heard this. I'm sorry that you've been hurt by her too." He gestured to Tate. "And I think we need to have a conversation after this, alone."

She nodded. As he was apologizing, fresh tears slipped down her cheeks and she brushed them away. Then she left and went outside.

Logan looked at the crowd. "Show's over. Get lost."

Everyone dispersed. Some ran into each other, but Logan wasn't one to be ignored when he spoke like that. Logan Fucking Kade was back. He stood there, shaking his head from side to side. I couldn't move. I didn't know if I dared. My eyes met Tate's. She was feeling the same way.

He motioned to her. "Get your pizza, or whatever the hell you came here for, and get out of my fucking life."

She sneered at us for a moment and left too.

There was an eerie silence over the customers, and Logan shook his head. A soft curse slipped from him as a manager came out from behind the counter. He started to lift his arm, but Logan shook his head. "No need. I'm leaving."

The manager looked from Logan to me.

"Sam," Logan said.

I jumped. The softness in his tone, the raw feeling that I heard from him, sent me into a full blown panic attack. My heart started racing. My chest grew tight. The storm that had been rolling over and over inside me during the confrontation had doubled.

I had hurt him.

He asked, "She told you last summer?"

I had lied to him. I forced myself to nod. "After graduation." That was seven months ago. I flinched as I realized how long I had kept this secret.

He turned and started for the door.

I went after him. Once we were outside, I paused on the sidewalk. "Logan?"

He was going to his Escalade, but he stopped. He didn't turn around, not right away. As I waited, my heart pounded against my chest, straining to get out. His head lifted, his shoulders dropped down, and his hands balled into fists. He turned slowly. The bleak look that had been in Kris' eyes was in his, but it was more intense.

That's when the fear came in. I could lose him. I could lose Mason. My nightmare was happening, right in front of me.

A ball was in my throat. I could barely talk around it. "I was scared."

He cocked his head to the side. "You better tell Mason." He started to turn back around, but stopped halfway. With his head down, he said softly, "Before I do."

A fresh wave of chills came over me. This wasn't the Logan who loved me, who called me his sister or family. This was the Logan I knew before he cared about me. He was a stranger in that moment, and when he got into his Escalade and drove away, I was suddenly very cold.

I had screwed up.

CHAPTER TWENTY-SIX

MASON

After the game, I stayed back to explain my tardiness to Coach. He hadn't been happy, but the fact that we won and I ran two of those touchdowns in helped lessen some of his anger. The locker room was empty when I came back out, and when I read a text left on my phone from Matteo, I understood why they'd left so fast. Everyone was grabbing their favorite alcohol and meeting at the house in two hours. A big party was planned with only the most trusted invited. That meant girlfriends, best friends, or family. As I was heading out to my Escalade, I was tempted to ask Sam if she could come. Seeing her for only a few moments wasn't good enough. The school year was almost half over, but that meant there was another half to go. I'd be out of season, though, which would give me free weekends. I already knew Logan was expecting me to go back for his basketball games. That was fine. I'd take Matteo with me. I grinned at the thought of Matteo in Fallen Crest.

I didn't realize it was raining until I pushed open the last door and felt the drops on me.

Shit.

I stepped back in, letting the door slam shut. It was pouring down. I'd be drenched if I walked out there, but I didn't want to wait. I was hungry, I was tired, and honestly, I just wanted to call Sam. With a scowl, I shoved back outside.

There were cars still parked in the lot, but I wasn't surprised. I had to park in a different lot because I had been so late. Hurrying through a few of the rows, I got to mine. It was dark. The light flickered above me, but half the bulb was out. Opening the door, I tossed my bag inside and started to climb in when I heard my name.

"Mason."

Marissa was on the other side of my door. The rain had drenched her, plastering her hair to her face. She was wearing a baggy sweatshirt, jeans, and sneakers. All of it must've felt like fifty extra pounds on her.

"Marissa?"

She stepped closer. Her eyes were bright and alert, skirting over my face. She swallowed, biting down on her lip for a moment. "I have to say this." She gestured to her chest, and her sleeve hung limp, barely moving as she did. "I have to get it out. It's just eating me alive."

"Okay." I was drenched too. "Can we have this conversation in my car? We can dry off?" I skimmed up and down her tiny figure. It was cold, she could get sick. "You should warm up too."

She shook her head. "No. It has to be here. It has to be now. I have to say this."

"Marissa," I started to argue. This was insane.

"No, Mason." She scooted back a step and pressed against the front of my Escalade. The door was still open between us, so I

349

closed it and leaned against it, facing her. She added, "I've been crazy these last few years."

"Marissa." *Fuck. Really?* "Let's go somewhere dry."

She shook her head again. "No." Her hand went up to her head and grabbed a fistful of hair. She kept shaking her head, swinging her elbow around with it. "You have no idea what it's like for people like me. I'm not even feeling the rain. I'm so hyped up. I have to get this off my chest, or I feel like it's going to swallow me whole. Mason," she stopped, and her eyes found mine, "when you became my friend our sophomore year, you have no idea what you did to me."

What I *did?*

She kept going, her voice rising as she did, "I was nothing. I am nothing. I had two friends. That was it. My life was all about studying, helping my uncle at Quickie's, and maybe a movie night with my friends. We read books. That was our excitement, then you came along and changed everything for me."

"I'm sorry."

"No." She released her hair, and her arm fell back against her side. "I think you helped me. I mean, there were bad times. Trust me. I was picked on. I was bullied. Girls beat me up. They called me names. They called my house constantly and just hung up when someone answered. We changed our number twice, but it never mattered. They always found out the number. We went to the principal, but he didn't do anything. That was the bad time, but you know, I got through it because of you. I kept thinking about you, daydreaming about you. I mean, look at you. Look at me." She gestured to me and her. "I felt like I was an ugly loser and a waste of space, and you became my friend anyway. I still have no idea why. And then, even when I moved away, you were still my friend. You protected me, when we were at the cabin. You had Nate stay with me the whole time. I know that was you. You were taking care of me in your own way."

I wasn't. I hadn't done a thing. "Marissa."

"No. Please, just let me talk. I know I sound crazy. I know I probably look crazy, but you don't know what it's like. I was invisible until you became my friend. No one cared about me. No one. Even my friends didn't care that much. We just stuck together because we were the three outcasts. We were on the outside, looking in, and you," she waved at me, moving her hand up and down, "you were *the* in. You were the god. Even the seniors respected you." Her voice kept rising, growing shrill. "I thought you were my romance story coming alive. You were the popular guy. I was the plain wallflower. No one saw me, but you did. You saw me."

"Marissa." She needed to stop this.

"NO!" She held her hand up. "I mean it. I know there's no chance. I know you have a girlfriend. I am aware of all of this in here," she tapped the side of her head, "but I feel all of it here," she said, pressing her hand to where her heart was. "I have to get this out, or I will never move on from you. You, you're in here, and you won't go away. You just keep building and building, but I saw you in the hallway. I saw how you looked at her. I know in my head how much you love her, but this," her other hand went to the middle of her chest too, "won't accept it."

351

"Fine." I surrendered, hanging my head. "Go ahead." I rested back on my heels, and she started again.

"I have convinced myself over the years that you loved me. I have comforted myself every time I felt lonely and, like a loser, felt that it was meant to be with you. The one guy who shouldn't have noticed me was the only one who did. I have planned our future together. I have everything worked out, from how I was going to come back into your life in college. We were going to be together. You were going to realize you loved me, and I was going to be your superstar girlfriend. I even told my friends here that I could see us dating. They laugh at me now." Her voice trembled, but I wasn't sure if it was from emotion, if she was crying, or if it was from being cold. "I never expected you to protect me in high school. Why would you? I didn't protect myself. I never fought back. I took it. A part of me thought I deserved it. I was a nobody, remember? Then the cabin, when you invited me there and had Nate take care of me, I convinced myself it was because you loved me. You loved me, but you couldn't be with me. It wasn't meant to be. That's how sick I was." She laughed at herself. "I even talked to Tate about it. I talked to her for hours about you and me."

"Marissa," I tried again. There was no her and me.

"No—"

I interrupted her, "—I had Nate take care of you because I was having sex with Sam."

She choked on her protest and fell back a step. Her hand flew out, grabbing hold of the Escalade, righting herself. Her mouth clamped shut. Even under the rain and in the darkness, I could see that she had paled. "No, you were protecting me from her. You didn't even want me to meet her—"

I clipped my head to the side, cutting her off again, "I didn't want you to meet her because I didn't want her to find out that I let people bully you. I never stopped them, and I should've. I was ashamed. I didn't want Sam to look down on me. I had Nate do my dirty work. He was on babysitting duty. The truth is that I never should've invited you, but I was trying to be nice. I was trying not to be an asshole *all* of the time."

"But—" She shook her head.

I could see the argument coming. She was going to spin it someway. I couldn't let her. "Stop, Marissa. I don't like you."

Her hand fell from the Escalade.

"You didn't want anything from me in high school. You were a vacation for me, but that was it. I was using you to escape from all the fucking piranhas everywhere else in my life. I'm sorry. I am. I'm sorry you got hurt and picked on, but I don't like you. I don't love you. I don't even want your friendship."

Her mouth fell open and lowered with each statement I delivered. By the end, she couldn't look me in the eyes anymore. She was hugging herself, as if warding off my words. She turned to the side, but stopped. She whispered, "I love you."

"You don't even know me."

When she looked up, the misery in her was so evident, and a twinge of regret flared in me. I pushed it down. She was affecting Sam. I needed her to go away and stay away. I made sure the coldest, fuck-you mask was on my face as I said, "Stop daydreaming about me. You were right the first time. I never should've given you attention. I didn't know what a head case you were going to be."

"Stop."

"And stop using Nate to get to me. That's the lowest you could go, screwing someone else and hoping they'll bring you around me."

Her shoulders seemed to shrink beneath my gaze. Her head lowered all the way down. I couldn't see the tip of her nose. If she could've curled up in a ball and disappeared, I had no doubt that's what she would do. For a moment, I regretted everything. I did. I remembered the hurt in Sam's eyes, how Logan warned me about her.

I was going to hell.

Marissa was already broken. I'd been her slight ray of hope, helping her get through the storm, and I just snuffed that out of her. I had broken her even more. Knowing I should probably stop soon, I added, "Just stop coming around. Leave me alone. Leave my relationship alone. Leave my friends alone. This is for you too. Stay. Away. Fall in love with some nice guy, someone who will care for you, but keep away from me. I mean it. I need you to go and never come back. I don't even want to see you in class."

I waited. I didn't know what she was going to do. I heard someone else call my name from behind me. "Mason!"

Park was standing in the other row of cars behind my Escalade. He stood between two trucks and waved at me. "Can I talk to you?" He was dressed in a black hooded sweatshirt and black pants. If he hadn't waved, I wouldn't have known he was there.

What the fuck was up with rainstorms and heart to hearts? I scowled at him. "Can it wait?"

"It's about Nate."

Crap. "Yeah." I glanced back to Marissa. She had turned the other way around. Her arms were still hugging herself, but she was bent forward, pressing against my Escalade.

Fuck. I had no idea what to do.

"Kade!" Park yelled again.

Suddenly, Marissa burst around me. She ran past my Escalade, heading in Park's direction. A burst of bright lights lit up. She stopped in the middle of the lot, frozen in place.

It happened so quickly, but it was in slow motion at the same time. Her eyes got big, her mouth opened, and she let out a scream as she held a hand up before a truck barreled into her. Her body hit the front of it and flew in the air. I watched as her body flipped an entire 360 degree circle and fell to the ground ten feet away. Her body bounced and settled back down with a thud.

I couldn't comprehend what had just happened, but as quick as that thought flashed through my mind, time slammed back into place and I took off running. "MARISSA!"

The truck had screeched to a halt as soon as it hit her, and a door flung open. As I raced past it to where Marissa laid ahead, I heard someone say inside, "SHIT! Who was that?"

I stopped paying attention. Marissa was my focus. Getting to her side, I felt for her pulse. It was there. She was alive, but she was unconscious. I looked back up. I was going to tell Park to call nine-one-one, but instead I saw him leap into the truck. Before he shut the door, he pounded his fist on the dashboard and yelled out, "PUT IT IN REVERSE! YOU HIT A GIRL! GET THE FUCK OUT OF HERE!"

"FUCK!" The truck sped backwards, its lights right on us. I couldn't see them, but I knew they were watching me.

They hit her on purpose. No. They hit her by mistake. I had been the target. My mind was reeling and I felt vomit coming up my throat; I shoved it down. *That fucker*. I reached for my phone in my pocket, but I had a hard time getting ahold of it. My fingers kept slipping. As I finally got a firm hold and pulled it out, I dialed nine-one-one. The truck got to the opening path and careened to the right, whipping the front around.

I lifted the phone to my ear, my one hand on Marissa's shoulder, and saw Park in the window. His eyes met mine. He flinched, and his eyes slid down to look at her. I saw fear come over him. *Good*. The fucker was going to burn.

Then I heard the operator answer, "Nine-one-one, what is the location of your emergency?"

CHAPTER TWENTY-SEVEN

SAMANTHA

The bus ride home was the longest thing I had ever endured. My heart was breaking a little more with each mile we passed. I couldn't stop envisioning Logan's face. He was hurt, by me. I had done that, and I knew, even before we talked, that it was because I had kept Tate's words from him. I should've confronted him right away, even if it was true, I should've. Mason would've wanted me to.

When we got to the school, any other time I would've received well wishes and congratulations. This time, everyone was silent. They were all watching me and Kris. As soon as we got off the bus, I was going to my car and heading home. I already knew what I was going to do when I got there, even if people were there or not. As it was, I was lucky. No one was home. A note was left on the kitchen counter for me. Malinda and David were out on a date. I shouldn't expect them home, and Mark was out with Cass. I scribbled my own note beside it.

I'm going to Mason's. Be home Sunday night. Late. Love, Sam.

I went downstairs and started packing a bag. Everything in me hurt. I had to get to Mason. I had to tell him the truth, and I had to know that everything was going to be okay.

Knock, knock

I stopped, my heart pounding. It was Logan. He had come to talk about this, deal with it, and get it out of the way, but when I whipped open the door, he wasn't standing there.

It was my dad.

"Garrett?"

"Hey, Samantha." He had a timid smile, holding a bag in front of him with his coat tucked over one of his arms. "I, uh, I know you wanted time. I'm supposed to wait for you, but I've never been good with being patient."

My lips pressed together and I crossed my arms over my chest. I had wanted it to be Logan. Badly. "What do you want?"

"Uh." He lifted a hand and raked it through his hair. It was then that I noticed he was dressed in a suit and tie. Even his shoes looked rich. The last time I saw him had been at Logan's football game. He always emanated wealth, even when he was dressed in jeans and a sweater.

He was not like me. He was so far from me.

"I have to fly back to Boston. I had hoped to come tomorrow. I wanted to give you a present. David told me about your race, that you won, and that you will probably get a scholarship. I wanted to say congratulations."

"I've wanted you to stay away. That didn't happen either."

His Adam's apple bobbed up and down. "Uh, yeah. Listen, Samantha, I know I messed up. I know that I was coming in at a bad time in your life. You probably wanted an escape. David's told me more about that time, that he had stepped away from you and you felt abandoned by him, then it was like I had abandoned you too. I get it. I do, but I'd really like to talk to you about that time. I'd like to explain what I did and why."

"I don't care." I didn't. I had. I'd been hurt. I hadn't wanted to trust him again, but after tonight, after the possibility of losing Mason and Logan, I didn't give two shits about anything else. "You're my dad. Whatever. Fine. We can have a relationship, just don't think you can pressure me to do what you want."

"I haven't been—"

I didn't have time for this. "You have. You call every fucking night."

"I don't." He glanced to the side.

"You're right. You don't. You just call the nights we have the ringer turned on. Thank you for correcting that for me."

He grimaced, then a grin crept over his face. "You're just like me."

Rage slammed into me at those words. I shot back, "I'm not. I'm not anything like you. I'm the product of a crazy abusive mother who's finally locked away and not able to hurt me. I am who I am because I lost my family. I got another one, and voila, you're back and you want another shot. Well, guess what, I'm more concerned about not losing *another* family. I don't care about you. That's the truth. Maybe I will. I have no idea. I don't really care to find out right now. All I care about is you leaving so that I can leave. I have places to be."

He'd been watching me. His eyes narrowed with each statement I said and as I finished, he noted, so softly, "You are like me, but it's my job to show you that. Give me a chance. Please, Sam."

I cursed.

He laughed. "Give me a shot."

I let out a sigh.

"I went back to Boston to make things right with my wife. Having a daughter changed everything for me. I didn't want to be a part of your life with Helen at my side. I needed the woman I loved, even if she cheated on me. I went back because of you. I wanted that family. Things are better. She moved here with me because of you, because I want to be a part of your life, but, Sam, the year's almost over. Let me have some time with you. I will never hurt you. I promise."

I watched him warily.

"Give me another shot."

Oh hell. I gave him a rueful look. "You're lucky that I'm all about second chances tonight. Fine. We can do dinner next week."

A smile lit up his face and for a second, I saw myself. He was right. I was like him. For some reason, the thought sobered me. It grounded everything for me. He was begging me. I'd be begging Mason. We had both messed up.

My throat went dry. I hated thinking I was like Garrett, but at the same time, this was blood standing before me. My other blood was gone. I didn't even want her around me. With everyone else, I was lucky they allowed me in with them. But Garrett...maybe there was a connection with him that I had never experienced?

He said, "Listen, I'll call when I'm coming back. Dinner. That sounds amazing, but I want to ask you early."

I grew wary again. "What?"

He laughed. "Nothing bad. I know you have your holiday break coming up and I'm going to be in Boston during it. I wanted to invite you to join me."

"In Boston?"

"Yes." He nodded. His eyes were bouncing with happiness. He looked elated. "I'll be there to close up some loose ends with the firm. It'll take a while. You can come. You and me. We can spend some good father/daughter time together. I can show you where I came from. You have cousins there too."

Cousins?

"And my mom has been calling me every day. She'd love to meet you."

His mom? "I have a grandma?" I had never realized. "My mom's estranged from her family so I just assumed…"

"I know. You don't have to say yes. Think about it. Please think about it, but I'd love for you to come. And hey, the championship game is already scheduled for Boston. If Mason's team keeps winning, they could be playing there the same time you're with me. My old firm has box seats. We could go and watch Mason play."

Mason. I had to go. "Yeah, uh, maybe. Look, I really have to go."

"I know. I'm going, but give me a call if you want to come. I'll get a plane ticket for you. I'll take care of everything." He left and on the way to his car, he turned to wave. I shut the door. I needed to finish packing.

I had just gone down the stairs to the basement, when I heard knocking again. Assuming it was Garrett, I laughed as I opened the door, "Forget about another trip you wanted to invite me on..." The words died in my throat.

Logan was standing there instead.

He grimaced, raked a hand through his hair, and grabbed a fistful before letting his hand drop back to his side. He jerked his head behind him. "Come on. Mason called. He wants us up there tonight."

Mason called him? Shock punched me in the chest. "But...I thought you were going to let me talk to him first?"

"I am. This is something different. Come on." His grimace deepened into a scowl.

"Logan, tell me what's going on."

He looked past me, saw the notes on the counter, and gestured to them. "That's you leaving a note, right? You're going to see Mason?"

"Yes."

"Let's go. Whatever Mason wants comes first."

"You want me to ride with you?"

A litany of curses left him and he held his arms out. "What do you want, Sam? I am pissed at you. No, I am goddamn furious at you. We're family and you being told that I love you, that's a huge thing to hold back from me. You should've talked to me. Trust me, I am brimming up to here," he lifted his hand to his head, "with anger. I want to talk this out and tell you a few things, but I can't.

363

Mason has to know first. He should've been told long before I found out. You two are dating. You guys have to talk first and bring me in. To be fair to my brother, to have his back, I can't say a fucking word. I want to." His eyes were almost bulging out. "Trust me, I have a lot that I want to say. So do me a favor, grab your bag, get in the Escalade, and keep fucking quiet the whole way there."

He didn't wait for me, just turned and went back to the vehicle.

I didn't think. I didn't let myself. I did as he told me. It was the longest three hour drive that I would ever endure.

*

MASON

I'd been at the hospital for three hours when Nate came through the front door. He saw me right away and held his hands up in surrender. Across the lobby, he said, "I'm here for Marissa. That's all."

I snorted and rolled my eyes. As he came to sit beside me, I said, "Think again, buddy."

"Okay."

He sat across from me. There were people around us, but when he took his seat, the ones closest to us moved away. I didn't blame them. I'd been pacing for three hours, and this was the first time I sat, then he walked in. They'd already been leery of me, watching me like I was a caged animal. I'm sure they were wondering if he would be the spark to set the bomb off. To be honest, as I watched him warily, I was wondering the same thing. I wasn't sure what was going to set me off.

We were both silent for a moment, just waiting for the other. Nate ran his hands down his pants, folded his hands together, and rested his elbows on his knees. He asked, "Have you heard anything?"

"No. She was unconscious and I think she's in surgery." I didn't know anything. They wanted to speak to her family. I had no clue who they were. They wanted friends. I couldn't give them names. They finally asked what I could give them. Nate. He was the only one I knew who would have information on her. I asked, "You gave them information on her?"

He nodded, running his hands together. "I had her cell number, but one of my frat brothers hooked up with her roommate. She lives in a house two blocks off campus. I think the hospital got ahold of her roommate and were going to have her parents called."

"One of your frat brothers, huh?"

"Yeah." He paused. "Why?"

"Don't fucking play dumb with me."

"What?"

"Nate. I mean it."

He'd been my best friend most my life. He'd been a sanctuary during my parent's divorce, putting up with me when I was a dumb shit, causing fights, wanting to destroy everything. Nate had my back. He was always at my side. He did whatever I wanted him to do, but looking at him, the last few years came back to me.

He continued to sleep with Parker even during the freeze-out.

They wanted him to drug Sam.

Logan stopped trusting him. I knew Sam never really had. And this year, with trying to shove Park Sebastian down my throat, then the final straw, bringing Marissa to that lunch.

He was watching me back, holding my gaze, but something flashed in his eyes. Something heated. He shot back, "What?"

"Playing dumb's been your forte the last few years."

"Fuck you, Mase."

"Fuck you, Mason."

"What?"

"Fuck you, Mason. I'm not Mase. We're not friends. You don't get to call me that."

The nerve in his jaw twitched and his eyes cooled, but other than that there was no reaction. A second later, he leaned back in his seat, shaking his head. "Man, you're messed up."

"Am I?" He had no clue, or he was faking it. "I thought you cared about Marissa."

"I do."

"You don't look it."

"Yes, I'm concerned. You said she was hit—"

"—by one of your guys."

Nate stopped. He heard me and judged me for a moment. I could feel him dissecting everything, those words, my tone of voice, how steady my gaze was, everything, even how I was sitting. Then he shook his head. His hand went to his jaw, and he started to rub his face. "No way, man. No way."

I'd already figured some of it out. "I punched you. You were out. The bro code says I have to be hurt too, but worse. Am I right? Isn't that what your fraternity is about?"

"No fucking way, Mase...Mason. Stop spitting this shit. There's no way." His voice rose on his last statement, but I heard an inflection of doubt in there too. He was remembering things. He was going over past conversations he might have heard or maybe even moments when he walked into a room and they stopped talking? There was something that triggered the doubt in his voice, because I saw the disbelief start to creep up on him. Then he shoved to his feet. He started pacing, his head caught in his hands, and his shoulders hunched over. "No way. No way."

I leaned back. I had him hooked. It was time to reel him in. "They were there for me. I was at my Escalade and Park called me over. I had to walk across to him. He said it was about you, and I was heading over there."

"But...no way. I mean, FUCK. Marissa? How'd she get hurt?"

"She ran out in front of me. I'm guessing the truck saw someone coming and went for her."

"But—"

"Her body flew ten feet. It did an entire flip in the air and they had to reverse out of there or they would've hit her again. And your buddy, Park, that truck was his getaway car. He was the bait. They hit the fucking wrong person."

"But that means," new horror filled his features, "they wanted to hurt you."

"Yeah." I shook my head, impatience clawing at me. "Come on, Nate. What'd you hear? You're not surprised. That means you heard something. What was it?"

"Nothing. I swear, except..." he trailed off. "No. I mean, no way. But..."

I wanted to stand, but kept myself down. "Either help me or help them. You can't be neutral."

"I know, but—" He stopped pacing, and his eyes closed tight. He pressed the palms of his hands to his eyes and shook his head back and forth. "I just can't believe this. I mean, yes, you hit me, but you're my friend. I was coming to apologize. Park knew that..."

Park knew that. I shot to my feet. "When?"

"What do you mean?"

"When did he know this?"

"This afternoon. They'd been waiting for me to decide what to do. He came to my room and I told him. I told him the fight was about him, that you didn't want to be friends with him, but he seemed chill about it. He was happy that I was going to work on our friendship. I swear, Mason. He didn't seem mad at all."

"Because you're the epitome of being perceptive."

Nate stepped to the side. "What do you mean?"

"A guy like that, what do you think he's going to do? He thinks he's the top of the food chain around here and some lowly freshman rejects him? Someone who could be a threat to him later on? Sebastian's not dumb and he's not nice. I'm sure he wanted to take out the threat—me—and do it early on."

"But hurting you would hurt the team. Park loves the team."

Nate was so dumb. "Right. He loves the team that has hated him since last year. He loves the team when it's well-known among us how big of a douche Sebastian is. He doesn't love the team. He tried to get in. He tried to see if he could use me, and it didn't work. I don't think he wanted to lose you, but if I'm in your ear, shedding light on how big of an ass he is, you're probably not going to be the devoted little pledge he wants you to be."

"But why?"

"Nate, your parents work in the movie business, they produce or whatever. You have more potential power to give him in the future than I do."

"Oh."

I sighed and patted him on the back. "Don't worry. Your brain will catch up. You'll see. I'm pretty sure I'm right."

"You usually are."

Two things happened at that moment. Sam and Logan came through the doors. Both looked fatigued and stressed. Then I heard my name from the hospital hallway.

"Mason Kade?"

I turned. A doctor stood there, dressed in dark blue scrubs, a mask hanging around his neck. He looked the same as my family, tired and stressed. His dark hair had been combed to the side, but parts were sticking up by his ears. As he waited for me, he ran a hand over his face and blinked a few times.

I went to him. "Yes?"

"You're Mason Kade?"

I nodded. "I am." *Please don't tell me she's dead.* I didn't want to hear those words. She would've been hurt *again* because of me.

369

"She's awake, and she's asking for you."

I closed my eyes and hung my head. Christ. I almost fell to the floor, but caught myself. I nodded. The doctor had been waiting for me. He gestured down the hallway. "If you follow me, I'll take you to her."

I turned. Logan and Sam had come closer. Logan shot a confused look at Nate and folded his arms over his chest. Sam never looked away from me. A wave of tenderness came over me. I just wanted to hold her, tell her everything was going to be fine, but I couldn't. I turned, without saying a word to my family, and followed the doctor. I had a different girl to comfort right now.

CHAPTER TWENTY-EIGHT

SAMANTHA

We were waiting in that lobby for what seemed like forever. I couldn't handle it anymore and went outside to get away. Nate had seemed dazed when we came in, but he told us what happened. Hearing that Marissa had been hit instead of Mason filled me with so many different emotions. I was grateful it hadn't been Mason. I was angry at Marissa, even though I didn't know why. That anger turned to Nate's fraternity. They wanted to hurt my soul mate. I breathed because of him, and they wanted to threaten that? To hurt him? I wanted to hurt them back. Then all of that faded as I pictured Marissa crumpled on the ground, then in a hospital bed. I'd been there almost a year ago.

I was a mess.

"I thought I would've found you on the phone with Jax."

Logan had come outside. His hands were pushed in his jeans, making them slip down an inch, accentuating his already lean body. As I stared at him, all the bullshit from the year came back to me and I admitted to myself that I could've loved Logan. I really could've, but it was Mason. It was always going to be Mason. I meant the words I had told Jackson, that all roads would've led to him.

He was my life. He was my breath. He was my heart.

I couldn't lose my heart.

"Sam?"

"Oh." A husky laugh came out of me. "No. Knowing Heather, she'd be in her car and headed here. I meant it, Logan, when I told you before that it's the Threesome Fearsome again."

"Oh." He sounded sad, but he shook his head and came to lean against the wall beside me. Keeping his hands in his pockets, he leaned forward, his head hanging down for a moment. He glanced up at me and gave me a brief smile. "That doesn't mean you can't have a friend. I didn't mean it like that."

He was hot and deadly to others, but he could be adorable. His brown hair had grown an inch longer and some of it had slipped over his forehead. His dark eyes had a slight mischievous glint in them, and the corner of his mouth was curved up in a half-grin, half-smirk. Without thinking, I reached out and pushed some of the strands of hair back, smoothing my hand over his forehead. He closed his eyes, and I finished, tucking more strands back behind his ear. As my hand fell away, he opened his eyes. A soft smile came over him. "That felt nice."

My heart was heavy. I loved them both so much, but I couldn't keep it in anymore. A whisper left me, "It's Mason for me."

He closed his eyes again. "Sam," he started in a murmur.

"Stop." I touched his shoulder. "I have to say this. I know you want to wait until he knows, but this is what I'm going to say to him, and you're wrong. We don't have to wait to talk about this before he knows. It won't make a difference. I love him. He will always be the one for me. There might've been the possibility of

373

others, but when Mason came into my life, all those possibilities left. My future's been set ever since I met him. I told Jackson before, my path will always lead to Mason. The only way it wouldn't have is if I had never met him."

"Sam." He straightened. He sounded so tired. "Stop. Please."

"No. Even if it isn't true, what Tate said, it doesn't matter."

"You're right." He pushed off from the wall and stood facing me. "It doesn't matter. What does matter is that you kept it to yourself. You never should've done that. Something like that, something that big, would only have caused distance and problems. Fuck, Sam." He lifted his hand and raked it through his hair.

I held back a grin at his gesture. Whenever he was frustrated or nervous, his hand always went to his hair. He'd grab a handful like he did now, and he would keep his hand there, just holding onto it.

He noticed my reaction. "What?"

"Nothing." But I couldn't keep it in. A slight chuckle slipped out and I pointed to his hand. "You always grab your hair."

"I do?" He released his hair and laughed. "I had no idea. That's embarrassing."

"It's cute. It's you. It's Logan."

He rolled his eyes and groaned. "What was I saying? Oh yeah." He snapped his fingers and pointed at me. "You."

"Me?"

"Yeah, you. This was the reason you've been freaking out since Mason left, even before he left. I could tell something was wrong.

You were always with him." He cursed. "The two of you were like rabbits for a while, always going at it. Now it makes sense."

"Logan."

Ignoring me, he kept going, "It hurt when you pulled away from me this year. We were already separated. You moved in with David and my mom moved back. Mason left me too. It wasn't just you. I needed you this year. I don't let people in, Sam, but I let you in. We both let you in. It fucking hurt. That's all I'm saying."

A lump sat on the bottom of my throat. It rested right there, blocking me from talking, from breathing. I struggled around it. My god, I could see the damage I had done. I choked out, "I'm sorry."

I was. God, *I was.*

"Yeah." He looked at me with dead eyes. "It's over and done with. Do you realize how much time it's going to take to for me get over this?"

"That I held this back or..." My heart rate picked up, thumping harder and harder. He had never confirmed or denied it. Was that what he meant...I was still too afraid to ask.

"Yes, that you held back." He gestured from himself to me. "Mason has to be told. I know it came from Tate, but this is a guy's worst nightmare, that his girl and his brother fall for each other. I'm hurting, but I'm pissed too. I'm pissed that this wasn't snuffed out right way. I think about my brother and what's going to go through his head. I mean..." He turned away sharply, then placed both his hands on the side of his head. Bending over, he let out a yell. When he looked back up, the deadness was there, but it was mixed with anger and just plain misery.

I wanted to look away. I couldn't, though.

Logan's chest lifted, and I heard him take a shuddering breath. "The girl I loved wanted my brother. I knew what he did for me, what he kept doing for me afterwards. Mason took care of me. He protected me, but I didn't love Tate like he loves you. You guys are epic. You guys are going to last forever and knowing that a wedge is between you, that the wedge is me, will haunt me."

He still hadn't denied or confirmed. I bit down on my lip. I didn't want to know, then it would be worse. I just knew it.

"Sam," he dropped his voice to a whisper.

I turned away.

His hand came to my shoulder and I held still. I kept biting down on my lip and my hands curled into themselves. I felt the first stabbing pain from my nails cutting into my skin, but it went numb. Flashbacks of my junior year, before Mason and Logan loved me, went through my mind. I had been so alone. I had been ostracized. I had no one. I was laughed at, jeered at. People wanted to hurt me.

I had nothing to lose then. I had everything to lose now.

"Stop." I was gritting my teeth. Everything had tensed inside me, but he didn't remove his hand. "Stop, Logan."

"Sam—"

"I said stop it!" I whirled around. It felt as if I had a never-ending stampede in my chest that would never slow down.

"Sam—"

"STOP! YOU DON'T LOVE ME!" I snapped.

In the back of my mind, I was telling myself to calm down. I should've been quieter. I *needed* to be quieter. We were outside, the front lobby just a few feet away. The only thing separating us and that room was a wall of windows. They could hear and someone could come outside.

Logan stepped back, his eyes wide. He looked taken aback.

I shook my head again. "You can't. I won't let you. You can't love me."

If he did, what then? What would happen? Would Mason still choose me? *No.* And that was the root of my fear. If Logan loved me, Mason wouldn't choose me. He had said over and again that he wouldn't ever let a girl get between them.

He would leave me.

"Sam," Logan hesitated. "I—"

"Shut up."

His eyes trailed past me and agony filled them.

I didn't recognize it in time. I should've, but I didn't. Instead, I whispered, "You can't love me. I won't let you."

I heard from behind me, "Sam."

Oh god. My stomach dropped to my feet.

Mason was there and I knew, from the soft tone of voice, from the small note of wariness, that he had heard.

I tried to prepare myself, but when I turned, I couldn't have. He wore a mask to me now. His green eyes were cold, staring through me, and it was like he was seeing behind me, not me anymore. He was so gorgeous. Even though my heart was breaking, I couldn't stop myself from feeling a surge of love just at the sight of him.

Football had made him leaner. He was an athlete, and he moved with a silent litheness, like a predator. I had never heard him, but even if I had, I didn't know if I could've stopped myself.

It was going to come out, no matter what. I just wish he hadn't heard it that way.

"Mason." I had no idea what to say, but I had to try. I wet my suddenly dry lips.

He shook his head in a savage motion. "Don't. Marissa wants to talk to you. Go do your duty, Sam."

"Mason."

"She wants to see you. Go and listen to her." Then he turned away from me and went back inside.

I watched him go. I watched my heart walk away from me.

*

I had no idea what Marissa would want to say to me, and I had no idea what to say to her either. I didn't know why she'd been in that parking lot with Mason. He said he would handle it, she would go away, but she hadn't and now this. She'd been hit instead of him, should I be thankful to her?

When I got to her room, I stayed in the hallway for a moment. I could see her through the window in the door. She was so tiny. Her hair had been brushed to the side, resting over her shoulder, but it was in clumps. It looked like she had tried raking her fingers through it, but it hadn't worked. Her skin was pale. She had her eyes closed and the bed sheet was folded perfectly over her chest. I wondered if she was cold. She wore the hospital gown, but it looked so thin. I caught sight of the goosebumps on her arms and knew she was.

I knocked once, saw her eyes open, and went in.

I had no idea what to do, what to say, so I stood there. The door shut behind me, and we continued to stare at each other. She looked even tinier now that I was in the same room as her. She didn't move, not a bit. She looked like a little statue. I watched her chest to make sure it was rising and falling. I know. Stupid of me, but there was an eerie stillness in the room. It was making me feel weird, like I had stepped into a different time zone. But that wasn't me. I knew whatever was in the air was coming from Marissa. I realized I wouldn't ever understand her. I wasn't going to try. I was going to listen to what she had to say and I was going to say whatever she wanted to hear from me, then I was leaving.

The bottom line was that she was still at school with Mason. She still had—

"I love him."

She interrupted my thoughts, but I was grateful for the break in silence. I ran my hand down the front of my jeans. I didn't know what to do with them, so I put them in my pockets. "Okay."

One of her eyelids twitched. "Okay?"

I shrugged. "It doesn't take a genius to figure that out. I'm sorry that truck hit you."

"I'm not."

I'd been looking everywhere but at her, and hearing that word, spoken from her calm tone of voice, my eyes flicked to hers. "What do you mean?"

Her lips pressed together, grimacing, and she gestured to the chair beside her bed. "Do you want to sit? I have a lot to tell you."

There was a chair immediately next to her and another positioned at the foot of her bed, angled so it was facing her. I took that chair. I still needed distance from her. When I sat and perched on the edge, my back straight in the air, a soft laugh slipped from her. She said, "I make you really uncomfortable, don't I?"

I didn't bat an eyelash. "Yes."

"I can't say I'm surprised."

She sounded normal. She sounded like someone I could be friends with.

She let out a sigh and sat up. The gown was strung together by a small string, tied into a knot behind her neck. As she leaned forward, the back of her gown fell forward. It exposed her back, and from the angle I was sitting, I could see bruising on the side and at the top of her shoulders. She seemed impervious, staring at me. She started to pick at the blanket in front of her as she spoke, "I hated you. Mason was still emailing me when you moved in, and he told me about you. He didn't say much, but I could tell that he liked you." She laughed and shrugged to herself. "It wasn't hard to figure out. Mason doesn't talk about anyone except Logan, and he had mentioned you more than a few times. Then I met you at the cabin and you punched Tate for me."

She looked up. Her eyes were sad, but there was regret in them too. She murmured, "It's ironic. Maybe not, but Tate was being mean and you defended me. You punched her. You were drunk and kept shaking your fists in a weird motion, saying something about being a survivor and being fifty. You were funny and came to my defense when no one else had. You didn't even know me and you marched right in and got in Tate's face. I liked you instantly, but that made me hate you even more." A small tear came to her eye. "I knew why Mason liked you. I should've left that room liking you too. You stood up for me, but instead I hated you and became friends with Tate. That's messed up, right?" The regret in her eyes was heard in her laugh as well. "I don't even know how to tell you the rest. I'm ashamed."

I asked the only real question I had for her, "What do you want from me?"

She bit down on her lip and her eyes widened. My question was direct and strong. She reacted; she shrank back in the bed but determination flashed over her face, and she straightened back up, sitting tall. "Nothing."

"Why am I here? I know you love Mason, but he's mine. I won't give him up without a damn good fight."

"No, I know." She rolled her eyes to the ceiling and muttered to herself, "This is so hard."

A bitter laugh wrung from me. She stiffened, looking back to me. I leaned forward in my seat. "This is hard for *you*? This is hard for me. Here you are, beaten up because you literally got hit by a car so my boyfriend didn't. Whether that was by accident or not, it doesn't matter. I should be grateful to you. You should be my best friend, but it's you. You've been in my life for over a year, but I don't know you. I know *of* you. Mason's told me about you, and about how he regrets not helping you. Then you go to that lunch and just stare at him. Then at his house? I mean, was that by accident? I don't believe you were that drunk. I think you manipulated that whole thing and were going to try and sleep with him. Now I'm summoned by you and what? I'm being put in a place where I should like you, I should be kissing your ass, and giving you hugs or balloons. But all I want is for you to say what the hell you need to get off your chest so I can leave and you can stay out of Mason's life." The word flashed in my mind, and I snapped my fingers at her. "You're being passive aggressive. You're controlling this whole thing. I should be yelling at you, but I'm not, well, I kinda am, but I'm just frustrated. Don't spin a pretty story, just spit it out."

She didn't shirk from me. She didn't look away. She held my gaze the entire time I spoke, and when I was done, she said, without blinking, "Tate lied to you."

I sat there for a second. I heard her say those words. For one split second, I wondered what she was talking about, but it clicked. Surging to my feet, I exploded. I yelled, "WHAT?!"

Again, she didn't cower from me. Marissa just watched me. "Tate made it all up. She laughed about it, said it could actually be true, but she doubted it. She was going to try anyway."

Oh my god.

Tate had lied. Tate had lied. Those words were repeating in my head, laughing at me. I couldn't stand still so I started to pace. As I did, she kept going, "Logan doesn't love you like that. Well, he might, but as for Tate knowing about it, that was a lie. She said that was her graduation gift to me."

This had to be a joke. It *had* to be.

"Tate knows how I feel about Mason. She's always known. It's why she bullied me in the first place, but she said she wanted to make it up to me somehow. I told her that I got into Cain University, and that I was excited. I didn't go to Cain U on purpose, because of Mason. I applied to a lot of schools, but when I got in, in my mind, it was like my fairytale was coming true. I always thought Mason was going to be my husband. We were going to be together, and I was no longer going to be that invisible girl that I had always been." She broke off and looked away. When she started again, the pain that came from her struck deep in me. It mirrored pain that I had gone through myself. She continued, so quietly, "She said the lie was going to eat you up inside. She told me that you wouldn't tell them, that you'd be too scared of losing them, so it would send you into a tailspin where you'd destroy yourself."

Each word she said was a blow to me. Tate had assumed right. I'd been manipulated and the end result was just pain, all around pain. All because of one lie.

"I didn't ask her to do that, but I didn't stop her either. I'm sorry. I realized this whole thing was wrong when I was standing in the rain, professing my love to Mason, and all he seemed was irritated. I don't know why, but I had this grand idea in my head that it would work. I would proclaim my love. We would have this fairytale scene, and he'd tell me he felt the same. I don't know what I actually expected. I wasn't thinking about you or what I was doing to Mason and his relationship with you. I was just thinking about myself." Her voice was so quiet again, it was barely a whisper. "I just wanted to be loved."

"No." I cursed, shaking my head. "You wanted Mason to love you. You're making it sound like you were nothing and he was going to make you someone. If you just wanted to be loved, you would've been loved. You're pretty, you might seem normal outside of this? I'm sure there are other guys who have liked you. You wanted Mason. You allowed Tate to lie to me, to make us all suffer. It was because you wanted one particular guy. Be honest about that."

God, I couldn't believe I was still listening to this. She was confessing, but it wasn't to make things right. It was to make herself feel better. A mangled sounding laugh ripped from me. "You have no idea what you did. Tate might've said the words, but you let her. You didn't say anything to stop this. You're just as guilty as she is."

The tears started. They began falling down her face and as I kept talking, they became a steady stream. I shook my head. Everything about her screamed victim. And she'd been hit by a truck. She was a victim, but what she did wasn't okay.

I couldn't stay there. I needed to leave, but there was one other thing. "That night, were you going to sneak into his bed?"

Her shoulders were shaking from sobbing. At my question, she stiffened and paused; a small whimper left her mouth as she nodded. She couldn't talk.

I heard all I needed to hear. Heading to the door, I thought of another question. Pausing, my hand on the handle, I asked, "Did you manipulate that whole night?"

A second slow nod, like she still didn't want to confess to that part.

"You pretended to be drunk?"

A third nod, even slower and just the bare minimum of motion.

I gripped the handle so tight. I knew my knuckles were probably white. "Were you there with friends? If Mason had found who you were with, what then? The whole lie would've been pointless."

She looked back down, but I heard her say, "I told them not to answer their phones. They knew. My phone was stuffed in my bra."

She set the whole thing up. She was going to try and seduce him. I felt sick, my stomach protested, and I realized I really was going to be sick. I hurried out of there and sprinted to a bathroom in the hallway.

CHAPTER TWENTY-NINE

MASON

Sam and Logan. Sam and Logan.

I couldn't get the images out of my mind: them standing so close together; her reaching up, tucking some of his hair back. I saw them through the lobby windows, even though Nate tried to block me from seeing them. Fuck that. He didn't try to block me. He tried to stall me. The two of them looked so intimate out there. They had looked like a couple, and it stuck a dagger in me.

My brother and a girl. This was Tate all over again, but worse. Even though Marissa told me the truth, all about the lie Tate had said to Sam, I was furious when she touched him. But this was Sam. A part of me wanted to grab her, take her somewhere, and remind her that she was mine. It was the animalistic side of me, but I couldn't do that. The other side, the one always in control, kept me from doing that. It told me to remain calm, think about it from her perspective.

She was scared. She had lost her family. She didn't want to lose me or Logan. I got that. It was pretty easy to figure out, but it wasn't helping my anger. Sam was mine. Not Logan's. But fuck, if he made her happy—no. Marissa said it was a lie.

"You okay?" Nate asked.

I glanced to him, and I knew he was my best friend again. He was there, he was waiting for what I was going to do, and he would have my back. It was the old Nate looking back at me, the same one that let me tear shit up at his own parents' party years ago.

Think, Mason. Stop. Fucking think about this. I forced myself to calm down and looked at everything that had happened. Marissa was hit. Park had done that. And Nate, he was back. No, I needed to make sure.

"I'm going after them." I waited, studying his reaction.

He didn't even blink. "I'm going with you."

"Good." I still wasn't sure, but my gut was telling me he was speaking the truth. He really was back, but hell, the image of Logan and Sam so close together had thrown me off balance. I needed to regroup and center. I nodded. "Go to the house. Pack your stuff and get out of there. Call me afterwards."

"Okay." He started to leave, but remembered who was out there and turned back. "You want me to go out there? Or..." He gestured out the door.

I knew what he was asking, and I moved ahead. "Let me go first. I'm going to have Logan go and get a hotel room, and I'll bring Sam later, after she's done talking to Marissa."

"Okay." He stepped back. "Wait. Marissa?"

"Yeah." I didn't explain it to him. I didn't want to. It'd be explained later in the hotel room, but for now, Marissa didn't know who hit her. It was my say only. When I questioned her, she claimed she never saw who called my name. She hadn't even remembered that someone had called my name until I told her. I pressed her, though. I needed to know if she remembered or not, and she held up under my interrogation. She really had no idea, which was good. I had no plans on going to the police. I wanted Marissa's hit and run to be just that, a hit and run. The camera feed from the parking lot wouldn't be good. It was dark and raining. There was no chance it could've picked much up. They'd question me, and I would handle those questions fine. As I went outside, I already had a plan set in mind, but it would take steps.

And the first step was dealing with Sam and my brother. I heard her say, "You can't love me!" and the dagger got shoved deeper in me and yanked to the side. She said something else, but my blood was boiling. I couldn't let my control slip. If it did, I didn't know if I'd be able to keep from hitting Logan.

When I spoke, Logan jerked away from her and Sam paled. She looked ready to either run or crumble. If she did, I'd have no sympathy for her. When I told her that Marissa wanted to talk to her, I was grateful. It was a break from the sudden tension, and I was literally counting down the seconds until she left and went inside. I wished that Marissa would prolong her apology to Sam.

Then my brother said, "I don't love her."

I snorted. "Don't fucking lie."

"I don't, Mason."

I shook my head. I didn't want to deal with this. "You've loved her since the cabin."

He was silent. I didn't give a shit. I continued to shake my head, laughing at myself. "I've known, Logan. I'm not stupid."

Then he sighed, and I heard his surrender in that sound. He murmured, "Yeah, well, it doesn't matter. I don't love her like you do, and I know she doesn't love me like she loves you."

This was a clusterfuck. The whole thing. My brother and my soul mate. "I should've seen this coming a long time ago. It should've been dealt with before now."

"Dealt with? How? By you not going for her?" Logan pushed off from the wall and started pacing in a small, tight circle. "This is bullshit. I'm going to lay all my cards out and whether you believe them or not is up to you, but this is the truth from me. I love Sam as a sister. I love her as family. I love her as a best friend, and yes, I *could've* loved her. I could've dated her, and maybe I could've married her. I don't know, but it doesn't matter because we're not meant to be together. I realized how I could have felt, and I stopped it. She's my sister. That's all she is to me. She's family. No guy would've held up against you. She's said that to me. No guy. Not as long as she knew you, and that tells me you're the one. You're the real deal for her. No one else even holds a slight shot against you."

He might've made her happier, though. That was the hardest piece to swallow. Maybe another guy would've made Sam happier than I could? As I forced myself to think about that, it was like Sam had reached down, grabbed my balls, and yanked them off. Then she started to play with them, even throwing them to Logan in a game of catch.

"I know what you're thinking."

I cursed, throwing him a sideways glance. "I highly doubt you do."

"That I would've made her happier."

Fuck. He did.

He added, "But not as much as you do. I don't know what to tell you to make you understand. You're like sunlight to her. I'm the fucking lamp in the corner." He paused and shook his head. "No, screw that. You're the sun to her, while I'm a chandelier. Still beautiful, but one drastically outshines the other."

I sighed. "Yeah, well, I'll talk to her later about this."

Logan gave me a half-grin. "Come on. The chandelier comment was funny. That's serious Golden Logan shit." He looked past me and the attempt at humor faded. "What's up, Traitor?"

Nate came to stand next to me. He shook his head. "I didn't know they were going after him. I swear."

"And now you do?" Logan was baiting him, watching him darkly. "What side are you picking?"

"Do you have to ask?"

"Yes," Logan threw back. "I do and that's what pisses me off. I shouldn't have to ask."

Nate was brimming with anger next to me. I could feel his tension. He gritted his teeth. "Back off, Logan. You have no idea how hard it is to be friends with you guys. I love you guys, but I'm nothing compared to you. Sue me for wanting to branch out and get some of my own friends this year. I'm sorry they turned out to be psychopathic assholes. Mason punched me, *me*, his best friend. That had nothing to do with the fraternity, and I had nothing to do with what they did to Mason, or tried to do. Park lied to me. I was wrong. I just wanted Mason to be a part of my other life, one where I'm not in third place every time."

Logan lifted an eyebrow, looked at me, then back to Nate. "That really touched me. I have no smartass comment to follow that." He patted Nate's shoulder. "Good job. I will call you Three from now on."

Nate groaned. "Really, Logan?"

He smirked at him. "I wasn't aware of how inferior you felt to me. I mean, that's a compliment since I'm a year younger and you're Nate Fucking Monson."

"Shut up." He shoved at him, laughed, and then grumbled, "I'm so stupid."

"Three, don't get so hard on yourself." Logan moved to pat him on the shoulder again, delicately, but Nate caught the arm and pretended to punch him instead. The two grinned at each other, and as the laughter died down, they turned to me.

It'd been squashed and buried. Just like that, in our way, that's how we dealt with things.

Logan asked, "So what's the plan?"

The other way we dealt with things? Payback.

I said, "Nate's going back to the house. He's going to pack his stuff and get out of there."

Logan nodded. "And me?"

"You go to a hotel. Get a big suite. We'll all stay there. I don't want anyone from the football house to know about this. I'll come with Sam later tonight."

Nate asked, "Is this going to hurt your career?"

I nodded. "It could, if it's not kept under wraps, but they were trying to hurt me, to either ruin my career anyway or something worse. They brought this to a whole new level. I'm not going to let them get away with it."

They left after that and I waited.

SAMANTHA

Mason was waiting for me when I left the hospital. He was outside, leaning against the wall, and for a moment, the sight of him stopped me in my tracks. His head was bent down with his shoulders hunched, and his hands were in his pockets. He was wearing dark grey athletic pants; they were light weight and stuck to his form. The wind picked up, rippling his shirt, and as it swept over him, some of his oblique muscles were exposed. He had always been defined, but since he had been training for his new position, he had become leaner. It had just made him more sculpted. For one slight second, everything melted away. Shit, I wanted him then and there. A surge of heat bloomed inside me.

He looked up and I felt pierced by his gaze. I'd forgotten how penetrating those green eyes could be. He saw through me, even if I didn't want him to. He still could and I felt stripped bare in front of him.

Wetting my lips, I started forward. "Marissa told me the truth."

He didn't react to that. Instead, he said, "He loves you."

I jerked back. The suddenness of that statement caught me unaware, and it took a moment for it to filter in. I gasped softly.

He straightened from the wall, his hands still in his pockets, and holy shit—he was hot. With a dark look in his eyes, he asked, "So, I need to know. Do you love him? Could he make you happier than me?"

Those two questions slammed me back into place, and I felt the world spinning from beneath me. "What?"

"Logan says he 'could've loved you.' Do you reciprocate?" A nerve clenched in his jawline. "I don't want to waste time thinking about this. The idea of you two together is a fucking cancer in me. I want it out, here and now. Do you love Logan?"

"No."

I didn't bat an eye and neither did he when he shot back, "Could you?"

"Yes."

He paused and turned away, but caught himself and continued looking me in the eye. "Would he make you happier than me?"

Again, there was no hesitation from my end. "No." When he didn't respond, I lifted my head higher and squared my shoulders. I was sure about this. There was no second guessing. There was no area of doubt. Everything else had fallen to shit in my life—my family, my mother, my friends—but the one thing that helped me remain strong was him. So I told him, "It's you. It's only been you for me. When I came into your life, I might've seemed strong, but I wasn't. I had nothing to lose. When you have nothing to lose, you're capable of doing a lot of damage, but suddenly I had something to lose. You. My mom put me through hell, and I will never forgive her for that. She threatened to take away your future and mine because of it. She damaged me, but you held me firm. Kate and her cronies came along. They tried to break me. It didn't happen. It was you. You held me up. You kept me strong. You loved me. I don't think you will ever understand how much I love you. I could love Logan. Yes. There was a small moment when it could've been him, but only if you were never in my life. ONLY then. You're the fucking moon and stars to me. Logan would've been fireworks on the Fourth of July. There's no comparison. You need to get that."

"Sam," he said, his voice dropped.

I took a step towards him. "Marissa just told me about Tate. I came here crying. I came here feeling broken and scared shitless of losing you. I go in there and find out everything was a lie? Tate's gift to her friend. I am furious, but I come out here and you're asking if I want to be with your brother. None of this is sitting well with me." I felt a rumbling in the pit of my stomach. It was like a wind-up toy, slowly being turned, cranking up, tighter and tighter until it couldn't be cranked anymore.

I was that toy, and I was ready to explode.

A wary expression came over him.

I took a step closer. Pressing a hand to my stomach, I felt that toy. It was waiting, ready to implode at any moment. "I was scared when Tate told me that. You've never wanted a girl to come between you two, and guess what, here I am. I could've loved Logan. Yes. But I don't. I love you. You and Logan were right. I should've told you guys immediately. This could've been dealt with, but I'm human. Can you stand there and tell me you didn't question the same thing?" His eyes shifted to the side and I knew I was right. "You did, didn't you?"

That sealed the deal. He questioned it. So had I. We both had kept quiet about it. A sad laugh ripped from me, and I shook my head. "We're the epitome of a great couple. Look at us, we're so perfect, but we don't talk."

"You don't talk," he shot at me. "I talk. I call you every night. I ask how things are going. You hold back. You don't tell me the big stuff. This! This was a big thing you should've told me."

"Neither did you." I was yelling. I didn't give a damn. "You kept this from me too!"

He jerked forward. His features tightened with fury. "Could you have handled it?"

I stopped, taken aback.

He ground out, "My god, Sam, you were almost falling apart. I didn't give a damn in the beginning. You were mine. I loved you. Yes, I thought Logan might've had feelings for you, but we weren't ready to deal with that. We were too new, then that crap with your mom and what she tried to pull happened. You looked like you were going to crumble. Then last year with Kate. When was I was supposed to have this earth shattering conversation about Logan's feelings with you?"

"SO WHAT IF HE DOES?!" I burst out. My blood was pumping. "SO WHAT?" I gasped for oxygen and added, "HE DOESN'T ANYWAY!" Pointing to the hospital, my voice broke, "Tate lied. Marissa lied. It's all a lie."

Mason lifted his hand, they were in fists, but they went to the sides of his face. He pressed them there and bent forward. As he stayed like that, for a brief moment, his shoulders heaved up and down. He lifted his head and a flash of pain splayed over his face. He rasped out, "It's not a lie."

My heart stopped.

He whispered, "It's not a lie. It was a guess, and Tate guessed right."

Logan loved me? I fell back a step. *No...*

"Oh." Mason shook his head in a savage motion. "It's not what you're thinking, but he *could* love you. It's the same damn thing as what you just said. He could've been with you. You could've been with him. Do you know the position that puts me in? It's a cancer, building in me, wondering if I might lose you one day."

I rested a hand on his head and with that one small gesture, the fight left him. His shoulders drooped. He expelled a sudden rush of air, and his forehead fell to my shoulder. I continued to cradle the back of his head. And, closing my eyes, I felt his hands rest on my waist. He pulled me close, but not too close. There was still space between us, and I had to blink back tears at the distance.

We weren't arguing about the what-if of Logan. He wasn't the issue. It was us. We were the problem.

His head was bent next to mine, and I rested mine against his. "I'm sorry I didn't tell you. I should've. I'm sorry that I've been so scared for the last year." I'd been weak. I'd been hurting. He had sheltered me too much. My hand tightened on his head, and without realizing it, he had pulled our bodies closer. We were clinging to each other. His arms were wrapped around me, holding on as if he needed me to breathe. I wound mine around him too. God. I loved him so much. I whispered again, "I'm sorry. I'm so sorry."

I was apologizing for more than keeping that damn secret. I was apologizing for letting him carry me so many times. I was apologizing for not doing the same with him. And with this one incident, I should've been the one to protect him, to shelter him. I was scared he would leave me, but he'd been scared that I was going to leave him. That alone, a shudder went through me, ripped me to pieces.

I loved this man so much. It filled me from my head to the tips of my toes, and it was powerful. So unbelievably powerful that knowing the damage done to us, I was ready to destroy Tate for planting that seed. I wanted to curse myself, for not being as strong as he needed me to be. Mason was the strongest person I would ever meet. He needed that in the woman who loved him. She needed to hold her own beside him, not behind him, not being held by him, or being dragged forward by him. Beside him. I hadn't done that.

I would now. I vowed that this was it. I wasn't going to lose him and anyone else who tried to take him from me, good luck. I would destroy them first.

"I love you." It swept through me, pushing the tension and fight away. As I said those words, they were burned into me with the promise to be strong, not to take his strength, but to have my own. A tear slipped out. I lifted my head, and he tilted his back as well. Cupping both sides of his face, my eyes met his and searched inside him. I was looking into him. I was piercing his walls, making him feel me slipping inside him. We stared into each other's gaze, and I knew he felt me there. His eyes widened a bit, and he tried to step back, but I kept hold of him and held firm. He stayed where he was, in my arms. I promised, "I will not leave you. I will not hold back anymore. I will not allow anyone to get in between us. They don't have to deal with just you anymore. They'll have to deal with me too."

This was different. It was in the air. Something in our relationship was changing, something that was for the future, for a better future. I couldn't explain it, but it was intoxicating and it was moving and it was making me feel like I could conquer anyone.

I whispered again, "I love you."

He continued to study me, then a wall fell away. Some of the weight from his shoulders slid to mine, and he closed his eyes. Drawing me back against him, he pressed his head into my neck, and his lips brushed against my skin. I heard him murmur, "I love you too, Sam."

I held him tight and thought, *So goddamn much.*

CHAPTER THIRTY

MASON

Sam and I were fine. We would be fine.

I'd like to spend more time sealing our renewed connection, especially with the possible rift of Logan being so damn close to heart. He was my brother. She was mine. The thought of a possible *them* was like a hot poker stabbing repeatedly into me, but the truth was that I couldn't do anything about it. I trusted both of them, and the only other thing I could do was trust in Sam's love for me and the integrity of our relationship. We weren't like other couples. We didn't mess with temptations and weak wills and petty bullshit. We were more than that, or I hoped to god we were. If we weren't, well...we'd have to deal with that in the future.

I wanted to take Sam home. I wanted to bury myself so deep inside her that there'd never be another thought of a 'could've been guy' in her life. It was me. It was her. It was us. I wanted to remind her of that, but the timing was shit.

Park had taken a swing at me. It could've been as payback because I punched Nate, but I was guessing there was more to it. Matteo told me earlier Park liked people with power around him. He tried to get me. Then he found out that Nate wanted to talk to me? The rift could've been smoothed over. If they knew I hit Nate, because I knew Nate didn't tell them, it meant they heard what else I'd been saying about Park.

If.

If we'd been given the chance to mend our relationship without their fraternity striking. If they hadn't meant to hit me and hit Marissa instead. If all of that hadn't happened and Nate had come to me, we would've fixed things. I hadn't known that after I punched him, but hearing what Nate told Sebastian, that he wanted to talk to me himself, I knew it would've been inevitable. Nate hadn't been too far gone, and with our friendship back on, I would've been in Nate's ear. I wouldn't have been able to keep my disdain quiet for his brother. That would've pulled Nate away from the fraternity. That would've pulled another powerful person away from Sebastian's control.

He put a stop to it. Or he would've, if I'd been hurt or worse. The hit and run could've just caused minor injuries like a sprained ankle or bruising that would've healed quickly. But it also could've torn a ligament or broke a bone, putting an end to my football career. If I'd been still breathing afterwards. Marissa still was and she was three times smaller than me.

Still. They went for the jugular. So would I.

I took Sam to the hotel instead of home. She was here, but I didn't want anyone in the football house to know. Logan mentioned later that he overheard Garrett at her house, when he went to pick her up. Her biological father had invited her to Boston over the holiday break, and whether Sam knew it or not, she was going. After what I had planned, I wanted her out of harm's way. The farther away the better, and when she came back, we'd have to deal with whatever was going on then. Everything would be touch and go for a while, but I was ready. What I had planned could hurt me. It could do more than just take my career away, but Park wasn't going to go away. I recognized his type. He'd keep coming. He'd want blood from me. He would want me destroyed. I intended to destroy him first.

Logan stood up when we walked inside. Skimming over us both, a smirk came to him, and he winked at Sam. "So, want to be my sister wife?"

I scowled, but hearing him joking helped lift some of the tension. "Not funny, asshole."

Logan laughed. "What? This is typical Logan Kade. This is good material. So how about it, Sam?"

Sam rolled her eyes. She was holding onto my hand, and for a second, her hold tightened, but at his first joke, she relaxed, relief settling over her.

A door that led to an accompanying room opened and Nate stepped through. Logan stood back up and gestured to him. "Just kidding. Nate already claimed me as his sister wife, even though we're both dudes. We'll figure a way. We don't need you guys. You can have your own Twosome Fearsome. Nate and I have realized our long-lost, deep...deeply buried love for each other. He's my Twosome Gaysome. Come to my bosom, my little horny husband."

Nate stopped, frowned at him, and looked at us. "What the fuck?"

Logan hushed him. "Don't listen to him. We're still basking in the honeymoon stage. He just doesn't want you guys to be jealous since it's obvious you two aren't."

Nate burst out laughing.

"Burn, bitches." Logan beamed at us. He licked his tongue and held it to the air, then made a hissing sound. "It's still sizzling."

Sam groaned, her fingers still entwined with mine. "Way to be sensitive to the issue."

"What issue?" My brother gestured to Nate, throwing his arm around his shoulder. "You two gotta duke it out over me. It's obvious you both want me."

Seeing the bag that Nate was holding, he held it up to me as Logan made another teasing comment. I took it and went over to the couch to look at what he brought. He'd gone with the directions to grab his stuff and get out of there. If he had something for me, there was a reason. As I started looking through it, aware of the other three watching me, I wanted to see what he had gotten for me first. And knowing this, Logan kept making offhanded comments. He was stalling for me. Well, they were all just waiting, but I knew the other reason for his jokes.

He and Sam had gotten close over the year. Now this shit of their 'could've been love' wasn't going to help me feel at ease, but he was breaking the tension. In his way, he was trying to reaffirm that everything would be fine. I knew this. Still. The sight of them talking together, standing so close was permanently etched in my brain. I didn't think it would ever leave. The entire image of them had seemed intimate, like I was the one intruding on them.

I found Nate's phone and held it up.

He turned and his slight grin vanished.

A sense of gravity filled the room and everyone knew the jokes were over.

I asked, "Is there something on here?" He had included it in the bag for a reason.

He nodded and came over to sit across from me. Sam sat next to me, and Logan stayed standing up. He'd be pacing soon; that's what he did.

"I recorded something." He took it, got it to the right recording, and hit play before handing it over. A crackling sound came out and then, "What are you doing, Monson?"

Nate's voice came from his phone, "I'm packing. I'm leaving."

"This is because of Kade?" The other voice scoffed. "You shouldn't pick your side so soon."

"What does that mean?"

"Look, we didn't mean to hit that girl. Trust me, we'll fix it. She'll never have to pay her college bills for the rest of the time she's in school. Her entire tuition will be covered; she'll find that out in due time. You don't need to worry about any of this blowing back on us."

"Right."

"I mean it. Kade didn't see shit."

"He saw you, Park."

There was silence, and a laugh came from the phone. "No, he didn't. He doesn't know what he saw. Trust me, Monson, you're picking too early. Put your stuff away. We can forget any of this happened."

"Yeah?"

"Yeah." His voice smoothed out, becoming persuasive. "Our dads are friends."

"Your dad is friends with Mason's too."

"This is between us. The sons. The fathers will stay out of this. Come on, Nate. Put everything away."

Another few seconds passed in silence, then Nate said, "I can't. Mason's been my best friend since we were little. We had a disagreement, but he's family."

More crackling sounds came from the phone and then Park laughed. The sound was mocking. "Fine, but you're going to regret this. Trust me. We're going to bury your friend."

"You don't know Mason."

"I don't have to. This is my school. This is my house. He thinks he's some big shot. Yeah, well, we'll see about that. Remember my other football buddy? The one I know Kade was telling you about, how heartless I was with his scholarship. He doesn't know anything about that story. That accident wasn't an accident. I can get at anyone, even your precious Mason Kade. Trust me, Nate. Go ahead. Go to his side. It's your funeral."

It cut out. I handed the phone to him, but Nate said, "No. I'll get a new one. That needs to stay how it is. I don't want to risk deleting it by accident."

Logan cursed. "What's the plan?"

I looked around the room. They were all waiting, all looking back at me. There were varying emotions in each of them. Logan was bristling. He wanted to fight. He was always down for anything. Nate was calm. I could see he was just ready for anything. I glanced at Sam. Other times she might've been fearful and slightly looking away. She wasn't this time.

She was looking right at me, and I could see her anger. There was a flame in her eye that I hadn't seen in a long time.

I sighed. Then I told them the plan.

*

We waited for a night Nate was certain his fraternity was going to be out of the house. Then he snuck inside. His job was to search every room, every closet, the bathrooms, even the showers. He searched every inch of that house. When a flashlight was turned on and then off, and it was repeated, that was our signal. The house was empty.

Logan was next to me. He expelled a deep breath, then took off. Both of them went through the house. They dumped gasoline over everything. When they were done, they tossed the containers inside and headed back to me.

This was it. This would change everything.

No one said a word. For a moment, we just stood there and thought about what we were going to do, then I held out my hand. Logan pulled the box of matches from his bag. For a second, everyone paused. There was a gravity in the air, a sense of stillness about what we were about to do, but I wasn't going back.

Logan tried to break a smile. He tried, but failed. He sighed. "Is this like fourth down, and we're going for the goal?"

I took out a match. No one else spoke. I shook my head. "No. This is kick off. They brought us to the game." I lit the match. "This is just the beginning."

I tossed it and watched it burn.

Fallen Crest Finale (tentative title) coming soon.

For more information, go to

http://www.tijansbooks.com

ACKNOWLEDGEMENTS

I'm just going to list everyone that I need to thank because there's a ton! My editor, honestly, she puts up with all my craziness and nagging! Ami! You do so much for me! And my proofreader, Chris! I give you such short notice and you always pull through. I'm so lucky for both of you. Then there's my team of encouragers/supporters/betas: Cami, Kerri, Eileen, Heather, Ker Dukey, Amanda, Amanda, Mari! I love you ladies! I can come to you for almost anything and you're there for me! It is so much appreciated. I don't know how I did it before when I didn't have this team to constantly reassure me or were just there for me to bounce ideas off of. Then my author friends: K.A. Robinson, Jay McLean, Debra Anastasia, Teresa Mummert, Sara Celi, L.B. Simmons, Ilsa Madden-Hills, there's so many more, but these ladies have helped with so much. Laughs. Venting. Tears. Sending me random pictures of penises. That's what friends are for, right? Lol

Then the ladies in my fan group, the Tijanettes!! Honestly, there's always something new in there that makes me smile and laugh. Just a heart-felt THANK YOU! Thank you for supporting me. Just thank you! And I have to add the customary last line of thank you to my other half, Bailey, my dog. Lol Jason, thank you for always understanding my crazy neurotic schedule and not getting too upset with me when I get too stressed out. He's my heart, my soul.

CPSIA information can be obtained
at www.ICGtesting.com
Printed in the USA
LVHW091530261219
641751LV00012B/428/P